H. E. Bates was born ... shire and was educated at Kettering Grammar School, worked as a journalist and clerk on a local newspaper before publishing his first book, *The Two Sisters*, when he was twenty. In the next fifteen years he acquired a distinguished reputation for his stories about English country life. During the Second World War, he was a Squadron Leader in the R.A.F. and some of his stories of service life, *The Greatest People in the World* (1942), *How Sleep the Brave* (1943) and *The Face of England* (1953), were written under the pseudonym of 'Flying Officer X'. His subsequent novels of Burma, *The Purple Plain* and *The Jacaranda Tree*, and of India, *The Scarlet Sword*, stemmed directly or indirectly from his war experience in the Eastern theatre of war.

In 1958 his writing took a new direction with the appearance of *The Darling Buds of May*, the first of the popular Larkin family novels, which was followed by *A Breath of French Air*, *When the Green Woods Laugh*, *Oh! To Be in England* and *A Little of What You Fancy*. His autobiography appeared in three volumes, *The Vanished World* (1969), *The Blossoming World* (1971) and *The World in Ripeness* (1972). His last works included the novel *The Triple Echo* (1971) and a collection of short stories, *The Song of the Wren* (1972). Perhaps one of his most famous works of fiction is the best-selling novel *Fair Stood the Wind for France* (1944). H. E. Bates also wrote miscellaneous works on gardening, essays on country life, several plays including *The Day of Glory* (1945); *The Modern Short Story* (1941) and a story for children, *The White Admiral* (1968). His works have been translated into sixteen languages and a posthumous collection of his stories, *The Yellow Meads of Asphodel*, appeared in 1976.

H. E. Bates was awarded the C.B.E. in 1973 and died in January 1974. He was married in 1931 and had four children.

H. E. BATES

The Distant Horns of Summer

PENGUIN BOOKS

PENGUIN BOOKS

Published by the Penguin Group
27 Wrights Lane, London W8 5TZ, England
Viking Penguin Inc., 40 West 23rd Street, New York, New York 10010, USA
Penguin Books Australia Ltd, Ringwood, Victoria, Australia
Penguin Books Canada Ltd, 2801 John Street, Markham, Ontario, Canada L3R 1B4
Penguin Books (NZ) Ltd, 182–190 Wairau Road, Auckland 10, New Zealand

Penguin Books Ltd, Registered Offices: Harmondsworth, Middlesex, England

First published by Michael Joseph Ltd 1967
Published in Penguin Books 1969
3 5 7 9 10 8 6 4 2

Printed and bound in Great Britain by
Cox & Wyman Ltd, Reading
Typeset in Baskerville

'WAVE good-bye.'

'They're too far away.'

'Wave good-bye, James.'

Today the clouds above the far end of the chestnut avenue across the park were like big balloons of ice-cream. Sometimes they were like fat, purple, crouching bears. Sometimes they were like sheep.

'Shall I wave with both hands? Then they'll see better.'

'It's too late now.'

Yes: the boy could see it was too late now. The white Jaguar was running swift as a mouse into and out of the gap at the end of the avenue. He watched it, heard it give a short hoot and then it was gone completely.

'Where is Tangier?'

'A long way away. Somewhere hot.'

'Will they be there long?'

'Perhaps a month. Perhaps longer. Perhaps six weeks.'

'Shall we look for birds' nests today?'

'There aren't any birds' nests. It's August now.'

'I saw a bird with a piece of straw in its mouth yesterday.'

'I expect it had been to the harvest field.'

He and Gilly were going to live in the little house; the big house was all shut up now. He liked the little house. It was thatched and brown and something like a cake. It smelled of floor polish and soot and honey. There was a well in the garden with a wooden roof over it and a big handle and a rope and a bucket on the end of it. There was a trap door and when you opened the trap door and looked down the well it was all dark and then suddenly there was a silver coin at the bottom of it, very bright.

'You're walking ever so slowly.'

'We're in no hurry to get anywhere that I know of.'

5

He liked Gilly; she was new. Miss Garfield, who had gone now, was old. She had a stuffy nose and hands like duck's feet, with funny sticking-up bones and a brown loose skin between them. The skin got all tight when she was cross. She wore spectacles with no rims and smelled of aniseed and she was gone now. He didn't know where.

Gilly was different. She was like the little house, friendly and brown. She didn't wear spectacles. Her hands were smooth and pale. Her eyes were brown and quiet and large. She had been with him only three days but he liked her as if she had been there all his life.

'Well, she's nearly seventeen. Yes, I know it's on the young side and she's a bit naïve sort of – but what are you to do? It's hell trying to get anybody. They simply don't want the work. You have to take what you can get and lump it.'

'Well, James seems to have taken to her. That's everything.'

'Two days and he'll probably have forgotten we ever existed.'

'More than likely.'

Once his father had stopped the car on a road and showed him a big dark building where an airship used to live. It was something to do with the war. Now the building was all shut up and the airship didn't live there and it all looked lonely and it didn't seem much use having it there, in the middle of a big flat field with sheep grazing about it, a bit like grey fat airships themselves.

The big house in the park was like that too. The shutters were all up. It didn't seem much use having it there. Sometimes there were sheep grazing in front of it too and once a few of them broke through a fence to where the big glass-house stood, with its many broken panes of glass and its grape-vine and its fig tree and its dark water tank and its froggy smell.

When the sheep had broken through the fence and came to the glass-house they just stood there and stared at the reflections of themselves in the glass, as if they were wondering how all the other sheep had got inside and couldn't get out again.

'Would the sheep eat the grapes?'

'Oh! no,' his father said. 'I don't think sheep care for grapes.'

6

'But if they could get in would they eat them?'

'I think not. The grapes would be too high for them to reach anyway.'

That was all there was in the glass-house: the grape vine, the grapes, the fig tree, the water tank and the froggy smell. But he liked going there. It wasn't dead or lonely or useless, like the big house, with nobody living there and nothing ever happening.

The narrow white road went right through the park, under the big avenue of chestnut trees. At one end was an iron gate that was never open. At the other end the gate was always open and it meant that cars always went out and never came right through.

'You said we could go and look for mushrooms today.'

Gilly's eyes were a strange grey-brown, like snails. Sometimes they looked shut even though they were open and they weren't looking at you.

'Gilly.'

'Yes? What did you say?'

'You said we could go and look for mushrooms.'

'Yes? What did you say? Did I? I was dreaming.'

'Shall we go. We could have them for lunch.'

'Not today. Not this morning. It's too dry. They don't grow when it's dry.'

'But when it rains next time.'

'Perhaps when it rains next time.'

'This evening?'

'Perhaps this evening.'

The day was like a sea-shell. You looked inside it and you couldn't see what was in the middle of it or at the end, except a big dim shadow. You put it to your ear and you heard strange sounds – the sea, waves, the wind, voices.

'If we aren't going to gather mushrooms could I go and see Mr Pimm for a little while?'

'Who is Mr Pimm?'

'He's a man.'

'Yes, but what man?'

'Oh! he's a man who comes to see me. He likes me. He's my friend.'

Gilly blinked her brown snail-like eyes and said she didn't know about going to see this Mr Pimm. She didn't think it was right to talk to a strange man.

'Oh! Mr Pimm isn't a strange man. He comes to see me a lot.'

'Oh! he does? I haven't seen him anywhere.'

'He only comes to see me.'

It seemed a long way up the road to where the little house stood to one side and the big empty house, all shuttered, on the other. Gilly was walking so slowly that he thought they would never get there.

'Is it time for lunch yet?'

'Good gracious me I should say not. It's only half past ten. We don't have lunch till half past twelve.'

'Couldn't we have it now if it feels like it?'

'Half past twelve.'

'Could Mr Pimm come to lunch today? I told him he could come one day.'

Gilly laughed, in a voice rather shrill and quivering. Mr Pimm come to lunch? He must be joking. You couldn't invite every Tom, Dick and Harry to lunch whenever you felt like it, just like that.

'Why not?'

She didn't know why not; you just couldn't, that was all. And once again, she said, her voice quiet but sharp this time, he mustn't talk to strange men.

'But Mr Pimm isn't a strange man. I know him ever so well. He calls me Jamesy. And sometimes Matey.'

'Oh! he does, does he? Well, that's no excuse for inviting him to lunch.'

'He doesn't eat much. He likes mushrooms though.'

'Oh! I'm sure.'

'He knows where they grow. He'll bring them if you say he can come.'

'Oh! I'll bet. No holding him back if it's all for free.'

'He likes you too.'

'Oh! I'm sure. And how does he know about me?'

'I told him. I said your name was Gilian and we called you Gilly for short.'

'Well, thank you. Who else have you been telling about me?
The more the merrier.'

'Nobody, only Mr Monday.'

Oh! so it was Mr Monday now, was it? And Mr Tuesday
and Mr Wednesday too? And what about Mr Thursday, Friday and Saturday? It was getting a bit crowded in these parts,
wasn't it? And Mr Sunday?

Gilly began laughing again, more shrilly than ever this time,
but he was quiet. He said he supposed she didn't believe him
about Mr Pimm and Mr Monday –

'Well, seeing's believing.'

He said he didn't know what she meant by that.

'Well, I haven't seen him, have I?'

'You haven't seen Tangier either.'

Oh! that was different. Tangier was there. It was on the
map. She might not have seen it but everyone knew it was
there.

'So are Mr Pimm and Mr Monday.'

'Oh! so you've seen them? Well.'

'No, not both. Only Mr Pimm.'

She laughed again. It was all getting a bit dodgy wasn't it?
First he was telling this Mr Monday about her and then it
turned out he'd never seen him.

'Yes, but Mr Pimm told him, I mean. Mr Monday's coming
one day next week. Mr Pimm betted he'd like to come to lunch
too.'

'Welcome Mr Monday. We'll get the roast duck and apple
sauce all ready.'

'Oh! that would be nice. Mr Pimm would like that. Shall I
tell him?'

'Oh! of course. Naturally. Why not? Don't let's have any
secrets from Mr Pimm.'

The park was so large that when you stood in the middle of
it, half-way up the road, as he and Gilly were now, you couldn't
see the ends of it. The most distant trees were a blacky green,
like mountains. Only the tips of the ice-cream clouds showed
above the dark tops of them.

He wondered often why his father bothered with the big

house when they only wanted to live in a tiny wing of it. You couldn't get the servants, his father said. It was dog eat dog. That was a funny expression: dog eat dog. He had never seen a dog eat another dog and he wondered if they ever did. It would have to be a very big dog eating a very little dog: like the big house swallowing up the little one.

'Do dogs eat dogs?'

'Of course not. You do say some funny things sometimes.'

'Father says they do.'

'Oh! it's an expression.'

'Are they in Tangier by now?'

'Oh! Good Lord, no. You and Tangier.'

And who wanted a glass-house as big as a barn? his father said. Who wanted a grape vine? When he wanted a bunch of grapes he would go out to the fruiterers and buy one.

'Could I go over to the glass-house this morning?'

'You're always over there. I wonder you don't get bored with it.'

'Would you come?'

'Me? Some hopes. I've got lunch to get and everything to tidy up.'

'What are we going to have for lunch? Shall I bring a bunch of grapes?'

'That would puzzle you.'

'Oh! they're getting ripe. You can see them. Right at the top, near the glass. Some are green and some are blue.'

'Well, not today. I don't think grapes today.'

'I could put them down on my list.'

'Oh! so you've got a list, have you? All right, put them down on the list.'

'What else shall I put down?'

'What have you got already?'

He consulted his list. He always pretended to carry his pencil behind his ear. He took it out now, ready to tick off things.

'Sausages, eggs, marmalade, ketchup, stamps, coffee, paper-clips, shag.'

'Shag? Whatever do we want with shag?'

'That's for Mr Pimm.'

Was there anything else? he said. He'd better be going now.

'Well, put down tooth-paste, toilet soap and honey.'

'I'll put down prawns too. I know Mr Pimm likes prawns.'

'Oh! of course. Prawns. We want to do the right thing for Mr Pimm, don't we?'

He had already started to walk away across the park, away from the road, before he answered. There were no sheep in the park today. Here and there browny-silver thistleheads stood like dry skeletons and already a few dry, ginger leaves from the horse-chestnut trees in the avenue were dancing slowly across the grass.

'Of course he might not be there today.'

'Who? Mr Pimm? Why not?'

'Oh! he isn't always there.'

'No?'

'No. He only comes on special days.'

He sat on the floor of the glass-house by the water-tank, talking to Mr Pimm. He always called Mr Pimm mate when they were talking together. Men always called each other mate. The electric light men who came to mend the cables called each other mate; and the telephone men and the men who came to collect the tins and bottles.

'Don't seem to get no rain, mate.'

No, Mr Pimm said, they didn't seem to get no rain.

'Any mushrooms, mate?'

Nivvy one. Not a smell. Too dry all the time.

'It's getting something chronic, mate.'

Men always said it was getting chronic, whatever it was.

'My folks have gone to Tangier.'

Ah! Yes? Tangier? Where was Tangier? Half-tidy way off, Mr Pimm supposed.

'It is that, mate.'

He picked up a vine-leaf that had fallen down and slowly stripped it down to the stalk and then put the stalk in his mouth, smoking it like Mr Pimm did and spitting sometimes.

Mr Pimm was somewhere behind some old mossy pots of ferns. You couldn't always see him very clearly. But you could hear him coughing while he smoked and striking matches and spitting sometimes.

'Might get a change with the next moon, mate, I expect.'

Shouldn't wonder, Mr Pimm said. Wanted the wind back up the hill, that's what they wanted. Gone for long? – Tangier, Mr Pimm meant.

'No bounds, mate. Weeks, Gilly says.'

Gilly?

'I told you about her, mate. She's come to look after me. She's new.'

Ah! yes, Mr Pimm remembered. Getting on well together?

'Oh! she's nice. I like her. You must come and see her. By the way, mate,' – his pipe was out and he struck a match and lit it up again, grunting – 'how's Mr Monday?'

Hadn't run across him lately, Mr Pimm said.

'Run down to Brighton for a few days I shouldn't wonder, mate.'

He spat again. He heard Mr Pimm spit too.

Shouldn't wonder, Mr Pimm said. Else on the beer.

'Talking about beer, mate, I brought a bottle along.'

Never? Mr Pimm said. Never?

'Expect you could do with a wet, couldn't you, mate?'

Mr Pimm expected he could. Too right. Should he tot out?

'No, I'll tot out, mate. You sit tight.' He totted out the beer into two glasses after first knocking his pipe out on the heel of his shoe. 'County-Pale: it ought to be all right. It's what my father always drinks.'

In that case it ought to be a drop o' good, Mr Pimm said. Cheers.

'Cheers, mate.'

He heard Mr Pimm give a big gasp. He gave one too and wiped his mouth with the back of his hand and then spat on the floor.

He heard Mr Pimm spit too. It was getting half-tidy warm in the glass-house, Mr Pimm said, and this was just what you wanted to quench you.

'Too right, mate.'

Drop o' bleedin' good, this, mate, Mr Pimm said, giving another gigantic spit that echoed all over the glass-house.

'Glad you like, it mate. Plenty more where this came from.'

Just up his alley, Mr Pimm said. You could hear Mr Pimm settling down with groans of comfort behind the pots of ferns. You could hear him smacking his lips over the beer and clearing his throat and saying how good it was and how it cleared the old gills.

'It does that, mate.' He cleared his throat too and smacked his lips and licked them. 'By the way, you coming up for lunch today?'

Well, he hadn't thought about it all that much, Mr Pimm said.

'Well, Gilly expects you. She says you can.'

Oh! she said that, did she? Mr Pimm said. Well, in that case –

'Good-oh, mate. We're going to start with prawns and then liver and fried onions and treacle tart.'

Treacle tart, eh? Mr Pimm supped softly at his beer. You could almost hear him tasting the treacle tart. Then he drank with sudden mighty thirstiness, giving a loud 'Ah!' and setting his glass down.

'Another tot, mate? Plenty more where that came from.'

Well, if you bent his arm, Mr Pimm said, This heat put a thirst on you. Hot where his folks had gone? Holiday, like?

'Gilly says it is.' He poured out two more new glasses of beer from the second bottle, handing one to Mr Pimm. 'A long way away and very hot.'

Well, they'd be wanting a lot o' this then, Mr Pimm said. He knew. He was out in Cyprus during the bleedin' war. That was bleedin' hot.

'Too right, mate.' Mr Pimm talked just like the men who had been laying the electric cable beyond the closed gate of the park. One of these had been in Cyprus too and it had given him the Willies. Like hell. He was browned off like a dinner. 'By the way, mate, could you reach and get me a bunch of grapes? I promised Gilly I'd take one.'

Green or black? Mr Pimm said, after another searching draught and a long spit. That was always the nice thing about Mr Pimm: he never said no. He never said things like well, we shall have to see what your father has to say or we shall have to cross that bridge when we come to it or it all depended or did we think that was very wise? Miss Garfield had always wondered if it was very wise. Even things like eating sweets and ice-cream and potato crisps had to be wondered about before you could have them and it was decided if they were very wise.

Gilly was better; but no one was like Mr Pimm. Mr Pimm would give you whatever you wanted, just like that. It was enormously nice and comforting, as a result, to be with Mr Pimm.

'Black, I think, mate.'

Well, if it was him, Mr Pimm said, he'd have the green. They were that bit riper. It was a bit early yet for the black.

'All right, mate, you get two bunches of green while I see if there's a fig or two left.'

At the far end of the glass-house was a fig tree. It was called Brown Turkey. He knew that because his father had told him so. Even Mr Pimm didn't know it was called Brown Turkey because one day he had asked him and Mr Pimm had said no, he didn't know that and he didn't like figs anyway, they turned him out so.

The brown-green figs were shaped like balloons: not like ordinary balloons but like the ones you saw in old picture books. He liked that shape. He liked the smell of them when you opened them too and all the seeds sat inside, juicy and pink, reminding him so much of the soft cod's roes his father sometimes had on toast. That smell was part of the smell of the glass-house: the smell of water and greenness and something froggy and Mr Pimm and his shag.

'Don't suppose you'd like roes on toast, mate, instead, would you, for lunch?'

He stood for some time sucking at the two figs he had gathered. It was only when he was licking up the juice of the second one from his chin that he suddenly realized that Mr Pimm was no longer there. For a moment or two he was disappointed that Mr Pimm had disappeared and then he remembered that Mr Pimm always skived off to the pub about twelve o'clock to get himself some shag. He had done it often before.

He liked that word skive. The electric cable man who had been in Cyprus had used it a lot. They were always skiving somewhere or other. Well, you had to, mate, didn't you, or else you never got nothing, did you?

It was time for him too to skive off and find Gilly. Sucking at the last of his Brown Turkey he walked slowly out of the glass-house and into the park. He thought he'd done everything on his list – no, there was just the cod's roes, in case Mr Pimm liked them to finish his lunch with.

He started to run. He had to be there first, to see where Mr Pimm had to sit and help to lay his place at table.

'Have you laid a place for Mr Pimm?'

Well, not yet, Gilly said. Give her time.

'Well, he's coming. He'll be here soon.'

Just as well she knew, wasn't it? Gilly said.

He and Gilly always ate in the kitchen. There really wasn't anywhere else to eat in fact: except the little front room with the sewing table and the sofa and the two easy chairs where Gilly sat sometimes, listening to the radio and reading magazines and staring out of the window as if she were half-expecting somebody like Mr Pimm to walk up the road through the park.

'I can't smell anything.'

'Smell what? Are you supposed to smell something?'

'I told Mr Pimm we were going to have liver and bacon and fried onions.'

Gilly laughed. She was starting to spread the cloth on the kitchen table and get the knives and forks out of the drawer.

'Liver and bacon and fried onions, eh? He'll be lucky.'

'Aren't we going to have it then? And treacle tart.'

'Oh! yes of course. And sausages and tomatoes and fried potatoes and strawberries and cream and soft roes on toast to finish up with.'

'Mr Pimm will like that. He likes all those things.'

'He does? Good luck to him.'

Gilly spread the red-checked kitchen cloth across the table and smoothed it with her hands.

'I think Mr Pimm could sit at the top here,' he said, 'don't you?'

'But that's your place.'

'Just for today Mr Pimm can sit there.'

'And where are you going to sit?'

'At the other end. Opposite. Then I can see him better.'

He started to lay Mr Pimm's knife and fork and spoon. It was awfully nice to have Mr Pimm to lunch. He reminded Gilly that Mr Pimm always had beer for his lunch, brown ale, like the electricity men did when they skived off to the pub, and hadn't she better get a glass for him?

'Oh! I'll get the best silver out and the red carpet.'

While Gilly found a tumbler and stood wiping and polishing it with a tea-cloth he told her how he had had two Brown Turkey figs to eat and how nice they were.

'I hope you left some for Mr Pimm?'

'Oh! he doesn't like figs. They turn him out so.'

Gilly laughed again and said so that was where he met Mr Pimm, was it, in the old vinery, the glass-house? What was he doing in there?

'Oh! he just comes.'

'Sends you a telegram? or just turns up?'

'Oh! I always know when he's coming.'

Gilly merely smiled this time and put a brown loaf of bread on the table, then a dish of butter and a salad of hard-boiled eggs and lettuce and tomatoes in the green glass bowl. There was just the pepper and salt to come and he got the two pots of them from the lower shelf of the cupboard by the kitchen window. On the window sill stood a milk jug with red and white dahlias in it, like balls of honeycomb.

'Shall we have the flowers on the table?'

'Oh! of course. We want to have everything right, don't we? Might as well have it posh.'

'I think Mr Pimm would like it.'

And Mr Pimm would like it too, Gilly said, if he washed his hands now. So he swilled his hands under the scullery tap and for a few minutes longer stood drying them on the roller towel, looking out of the window, and then suddenly Mr Pimm was there, coming up the garden path.

'Mr Pimm's coming. He's just opening the garden gate.'

'He's fast on the ball, isn't he? I'm not ready. You just entertain him a minute while I go upstairs and straighten my hair.'

While Gilly had gone upstairs, untying her apron as she went and leaving it on the back of a chair, he opened the kitchen door.

'Oh! there you are, mate. Dead on time.'

It was wonderful to see Mr Pimm standing there on the doorstep.

'Well, come in, mate. Don't stand there.'

He always used a special voice for Mr Pimm, low and matey. Sometimes too he wiped his mouth with the back of his hand, like the electricity men did, and pushed bits of something out of his back teeth with his tongue.

'Sit here, mate. This is your place.'

He lifted the chair that stood at the top of the table and pulled it back so that Mr Pimm could sit down.

'Make yourself comfortable, mate. Smell the liver and onions? Gilly's just gone upstairs. She won't be long.'

Mr Pimm sat down at table. Wouldn't say no to a glass of beer, either, while he was waiting, would he? No, Mr Pimm said, he daresay he wouldn't.

'I'll tot you one out, mate.'

He poured a glass of beer for Mr Pimm and solemnly hoped it was about right? He could smell the liver and bacon and onions himself now. He was fairly tasting them already. He expected Mr Pimm was too and wouldn't he like a piece of bread to be going on with?

Mr Pimm indicated that he would, at the same time knocking off the rest of his beer, grunting pleasure, wiping his mouth with the back of his hand.

'Drop of all right, mate?' He started to fill up Mr Pimm's glass again, wiping his mouth with the back of his hand too. 'Quenches you?'

It was pretty well all right, mate, Mr Pimm said. It quenched you.

'Ah! it does that.' He dug at the back of his teeth with his tongue, just like the electricity men did. 'No sign of rain yet, though, mate. Ah! here's Gilly coming.'

Gilly came downstairs and into the kitchen, her brown hair brushed neatly back, noting with slow, surprised eyes that there was no sign of Mr Pimm.

'Oh! yes there is. He's sitting there at the top of the table. Where I said.'

'Oh! so he is. For a minute I didn't see him.'

'Mr Pimm, this is Gilly.'

'Good morning, Mr Pimm. So you've come to lunch with us?'

'I gave him a glass of beer and a piece of bread already because he was hungry and he said he couldn't wait. Was that all right?'

'Oh! that's all right. Make yourself at home, Mr Pimm.'

'That's it, make yourself at home, mate.' He got up and went to the top of the table to pour Mr Pimm more beer. 'I expect he could smell the liver and onions, couldn't he?'

Gilly said she expected so and went over to the kitchen dresser to find plates and the wooden salad spoon and fork for the salad.

'But you've only brought two plates. Where's Mr Pimm's?'

'So I have. Silly. I forgot.'

While Gilly had gone back to the dresser to find another plate he picked up the salad spoon and fork and said could he serve Mr Pimm?

'Yes, you do that.'

'How do you like your liver, mate? Well done?'

He nodded his head in sage approval as Mr Pimm indicated, nodding his head, too, that he liked his liver pretty well done. He spooned generous piles of liver, bacon, onions and fried potatoes on to Mr Pimm's plate and then passed the plate to Gilly, who took it and passed it to Mr Pimm.

'Don't let it get cold, mate. Start. Mustard?'

Gilly got up from the table and went to the dresser to find the mustard pot. As she stood there she turned and said:

'Shall we give Mr Pimm the funny mustard pot? You know, the joke one. The one that lets the snake out of the top when you undo it.'

'Mr Pimm doesn't like that sort of mustard.'

'No! It always makes you laugh.'

He stared at Gilly with severe, still eyes.

'Mr Pimm only likes proper mustard.'

Gilly sat down at the table, quiet. James took the mustard pot to the top of the table, where Mr Pimm was sitting.

'I'll help you, mate, shall I? Say when.'

He unscrewed the top of the mustard pot and helped Mr Pimm to a generous spoonful or two of mustard, dropping it in yellow blobs on the side of his plate, afterwards topping up his beer.

When he got back to his place again Gilly was eating her salad.

'Shall I give you some salad now or would you like to help yourself?'

'I'm not having salad. I'm having liver and onions like Mr Pimm is.'

'Oh! yes, I forgot. One piece of liver or two?'

'Two.'

'Two what?'

'Two please. And two bits of bacon.'

Gilly gave him two pieces of tomato, two lettuce leaves and half a boiled egg.

'Would you like me to cut it up for you?'

'I can cut it up myself. I don't want anybody to cut it up.'

'All right, you cut it up. Knife in the other hand.'

'Why? Mr Pimm has it in that hand.'

Several times in the course of eating his liver, bacon and onions he looked up to the top of the table to see how Mr Pimm was getting on. Mr Pimm was getting on very well, it seemed, thank you, except that he ate with his knife in his left hand: at least James supposed it was the left hand. He didn't really know.

More bread, mate? Yes, Mr Pimm would have more bread. And if there was a bit more liver left?

'Is there some more liver left, Gilly?'

'I think I left a piece in the frying pan on the stove.'

'Bit of luck, mate. There's a bit more left. I'll get it.'

He went to the stove and picked up the frying pan and then helped Mr Pimm to the last piece of liver and a final spoonful of onions. He gave Mr Pimm more mustard too and again topped up his beer. Then when he had seen Mr Pimm happily settled again he went back to his place at table, picked up his glass of water with a loud 'Ah!', wiped his mouth with the back of his hand, grunted and said:

'Cheers, mate. Treacle tart after this.'

Then he finished off his own liver and bacon and onions and dug his tongue into the back of his teeth, at the same time telling Gilly that he expected Mr Pimm was ready for the treacle tart now.

'It's custard and raspberry *mousse* today.'

He made grim dark noises, deep in his throat.

'Men like Mr Pimm don't have *mousse*. Men can't work on muck like that. They have to have something that wears well. Don't they, mate?'

Under the silent, approving stare of Mr Pimm Gilly got up to fetch the raspberry *mousse*.

'Been waiting for this, mate, I expect?'

There was no doubt at all that Mr Pimm had been waiting for this. The echo of his approval came up from the other end of the table with a grunt, a smacking of lips and a muscular scraping of fork and spoon.

'You don't have to shovel it in so, do you?'

'Working men do. They shovel it in.'

'Well, you're not a working man.'

'Yes, I am. Me and Mr Pimm are working men. That right, mate?'

Without waiting for an answer he extended an invitation to Mr Pimm to have more treacle tart. There was plenty more where that came from. Mr Pimm's plate now being empty for the third or fourth time, Gilly actually got up to go and fetch it herself, only to be stopped with a snake-like hiss, as if the comic mustard-pot had suddenly appeared and exploded.

'Mr Pimm doesn't want to be waited on by you. I have to wait on him. Don't I, mate?'

Gilly was silent, crushed.

'Might as well clear it up, mate.' He proceeded to cut Mr Pimm an ample slice of treacle tart as big as a man's hand and then took it up the table and put it on his plate. 'We don't want anything left, do we, Gilly?'

'No, that's right, we don't want anything left.'

Gilly was quite solemn now; she was beginning, he thought, to understand Mr Pimm. She hadn't so far said anything to Mr Pimm, he noticed, but perhaps when he came another day, to-morrow he hoped, she might begin to talk to him. You had to talk to Mr Pimm just the way Mr Pimm talked and it wasn't easy until you got to know.

'Well, ought to be getting back on the job, mate, I suppose.'

It was clear that Mr Pimm supposed he ought. The last crumb of treacle tart had gone. There was nothing left to keep him at all.

'Well, see you tomorrow then, mate.'

He got up to go and shake hands with Mr Pimm.

'Could we have roast beef tomorrow, Gilly? Mr Pimm likes roast beef. And Yorkshire?'

'I expect we could.'

'Well, so long then, mate. Same time tomorrow.'

Soon Mr Pimm was far away across the park. The skeleton thistleheads glistened like white bone in the sun and except for them the park was empty.

'Mr Pimm is nice, isn't he?'

'Mr Pimm is very nice.'

Together they watched the road across the park. Suddenly, without Mr Pimm, the afternoon was nothing. Like a sea-shell with only its shadows and echoes, the day was empty.

After that, for a week. Mr Pimm came to lunch every day.

'Shall we have sausage and eggs and baked beans today? Mr Pimm likes sausage and eggs and baked beans very much.'

'We were going to have pork pie and salad.'

'Oh! Mr Pimm doesn't like that. If we don't have what Mr Pimm likes he won't come again.'

'All right. We'll have what Mr Pimm likes.'

'Tomorrow could we have lamb chops and mint sauce and baked apples? Mr Pimm always has baked apples when he's at home. He has apples every day.'

'All right. By the way, where does Mr Pimm live?'

'Over there somewhere. On the other side of the park.'

'Is Mr Pimm married?'

'I don't think so. He lives with his old lady.'

'How do you know?'

'One of the electricity men told me and then I asked Mr Pimm and he said, yes, he did.'

Sometimes during these conversations a figure briefly intruded. It was his father, far away in Tangier, saying: 'Plenty of salads. And fruit. Not much meat. You can buy him a Coca-Cola at the week-ends but not too much of that sort of thing. The main thing is to watch him. He will wander off so. He used to wander off every day when the electricians were connecting the new cable. But they've gone now.'

For Gilly there was also another figure, tall and elegant, with a dark, arresting head. Her aloofness was heightened by the long black stockings and bright turquoise blue shoes she always wore. The shining pools of her eye-shadow were turquoise too.

'The job doesn't permit you to go out much, I'm afraid. You'll have to make your own amusement. I spoke to Mr Sampson about changing the television over to the cottage but it means a new aerial and it's expensive into the bargain and there really isn't time. You don't mind about the television, do you? You've got the radio.'

The tall, elegant figure had also spoken about men. She had hinted that she hoped there wouldn't be any of that sort of thing. She had chosen Gilly out of a number of applicants largely because of those inoffensive, mild, brown snail-like eyes. They didn't look like the eyes of a girl of restless temperament. She wasn't pretty either: just passable.

'This is our address in Tangier. If we move I'll telegraph you. I'll send you postcards anyway, but if James doesn't ask for them – well, I mean don't over-fuss about them. He'll only start wondering. We don't want him fretting. Is there anything else I could say?'

'I just wondered if I could teach him to read. I think he'd read very quickly if I started him.'

'Oh! no I don't think so. He's not quite six. It's too early. If you start them reading at that age it sort of retards them in a way. They run before they can walk, sort of.'

'You said something about a night-light. Does he still need to have that?'

'Well, you'll see. Perhaps it's a good time to break him of it.'

'Is it all right if I take him down to the sea now and then?'

'I think we'd rather you didn't. The beaches are awfully scruffy this time of year and the water's pretty grim. Well, you think you'll manage?'

'I think I shall manage.'

'Well, we shall be five, six weeks. More if we get the sun. It's the sun that matters – I don't give a damn about anything else if we get the sun.'

The second day Mr Pimm came to lunch the roast beef and Yorkshire and roast potatoes and carrots, in reality fish fingers and fried egg, was very popular. It was a race to see who finished first. There was much scraping of plates and sucking of teeth and throaty gruntings of satisfaction.

'Not knives in mouths, please. I told you.'

'Mr Pimm puts his knife in his mouth.'

'Never mind what Mr Pimm does.'

'If Mr Pimm does it why can't I? It doesn't do Mr Pimm any harm. He eats everything up. He's strong.'

'What's all right for Mr Pimm isn't always all right for you.'

'Oh! yes it is. You don't want me to be like Mr Monday, do you?'

'What about Mr Monday?'

'Mr Monday's broken his arm and he's on the club.'

'I'm sorry to hear that. When did this happen?'

'Yesterday afternoon. He fell off a ladder.'

'What awful bad luck.'

'Now he has to have his food cut up for him. I don't have to have my food cut up for me, do I?'

'I should think not, a big boy like you.'

'Well, that's what I meant about Mr Pimm.'

For the first two days she forgot to lay Mr Pimm's place at table; it was a mere passing phase, she thought, this business of Mr Pimm. On the third day she remembered; she even put out a clean napkin for Mr Pimm. The next day she was standing at the garden gate, on the stroke of half past twelve, waiting for Mr Pimm.

'I think Mr Pimm's late today, don't you, Gilly?'

'No, I don't think so. It's barely half past twelve.'

'Perhaps he isn't coming today.'

'Oh! don't say that. He'll come.'

'Perhaps it's his day off and he's had to go out with his old lady.'

'I shouldn't think so. It's only Thursday.'

'Perhaps he's gone to see Mr Monday.'

'Well, he might have, I suppose. How is Mr Monday?'

'As well as can be expected.'

'Oh! good. I'm so pleased.'

'Oh! there's Mr Pimm now. Coming across the park. Can we go and meet him? He's got a red shirt on today.'

They ran together for some distance down the road to meet Mr Pimm. A little rain had fallen in the night. The grass was freshened and wet and there were shallow pools, blue and white under a clear washed sky, all along the road.

'Thought you were never coming, mate. Nice shower. Do more good than we shall.'

James shook hands with Mr Pimm and then Gilly shook hands with Mr Pimm.

'It is nice to see you. How are you, Mr Pimm?'

'Could do with a wet, I expect, couldn't you, mate?'

It was, it seemed, Mr Pimm's day off after all.

'Could we go fishing with Mr Pimm after lunch? Mr Pimm thinks it would be good for fishing after the rain.'

'I don't think we've got rods and lines and things, have we?'

'Oh! Mr Pimm's got all that. He's brought his rods and everything with him.'

'Oh! of course. I never noticed. We don't have to dig worms and things, though, do we? I hate worms.'

'No, no. Mr Pimm's got all that. The worms and the gentiles and everything.'

'The what? The gentiles?'

'Gentiles and bread and everything.'

'What are gentiles?'

'Oh! they're maggots. Mr Pimm gets them out of bad meat. You catch all the best fish with gentiles.'

'Oh! please. Do you mind? You'll spoil my lunch.'

After lunch, when she had washed up, Gilly always made a cup of tea. Then she sat for half an hour in the little front sitting-room, slowly sipping tea and reading the morning paper. Mr Pimm didn't always stay for the tea; some days, he said, he could do with a cup and some days he couldn't.

But today, Mr Pimm's day off, they all three had tea. Gilly brought it in on a tray. There were three cups and Mr Pimm, who had a sweet tooth, had five lumps of sugar in his tea.

'Not spoons in cups, please.'

'Mr Pimm's got his spoon in his cup.'

The electricity men always had their spoons in their tea mugs too. They were always drinking tea, whenever you went to look at them.

'It's not very nice, spoons in cups.'

James drank his tea with low, dark noises.

'Re-fill, mate?'

The golden afternoon, windlessly quiet, the sky washed pure after rain, was perfect for fishing. A stream about the width of the road and about fifty yards from it flowed southward, a coil of rope casually thrown down between grey-green willows and clumps of alder and hawthorns already berrying crimson, across the park.

The shadows under the alders were dark with mystery. The

water was black and still and deep. You couldn't see to the bottom of it. The air above it was drowsy with golden crowds of little flies.

'Look, there's a water boatman going across the pool.'

'Don't talk. You mustn't talk. Mr Pimm says the fish will hear.'

Gilly had broken off three wands of willow from a tree and stripped them clean of leaves. She sat on the bank of the stream with one in her hand, James with the other and Mr Pimm with the third. Every twenty seconds or so Mr Pimm snapped his rod out of the water with a bite. James had several bites too but never as many, quite, as Mr Pimm. It was marvellous the bites Mr Pimm had.

'That's a good one, Mr Pimm. That's a fair old whopper. What are you on, mate? Gentiles? or paste?'

Mr Pimm was on gentiles; it was just the day for them.

'Don't go to sleep, Gilly. You'll miss a bite if you go to sleep.'

The air was so drowsy that it intoxicated deeply. Thick patches of willow herb lying along the banks, pink with drooping flowers, moved with less than the flicker of a gnat's wing. A fish that plopped to the surface some way downstream made a sound like a cork of velvet being pulled.

Half asleep with warmth and silence and enfolding shadow Gilly drowsed and woke and drowsed again, the willow wand half in the water. To what she thought was the rising sound of music she heard fish after fish being caught. In an air unreal and compelling as Mr Pimm himself she became aware, slowly, that the sound of music was increasing and coming nearer, worrying her ear like the echo of an intrusive distant radio.

'Gilly, don't go to sleep. There's a man looking at you.'

Startled she awoke. The willow wand fell from her hand, dropped into the water and started spinning in the slowest of circles downstream.

'Oh! I'm sorry. I'm afraid my transistor startled you.'

'Ulrica Lehmann will now sing three songs by Schumann. The first *Der Nussbaum*, the Nut Tree – '

The voice from the transistor swooned away, increased in strength again and then suddenly, with the snap of a switch, died completely. The transistor itself was no bigger than a blue box of playing cards. It sat comfortably in the hand of a man of thirty-five or so, wearing greyish leather shorts, a green check shirt and open brown sandals. In his other hand he carried a map sheathed in a Perspex case and on his back a rucksack that seemed altogether too heavy for his tall, narrow shoulders.

'Oh! it didn't startle me. You needn't switch it off.'

'Off now. I only listen when I'm alone.'

With casual bemusement he stood gazing down on the two willow wands and the third floating slowly away downstream.

'Intensive fishing going on I see.'

'Yes.'

'Any luck?'

'I think James caught a few and Mr Pimm quite a lot – '

Mr Pimm? With intense blue eyes that somehow succeeded in looking casual too the man looked up and down the banks of the stream, again at the two willow wands and again at the third floating away. Mr Pimm? Who and where was Mr Pimm?

'Mr Pimm's gone home,' James said.

The man stared at the willow wands again, at the one in the boy's hand, the empty one propped up on the bank and at the third floating away.

'Mr Pimm's gone home, it seems.'

'Yes.'

Gilly moved swift fingers across her hair, slightly irritated, aware of being mocked.

'Caught enough for his supper, I suppose?'

'Mr Pimm caught twenty,' James said.

'Lucky Mr Pimm. How many have you caught?'

'They're all in my basket.'

'Ah! yes, I see. In the basket.'

There was an awkward silence while the man looked this way and that for the basket and then at last, casual and slightly mocking again, at Gilly. His voice, when he spoke, was deliberately low.

'The basket, like our Mr Pimm, seems to be no longer with us.'

Gilly had nothing to say. The man seemed inclined to treat the absence of Mr Pimm and the basket more than ever lightly.

'What sort of fish do you get in here?'

'Roach and perch,' James said, 'and sometimes gudgeon. And one of the men from the electricity caught a trout one day.'

'A trout? I say, that's good. How big?' Half-mockingly the man spread out his arms to the length of a foot or so, then wider and then wider again. 'As big as that?'

'Not quite so big.'

During another awkward silence the man looked at his map and then across the park at the empty, shuttered house and then back at the map again.

'If the next village is Fairhurst this must be Fairhurst House. Regency, I suppose, or probably earlier and re-fronted. Looks very empty. Still I sometimes think they look better empty, don't you?'

'Think what?'

The man, more closely intent on the map now, gave a brief dry laugh.

'Funny.'

'Is it? What is? – the house?'

'No, no. I mean the stream. It really shouldn't be here.'

'Oh! shouldn't it? Where should it be?'

He laughed again, letting a forefinger trace a line across the map. 'Well, more over there.' He pointed some thirty or forty yards across the park, away from the direction of the house. 'It probably went round there in a great bend. They straightened it out at some time.'

'Did they? It still winds pretty much.'

'Oh! but not so much as it did. If you got up there in a helicopter and looked down you'd probably still see traces of the old course. One of those big ox-bow bends. They did that sometimes when they re-made these old houses – straightened the streams out, planted avenues, made lakes and all that – like this one – and did a general tarting up.'

'They did?'

'Sort of keeping up with the Joneses. Lady Elizabeth got

jealous because Lady Witchcraft had a new portico on her house and so she had to have one too, nice modern Regency – what are you laughing at? – '

'Lady Witchcraft.'

'Oh! yes. Well, you know how those old trouts must have been. They don't change much.'

Suddenly he sat down on the river bank, slipping off his ruck-sack, at the same time giving the transistor radio switch a flick with his finger. A soprano voice came forth, singing in German, with a slow delicacy, expressing some longing not quite tangible.

'Care for Schumann? No?'

He switched the trannsistor off again.

'Amusing, these old maps. Very interesting. This one's 1870. Prussians at the gates of Paris and all that and the stream on a different track altogether, right over there. And probably no road.'

'No road?'

'Not according to this map. Probably planted the avenue first and then couldn't afford the road. Bankruptcy rearing its ugly head again, I expect. Gosh, it's warm.'

'Yes, it seems terribly close after the rain.'

His finger became restless on the switch of the transistor. He flicked it on and off again so swiftly that only the merest brittle note came forth, rudely broken, restless itself, on the drowsy afternoon.

'And how's our fisherman getting on?'

The sleepy silence of the afternoon remained unbroken.

'Answer came there none.'

'He doesn't like to talk when he's fishing.'

'Of course. Sorry. I forgot.'

After this it was necessary to talk in whispers. From time to time he seemed suddenly driven by some restless force, more out of sheer habit than anything conscious, to switch on the radio. Then as suddenly he checked himself, peered at the map and wondered, half to himself, in whispers, what life could have been like all that way back, almost a century away.

'Is the house really empty?'

Except for one small wing, she explained. And even that was

used, mostly, only for the summer. She explained too, briefly, about Tangier and the long, long holiday stretching ahead.

'Ah! the sun craze.'

'Yes, it's the sun she's after.'

'The sun madness. All this and heaven too and not enough.'

She was quiet, watching the stream, the boy and the motionless willow wand. She was not sure, now, what he was talking about. He moved a bit too far ahead and too fast for her sometimes and it didn't improve things when he suddenly said:

'Pub in the village any good? The White Hart, isn't it?'

'Yes.'

'I'm putting up there for a couple of days or so.'

'You are?'

He looked at her rather hard, almost as if in reproval about something. All this time they had been talking in whispers, or a little above whispers, but now when he suddenly raised his voice the contrast was so great that he might well have been shouting to someone else, far downstream.

'Ah! it's heaven all right. I love August, don't you? Beautiful month. Do you know I've walked on over fifty miles of roads that are no longer on the map?'

'You have?'

'Green tracks, lost tracks, the lot. You'd be surprised. No cars, no anything.'

'How do you find them if they're lost?'

'Well, they're there and they're not there, lost and not lost, if you see what I mean. It's just a question of looking. Well, not quite. Knowing where and how to look.'

'I expect it'll soon be like that with the railways.'

'Exactly. Same thing. When that boy grows up' – he pointed suddenly to the motionless watching figure of James on the bank of the stream – 'he'll probably be tracking lost railway lines and saying "Isn't it marvellous? People actually travelled on here".'

'You think so?'

'Sure of it. Passionate interest in what's lost and all that. Anyway it makes a damn good holiday.'

'Oh! you're on holiday, are you?'

He gave her another hard, searching but slightly disbelieving look, clearly as if to say 'You catch on quickly, don't you?' This time the inference was not lost on her and she sat very quiet, staring down at the grass, biting her lip.

For fully half a minute he was quiet too and then suddenly he again flicked on the switch of the transistor radio. Again the soprano voice came forth and this time he let it sing on, inexpressibly sad, for a little while, during which he stared at the chestnut trees.

'The chestnuts are turning early this year.'

'They are?'

'Quite a lot of colour already. I suppose it's the wet summer. They say it's something to do with the amount of sugar in the leaves.'

'Sugar?'

'Oh! yes. If there's not enough sun there isn't the sugar and then the leaves turn colour that much earlier – Hullo, where's our fisherman friend?'

'You mean James? James! James, where are you?'

She leapt to her feet, her voice rising too.

'James!' For a few moments she could see no sign of the boy; then abruptly she caught sight of him, leaning against a willow trunk, motionless, thirty yards or so downstream. 'James! Don't go too far away, will you? No farther – do you hear?'

She stood for some moments longer, watching, slightly troubled, again biting her lip.

'You scared me for a moment. I thought he'd gone off – I thought I'd lost him.'

'But doesn't he often go off? Boys do.'

'Yes, but he's a terrible wanderer. Wandering off and talking to people and making friends – '

'Like Mr Pimm.'

She sat down on the grass again, quiet, her silence defensive. The way he spoke of Mr Pimm slightly irritated her. Clearly, he didn't believe in Mr Pimm.

'Mr Pimm's different.'

'Oh! yes? How?'

'We know where we are with Mr Pimm.'

She suddenly found that she not merely resented the intrusion of a stranger on the privacy of Mr Pimm. Silently she was defending it. Mr Pimm wasn't for any Tom, Dick or Harry; Mr Pimm didn't belong to any stranger.

When she looked up at him again she found that even his brief casual interest in Mr Pimm had passed. Instead he was staring at the house. He was actually framing his two hands into a square, as if preparing to take a photograph.

'Of course they'll pull it down. Bound to.'

'They will?'

'They always do. Progress and all that – ever heard of it? I'd like to get a picture of it. How's the light?'

He looked quickly at the sky. For a moment the sharp upcast eyes might actually have been cut out of the fabric of blue space between the clouds. She found herself still watching them, still fascinated, as he took a light meter from his pocket, at the same time saying he didn't know why he bothered, it was clearly no good. Finally he swung his camera round from behind his back and held it to his eye.

'No. Too far away. What's it like inside?'

'The house? I've never been in.'

'Oh! really? I thought you were part of the family and all that.'

'Only for the last three days. Anyway we only live in the little house. The cottage.'

'Pity. I'd have liked some shots of the inside. Still, I can get the outside, tomorrow perhaps, in colour. Hold still – no, like that – just hold it like that –'

He was suddenly swivelling the camera this way and that, swiftly, at odd angles, stooping, once down on one knee, once actually half-lying on the grass, on one elbow.

'Oh! you're not taking pictures of me?'

'That's it. Keep looking over that way. That's it. Towards the house.'

'You're not taking me in colour?'

'Oh! no. Just using a film up. I'll get colour tomorrow.'

She didn't know what to say except that he had caught her unawares. He merely smiled. Already he was putting the camera back into its case, saying at the same time that colour was expensive, that he only used it for special things. Then he sat for a time crouching on his haunches, looking at the house, the park and the chestnut trees with their scarcely discernible fingers of copper faintly showing among the leaves, saying that he expected there was a shop in the village and he could get film there.

'There's a shop but they don't have film. I don't think so.'

'Well, I'll have to track around. Where's the next place?'

'Grafton Heath. About four miles.'

'More walking. My fault anyway. I should have got some this morning.'

She watched him fix the camera finally into its leather holder, her face bemused, in a half smile.

'Do you always take so many pictures all at once? Of one person, I mean? You must have taken dozens.'

'Oh! generally. That's what these cameras are for.'

'When will they be ready? Could I see them?'

'Oh! I'll probably keep the whole shoot until I get back home and then develop them altogether. I do my own. Much cheaper and more fun.'

'You say you might come and take the house in colour tomorrow?'

'Did I say that? Oh! might do. No, can't, can I? Can't get the film in time. Tomorrow's Sunday.'

He stood up, hitching rucksack, camera and map into place over his shoulder. For a moment she stared at him with the impression that he was some sort of explorer, bound for distant adventure, in strange parts, and that she would never see him again. Like the lost roads and tracks he discovered he was about to slip away into a countryside that, to her, was just as much an unknown region.

'Well, must go. Got to get some stamps before the post office closes. Good-bye. Might see you.'

'Yes. Good-bye.'

He started walking and was already a dozen yards away when she suddenly remembered something.

'I've just thought of something. If you really wanted to look at the inside of the house I've got a key.'

'Good girl.'

'I think it would be all right. I'm supposed to go in every few days anyway and see – '

'Good. Come Monday, I'll take you up on that.'

He swung away from the river, across the grass and on to the road. For a few brief moments she watched him, again biting her lip, and as she did so the impression that he was an explorer, an adventurer about to disappear into some strange unknown region, sharpened to a point of pain. It was Sunday tomorrow, she remembered, and she hated Sunday. It was the very death of a day.

She was aware, presently, of another figure standing beside her, willow wand raised like a whip.

'Hullo, you're back again. Did you catch anything down there?'

'No. But Mr Pimm did.'

'Mr Pimm? I thought Mr Pimm had gone home.'

'He did, but he's back again. Didn't you see him? He's sitting over there.'

She woke on Sunday morning to the sound of church bells. They sounded dull and flat, as if someone were beating old kettles against a wall.

She stood for a long time in the kitchen, in her dressing gown and slippers, staring at the rain. It was one of those gentle, misted, irritating rains of late summer, almost feathery, the colour of lead pencil. In the park the chestnut trees looked as if they had partly rusted overnight. The grass everywhere was overlaid with a film that looked like tarnished dew.

'The clouds look like big old bears today, don't they?'

'Do they? I never noticed.'

'I can hear the church bells. Are we going to church?'

'I don't know. Are you supposed to go to church?'

James was trying to eat his tomato and scrambled egg the grown-up way, with a knife and fork. The scrambled egg was leathery and cold.

'Would you like to go to church?'

'It's raining, isn't it?'

'Yes I know it's raining, but would you like to go to church?'

'Would you?'

She poured herself another cup of tea, still staring at the rain. The rain would have been less irritating if it had fallen heavily, with visible force. As it was it merely gathered in the air, a grey imprisoning web.

'Do we have newspapers on Sunday?' she said.

'I think so.'

'What time do they get here?'

'I don't know. Sometimes we walk and get them from the shop.'

The clouds, she thought, were not so much like big old bears as crumpled umbrellas, the grey fabric saturated. There was no wind to tear a hole in them.

'Does Mr Pimm come to lunch today?' she said.

'No. Not today.'

'Why not? He comes every other day.'

'Yes, but he never comes on Sunday.'

'Why not?'

'He has a lot of things to do on Sunday.'

'He does? What sort of things?'

'He digs his garden and goes ferreting and getting mushrooms and things like that.'

'Ferreting? How do you know that?'

'He told me. He never has time to turn round on Sundays.'

She sipped her tea, thinking of church, newspapers, rain, the clouds that never broke. It was the sort of morning that made you think that summer had died for ever. You were on the edge of winter. The echoes of summer, flat as the church bells, were drowned in the distances. She had always hated Sunday: it was the death of a day.

'I was going to cook roast beef and Yorkshire. You know, a real Sunday lunch.'

'We had that once in the week.'

'Yes, but that wasn't really – you know, it was – Wouldn't you like it, I mean real roast beef and Yorkshire and nice beans from the garden? I thought Mr Pimm would like it.'

'He doesn't come on Sundays.'

She poured herself another cup of tea, nursed it in her hands for a moment or so and then got up and went to the kitchen cupboard.

'Are you taking pills?'

'Just a couple of aspirins.'

'Why are you having to take aspirins?'

'I feel rotten.'

'Why do you feel rotten?'

'Oh! do you mind!'

She sat in brooding silence. Then she started to swallow the aspirins, washing them down with tea. One of the aspirins got partially stuck in her throat and she started coughing.

'Why are you coughing?'

A broken fragment of aspirin came up and lay on her tongue. It was bitter and she swallowed it again.

'Couldn't we go fishing?'

She gulped at the tea, trying to wash the aspirin finally down her throat.

'Couldn't we? It's better when it's raining.'

'I should look well. What do you think I am? – a duck or something?'

'Mr Pimm says it's better when it rains.'

'Oh! could we have less of Mr Pimm? He's not coming today, is he? All right, let's forget about him.'

Abruptly she swallowed the last of her tea and then rattled the cup into the kitchen sink, letting the tap run cold water over it and over her hands.

'Sit and finish your breakfast. I'm going upstairs.'

'What are you going upstairs for?'

'I'm going to have a bath.'

'What are you going to do then?'

'We'll walk and get the papers. Would that suit you?'

'You mustn't go out after a bath. You'll catch your death.'

'All right. I'll catch my death. That'll be a bit of excitement.'

She slammed her way out of the kitchen, tramping upstairs.

'Is it exciting when you're dead?'

The rain had stopped. The merest finger of white light, like fluffy trimmings of fur, had begun to show on the breaking outlines of western cloud. The sound of church bells had stopped too. The surface of the road beyond the park was actually steaming slightly in the warmer air.

'Is it?'

'Is what?'

'Is it exciting when you're dead?'

The village street was long and rather wide. The church, squat-towered, tawny-roofed, grey, stood at one end of it. Half-way down stood The White Hart. Normally a sign hung above the door, but now the sign had gone away for re-painting and only the bare wrought iron frame stuck out from the red brick-work, an empty skeleton.

'That's what you said.'

'Oh! don't keep on about what I said. It isn't important.'

'Isn't being dead important?'

'No, it's not. Good gracious I should think not.'

'I heard you say it's better to be dead than stuck in this hole on a Sunday.'

'Well, that was just an expression. I was only talking to myself.'

'Well, somebody else might hear.'

He stopped to stamp his feet in a pool of water.

'And don't do that! You'll splash my stockings. They're clean on too.'

He stopped stamping his feet and merely dragged the sole of one shoe across the surface of the puddle, slowly.

'I told you, don't do that. It's messy. Look at your shoes. You'll get me six months.'

'Six months what?'

'Go into the shop and get the papers. Do something useful. Ask for the papers for Mr Sampson.'

While she waited for him to come back from the shop the first fragmentary glimpse of sun appeared. It merely served to illuminate the street's Sunday emptiness, the skeleton pub-sign, the cracked flag-stones of the pavement drying like white bones after rain.

'The lady in the shop says the boy has already gone with the papers.'

'Oh! he would. Of course.'

Driven by a wave of new irritation she turned away to hear a voice saying:

'No fishing today?'

No camera today, either, she thought: no rucksack. No map. No shorts. No transistor, especially no transistor. He looked very different without it all: a pair of creased but otherwise clean linen slacks of a bluish grey shade making him look even taller than before, and a long-sleeved cream shirt, buttoned at the cuffs, giving him an unexpectedly well-laundered, Sunday-fied air.

'I bar it in the rain.'

'What, the fishing? Well, it's stopped raining now. I see bits of blue as big as a man's shirt. By the way, splendid pub. Every comfort. Fabulous breakfast. Porridge, kippers, grilled ham, a dozen eggs if I'd asked for them. My God, she knows how to lay it on.'

'Who does?'

'Mrs Fitzsimmons. The woman who keeps it. Know her? Had a long, long chat with her last night after the bar closed.'

No, she said, she didn't know Mrs Fitzsimmons. She stared at the empty street again, still aware, in spite of growing sunlight, of her Sunday morning shroud.

'She knows your people a bit, the Sampsons. They drop in quite a lot at week-ends. My God, she's got that place hopping. The vitality – Not going, are you?'

'Well –'

'Come in for a drink. It must be opening time.'

Her? With the boy? And did they serve girls of seventeen now?

'Oh! of course. Sorry. I forgot. I somehow thought you were older.' He looked at her figure up and down, appraising it quickly. 'You look older.'

'I feel older.'

'Oh! don't say it like that.'

'Say it like what? I hate Sundays, that's all.'

Curiously enough, he said, he felt quite differently about them. He thought Sunday stimulated. He liked the air of Sunday. He liked dressing for the day. Weekdays he didn't mind knocking about in any old thing, but Sundays – no, he couldn't agree about Sundays.

'Well, everybody has different ideas.'

Yes. And what, he said to the boy, about Mr Pimm? How was Mr Pimm today?

'I expect he's all right.'

'Not coming fishing today?'

'Not today,' she said. 'We don't see Mr Pimm on Sundays.'

No? Ah! yes, he caught on. Mr Pimm sort of – well, appeared as and when required? Was that it?

'Mr Pimm doesn't like people who don't like him.'

'Now you know,' she said.

They walked slowly down the street. A miraculously wide space of sky, brilliantly blue and rain-washed, was enlarging every moment from the west. Presently the sun slipped into it, swam clear and poured down bright and hot.

'People are coming out of church,' the boy said and stopped to draw the sole of his shoe across another puddle.

'You said something about coming to look at the house.'

'Did I? Oh! yes. I forgot. I've got to get the films, haven't I?'

'Come out of that puddle! I've told you a million times.'

They stopped for a moment or two, waiting for the boy to catch up.

'Now do as I say. Walk on ahead and keep in front where I can see you.'

'Gone to Majorca, I hear, his parents.'

'Tangier.'

'Oh! Tangier. Mrs Fitzsimmons thought it was Majorca. Tangier – Know it?'

'Never heard of it till they went there.'

'A friend of mine went there last spring. Rained every day.'

'That won't suit her. It had better be hot.'

'Ah! the sun-worshipping type. I know a woman who doesn't eat because she's convinced the sun is food. Thin as a rake. Puts on half a gramme and then goes round in circles, thinks she's getting fat.'

'Some people are crazy.'

Several times, as they walked on, she felt his eyes appraising her again. Once the boy dropped behind and momentarily he dropped behind too. Without turning round she knew quite well his eyes were fixed on her, sizing her up.

'Pity you couldn't come in for a drink. Are they so particular nowadays? You'd pass for eighteen.'

'How could I leave James? I'm in charge of him, remember?'

'Perhaps Mr Pimm would look after him.'

She felt herself go rigid with resentment. Her mind bristled at the thought of Mr Pimm being mocked. Mr Pimm had to be believed in; Mr Pimm was real; it was despicably cheap to doubt Mr Pimm. In a silence both frigid and distant she felt herself protecting him.

'Did I say something?'

'Did you? You should know.'

'I mean, to offend you.'

'Oh! you haven't offended me.'

'No? Well, sorry if I did.'

She laughed, dryly, grittily, for the first time that morning. 'What's the use of being sorry for something you haven't said?'

He laughed too, at the same time disarming her by changing the subject completely.

'Thanks for reminding me about the house. I'll have to do the pictures tomorrow. I plan to push on sometime on Tuesday.'

'You do?'

'Got a long way to go. Mustn't miss the house, though. Quite a passion of mine, these houses. The empty ones especially. You know – wondering who lived there, what they did, eating and drinking, quarrelling, love affairs and so on, the lot. This house, I mean – it's the period, it could be Jane Austen.'

'Who was she?'

'What sort of size is it? Oh! Jane? – she was quite the girl. She had them weighed up. It doesn't look all that big from the outside but they're quite often deceptive, a lot bigger than they seem.'

'Great big deadly hole it looks to me.'

'Oh! you've seen it all?'

'No, only that one bit. The wing they use. I just went up there once for the interview.'

'But the key does for the whole lot?'

'Oh! yes, wander where you like as far as I'm concerned. Any idea what time you might come along?'

'My God, look how the sky's cleared. In that short time. You'd never have thought it. Deadly first thing and now look at it. Made you think summer had gone and now –'

'Some time in the afternoon? or morning?'

'Gosh, it's quite hot. Oh! afternoon I think. I'll have to get the film in the morning. I'd like to have the light about right. I should think between three and four.'

'I see. Where's James? James? – that boy! he's out of my sight like a rabbit.'

'It's all right. He's just round the corner of the road there. I just saw him go. He doesn't talk much, does he?'

'Oh yes he does.'

'He hasn't said a word.'

'You wait till you're gone. Then he'll start.'

He laughed. That, he thought, was very interesting. He had to wait till he had gone so that he could hear something that couldn't be said while he was here – interesting, most interesting, extraordinarily interesting.

'Well, you know what I mean. You're a stranger.'

For some reason she suddenly felt impossibly shy. The slow look she started to give him never resolved itself. She actually felt the light in her eyes drain away like a tide, leaving everything in her dry and withdrawn.

'Well, that's inevitable when people first meet, I suppose.'

Inevitable? In shyness she felt herself also, and for the first time, confused. For some ridiculous reason she suddenly wanted to apologize for the way she had talked, Sunday-grousing, a bit sour and sore-headed, but the pressure of the moment was too great, too intimate altogether. She simply stared ahead, unaware that she had also stopped walking.

'Well, this is your park gate.'

'Yes.'

'The one that's kept closed. Why's that? Ought to have a notice on it – *Strangers Keep Out*.'

She was going to say that she didn't know why and that in any case you could always use the other gate, you could always get in at the other end, but the words never came.

'Well, it doesn't stop James. He's over the damn thing like a shot. Wants his lunch, I expect.'

'He can wait for a bit. I haven't cleared the breakfast things.'

'Well, I could do with mine. Mrs Fitzsimmons tells me it's roast pork today. I ought to get back.'

'Oh! yes, mustn't keep Mrs Fitzsimmons waiting.'

'She's really marvellous. She really can cook. She's Irish. You knew that? Calls everything and everybody beautiful. A man comes into the bar and orders himself a pint of bitter and says it feels like thunder and she says "Does it now? Ah! you're a beautiful man". You should see them melt – no wonder she's got the place hopping.'

'So you'll come some time tomorrow then.'

'Ah! yes, tomorrow. Between three and four did I say?'

Her shyness, now amounting almost to mistrust, deepened still further. She tried again to say something, but the grey Sunday mood held her shackled.

'My God, I'm looking forward to that roast pork I can tell you.'

She climbed the gate into the park. She walked slowly up the road, alone except for the boy running in the distance, feeling like a stranger herself.

After the long desolation of Sunday it was good, on Monday, to have Mr Pimm to lunch again. The reality of Mr Pimm asserted itself in bright new terms. Mr Pimm had been down to the sea for the week-end. Mr Pimm looked sun-burnt. He had been round the whelk stalls and on the dodg'ems and everything was smashing. It seemed almost an insult to give Mr Pimm only

Welsh rarebit for lunch but Mr Pimm seemed to enjoy it enormously.

'How's the roast lamb, Mr Pimm? Have some mint sauce, mate.'

There was no doubt that Mr Pimm thought the lamb pretty hot stuff. The presence of Mr Pimm was not merely real. It was uplifting. It exhilarated Gilly so much that she felt not merely its warmth and reality but the final extinction, in herself, of the cold, sour mood of Sunday.

'Do you think if we asked Mr Pimm we could go down to the sea with him next Sunday?'

'I expect we might.'

In a flash she saw the sea. It was a great wide space of blue and white, all glittering, beyond a barrier, open to the sky. It shone before her suddenly as a great shimmering avenue of escape.

She was so absorbed in this dream of inner solitude that for some moments she let the talk between James and Mr Pimm go on as in a dream too, fluidly, uninterrupted. She felt she could never endure another Sunday. The fact that there were five of them, perhaps six, perhaps more, stretching ahead like grave-stones marking the passage of the weeks had depressed her, only yesterday, like the wearing of a shroud. She was stuck with Sunday, the boy, the job, the house and there was no way out of it. Today, miraculously, it hardly seemed to matter.

Had Mr Pimm been alone to the sea? or with someone else? Oh! Mr Pimm had been with Mr Monday.

Aroused by the name of Mr Monday she inquired if James hadn't asked how Mr Monday was today?

'He's about the same, Mr Pimm says, but he won't make old bones.'

She said she was sorry about that; it was a pity for Mr Monday.

'Will you make old bones?'

She didn't know; she expected she might do.

'Should we ask Mr Pimm if he'll come fishing this afternoon?'

No, she said, she didn't think they could ask Mr Pimm to come fishing today.

'Why can't we?'

Because they had that young man coming, the one who had the camera. He was going to take pictures.

'Oh! him.'

Well, they sometimes had to have other people, didn't they? They couldn't have Mr Pimm by himself all the time. If they had Mr Pimm all the time they might get tired of him, mightn't they?

'I like having Mr Pimm all the time. I never get tired of him.'

'Well, let's not sulk then. Let's make the most of Mr Pimm while he's here.'

'Mr Pimm doesn't like being here with other people.'

'Well, he'll have gone home by then anyway.'

'Don't you like having Mr Pimm now?'

'Yes, I do. I love having Mr Pimm.'

'That man didn't like him.'

'Yes, but that's not the same. He doesn't know Mr Pimm. He doesn't see him like we do. Other people don't always see things like we do.'

'Mr Pimm does.'

After lunch it began to rain again. The clouds above the chestnuts at the far end of the avenue were, as he so often imagined, like fat, purple, crouching bears. Again the feeling that summer had died for ever and had been wrapped away in a dingy August shroud enveloped and oppressed the little sitting-room.

For this reason it was also nice that Mr Pimm stayed on for coffee. It relieved the oppression, shutting out the stormy stream of western rain snapping on the windows. It helped to pass the time away.

Mr Pimm also had a smoke. Cigar? He might just as well, mate, because it wasn't going to let up yet – once the wind got up the hill there was no telling what they'd get. James had a cigar too. He clipped off the end, lit it with a care almost reverent, gazed with benign approval at the burning tip of it and went on to smoke it with care, looking somehow old and content.

'Care for a game of dominoes, mate?'

Mr Pimm indicated that he would indeed. He was a great one for dominoes.

'Spot more coffee first? How's the cigar?'

Yes, Mr Pimm said, he would have a spot more coffee. James gazed with reverent adult approval at the tip of his cigar, holding it out with the hand of a connoisseur, little finger extended.

Somehow, by the time Gilly had found the dominoes, a feeling of great opulence filled the room. It wrapped itself round everything like velvet. It enfolded itself softly about the conversation, the coffee cups, the dominoes actually laid out like an architectural black-and-white cortège on the table. It even had on Gilly the effect of tranquillizing her into a belief that she was no longer herself. She was Mr Pimm, smoking a cigar, sucking loudly at coffee and playing dominoes.

She even began to talk like Mr Pimm.

'Double six, mate, eh? That's a bit ripe.'

'I laid the double six already. That's a double five.'

'So it is, burn me. It's my eyes. Can't see the pips nowadays.'

'You want new glasses. Your go.'

The rain beat with an almost winter frenzy on the windows. The farthest trees across the park melted into grey dank cloud, a glowering primeval forest in which not even a bird was seen to move.

'Well, you beat me that time, mate. You fair tanned me that time. Another game?'

Yes, she said, speaking as and for Mr Pimm, she wouldn't say no to another. Yes, the cigar was going a treat, thank you. Beautiful. Nice feeling they gave you, cigars.

'Ever so difficult to get nowadays.'

You were telling him. Didn't get these Havanas very often. Except perhaps at Christmas time.

'Going away for Christmas?'

No, Mr Pimm said, he didn't somehow think he was. He loved the old home fires at Christmas.

'I reckon my people are going to St Moritz.'

Never? Where was that, like?

'Snow place. You always have snow. Snow-balling all day long. Twos or fives wanted. Your go.'

Never? Snow all the time? Double two. That wouldn't suit him, snow all the time.

'Blimey, twos and fives again. Turn it up, mate. I'm running out.'

Mr Pimm said he was very sorry, but you couldn't help how they ran. Was it all right if he helped himself to a spot more coffee? Perfectly all right. Thanks. Mr Pimm, after pouring out more coffee, dragged hard on his cigar, leaning back on one elbow with relaxed content, blowing opulent smoke clouds. This was the stuff. Still raining? You bet. Pelting down.

'Let it. We're all right in here, mate, eh? Nothing to worry about here. Twos and sixes wanted.'

As the afternoon went on, with rain squalling at the windows with grey bullets, the distances more deeply, and more waterily unbalanced in mist, it became more and more easy for Gilly to slip into the body and mind of Mr Pimm, to think the thoughts of Mr Pimm, to use the language of Mr Pimm and, with a benign opulence that almost drugged the senses, smoke Mr Pimm's cigar.

So much was she enshrouded in the reality of it all that if anything belonged to the world of make-believe it was the re-collection of her sour-grey mood of Sunday. It was no use, though; that was how Sunday affected her. Now, on Monday, it could rain hell and donkeys all day and it didn't matter.

'You always go down to the sea for your holidays, mate?'

Mr Pimm reckoned he did. Suited him all right down there.

'My folks are in Tangier.'

Never? Where was that then?

'Near Paris. You go by plane.'

Ah! near Paris, eh? Tidy step away, like? Did he ever miss them?

'Can't say I do, mate, not all that. Long as I got company.'

Mr Pimm said he was glad to hear that. He liked company too. Of course there was company and company.

'Too right, mate.'

He actually paused, and looking up from the dominoes, winked at Mr Pimm. With grave solemnity, sagely, Mr Pimm winked back.

In that moment of mutual affection she felt a sudden driving desire to escape from being Mr Pimm. The emotions now engendered in her as Mr Pimm's emotions were somehow greater than those she felt as herself. She was suddenly too much part of Mr Pimm. For a few moments she wanted to slip out of his skin and shake herself free.

'What about another game, mate?'

'Do you think you should?' She was herself now, speaking as herself. 'Don't you think Mr Pimm ought to go?'

'What, in this lot? He'll get soaked.'

'I could lend him an umbrella.'

'Umbrella? Mr Pimm? People like Mr Pimm don't have umbrellas.'

'Well, it's letting up a little bit. It doesn't rain quite so hard. I think he should go before it comes on too fast again.'

She was standing by the window now, staring at the rain-drenched park. Half-way along the road a postman was cycling, rain-cape shining, head down, struggling towards the house against the rain.

'There's the afternoon post. Let's see if he comes here.'

'Is there a bit of blue as big as a man's shirt?'

'No. Not yet.'

'Then it's not clearing up. Mr Pimm can't go. That's what that man said yesterday. About the sky.'

'Well, it isn't quite so hard. Perhaps he would like to walk with the postman.'

'The postman isn't stopping here.'

No: the postman wasn't stopping. He struggled past the house, head down, wind-blown. And watching him, she thought of Tangier, post-cards. Of course it was too early for post-cards.

Thinking of Tangier, she suddenly started thinking also of the big house, the man with the camera and the transistor, the films and the pictures. Incredibly, far off to the west, a strip of light long and thin as a yellow eel suddenly swam low down into the grey horizon. In silence she watched it slowly enlarge until she could actually see the fingers of tree branches grow green against the light.

'You see, it's clearing up now. I think Mr Pimm should go while he can.'

'It's not blue like a man's shirt, though, is it?'

'No, not yet, but it will be.'

'It's got to be a lot bigger than that. It's still raining anyway.'

'Well, Mr Pimm can run between the showers.'

'It's raining hard again. If we had the telephone we could ring for a taxi.'

'If Mr Pimm doesn't have umbrellas I don't think he has taxis.'

'Well, can he come again tomorrow?'

'You'd better ask him first if he'd like to.'

'Would you like to come to lunch again tomorrow, Mr Pimm?'

Mr Pimm said not half he wouldn't. Thanks. Briefly, with gravity, she lent Mr Pimm's old gestures to the air, giving a last puff at the cigar before laying the stub down on the table. Well, Mr Pimm said, he'd push off now. Thanks for everything.

'What shall we give Mr Pimm for lunch tomorrow?'

'Shall we ask him or let it be a surprise?'

'A surprise.'

'All right. We'll think something up. Good-bye, Mr Pimm.'

Good-bye, miss, Mr Pimm said. Good-bye.

'So long, old mate. Sorry we can't say what we'll have for lunch tomorrow, but it'll be good.'

'You bet it would, Mr Pimm said. You bet. Well, thanks again for everything. So long.

'So long, mate. So long.'

She opened the front door so that Mr Pimm could go out. The rain was slackening now to a light beady drizzle. Great drops of water, like huge bird droppings, were everywhere slopping down from the trees.

Together they watched Mr Pimm go down the garden path, between rain-drooping dahlias, marigolds splashed with mud, asters bowed like dirty feathers, and so out on to the road beyond. Waving occasional hands, they stood there for some time watching, until at last Mr Pimm disappeared.

'What about jugged hare?'

'All right. Good. Let's have jugged hare.'
'And red currant jelly.'

As the strip of light in the west enlarged and became less like a yellow eel than a broad-bellied fish, its grey cloud-scales tipped more and more with flecks of sun, she became acutely aware of a rising restlessness inside herself. Mr Pimm and the rain, all afternoon, had held her content and secure. Now she was breaking away from the body, the mind, the speech and the gestures of Mr Pimm. She was completely herself again and was free.

When she looked at the kitchen clock, a few minutes later, she was astonished to find that it was almost half past four. It was hard to believe that the imprisoned afternoon had gone so quickly; hard to believe, too, that she was still in her working morning dress, hair still half scraggy, the lunch things unwashed.

'You look at a book or something while I rush upstairs. I've been sitting here all afternoon and haven't done a thing. Look at me.'

'I'll build a house with the dominoes.'

'You do that. I'll be a few minutes yet.'

From the window of her bedroom, as she changed her working dress for a green jumper and skirt, she saw the sun break through. A huge triangle of light, a theatrical cone of gold, poured down in almost violent illumination on the house across the park. She brushed her hair with vigour; its dark brown tones shimmered as she faced her reflection in the mirror, powdering her face and putting on new lipstick.

Suddenly, in the electrifying and almost harsh new light of sun, the green jumper looked shabby. Under the armpits it was stretched to bursting point. She remembered suddenly a box of clothes Mrs Sampson had given her just before going away. 'Just a few bits I won't need. Heave them into the rag-bag if they're not your size.'

She found in the box a jumper, cashmere, long-sleeved, of a curious gold-pink shade. When she put it on it was slightly too

49

tight for her. Its clinging softness was like that of a squirrel. Then the slight discomfort of it made her take it off again. Then she took off her bra too and put the jumper on again. The slight difference of wearing the jumper next to her skin gave her a new degree of comfort. Her breasts stood easy and free.

As she went downstairs she was increasingly aware of a new sense of pleasure. The squirrel softness of the long sleeves as she drew her fingers up and down them was exquisite. 'I suppose I shouldn't be wearing it in the afternoon like this. It's too good,' she thought and the boy said:

'You look like someone else.'

'Well, it's really someone else's jumper. She gave it to me.'

'You're not supposed to wear the things belonging to someone else.'

'Well, if someone else doesn't wear it any longer. If she doesn't want it – '

'You don't look the same. You don't look like you.'

'I am me. It's just the jumper. You'll get used to it. Don't you like it?'

The conversation with James, together with the new strength of light in the sky, started to make her impatient. In almost her first moment of irritation with him she turned on him sharply and said:

'You'll be telling me next you don't want me to wear it, I suppose.'

'I don't mind.'

'Well, I'm wearing it whether you like it or not.'

He stood at an unfriendly distance from her, staring.

'And don't give me the old milord look either. I don't like it and I won't have it.'

He continued to stand away from her, unfriendly, not speaking.

'All right! I'll go up and change the damn thing!'

Her sudden surge from the room had hardly taken her to the foot of the stairs before she heard the front door bell ring.

'Oh! who the hell's that now? I'll go. You go and play with your blessed dominoes.'

At the door, when she opened it, stood the man, in a light

mackintosh, with the camera slung round his neck, his light-meter held in one hand like a watch.

'Oh! it's you.'

'Yes, me. Unwelcome intruder? Sorry.'

'Oh! I didn't mean – I – '

'I know. Don't press it. It's Monday.'

Struggling desperately to free herself from irritation she tried to smile. His eyes were fixed, she noticed, not on her face but unashamedly on the gold-pink jumper.

'I'm not really late, am I? I said between four and five.'

'Oh! you're not late. The afternoon went like wildfire, that's all. Won't you come in a minute? I'm only just ready.'

He paused on the threshold, taking off his mackintosh.

'I'll just take this thing off. Hell of a day.'

'I thought it would never let up.'

'I didn't get up till one. Couldn't face the thought of summer. I hate Mondays anyway, don't you?'

'No, it's Sundays I hate.'

'Ah! yes, I remember.'

He stepped into the house. From the direction of the sitting-room, from the dominoes, came nothing but silence.

'I thought you might be fishing.' He peered round the half open door of the sitting-room. On the table the dominoes were no longer spread out in a black and white cortège. They were rising in a tower. The boy pored over it like a student locked with problems. 'No fishing. No Mr Pimm.'

'I should leave him.'

'Being difficult?'

'No, no. Just leave him.'

The silence from the domino tower was absolute, bleak and dark.

'You want to go? I'll get the key.'

She went upstairs. For half a minute he stood contemplating James.

'Building up nicely. You have to be careful of the last one, though. That's the one that brings it down.'

The silence that greeted these remarks merely made them seem more pointless.

'Well, I've got the key.' Gilly came downstairs and went into the sitting-room, half-way towards the boy. 'I'm going over to the house with this gentleman for a little while. You want to come?'

The silence from the dark domino tower was again bleak and absolute.

'We shan't be long. Will you be all right there, building?'

The boy put another domino, precariously, on the top of the tower.

'You want a glass of milk or something? Say if you do. No?'

The silence, she felt, was almost black. She managed to suppress inside herself a fresh hot stab of irritation.

'Well, do you want milk or something or not? Answer me.'

'Answer came there none – again –'

'Oh! leave him. He'll come out of it. If you let him he'll drive you – Well, make a nice tower, if that's the way you feel.'

As she and the young man went out of the house, across the road and into the park she felt a certain ruthless satisfaction in telling herself over and over again that absence would teach its lesson.

'You think he'll be all right there? By himself?'

'Oh! leave them alone and they'll come home – I see you keep looking at your light-meter. Is the light going to be all right?'

'Perfect – outside, that is. I can't tell about inside.'

Pellucidly, in steaming brilliance, the sky washed utterly clear of cloud, sunlight poured down on wet acres of grass, giving its summer emerald the shine of pure enamel. The white façade of the house, the balustrades of the front terrace and the big fanlight of the doorway looked almost as if built in salt. Against the high blue sky of the August afternoon they seemed to glisten, almost crystallized.

He took several shots of it all, now and then bending down on one knee, once leaning half-prostrate on the balustrade of the terrace, several times squatting on his haunches in the grass, the camera to his eye, the shutter clicking tirelessly: so industriously absorbed it was even a surprise to her to hear him say:

'Beautiful house. A peach. Proportions quite marvellous.'

'Are they?'

'Which key have you got? Back or front? I've about finished outside.'

'Front, I think. I've never tried it.'

'Well, let's try.'

As they stood on the sunlit terrace and while she found the key and fitted it into the front door lock she was acutely aware again that he was looking not so much at her as at the gold-pink jumper. She was aware too that wearing it gave her a sense of style, a feeling of quite unaccustomed illumination.

'Ah! that's it.' The key turned in the lock. The front door swung open. 'Thought for a moment you hadn't the right key. Oh! your name's Gilly, that right?'

'That's right. What's yours?'

'A – ' He seemed for a moment to hesitate. In a half absent-minded way he seemed to start to say something and then corrected himself and said another. 'A – Ainsworth.'

'That's not your Christian name.'

'Oh! Christian. Alex.'

Together they walked over the threshold, on to a floor of bare wood, carpetless. Rising centrally from it a staircase of thinnest wrought iron rails spiralled up beyond a high window like the twisting horn of a sea shell. He stood for fully half a minute enraptured by this, blue eyes intensely uplifted, before coming suddenly down to the business of reading some mundane message in the light-meter.

'Not bad. Not bad. Could try it. Probably better with a flash. But perfect, isn't it? Quite perfect. Fancy not living in this, I ask you – fancy – . But they do, don't they? I mean, in part?'

'It smells musty. Like a church. Old.'

'But didn't you say they did?'

'Say what?'

'They lived in it.'

'Oh! yes, in the wing. That's over the other side. We have to go behind the staircase and through that way. Aren't you going to take pictures?'

'I'd like to try the morning light. The light's awfully strong from that big window. Difficult at this time of day.'

'There's not much colour, is there? Wouldn't it be better in black and white?'

'No, there's not much colour. Except you. Stand over there, would you? Anywhere there. At the foot of the stairs.'

She stood at the foot of the stairs. Just casually, he said, anyhow. No pose. It was just to have a look at the colour. He focused the camera on her, held it watchfully for some moments, whipped it away and then stood staring at her with the naked eye. That was an extraordinary shade, that jumper of hers. What colour would she say that was?

'Don't really know.'

'Looks marvellous against the black ironwork and the white. Ah! yes, I know – you get that colour in some flower or other. God, what is it? I can see it clear as – my father used to grow it in his greenhouse. A sort of lily thing – long, just that shade. Marvellous – it sort of flowers out of that green skirt of yours.'

'It does?'

'I think the morning would be better after all. Shall we look at the rest of the house now? Yes, it'll be better for indoors tomorrow.'

Beyond the stairway there were unexpectedly wide passages of bare stone, leading to kitchens. The air was damp. The floor stones sweated underfoot. A sack of coal, uncollected for some reason, stood outside a door, a shovel beside it. From another passage beyond the kitchens a back stair twisted up, at last coming out on a landing lit by one small circular window.

'Did you say tomorrow?' she said. 'I thought you were going away tomorrow?'

They had reached the head of the narrow stairway by the time she remembered this. He shook his head very slightly, with some vagueness, as if at first not really hearing her.

'What? Oh! yes – no, no I'm not going tomorrow after all. I decided to stay on a bit. It's a good centre and all that – I can walk to places – the pub's nice. I say, this looks as if it's gone off a bit, doesn't it?' He actually sniffed at the stale stairway air, his nose turned up. 'Sure we've come the right way?'

'It's along this way. The wing's shut off. I need the other key.'

With a second key she opened a door at the end of the landing. It gave on to a small hallway with an umbrella stand and a coat rack on which hung several raincoats, an old polo sweater and a hat or two. One raincoat had fallen to the floor. She picked it up, shook it and hung it up again.

'Careful of the moths,' he said.

From the hallway they went into a drawing-room unexpectedly expansive, with a tall, shuttered window on the western side. She opened one of the shutters and sunlight poured in on a grand piano on which stood a black urn of dead chrysanthemums. Magazines were everywhere littered about on chairs and tables, newspapers and letters on mantelpiece and window sills. One newspaper had actually been screwed up into a ragged ball and lay in the fireplace, as if someone had thrown it there in a fit of temper. Grey cigarette ash seeded itself everywhere; cigarette stumps lay about tables and carpets like fat white ants. The lid of the grand piano was open and a tray of unwashed glasses still stood by the chrysanthemums. Half moons of dry lemon stuck to the glass rims.

'It's a sort of flat. I think they've got two bedrooms.'

She led the way into one of the bedrooms. Two single beds stood unmade, bedclothes strewn about the floor. A breakfast tray, coffee-cups unwashed, fragments of toast in blackish ruins among red daubs of jam, stood on a dressing table.

'Hurried departure? – moonlight flit or something?'

'I wouldn't know.'

'Is it supposed to stay like this until they come back? Isn't somebody supposed to clear it up or something?'

'Not me. They never asked me.'

'It stinks. It's festering.'

He went out of the bedroom and back into the drawing-room and said angrily:

'And, Good God, to do that to a piano. A Bluthner too. Look at it.' He seized the urn of chrysanthemums, from which water had poured over the piano top in a grey staining stream. 'It's nothing but bloody sacrilege.' Savagely he took the urn of dead chrysanthemums over to the window, rattling hard at the window-catch until it opened. 'That's what it is – nothing but bloody sacrilege. God, how I hate that smell of dead flowers. Don't you hate that?'

She was about to say that she hated it too when she saw him throw the chrysanthemums out of the window. At the last moment his hand slipped and she heard the urn crack against the window frame.

'You've gone and broken the vase. You shouldn't have done that.'

'Oh! who cares?'

Angrily he pushed the window open wider, taking a sharp deep breath of air. He then went back to the piano and impatiently played a few scrambling notes on it, one hand.

'What sort of people are they? God, it's the piano that gets me – to do that to a piano like that.'

'They've got money. It isn't that.'

He gave her a short pitying glance, not even angry now.

'Go on, tell me they're musical too. The piano's in good tune.'

Calmer now, he ran his fingers up and down the piano playing a few light absent chords, deliberately, with his right hand.

'I think it's she who plays. She was playing when I came for the interview. Mr Sampson let me in.'

'God save the Sampsons. Let's get some fresh air.'

He was through the doorway and into the hall before she remembered the window. She would have to shut the window, she called, she couldn't leave that open, and he called back:

'Damn the window. Leave it open. Give the place some air.'

She shut the window. She caught a last lingering breath of the wet, deathly odour of dead flowers and then went out of the room, shutting the door to.

By the time she caught up with him he was half-way down the back stairs. His footsteps scurried down so fast on the bare wooden treads that she was oppressed for some moments by the idea that he was running away from her and that she would never catch up. In the broad damp flagged passage below he actually started running. It was only in the big entrance hall beyond that he stopped for a moment, pausing at the foot of the staircase to look up at the elegant spiralling horn, his face pained.

She caught up with him, at last, on the terrace. He was sitting on a stone seat, staring at the park.

'Didn't you want to see the rest of it? There's two beautiful big rooms on this side, downstairs. I think they call one the music room.'

'Do they indeed?'

For several minutes he sat staring across the empty parkland without another word. At last she said:

'I don't know what you're going to do, but I ought to get back.'

'What? – Oh! yes. Why?'

'I've left the boy all by himself.'

'Oh! yes. Won't he be all right?'

'I suppose so, but I'm responsible – '

'Don't go for a minute. Sit here. Does he mind being alone?'

'Not really. He plays very well by himself.'

'And when you're not there, of course, he's always got Mr Pimm?'

He gave a slight laugh. Once again she thought she detected an echo of disbelief in Mr Pimm, a slight touch of mockery. As a result she found herself more than ever believing in the existence of Mr Pimm. She felt suddenly affronted, quick to defend him.

But suddenly the existence of Mr Pimm and the boy no longer seemed to matter:

'I ought to have learned my lesson by now,' he said.

'What lesson?'

'These houses. They all look so marvellous from outside and then inside – God, isn't someone going to close that place up? Is it going to stay like that until they come back? Doesn't anyone come in to clean?'

'They have a daily help, a Mrs Chapman, but they had a row the day before they left. She said she'd never come in again.'

'What about you?'

'Me?'

'You can't let it stay like that. I shouldn't sleep at nights thinking of it if I were you. It haunts me.'

'It does?'

'I don't think I'll sleep myself. I can taste it, that smell. It's in my mouth now.'

Together they stared across the park, at the tranquillized rain-washed spaces of western sky, all trace of cloud dispersed. Her eyes as she stared at these cloudless distances were as wide and slow and reflective as ever. The white light of afternoon seemed to fill them with an enormous innocence and again she seemed to be thinking of something remotely far away.

At last she said that she supposed if he thought it was all so awful he wouldn't be coming to take pictures tomorrow?

'Don't know. Not of these rooms anyway. You can bet on that.'

'You don't have to go upstairs.'

'Yes, but they're there. You can't escape them.'

'But there's the two big rooms downstairs. You haven't seen those.'

'I'll see. I may push on after all.'

For some moments she stared across the park without speaking. Then all of a sudden she seemed to be struck by a touch of conscience.

'You think I should clear it up? You think they'd expect me to?'

'They strike me as the sort of people who'd expect anything.'

'You think I should?'

'I think it's a bit much to expect.'

'You said just now you wouldn't sleep for thinking of it.'

He suddenly got up and started to walk across the terrace. Almost as if tired of the conversation he said he thought he ought to get back. He had a couple of post-cards he wanted to get written before the post went out. He wanted to get a bath before dinner.

'Good gracious me I ought to get back too. What on earth am I thinking about? I left James.'

'Probably perfectly happy with our Mr Pimm.'

'Yes, but if all of a sudden he finds I'm not there –'

He started walking quickly across the park. By the time she had caught up with him he hardly seemed to notice her. His eyes, as always, were quick. They roamed in restless search about the landscape, seeking pictures. His hands at the same time were equally restless with the camera. Almost hungrily he kept looking at the light and the sky, itching to record something, unaware of her.

Suddenly, from being utterly oblivious of her, his eye caught her as it might have caught at something ephemeral, a butterfly, a passing subject that had to be grabbed before it disappeared.

'Hold it. Hold it just like that.' He was down on one knee; the eye of the camera looked curiously like that of a big beetle. 'Head up a bit. A bit more. I want you against the sky.' The camera shutter made innumerable nervous clicks. He crept, then bounced, from one knee to another. 'No, a bit higher yet.'

She was aware of a stiffness in herself; she found a pose and then clung to it, rigidly.

'No, no, you're too conscious of me. I don't want you to be conscious of me.'

'How then? – is that better?'

'I know – walk away from me. Walk away and then start walking back. Walk back until I tell you and then stop. No, no, don't look at me.'

She walked away from him for ten or a dozen paces, stiffly, almost as if drilled, and then at the words 'Now turn,' she turned and walked back. He was down on both knees and now she walked on without a word of command to stop until at last it seemed that she would walk right into him and trample him down. At the very last moment he suddenly called 'Stop' and she halted.

'That's it. Turn your head a bit. Not this way – away from me. That's it – away from me. Head up. Look at the sky.'

Looking at the sky, covertly, she smiled.

'No, no. No smile. I don't want you to smile.'

She stood transfixed, stiff again, eyes on the sky, this time without a smile.

'You've got such a natural air of – I tell you what, stand there as if you're listening to something. Something a long way away. No, I'll tell you what's better. Stand there as if you're talking to somebody.'

Obediently, at once, her lips started to move.

'No, no, not you talking. The other person. Someone else.' Suddenly he was sure he had a brain-wave. 'Just listen, that's all. That's it – listen. As if you're listening to someone who isn't there.'

Her air of trustful innocence, serene but somehow on the very edge of being startled, was just what he wanted. He bombarded it several times with repeated nervous clicks of the shutter without her once moving an eyelid or in any way indicating that she was conscious of his being there. Even the slightest movement of a strand or two of her brown hair blowing across her face seemed not to disturb her at all.

'Perfect. Good girl,' he said. 'Perfect. You can relax now.'

Her way of relaxing was to stay as she was except for a slight turn of her head to one side, like a bird listening.

'That ought to be marvellous. You know, you've got that lovely way of – You looked just as if you were really listening to somebody. Or something. Music perhaps. Were you listening to music?'

This exceptional question was enough, at last, to disturb her serenity. She smiled. No, she hadn't been listening to music.

'Do you like music?'

'Oh! yes, I suppose I do. But I didn't hear any then.'

When James had been put to bed in the last half hour of twilight she sat in the sitting-room and turned on the radio. She liked the presence of the radio; it gave her a feeling of ever-present company. She liked the voices and the music that came out of it without ever troubling to wonder who made them and from where they came. The only trouble with a radio was that you had to sit with it. With a transistor you could take the voices and the music anywhere. Wherever you went you had music for company.

She greatly envied the man his transistor. The camera was wonderful too of course. But the camera wasn't company. It couldn't stop you from being lonely. With the radio she wasn't lonely. Nor was she afraid of the dark.

Once she went for a short time out of the house, leaving the radio still on in the sitting-room, and walked down the garden path and stood at the gate at the end of it in the summer darkness. The fragrance of tobacco flowers was strong and sweet as the night air. Through the open door of the house a long shaft of light shone on pools of flowers, red and orange and purple, still wet and glistening from the rain of afternoon. The sound of the radio came through the open door too and as she stood and listened to it she again held her head slightly to one side, like a listening, attentive bird.

What had he meant about listening to music? She hadn't been listening to music. You couldn't listen to music that wasn't there. The radio was real and you could listen to that. But that afternoon, standing there, looking at the sky, just staring emptily, waiting for the click of the camera, she hadn't thought or listened to anything. There hadn't been a thought or a sound in her head.

There might have been, she thought, something in her face that had made him think of her like that, perhaps something about her way of looking? She remembered how, in a sentence that he had never finished, he had said that she had that lovely way of – That was all. But then he was always beginning sentences and never finishing them. He was always a jump ahead of her.

That lovely way of what? – the perplexing, unfinished sentence hung on the night air. Elusive and sharply real, it meant more than if he had ever finished it. That was the odd and baffling thing about him – that way of never finishing things. You never knew, quite, if he meant things or not. Did he mean it about the rooms in the big house, for instance? Did he mean it about not sleeping at night? Did he mean it about her cleaning up? She couldn't be certain. Then as she looked back on the afternoon she felt she couldn't be certain about anything except perhaps the camera, the urn and its dead chrysanthemums thrown down on the terrace, the way he had looked at her at the foot of the staircase and the few one-handed chords he had played on the piano in the messy upper room.

All of a sudden she was telling herself, surprisingly, that of course you could hear music that wasn't there. Again she could hear the few brief chords on the piano. They echoed across her mind as clear as bells.

'Of course, I know what you meant now.' With her head to one side she actually smiled to herself, in the act of listening to someone who wasn't there.

In the morning, by nine o'clock, she had started to clean the first of the five upstairs rooms in the big house.

It seemed natural to start with the kitchen. The sink was half full of unwashed dishes, food-stained cutlery. The stove dripped with grease. The air was oily, rancid and dead. On the table stood a carrier paper-bag half full of fish bones, stale bread, coffee grounds, lumps of grey potato. In the window stood several empty milk bottles and a milk jug in which a handful of poppies, wild scabious and grass had died.

She opened the window. Today there were sheep in the park. Miraculously, like mushrooms, the white flock had sprung up overnight.

'We used to live here, didn't we?'

She was wearing her oldest skirt and apron. The sleeves of her sloppy brown jumper were rolled up. James had his sleeves rolled up too. She stood at the window, half sick, breathing fresh air.

'Didn't we used to live here?'

'You did.'

'Why don't we live here now?'

'Because they're away, your father and –'

'Are we coming back to live here?'

'Not yet.'

He climbed up on a chair and stood looking out of the window. The sight of the sheep in the park gave him a nice, happy feeling. The sheep were his friends. He remembered how once some of them had broken through the wire fence that surrounded the glass-house and how they had stared at the reflections of themselves in the glass and stood wondering how all the other sheep had got inside.

'If we're not coming to live here why have we come here today?'

62

'Because I'm going to give it a bit of a once over.'

His father was sometimes a misty figure, sometimes quite clear. Already he couldn't remember him properly. He remembered quite well how he had said the sheep wouldn't eat the grapes in the glass-house but he couldn't always remember other things. He remembered Miss Garfield and the funny way her skin got tight when she was angry and how she smelled of aniseed. Most of the time his father was in London and only came down to the country at week-ends. One thing he did remember was how his father had once said the whole place was a bloody bore and how he'd had a belly full. He wanted to know what that meant and his father shook him like a rat.

'I don't like it here very much. I don't like the smell.'

'I don't like it either but we've got to put up with it for a while until it's a bit sweeter, haven't we?'

'Couldn't I go and play in the glass-house?'

'Not yet. If you don't like it here go and play in the sitting-room. I won't be all that long.'

She started scouring the kitchen sink. Then from the sitting-room she heard the sound of notes being played, one finger, on the piano. She turned on the tap and let water run down the sink and stood listening to it, remembering at the same time the brief, one-handed chords she had heard played on the piano the day before and how, if you tried, you could listen to music that wasn't there.

Presently James came back from the sitting-room. By now she had lit a fire in the stove. She was feeding it with rubbish and the air was smoking.

'Somebody's thrown chrysanthemums out of the window. They're down on the terrace.'

'Oh! are they?'

'The vase is cracked. The one that used to stand on the piano.'

'Oh! is it? It doesn't matter.'

'Did my father throw it at Miss Garfield? He nearly did one day.'

'I don't think your father would do a thing like that.'

'He nearly threw the vase at her and then he called her a bitch – '

'Now, now – '

'An interfering old bitch and told her to keep her stinking nose out of things. That was the day she left. Not long before you came.'

'Now, now. We won't have that kind of talk. Where's Mr Pimm today?'

'That's why Miss Garfield left. Because he called her a bitch too. What is it, a bitch?'

'I said where's Mr Pimm today?'

'I think he's gone to market. He won't be back yet. How did the vase – '

'I wish you wouldn't ask so many questions. I never knew a boy ask so many questions.'

He stood on the chair and gazed out of the window again, at the many sheep grazing in utter peace on grass made brilliant by summer rain, at the long browning avenue of chestnuts and the windy sky.

'The clouds are all running about today, like dogs. Like you see those dogs running across the fields when they go hunting foxes.'

'Oh! are they? I never had time to look.'

'Why didn't you have time to look?'

'Because I'm working myself silly trying to get this place civilized.'

'What's civilized?'

'I sometimes ask myself.'

The morning went past her, it seemed, like a litter of casual and unimportant objects scattered by a wind: washing up, chatter, scrubbing a floor, chatter, burning rubbish, chatter, occasional one-fingered notes on the piano.

'How long are we going to stay here?'

'Like I said before we've got nowhere to go and a long time to go it in. As long as we're here we're out of mischief. I don't mind if we stay all day.'

'Oh! not all day?'

'Well, this afternoon then. I'll get the fire hot by then and give myself a good soaking bath. I'll need it, I'll tell you.'

She was scouring grease from the stove, just before noon,

when she thought she heard a voice calling something from the terrace below. She dropped her scrubbing brush and went, wiping her hands on her apron, to the window. She leaned out, only to find herself instantly caught up in the beetle eye of the camera.

'Oh! not like this! Oh! not in this mess – that isn't fair.'

'Sort of shot I like. A beauty. Absolute natural.'

'A beauty? – I think that's mean.'

She was aware of the sound of music; today he had the transistor with him again.

'I don't think you're fair. How did you know I was here?'

'I've been taking shots of the outside for the last half hour or so. Then I thought I heard your voice.'

The music broke off; after a silence a voice said *'Now we shall hear the orchestra dell' Opera di Roma playing –'* and once again, like a small pistol firing, the camera shutter started clicking rapidly.

'I wish you wouldn't keep doing that. I look an awful sight.'

'Can't hear.'

The music of the orchestra rose to full volume. She put her fingers to her ears. He smiled up at her, made a half-mocking gesture of apology with one upraised hand and then switched the volume down.

'Sorry. What did you say?'

'I said I couldn't hear either, that's all.'

'I'd got it a bit loud, I'm afraid. Busy up there?'

'It's like chasing my own tail.'

'Need any help?'

'If you've got forty pairs of hands.'

'I'll come up.'

'Come in by the back door,' she said, 'that's open.'

While she waited for him to come upstairs she hastily went into the bathroom, washed her hands, took off her apron and combed her hair.

'What are you doing all that for?'

'All what for?'

'Combing your hair and powdering and getting ready to go out.'

'I'm not getting ready to go out. Don't pester so. Go and sit down and do something quietly for a change. Go and play the piano.'

'That isn't doing something quietly.'

'Well, do *something*.'

'That man's here, isn't he? The one with the camera.'

When at last she let Ainsworth into the hallway and he came through to the kitchen, whose chairs were stacked on the table and floor mats on the sink board he said Good God, she had a task on her hands.

'I thought I'd get stuck in. You said you wouldn't sleep for thinking of it.'

'Did I say that? You shouldn't take that notice of me.'

'No? Didn't you mean it then?'

'Me? I never lose sleep about anything.'

It was hard to know, she thought, whether to believe him or not. From the sitting-room came the sound of a few discordant one-fingered notes on the piano. The discords irritated her slightly and she said:

'Well, anyway, you're just in time to help me move this table. Catch hold of that end. I want it over there. I've got to scrub underneath it.'

Together they moved the table.

'I'll scrub,' he said. 'I adore scrubbing.'

Before she could make any answer about this James came to the doorway of the kitchen and said:

'I think Mr Pimm's back from market. I think he's in the glass-house. Can I go down and talk to him?'

'Ah yes,' Ainsworth said. 'Mr Pimm. I saw him too. I saw him in the glass-house as I came by.'

'You didn't. Because he's only just got here. I watched him come across the park just now.'

'All right, James, but not for long. We're having lunch up here today. Just sandwiches. Just ourselves. No Mr Pimm today.'

As James went out of the kitchen and into the hallway and disappeared she heard music from the transistor begin again. She didn't mind, did she, the music? No, she told him, she didn't mind. The music, strange to her, nevertheless awoke in her an odd sense of disturbance. She suddenly felt self-con-

66

scious and awkward, uneasy at the sight of him in the half-squalor of the kitchen, a scrubbing brush in his hands.

'You shouldn't bother about this. Haven't you got something more important to do?'

'This is important.' He took the transistor over to the kitchen dresser, set it down and cut the sound until it was dreaming and muted. 'Where's the soap? Better have a bucket of clean water.'

'I thought you said you were going off to trace that road or something.'

'Did I say that? Well, the road's been there for three thousand years and I daresay it'll still be there tomorrow.'

'Three thousand years? How do you know?'

'I don't. I'm guessing. It might not even be there.'

'No? How can you look for something that isn't there?'

'Well, that's part of the fun of it, isn't it? The not knowing.'

By this time he was down on his knees, scrubbing the floor. She started to wipe dead flies and odd coloured petals of dead flowers from the window sill. Suddenly she heard him laugh, not loudly, as if at a sudden joke, but to himself, reflectively.

'He takes his Mr Pimm very seriously, doesn't he?'

'He's only just six.'

'Yes? He seems older than that sometimes. Funny, this talking and playing with someone who isn't there.'

'Funny? No funnier than your road. That isn't there.'

It was her turn to laugh. He laughed with her. He remarked how she said amusing things sometimes. Did she? she said and once again, as when he had taken her picture framed against the clear sky of late afternoon, he found himself captured by an air of innocence that was somehow, in a way he found hard to explain, profound too.

With this same air of profound simplicity her large brown eyes held him for fully half a minute while he scrubbed the floor. Finally when he became aware of this he looked up and said:

'Not doing it right, am I? You don't approve.'

It wasn't that, she said. It was only that she found it hard to believe that he could find time to come up here, among all the mess, and help her. It was nothing to do with him. He'd got so much better things to do.

'Oh! the day's free. I go where the fancy takes me. Mrs Fitzsimmons put me up some sandwiches. By the way any news of Tangier yet? Any post-cards?'

No, she said, there were no post-cards. Once again his mind, alert, for ever jumping ahead, baffled her. Her air of enraptured simplicity seemed to deepen.

'By the way, what does he do, Sampson?'

'I think he's something in London.'

'Mrs Fitzsimmons says they were in coffee or something. Kenya or somewhere. Had to sell up and get out.'

'Oh! did they?'

'Mrs Fitzsimmons says Mrs S is always beefing about servants and how she had eight or something, three cooks and two houseboys and so on. Never had to lift a finger.'

'Now she's only got you and me.'

He laughed. Once again he told her that she sometimes said the most amusing things. It was exactly as if he had told her frankly, face to face, in so many words, that he liked her very much. An elusive start of pleasure skimmed briefly across her face as she flicked a duster from the window and let the last of the dead flower petals float away.

'Well, we're getting on with the kitchen,' he said. 'What's next?'

Oh! she hadn't got as far as thinking about that yet. What she really thought was that she'd get the kitchen done first and then they could sit down, her and James, something like civilized, and have their bit of lunch, and then in the afternoon –

'Do you mind if I have my lunch here too?'

No, she didn't mind, she said, not if he didn't. They were just going to have the sandwiches and she'd make a cup of tea. She'd have to go down and fetch James first.

'I'll fetch James.'

No, she said, it would be better if she fetched him. He was rather funny about that sometimes. He had a funny way of hiding himself if he felt that way. One day she hadn't been able to find him for nearly an hour and when at last she did he merely said he hadn't been anywhere at all. He was just hiding in the clouds.

'In the clouds? That's odd.'

Oh! he often talked about clouds. They meant something. Clouds had a great fascination for him. Sometimes he said they were like ice-creams and once they were like elephants and another like bands. That was when there was thunder. They were often like sheep too.

'Wonder why they had a piano.'

His mind, yet again, leapt away from her like a spark struck from a stone. She felt awkward and uneasy. She picked up one end of the kitchen table and said would he mind getting hold of the other, so that they could put it back in its place again!

'Don't seem at all the right people to have a piano. Somehow doesn't go. They couldn't care a damn anyway, otherwise they wouldn't have treated it like that, would they?'

In a voice barely audible she said she didn't know. Together they picked up the table and put it down in the centre of the kitchen.

'They sound like bridge parties. And endless cocktails. And duck-shooting. And Lady Plonk.'

Her laughter exploded like a jack-in-the-box, almost foolishly.

'What now? Something funny?'

'Last time it was Lady Witchcraft.'

'Oh! they're sisters, didn't you know? They're the daughters of Lord Cockshott, the punt-gun wallah.'

Still captivated by this note of flippant gaiety she went downstairs and into the glass-house, to fetch James.

'It's time to come up for lunch now.'

'Me and Mr Pimm are having our dinner.'

'I think it's time to say good-bye to Mr Pimm now.'

'Not in the middle of his dinner.'

'You can come again this afternoon.'

'Mr Pimm doesn't want to come this afternoon.'

James had a ripe purple-brown fig in his hands. He looked at it moodily.

'Oh! I think Mr Pimm would like to come, wouldn't you, Mr Pimm?'

In answer she conjured from the air the deep, crusty voice of Mr Pimm. Well, he daresay he could, come to that. He was only thinking of the mushrooms –

'Mushrooms?'

Mushrooms, Mr Pimm said. He'd thought he might go and look for mushrooms. There were a tidy few about now again. They'd come on with the rain.

They went upstairs together, James still carrying the purple-brown fig in his hands. From the sitting-room came the light clear sound of music. For a moment or two she was sure it was the transistor again. Then she went to the open door of the sitting-room and saw Ainsworth there, playing the piano. A haunting, half-familiar air about the piece he was playing held her captivated too and again she listened to it like a bird, her head to one side.

While he was still playing she went back to the kitchen and filled the kettle and put it on the stove. She found plates and cups and teapot and the cheese sandwiches she had made. James sat at the table, which had no cloth on it, and stared at the purple-brown fig, sullenly.

After the kettle boiled she made the tea and went back to the sitting-room. This time she stood near to the piano and, again with her head to one side but now more like a dutiful bird waiting to be fed than one trying to capture the sound of something elusive and not quite there, she stared at the hands moving up and down the keys of the piano.

With considerable gentleness of touch Ainsworth played to the end of the piece, then smiled up at her and said:

'All over. Nice piano.'

Something about the piece continued to haunt her and she simply stood staring, not knowing what to say.

'Odd thing is that it's in perfect tune.'

As if to demonstrate this he played the few final bars of the piece again.

'Haven't I heard what you're playing before?'

'Oh! this. You might have done. Where?'

'It sounds like something they were playing on your transistor – that other afternoon, Saturday, by the river –'

'Ah! yes, our old friend Schumann.'

They went back into the kitchen to eat. He sat at one end of the table, she at the opposite end, James between them, the purple-brown fig remote in the middle of the table.

'Would you like some tea now or will you wait till afterwards?'

'Oh! please, now.' He unwrapped his package of sandwiches and peered into them. 'Oh! good for Mrs Fitzsimmons. Chicken. And sausage. Liver, I think. What have you got?'

'Just cheese.'

'Oh! we must share. Start with some of my chicken.'

'No, really – '

'Oh! please. There are mountains. She's so generous, that woman. You order a grilled sole and it comes up as big as a tennis racket. James – liver or chicken?'

James, silently staring at the fig, needed neither liver nor chicken.

'Oh! do. Breast of chicken – you like that? Not hungry? Oh! I am. And Gilly too. You don't like chicken?'

'The birds are hungry when you don't put the food out,' Gilly said.

'Oh! yes, of course. And the birds have to eat too. They have to eat a lot. They have to keep their blood temperature up or else they wouldn't be able to fly or they'd drop down dead, wouldn't they?'

James said nothing.

'There's still some eggs in the fridge,' Gilly said. 'Would you like a boiled egg? James, it's you I'm talking to.'

'No.'

'No? I don't hear anything else.'

'No thank you.'

Gilly went to the kitchen cupboard and found an egg-cup and put it on the table.

'Could I have a boiled egg too?' Ainsworth said. 'I love boiled eggs.'

He gave Gilly a slow, sideways wink. Gilly put a second egg-cup on the table.

'I'll have mine soft-boiled,' Ainsworth said. 'I hate them when they're hard, don't you? How do you like yours?'

James stared at the bare kitchen table and had nothing to say. Ainsworth laughed, inspired by a sudden bright idea. He picked up the Brown Turkey fig and dropped it into the egg-cup. Then he picked up a spoon and tapped the top of the fig and made as if to peel the top off, at the same time making hungry, sucking sounds.

'Looks marvellously good, this egg. A brown one too. They always taste better, the brown ones, I think.'

He spooned up a luscious mouthful of egg, smacking his lips over it.

'Yours good too?'

'He's eating my fig.'

'Oh! no, no. This is that nice boiled egg Gilly just got for me. Won't you have one too? And would you mind passing the salt please?' He gave Gilly another low, secret wink. 'I think it needs a little salt. Thank you.'

James stared at the table. Gilly poured out a glass of milk and set it down in front of him. Ainsworth sliced a finger of bread from one of his sandwiches and proceeded to dip it into the top of the fig and said he always ate his eggs that way. It made them last longer.

'I don't think the birds are very hungry today,' he said.

'No. Sometimes I let them fly away and then they come back again when you're not watching. More tea?'

'Oh! please.'

He suddenly got up from the table, a sandwich in his hands, munching it in apparently distant thought.

'You shouldn't get up from the table, not when you're eating.'

Ah! yes, of course, he knew that, Ainsworth said. But he was really getting up to go and open the other window. It was rather warm in the kitchen, he thought.

He opened the window. Then he stood by it for some moments, looking out. The sound of a wood pigeon repeating its soft low moan in one of the trees across the park seemed to saturate the air with the deep sound of summer. He turned at last and started to say that it always seemed farther away than you thought, that sound, and then stopped, seeing Gilly listening too, with her head to one side. He said instead:

'Whenever I see you standing like that I feel I want to take a picture of you.'

'You do?'

She smiled and for a moment she was alone in the kitchen with him.

'The trouble is that it's so spontaneous and if you're not there at the right moment – '

'Can I go back and see Mr Pimm now?' James said. 'He's going to get mushrooms.'

'Drink your milk first.'

'Oh! yes and you'd better take your egg too, hadn't you?' Ainsworth said. 'I hope it's as nice as mine was. Mine was delicious.'

James took a drink of milk. He stared at the fig and then took another drink of milk. Then he picked up the fig and put it, slowly, into his pocket.

'Can I go now?'

'Yes, but don't go wandering.'

'Mr Pimm and me are going to get mushrooms.'

'Yes, but only in the park. Don't you dare go out of the park.'

When James had gone downstairs Gilly poured out more tea and sat with her elbows on the table, resting her chin in her hands. The voice of the wood pigeon, swooning, breaking, pausing and swooning on again, poured through the open window. Ainsworth sat drinking tea too, lazily stirring a spoon into his cup, watching her.

'What are you going to do this afternoon?'

'Nothing. If I had my way.'

'Then do nothing.'

'There's the sitting-room. I'll have to give that a lick and a promise.'

'Two more sandwiches left. Chicken, I think. Shall we share?'

For a moment she didn't answer. She sat again with her head slightly to one side, as if listening to the sound of the wood pigeon, and then suddenly came to herself and said:

'Oh! what? Oh! sandwiches? – Oh! no I won't, thank you.'

'Damn it, damn it, damn it – there you were again and I missed you.'

The air of astonishment on her face was great enough to make him laugh. When he was quiet again she said:

'And what about you? What are you going to do?'

'Like you – if I had my way – nothing.'

'You know what I'd like to do?'

'Tell me.'

'I'd-like to curl up on that big sofa in there and you play the piano to me.'

'I daresay that could be arranged. You like music?'

'I'm always having the radio on.'

'What shall it be? Our old friend Schumann?'

It didn't really matter all that much, she said, what he played.

'He was mad, of course.'

'Who was?'

'Old Schumann. Really two people. Not knowing which he wanted to be. All rather sad – '

It must have been half past two before he at last got up from the kitchen table and went into the sitting-room and started to play the piano. She still had a few things to straighten up in the kitchen and a few plates and cups to wash. For some time she stood dreamily over the kitchen sink, half listening to the sound of the wood pigeon and half to the piano, the one almost an echo of the other.

When everything was finally washed and dried and cleared away she went into the bathroom and combed her hair again and powdered her face and put on fresh lipstick, keeping the door open so that she could still hear the sound of music. Then she remembered something. She was going to have a bath. She was going to wash the morning's grease and dust away.

She went back into the kitchen and then stood at the door of the sitting-room and said, lifting her voice above the sound of the piano:

'I just remembered. I was going to get a bath. Do you want to go?'

'Perfectly happy here.'

'I'll just straighten a few books and papers up and then give it a good do tomorrow. I can't very well sit down in all my kitchen muck. You don't mind? I won't be all that long.'

'Oh! don't mind me. Take all the time in the world. Beautiful piano.'

By now she was on the far side of the room, packing up magazines, books and papers. A big Victorian sofa in dark green velvet stood under one of the high, shuttered windows. She opened the shutters and a glow of sunlight, pouring in, showed a coffee-brown stain smeared down the side of it, with the coffee cup and saucer wrecked on the rose carpet underneath it. She picked up the wrecked cup and saucer and only half-heard him say, above the notes of the piano:

'Beautiful instrument,' he said. 'Quite exceptional.'

'It's what? I shall have to get this stain off in the morning. It ought to have had hot water at the time. What is it you're playing?'

'Oh! just making it up as I go along.'

She packed up a few remaining magazines and papers, occasionally pausing to listen. For a few moments she actually allowed herself to become part of the soft distillation of sounds falling on the room and the afternoon like a mood of half-sleep and then suddenly she roused herself to say:

'Well, this won't get my neck scrubbed. I'd better be off now. If James comes back before I'm out just see that he doesn't get into mischief, won't you?'

'I don't think I'm his friend.'

'Oh! yes, you are. That's his way. Play to him – perhaps he'd like that.'

'Or perhaps I could play at being Mr Pimm.'

'No,' she said. 'No. Don't do that.'

'Not cut out for Mr Pimm?'

'No, no, don't do that. Just be you – '

He suddenly broke from his own improvised rhythms and started to play with one finger.

'Something simple? Like that? *Every week day Mary Jane.*' He half sang the accompanying words to the simple pattern of notes. '*Seems to have another pain. But on Sundays –* ' He suddenly stopped the words and turned to smile at her. 'Simple, eh? Basis of half the tunes in the world. Mozart used it, Haydn – also our old friend Schumann – '

She simply stood staring at him, transfixed, holding the dirty coffee cup and saucer in front of her, the cup in one hand, the saucer in the other.

'Can he play? James, I mean. I'll teach him. Never too young to learn. I was five.'

He turned from the simplicity of his one-finger exercise into fresh rhythms of his own so absorbing that it was some minutes before he realized she had left the room. Unsurprised, he played on for another half an hour or so and then abruptly came to himself in one of those inconsequent changes of thought and mood that so often bewildered her.

'Good God, where on earth's she got to?' He spoke to himself aloud. 'She's been gone hours.'

He went out of the sitting-room, through the kitchen and into the passage that led to the bathroom. There was no sound of water running and in a silence that for some reason seemed to him unpleasantly ominous he knocked on the bathroom door and said:

'Are you there? Is everything all right?'

'No, I'm over here.' Her voice came unexpectedly from an open door at the end of the corridor. 'In the bedroom. I've been out ages. I was just looking for a dressing-gown I could borrow.'

'Well, that's a relief. I thought something might have happened to you.'

As she came out of the bedroom, wearing a padded dressing-gown of deep warm pink, not unlike the colour of the jumper she had worn the day before, she was so struck by the wide expression of disturbance on his face that she actually laughed and said:

'It isn't as bad as that, is it? I called you once, when I came out, but you didn't answer.'

Her dark brown hair was still slightly wet; she ruffled it half into place with her two hands. The effect of it, untidy but fresh, made him stand for some moments and look at her exactly as he had looked at her the day before: not so much at herself as at the dressing-gown, not so much entranced by a person standing there as by the colour about her.

'I think I must have got the bath too hot. I felt quite faint when I came out. That's why I thought I'd cool off in a dressing-gown. You didn't really think anything had happened to me, did you?'

'Well, you never quite know. I'm always a bit uneasy about bathrooms. They say you should never lock the door at home.'

'Oh! don't worry, I always lock mine.'

They went back into the sitting-room. She sat, as she had promised herself, on the long green sofa, her legs stretched out, her dark still wet head on a cushion. The unexpected air of entrancement created for him by the dressing-gown increased whenever he turned his head and looked at her from the piano and saw the light and dark of her figure against the deep green velvet and the high blue-white sky beyond.

'Have you given up playing? Or are we back on one finger again?'

'Oh! we're playing. When it comes. It isn't arithmetic.'

He noticed presently that her eyes were closed. He wasn't at all sure, as he began to play a few dismembered chords without bothering to pick them up for more than a bar or two, that she wasn't asleep. Before lying down she had opened the window behind her, in order to get a little air, and now he could hear once again the voice of the wood pigeon floating in on its rising and dying fall across the park. The breathless serenity of the afternoon was so deep that after asking once if she would like that tune again, the simple one, the Mary Jane, – it lent itself to rather nice variations and he could play a few – he not only stopped talking completely but let the notes of the piano themselves die away.

'Why aren't you playing? I thought you were going to play.'

'I didn't want to disturb you.'

'You're not disturbing me. I was just beginning to like it.'

He played again. After some time he once more got the impression that she was asleep. Her breathing was serene and steady. Her breast rose and fell with deep regularity under the dressing-gown. One of the red bedroom slippers she was wearing had slipped off and presently he found himself staring at her outstretched bare foot and the calf of her leg. In imagination he started to follow the line of the calf up to her thigh and beyond. The cord of the dressing-gown was so loosely tied that he had only to go over and flick it with one finger, he thought, and find the shape he imagined below. Excitement rose inside him in deep pulsings, with now and then a sharpness like a discord on the piano, until the whole central core of himself was throbbing.

Suddenly he stopped playing and got up and went over to her. This time the silence after the notes of the piano had died made no effect on her. She simply lay there, lips very slightly parted, in complete serenity.

Without waiting for her to open her eyes or move at all he bent down and kissed her full on the mouth. She made some faint disturbance of half-resistance for the space of a second or two and then he felt the lips part themselves, accepting him.

They went on accepting him without even the merest flutter of a movement for what seemed a long time. Her unwillingness to let him go became part of a trance as fixed and deep as the drowsy stillness of the August afternoon. When finally she moved her head slightly backwards and freed her lips it was to say:

'That's the trouble with you. I never know what you're going to do next.'

'The trouble? You'd like me to send you a post-card next time? Fair warning, I mean?'

'No.'

Her slow brown eyes that in occasional turns of light were so like the shells of brown-green snails gazed up at him without a flicker. It wasn't until some time afterwards that he was able to grasp that, sleepy as they seemed to be, they were really waking into a burning adoration. It didn't even occur to him that he might already have woken in her an amazed fondness for him, even when she stared at him with a long solemn look and said:

'No. Don't do that. No warning. Don't tell me. That's the way I like you.'

It was nice to be in the glass-house again, alone with Mr Pimm, under the big fig-tree. It was nice to stare out of the windows and look at all the sheep peering in through the glass from the park. If you half shut your eyes you could look at the sheep until they got smaller and smaller and rounder and rounder and farther and farther away, so that they all looked like so many mushrooms.

The nicest thing of all was that Mr Monday was coming. Mr Pimm said so. Mr Monday was out of hospital and was coming over to blow his bacca and have a bit of a chinwag. Mr Pimm was already settled in nicely, blowing his shag under the fig-tree.

Under the fig-tree it was just like being under the tent where the electric light men sat for so long every day and brewed their tea and chinwagged and read newspapers and talked about horses and form and sometimes played cards. It gave you the same nice brown feeling. It was like being in a cave and nobody outside could see you.

'How's the brew-up coming on, mate? I see old Monday's coming across the park.'

Yes: there was old Monday coming across the park with his arm in plaster.

'How did he break his arm, Mr Monday?'

'Fell arse-over-head in a trench. Should've knowed better. Should've took more water with it.'

Ah! that was right: of course. He remembered now. Mr Monday had fallen in a trench, just like one of the electric light men.

'Come in, mate. Sit yourself down. Make yourself at home.'

James, going over to the door to let Mr Monday in, spoke with a voice guttural with infinite age, and spat.

'How's the old arm, mate? That's it – sit yourself down on the box there.'

Ah! that was better beer, Mr Monday said and sat himself down on the box, grunting. Arm? Gittin' on fairish like now, but it give him the old pepper, salt and mustard sometimes.

'You bet.'

Mr Monday took his pipe and his tobacco pouch out of his pocket and started to try to fill the pipe just like the electric light man used to do, one hand. It was fascinating to see Mr

Monday do his. Mr Monday got the bowl of his pipe and somehow tucked it under the ball of his thumb and then tucked the stem of the pipe between his two little fingers. Then he coaxed the tobacco out of the pouch with his two big fingers until it sat in his hand looking like a dark brown mouse ready to run into a little hole.

While Mr Monday was doing all this Mr Pimm blew his shag and coughed now and then and asked if Mr Monday had had anything come up like, yesterday? Mr Monday said he'd had *Ajax* in the two o'clock and *Pretty Lizzie* in the three-thirty but neither one of the bleeders had come up. Bloke he knowed had a double on *Skipper's Torch* and *Toffee Apple* though.

Mr Pimm groaned and said some people had the luck of the devil, and spat. It was a very long spit and went half-way across the glass-house. Nobody could spit like Mr Pimm. The spit shot out straight and clean as an arrow and very far and what was even better was that Mr Pimm did it without trying.

'Done anything for today?'

No, Mr Monday said, he hadn't done nothing for today. Matter of fact he was trying to pack it up. He was a quid or two short on the week what with the old arm an' all – it was either that or the beer and you had to have something to keep the old woman sweet. Mr Pimm said too bleedin' right and how much longer was he going to be on the club?

Mr Monday half lifted his broken arm and looked at it hard and gave a twinge. A month or more yet, he thought. Mr Monday had a moustache that was a sort of froggy yellow underneath it where the tobacco stained it and a cap that looked like an old brown cow-pat that hung on one side of his head and nearly fell off every time he wagged his head and then never did.

'By God,' Mr Monday said, 'that don't half work me up sometimes just afore I'm droppin' off of a night. Like a bloody old lot o' squirrels gnawin' at nuts under me elbow.'

Mr Monday screwed his face up so sharply that his cap nearly fell off and you could feel the pain of his arm in your own, just as you could fairly see the smoke of shag across the glass-house and could taste the smell of it mixed with the froggy dark smell of the water tank and the damp greeny smell of the ferns.

'Have to take more water with it, next time, mate,' Mr Pimm said.

'Somebody left a bleedin' shovel there and I went arse-over-tip afore you could wink.'

'Still, you git the compensation.'

'Everybody talks about compensation. Just like Christmas. Everybody talks about Christmas. Christ, Christmas, Christmas. They don't have the squirrels gnawing up their arm.'

Every time Mr Monday talked about the squirrels gnawing up his arm you could feel the pain gnawing up your own arm too. It made you bite your teeth into your lips. It made your legs go empty and your arm started to jump and you felt it would drop off like Mr Monday's cap but it never did. It was an awful dry sort of pain.

It was better when you put your arm into your anorak and let it stop there as if it was really broken. It made you feel old too. It was like having a moustache and smoking shag and spitting a long way.

'How's the old brew-up coming on, mate? Seems a bit on the never-never, don't it?'

'Just on the boil. How's Mr Monday like his?'

'Hot as mustard,' Mr Monday said, 'and sweet as a barmaid's breath.'

Talking about barmaids, Mr Pimm said, did he ever see Nelly nowadays? Mr Monday said Nelly wasn't there no more. The electric light men were always talking about barmaids too.

'Nelly gone?' Mr Pimm said. 'How long ago was that then?'

A month or more, Mr Monday said. Since this woman took over. This Irish bit.

'Irish bit, eh?' Mr Pimm said and looked as if candles were shining in his eyes.

Well, doing her injustice, really, Mr Monday supposed. A bit more varnish on her than that. Very smart. Too smart to draw a pint anyway. Got a tame canary to do that for her. Mr Pimm needn't look like that either. She'd eat him like hot potato with butter on a frosty morning.

It was funny how Mr Pimm and Mr Monday so often talked like the electric light men and how clear and real their voices were.

When the brew-up was ready and the tea was poured out into mugs, that was real too. You could taste it hot and strong, like Mr Monday said, and when you drank it you drew it in deep gasping breaths and said things like 'that was a drop o' the old right an' proper' and then wiped your mouth with the back of your hand and wagged your head as if you knew about a lot of things that you weren't going to talk about. Once he got up and picked himself a brown fig from the fig-tree and then put the stalk of it into his mouth and smoked it, like a pipe. Sometimes, like Mr Pimm, he'd be damned if it would draw and he blew hard on it with a long whistling sound and then knocked it out on the heel of his shoe and started again. Then when it was going well again he leaned back and half-closed his eyes and looked sleepy and, as Mr Pimm said, very cunning, as if he knew about all what was going on in the world.

It was so easy for the afternoon to slip away like this that it was some time before he became fully aware that it was growing darker. The sun had disappeared some time before. Now the clouds were creeping up like big blue bears. At first the darkness had a queer yellow streak in it, so vivid that the grass outside looked burning bright like the flames sometimes did in the grate when it was frosty weather in winter time. The leaves of the fig-tree were like big bright green hands, with fat enfolding fingers, and in the water tank there was a great bottomless darkness.

Soon the yellow streak in the strange twilight of mid-afternoon had gone. The vivid green of grass and fig-leaves died. The first burst of rain swept across the roof of the glass-house like the swish of a great birch broom. First it swept in one big swish and then over and over again, madly and hard, so that it was no longer like the sound of a broom but like nails flying and crashing on the glass. At first you could see the nail heads shining like iron and then they were white, like snow. At first they were no bigger than grains of wheat and then they were as big as peas and soon like fat white bumble-bees. You could see them jumping and slithering down the long slope of glass, sometimes with their scratching shrieks, and down into the gutterings. Presently the pipe leading down into the water tank began to be strangled with mad sounds that gurped and trembled until the pipe at last gave a long coughing retch. Suddenly it sicked out black leaves and let the first great spew of water down.

The first dark explosion of water frightened him. He turned and rushed to the door of the glass-house. The faces of the many staring sheep had disappeared. The grass was green no longer. It shone white now, littered with a broken canopy of hail. Outside the door hailstones were hopping wildly up and down like white frightened insects on the flagstones.

The parts of the fence that kept the sheep away stuck up like headstones in a graveyard. In fear he turned back to the darkness of the glass-house. The darkness was alive with sounds and the sharp shadows of sounds. Hail squealed on the glass. It ran screeching away from itself down the slopes of the roof. Water pitched and squobbed and hissed in the down-pipe before finally belching free into the tank below. With every burst of hail the thin branch of a tree scratched against the glass. Wherever a pane or two of glass was broken wild handfuls of hail lashed at the flat crowded hands of vine leaves.

For some time the continued darkness imprisoned him. It held him hard in a corner, away from the spew of the water tank. Once he shut his eyes and then opened them suddenly again to see lights shining brightly in houses across the park. Then he knew that it wasn't daytime any more.

This feeling of dark imprisonment made him want to cry. Somehow he didn't cry. He simply sat with his arms in his anorak tight and stony, gripping his fingers together. Every time he told himself that the screech of hail and retch of water were lessening the sounds simply lashed at him with new frenzy.

When the sound of hail stopped at last the silence of the afternoon imprisoned and held him for a time more rigidly and fearfully than the storm had done. He found himself waking from dreams too loud and dark to be real. For a long time he was afraid to move at all. When at last he did move it was to discover suddenly that a long uncanny tongue of light had licked its way across the park again, that big bears of cloud were stumbling away in the light of it across the sky. Sheep were back in the park, too, actually grazing at the white spread of hail in the grass, calm as if nothing had happened.

In a wild hope he looked about the glass-house for Mr Pimm and Mr Monday. The air was drenched and icy. Neither Mr Pimm nor Mr Monday appeared out of the growing daylight, in the strange afterglow of storm where every colour looked as if freshly dipped in paint fierce and vivid and sickly. Nor was there any smell of shag.

At the first renewed burst of sunlight he opened the door of the glass-house and started to run. The park was printed white with its fresh coating of summer hail. Here and there lay deeper drifts and you could imagine that suddenly, in the great brilliance of sunlight, it was winter and everywhere was snow.

Momentarily, in the light of this new excitement, he forgot the fear and darkness of the glass-house. He even forgot Mr Pimm and Mr Monday. He was filled only with the thought of Gilly. He felt he must find her and tell her of the miracle of how, that afternoon, there had been snow in summer.

'Gilly! Gilly! Did you see? It snowed. It came all white. Gilly! – did you see it snow?'

As he burst through the door of the sitting-room he stopped. The sun was shining with full brilliance now. Everywhere was like summer again and Gilly's naked shoulders glowed with startling brightness on the sofa, lying under the window.

'Gilly, did you see how dark it was?'

Ainsworth, who had been lying on the sofa too, got up quickly and walked away, behind the piano.

'Gilly, it was all dark and it snowed, like winter. Did you think it was time to go to bed when it was dark and it snowed?'

'It was hail, not snow.'

'But it looked like snow. Didn't you think it was time to go to bed?'

Gilly laughed, a little oddly, he thought, and said no, she didn't think so.

'Why are you nearly undressed then?'

He stood still, very tense, as if listening to the dark sounds behind him, and waited for an answer.

'Look James, it's the first post-card. Isn't that quick, really? It wasn't posted until the twenty-fourth and it's only the thirtieth now. I call that good. All that long way.'

Gilly first propped the post-card up on the breakfast-table, by the sugar basin. Then she picked it up and turned it over several times. Then she read the writing part of it to herself, not aloud. All the time James stared up from his toast and scrambled egg, watching her lips move.

'Look, that's the hotel. Isn't that marvellous? And the beach. Doesn't it look hot? It's over ninety every day.' She picked up the postcard and handed it to him across the breakfast table. 'Look how blue and hot it all is. You can fairly feel the heat.'

He took the post-card from her. He felt it carefully with his finger tips, staring at the picture showing a big white hotel, many palm trees sticking up like floppy green umbrellas from white sand and over it all a fierce unreal blue sky.

'I can't feel anything.'

Gilly laughed. She was amused to see him touching the post-card with his finger tips as if it were something hot from an oven.

'Oh! I didn't mean hot like that. I meant you could feel it hot because of the sand and the sky. Shall I read it out to you?'

Without saying anything he handed the postcard back to her and then started to eat his scrambled egg.

'It says "Arrived two hours late after rather dicey flight" –'

'What's dicey?'

'Oh! it's a word. They were late taking off. "Otherwise all well. Hotel pretty good, beach marvellous, bathing from morn to night. Temperature over ninety every day but feels less because of strong sea wind. Met the Dawsons from Richmond in plane – and lo! and behold they're in the same hotel. Didn't even know they were coming. Love to James. Tell him I tried to get a picture of a camel but no luck. Will send one tomorrow." There! – she's sending a picture of a camel.'

'When will it come?'

'Oh! tomorrow, I expect. It says tomorrow.'

He speared a piece of scrambled egg with his fork and stared at it for some time before putting it into his mouth.

'Why didn't my father write the postcard?'

'What? –' Gilly turned the post-card over and over and then gave a sudden sharp exclamation. 'Oh! here's an extra bit. On the top here. I thought it was part of the postmark. What's it say? – it says – I can't read it – it doesn't say anything, I think. Oh! yes it does – Silly – it's a camel. Your father has drawn a camel.'

'Where?'

'Here – look here. Just in the corner – see? There it is.'

He took the post-card from her. He looked at it and saw that his father had drawn odd squiggly marks in one corner and that someone had smudged across them.

'It doesn't look much like a camel. It's all smudged over.'

'Oh! I think it's a very good camel.'

He put the post-card back on the breakfast table. Gilly picked it up again and peered at it and suddenly said:

'Oh! there's something else here. Some more writing. I can't make a thing out of it – Oh! yes, wait a minute, it should be the other way up.' Gilly turned the post-card upside down. 'Oh! yes, that's better, that's it. What does it say? – oh! yes, it says "A man sits just over there charming snakes with a whistle. Like this." Oh! I see, it's snakes. It isn't a camel at all.'

'Why?'

'Oh! I just thought it was. Just at first it looked like it. No, it isn't though. It's a snake all right. Not a camel.'

'You said it was a very good camel.'

'Well, at first I thought it was and now it isn't.'

'How can a snake look like a camel?'

'Well, it could, couldn't it? When it humps up like that, like snakes do.'

'Camels have got long legs and snakes don't have any legs. They slide. What did you say it was a camel for?'

'Because I thought it was at first. It's easy to make mistakes. We all make mistakes.'

86

'What does charming snakes mean?'

'Oh! well – a man plays music. On a sort of tin whistle. He sits cross-legged and then plays the whistle to the snake and then the snake gradually sits up and listens.'

'Why?'

'Because it likes it I suppose.'

'How can it listen? Snakes don't have ears.'

'Oh! well it sort of hypnotizes it. I suppose it goes into a sort of trance.'

'What's that?'

'Oh! it's a sort of dream and you don't know what you're doing.'

'So it doesn't sting?'

'The snake, you mean? Something like that.'

'Do you ever go into a trance and don't know what you're doing?'

'Everybody does. Some time.'

'Does it hurt?'

'Oh! don't keep on. Eat your egg. I'm trying to read the paper.'

He knew suddenly, by the way she put her head behind the morning paper, that she had turned cold and irritable. The morning sky looked cold too. The clouds were big and podgy and blue underneath, with frothy crust on top, like snow. Several times he half-closed his eyes and stared at them and went into a trance of his own, squinting hard, trying to mould them to shapes he knew. Today they were neither like bears nor ice-creams, neither snakes nor camels.

Oh! yes, at last there was one like a snake. Pure white and curled and twisting, it slid from behind a bank of heavier cloud and into a lake of sharp windy blue. He started at once to whistle, his eyes still half closed. To his excited astonishment he saw the cloud twist and writhe and lengthen itself, head in air. He whistled harder and again it gave its white response, obediently charmed.

'James, what are you whistling for? I thought you knew it was rude to whistle at table.'

He had no answer except a sharper and finer whistle to the snake-cloud.

'James! I said no whistling. Do you hear?'

He whistled harder still. He could have sworn the cloud darted its tongue at the sky.

'James, don't you ever take notice of anything I say? Don't you hear me?'

'I'm whistling to a snake up there.'

'Up where?'

'It's going away now. It's going back into its hole. Behind that big cloud. It sat up and listened to me. You didn't see, did you?'

'I've got plenty to do and see without looking at snakes in the sky.'

He escaped from the fresh narrowed irritation in her voice by getting up from the breakfast table. He stood at the kitchen window, looking out for a last glimpse of his snake-cloud. The wonder of being able to charm a cloud into any shape he wanted held him in captivated silence for fully half a minute longer, his eyes still half-closed. Then, suddenly opening them, he looked down at the kitchen sink and saw that a glass had been broken, the splinters scattered where they had fallen.

'Somebody's broken a glass. Look, the bits of glass are all over the sink.'

'I know. No need to get so excited. I broke it.'

'When?'

Gilly was speaking all the time from behind the morning paper. You couldn't see her face. But all the time you could hear exactly how it looked.

'Oh! in the night. I came down for a drink of water and knocked it against the tap.'

'Why?'

'I was thirsty. I wanted to take an aspirin too.'

'Why? Did your head ache?'

'I couldn't sleep very well. Oh! do you have to keep on?'

'Perhaps if you can't sleep another time I could whistle and charm you like I did the snake up there.'

'I'm not a snake, thank you!'

In the garden there were many fuchsias. After Gilly had told him, for the third or fourth time, not to keep on so but to go into the garden and let the wind cool his tongue for a while he walked up and down the path and among the flower beds, popping fuchsia buds into small explosions with his fingers. He stopped once at the head of the well and lay flat on his face and looked through the crack in the round wooden board that fitted like a cap on the top of it. When the well was wide open the round silver coin that lay far down in the darkness at the bottom of it was like a bright full moon. Now it was a mere slit of silver. After watching it for a minute or so he dropped a half-open fuchsia flower through the crack in the well top and then watched it float quickly down, like a pink and purple parachute, until it was swallowed in blackness.

'Careful of that well top. It doesn't look too safe.'

He turned to see Ainsworth standing in the garden, looking down at him with some concern. He carried his camera in his hands.

'It's got a lock on it. It can't come open.'

'Still, can't be too careful. Look, how about that?'

'What?'

James got up off his knees at last, and stood up.

'I bought you a float for fishing.'

The float was bright orange at one end, dark brilliant blue at the other. Ainsworth held it like a dart.

'How about that? With a float like that you'll catch fish like mad.'

'I will? How many?'

'Oh! millions. Simply millions.'

Ainsworth held out the float. James took it, holding it too like a dart.

'It's like a kingfisher.'

'Like what? A kingfisher? How?'

'It's like the colour they have on them.'

'Observant boy.' Ainsworth laughed and looked towards the house. 'Where's Gilly this morning?'

Before he could answer a voice said, suddenly, 'Oh! my God,' and Gilly looked out of an upstairs window.

'Hullo there. Not up yet?'

'Good grief, what brings you out so early?'

'Mrs Fitzsimmons lent me her car. I thought I'd run over to

Market Easton. It's about thirty miles from here. There's a Roman site there. Thought I'd take a picture or two.'

'And you came all the way over to tell me the good news.'

'Great Heavens, no. I thought you'd like to come with me.'

All the cold irritation seemed to float from Gilly's face as swiftly as if, as with the snake in the clouds, something had charmed it away.

'Well, give me a chance. I'm not dressed. I never know what you'll do next, do I?'

'Can you come?'

She wrinkled her face. She pointed down at James, who was popping fuchsias with his finger tips again. Did it mean they had to –? And what had he got in his hand?

'A float. I bought him a float. Will you come?'

Before she could answer she heard the voices of geese harshly honking across the park.

'There are the geese,' she said. 'I can see them coming across now. Take the bread that's on the table. Yes, all of it. It doesn't matter. All of it. It's yesterday's.'

James ran into the house, snatching half a loaf from the breakfast table. He tried to break it with his hands as he ran out again. Most mornings he fed the geese. Obedient as sheep, they came over from the farm and, again like the sheep, stood outside the wire fence beyond the garden, staring, necks high, waiting to be fed.

Sometimes he thought he liked geese better than sheep. You could talk to them. One of the geese was very old. He called her Biddy. You could tell her at once from the rest because her head was nearly the colour of pumice stone. He called another Croaky. You held the bread high up for him and all the time he croaked loudly and madly and begged like a dog.

As he began to break the bread into pieces Gilly came downstairs. She was still wearing her dressing-gown. She was laughing and she drew Ainsworth into the kitchen.

'Dressed for the part,' he said. He put both arms round her. He kissed her full on the lips and then let one hand slide inside the dressing-gown, his fingers running down to her breasts. 'Warm as a bird's egg.'

'God, the things you say.'

She fingered his hair with both hands, staring up at him, lips apart. Then she fingered her own hair and laughed and said what a sight she was. She hadn't done a thing. Even when she confessed she hadn't slept well and had tossed and turned half the night long there was a look on her face of unrelieved rapture as if she too had been charmed by music.

'Do we have to go? Couldn't we stay here? We could go over to the house again. He'd play all morning in the glass-house.'

'But you see Mrs Fitzsimmons lent me her car.'

'Couldn't you go this morning and come back for this afternoon? Sometimes he goes to bed in the afternoon. He was up early today.'

'I thought we could picnic. Mrs Fitzsimmons put up some sandwiches and I brought some beer.'

'Stay here. Let's stay here and go over to the house. I liked it over there in the house yesterday.'

'We could go over to the house tomorrow. It might rain tomorrow. I feel somehow I ought to use the car now that she's been good enough to let me have it for the day. If you can't come I feel I must – '

'Oh! God, don't go.'

In answer he kissed her again. He ran his hands quickly over both her breasts. Her lips parted themselves and she started to tremble, making small sobbing sounds. Then she gripped him hard and drew him centrally against herself, feeling his body like a rock. He begged her, half-laughing, to be careful. Did she want to make it too hard to bear?

'God, I can't bear it anyway.'

Some time later she managed to shake herself out of a long half trance to say:

'Well, what do we do? Do we stay or go? I have to get dressed anyway.'

'He'll be around whatever we do.'

Now she was gifted with a sudden thought.

'Perhaps Mrs Barton would have him for an hour or two.'

'Who's Mrs Barton?'

'Over at the farm. She said once – no, you go. It wouldn't do.

Anyway, I believe it's market day today.'

The struggle inside herself was sharp and real enough to be reflected miserably on her face. The effect of it was so plain and open that he laughed.

'Do you have to be so conscientious?'

'Yes, I have to be conscientious. That's the way I'm made.'

'The way you're made is like a bird's egg – warm. All smooth and warm – '

'You mustn't do that again. I can't bear it if you do that again. Just let me go, will you? – I have to go and get dressed now.'

Half an hour later they were ready to drive off in Mrs Fitzsimmons' blue-grey Vanguard.

'Say good-bye to the geese now. We're ready to go.'

'I don't want to say good-bye to the geese. They've only just come.'

'Say good-bye to the geese. Mr Ainsworth's going to take us out in his car.'

'Why?'

'You've got that nice float Mr Ainsworth gave you. Perhaps we'll find somewhere to go fishing.'

'Fishing? Can Mr Pimm come?'

'No. Mr Pimm can't come. Not today.'

'Why can't Mr Pimm come? Why not?'

'I'm fed up with Mr Pimm!'

As Ainsworth turned the car away from the house she spoke the only words she was to say for another ten minutes or so.

'Not that way. The gate's closed that way. You'll have to turn round and go the other way.'

With silent unconcern Ainsworth turned the car round and started to drive towards the gate that was open. Across the park the empty house stood stark white in the morning sunlight. Along the avenue the chestnuts were turning fast. There was a real touch of autumn in the air.

Well, it was September tomorrow, he said, and she listened in silence. He went on to speak of the morning with light enthusiasm. It had that marvellous something in it, that lifted up feeling that you got after storms, that light that never was on land or sea. One day you thought the summer had gone for ever. It rained or hailed or some other damn thing and you said good-bye to it and thought of winter. Next morning it was all back again, marvellous and brilliant and all warm – warm as – He was about to make some comparison with a bird's egg, and then her breasts, but he turned from the driving wheel and looked at her face, stonily staring ahead, and found he had no words.

'Gilly!'

'Yes, what is it now?'

'I haven't got my float.'

She turned and banged her hand flat on the seat behind her.

'Well, if you're too stupid to remember it you must go without it!'

'Oh! don't worry. I'll buy him another.'

'I don't want another. I like that one. It's like a kingfisher.'

'Oh! go back,' she said. 'Go back. Turn back. We might as well go back for the wretched thing first as last. We'll save ourselves time and trouble. Where did you leave it then?'

'I dropped it down the well.'

Speechlessly she stared ahead, grimly silent, actually hearing the man laughing.

'Well, that at least solves that problem. What did you hope to catch in the well, James? A nice big fat smoked salmon?'

'Oh! very amusing.'

Now and then, as they drove on in complete silence, a light shower of leaves, like yellow petals, detached themselves and floated down on the road or the verges of grass in the late summer air. And looking at them, he was again enthusiastically reminded of the magical changes that could so swiftly come over things. The hail of the day before had been pretty stiff. It had broken half a dozen panes of glass in Mrs Fitzsimmons' greenhouse, behind the pub. One hailstone, big as a halfpenny, had actually cut a tomato clean in half, clean as a whistle, clean like a knife. It was so remarkable a cut that Mrs Fitzsimmons had put the tomato, severed exactly in half, on the bar, for all customers to see. It sat there to be argued about all night. Some thought it was really the work of a hailstone; some were equally positive it must have been a slivered pane of glass. It was just the sort of thing people liked to argue about in pubs. It went on and on. He himself inclined to the pane of glass theory. A hailstone was altogether too round to have made a cut like that.

In a long silence she stared ahead. A suffocating sensation of having left some part of herself behind kept her cold, almost antagonistic. Her warm other self was still behind her, in the kitchen, her lips parted and unsatisfied.

'You're very quiet this morning.'

'It's a quiet morning, isn't it?'

Cheerfully ignoring this, he said that Mrs Fitzsimmons' car went well. It was very sweet of her to have offered to lend him the car. He actually felt a bit of a hypocrite about the car. He had really set off with the avowed intention of walking every step. No transport, no cheating, doing it the hard way. But Mrs Fitzsimmons had been so insistent and sweet and persuasive about the whole thing that he hadn't had the heart to refuse and offend her.

'She's very persuasive, that woman. She's got that Irish way.'

Her latent antagonism, quiet until that moment, suddenly twisted itself inside her like a knotted fist. She was poised to say 'Oh! really? I wonder you didn't bring her with you,' when he suddenly said:

'Blast. Now I've gone and done a damn silly thing.'

'Don't say you've forgotten your float too.'

'No, but I've gone and forgotten my transistor.'

'So important?'

'Damn. Yes, it's important. I miss it terribly. The music I mean. It makes me feel so alone.'

'Thank you.'

He half smiled, introducing into his voice a note of true apology, of genuine affection.

'No, sweetheart, no. I'm sorry. I didn't mean it like that. Really. But there was a programme at half past twelve – Schubert, rather special – I wanted – Oh! blast, it doesn't matter now.'

Suddenly, from the back seat, James said:

'I just saw two magpies. What does that mean?'

'It means there are two of us. That's what. Two stupid twits.'

'What's a twit?'

'You and me. Two for silver, is it? I can never remember.'

'Is a twit the same as a bit?'

'No, two for joy, that's it. The same as what? A bit? Why?'

'Mr Pimm says there's an Irish bit at the pub.'

Gilly felt antagonism break, running free in an impossible burst of laughter.

'You see,' she said, 'what big ears they've got.'

She laughed again. Ainsworth, gloomy, stared at the road ahead.

'I don't see anything particularly funny about it.'

'No?' Suddenly she felt almost gay. 'After all, two for joy.'

Ainsworth had nothing to say for some moments longer. Finally James leaned over from the back seat and said:

'When are we going fishing?'

'I didn't think we were going fishing.'

'Then what did you buy me a float for?'

A good question, Gilly thought, and laughed again.

'All right,' Ainsworth said, 'we're coming into Market Easton now. I'll stop and buy him another float.'

'Then you'll have to find a river. Or a pond or –'

'The river's the same one that runs through the park. I've got a map, haven't I?'

After another thirty minutes or so the river, broader now, feathered with brown-grey plumes of reed, appeared suddenly below them, a tranquil sleeping snake in a small valley. Ainsworth pulled the car into the side of the road, directly against a gate on which a nailed notice said in militant white letters: *Private. No Fishing. All Trespassers will be prosecuted.*

'This will do,' he said.

'But it says trespassers –'

'It always does,' he said, 'and they never do anything about it.'

Suddenly some of Ainsworth's gloom seemed to lift. Perhaps it was because James, bounding from the car, started running up and down the grass verge, waving a new scarlet and white fishing float above his head like a firework.

'Shall we picnic on the side of the road,' Gilly said, 'or in the field?'

'Oh! in the field. That's what trespassing notices are for.'

'Are they? I thought they were to keep people out.'

'No. They're really to invite people in.'

By the time sandwiches and apples and bottles of beer and tomatoes and glasses had been spread out on the river bank, half in the shade of an ash-tree, Ainsworth was cheerful again. He even paused in the act of opening a bottle of beer to smile and say to her, suddenly, inconsequently:

'Why so thoughtful?'

'Me? I'm all right. I thought it was you.'

'Good God, what's up with me?'

'I thought you were angry with me.'

Angry with her? He gave her the softest of smiles. How could she think he was angry with her? How could she come to have a thought like that?

She couldn't explain, she said, she just thought, and gave him a quiet sideways smile of her own in return.

Ainsworth hardly noticed the smile. He was busy with bottles, sandwiches, glasses. He rustled unopened packets, caressed shining tomatoes and started to peel a cucumber.

'Gosh, Mrs Fitzsimmons has done us well. Ham, chicken – and Good God. Steak pies. Oh! they're marvellous, the steak pies. She has them on the bar every night. Strong men go mad for them. Like kids for ice-cream.'

'Ice-cream?' James said.

There was no ice-cream. There was a brand new float, a real brand new rod, a packet of hooks and a fishing line. He should be grateful for that, Gilly said, without ice-cream. It was very good of Mr –

'Marvellous, these pies. I think she puts mushroom in them. They've got that something – Yes it's mushroom.'

Ainsworth gave off sighs of praise and content. He took deep gulps of warm midday air. He looked with contentment at the river, the meadows through which it flowed with undisturbed tranquillity, between plumes of reed that hardly turned in the air, and said how good it was to feel that summer, after all, hadn't gone. He was looking forward to a long, dozy afternoon.

'Can I have some ice-cream?'

'No.'

'Why not?'

'Now don't start on about ice-cream.'

'Why not?'

'Because we're a long way out in the country and there isn't any ice-cream out here.'

'There was ice-cream in that town we came through. Where we bought the float and things. I saw one of those vans that have bells on them.'

'There'll be bells on you if you don't sit still and eat your lunch and stop ding-donging about ice-cream.'

'You said I could have ice-cream.'

'When did I say that? I said no such thing.'

'Yesterday.'

'Yes, but yesterday isn't today!'

'Look,' Ainsworth said, 'if it will make for peace and quiet I will go and get ice-cream. I saw a sign back there –'

'No, you don't. Don't pamper him.'

'It said Easton Green 1 mile. They're bound to have ice-cream there. It won't take five minutes. They all have their deep freezes nowadays.'

'You are not to pamper him.'

'I know how I felt about ice-cream. All kids –'

'Not until he's eaten his lunch. Now James, eat your lunch. You've started that nice chicken sandwich – eat it up now and stop mauling it about. You've got that nice float and rod and line and everything – what more do you want?'

'Ice-cream.'

'Look, if we have any more of that – my nerves are jangled up enough already –'

'The solution,' Ainsworth suddenly said, 'is simple. My system is – if you want something, have it. If the man says ice-cream – then let it be ice-cream. Let's all have ice-cream.'

'Oh! you'd spoil him, you would. Of course!'

'I'll be back in a quarter of an hour.'

She ate moodily through a ham sandwich, in silence, not turning to watch him cross the meadow, climb the gate and go out to the car on the verge beyond.

Twenty minutes later he was back with two tubs of vanilla, one of chocolate and raspberry and one large multi-coloured super-duper on a stick.

'Where's James?'

'He pestered so I fitted up his rod and made bread paste – '

'Where is he? Doesn't he want his ice-cream?'

'Oh! somewhere just up the river. Oh! just like a man – craves for something he can't have and then when he's got it doesn't want it.'

'I'd better take him his ice-cream. Want one? Vanilla or chocolate and raspberry? I'll put the rest in the shade – '

'Oh! don't pamper – '

Five minutes later, coming back from where James sat watching float and line at a point up river, Ainsworth found Gilly lying flat on her back, eyes open, in full sun. Without evident recognition she saw him arrive, pour himself another glass of beer, sip at it and start to eat a second meat pie.

'It really wasn't far. It actually wasn't even a mile.'

The few words he spoke from time to time had no effect on her. The blank brown eyes might have been in a state of gloom or withdrawal or more dreaminess: he couldn't tell. But at last he leaned down to her, pressed his lips against her face and said simply:

'Who's angry now?'

'You baffle me. You switch from one thing to another. I never know where I am with you.'

He lay down beside her, his body close to her legs, one hand casually across her breast.

'Then I'll tell you. It's August. Alice was sitting by the river – '

'And you tease me too, don't you?'

'I think you're sweet. Are your eyes closed?'

'No.'

'Then close them. I've closed mine. Then we can say we've slept together.'

'We've done that already, haven't we? That's what I mean.'

'It was lovely.'

'I know it was but you can't expect me suddenly to be all calm and nice and tidy about it, can you? It's never happened to me before.'

'It will again.'

She started to say something but whatever it was she had to say was smothered by his mouth, lightly caressing her lips from side to side. She responded to this by at last closing her eyes and then holding his head with her two hands. Some long time later he drew away from her and looked down at her and finally said:

'What are you listening to?'

'Listening?' She suddenly opened her eyes. 'I wasn't listening to anything.'

'You looked as if you were listening to something a long way away.'

'Did I?'

'Damn about that transistor. They were playing just the piece of music for you, that Schubert. It's the bit in the slow movement – you hear the horns in the background, a long, long way away. The same one soft note – they play it over and over again.'

'Do they?'

'That's what you looked like. Just as if you were listening to something like that.'

She lay completely still, eyes open now, and her head slightly to one side. It might have been that she was in fact now listening to a distant, repeated, uncapturable sound, elusive and very far away. She was full of an amazed, repressed stillness that it seemed nothing could ever break. Suddenly Ainsworth said:

'What did you do before you came here?'

'There you go again. Fancy asking a question like that. At a time like this. One minute you're talking about me listening to some music somewhere – I don't know where – and then – all of a sudden – that's what I say, I never know where I am with you.'

'What did you do, I mean? Did you always look after children?'

'Worked in a baker's shop.'

'Doesn't sound very exciting.'

'It was too exciting.'

'Hard to believe.' He gave a short laugh, more at the joke he now made than at anything she had said. 'Got too terrific, I suppose, counting the currants in the buns.'

To his surprise she said: 'Something like that. I started to get nervous about all the faces. I couldn't stand the faces.'

'The faces? What faces?'

The faces coming in. The faces in the shop. In and out, all day long. Staring at you. Asking questions. You never think about faces until you stand behind a counter and they start coming at you, all day long, six days a week.'

'I never thought of that.'

That's why she left, she went on to say – well not exactly. The faces were getting her down -- well, not really, not all the faces, just one face. She was always looking for one face and it was never there. Did he understand what it was like, looking up every minute hundreds of minutes a week, and expecting to see one face and it never came?

Ainsworth didn't answer her question simply because he supposed she didn't need an answer.

'Oh! well, let's not talk about it. He's gone now – I mean it's all over and done with now. But at the time I thought I'd go mad. I got so I couldn't count up properly – it sounds daft, I know, but I couldn't count and I even started to see faces in the bread.'

He sat up suddenly. Without a word he reached out and helped himself to a chicken sandwich.

'Then I saw this advert. This job. It sounded just what I wanted. Away from everything, in the country, quiet, just for five or six weeks – and good money.'

She broke off, closing her eyes again. It wasn't ten days since she had taken the job. Now the beginning of it seemed a thousand miles away. The beginning had been so simple. The beginning had soothed and quietened her and taken her out of herself. She liked the beginning: only herself and the boy and Mr Pimm and Mr Monday to bother about. A world uncomplicated by figures who didn't exist might have seemed to other people too complicated to bear but for her, in a still distraught mood where she was looking for a face that was never there, it was very comforting. She liked the world of Mr Pimm; she liked the make-believe. It took you out of yourself in a wonderful way, listening to Mr Pimm, pretending you were Mr Pimm, living for a while in the skin of other people. It wasn't fantastic really, or silly or far-fetched. It was no more far-fetched than a road that wasn't there, some bit of Roman wall, a river that had changed its course. It had all been very simple in the beginning, but it wasn't so simple now.

She opened her eyes at last to hear Ainsworth say:

'It's no use waking up now and asking for sandwiches because I've eaten them all.'

'I wasn't asleep.'

'You were a-sleeping and you took me in.'

'What?'

'Oh! no, it's too complicated.'

She lay drowsily quiet for a little longer. She had kicked off her shoes. Her feet were warm in the sun.

'Who was this Schubert?' she suddenly said. 'Does he sing? I never heard of him in the pops or anything.'

'If I hadn't forgotten the damned transistor I could have shown you.' Ainsworth gave a long, easing sigh and, wiping the last of the sandwich crumbs from his lips, stretched himself on the grass, close to her. 'Mind if I come into your bed?'

'I think you're in, aren't you?'

'I'm very close to you, if that's what you mean.'

He pressed his body against her. She touched his face with both hands. She seemed about to draw him towards her and then, as if unconsciously troubled about something, simply stared at him instead.

'Why the complicated frown?'

'I didn't know I was frowning. I didn't mean to frown.'

'Never,' he said, 'let it get complicated.'

'No?'

'Never,' he said, 'let it get too serious. It may never happen and there's always tomorrow.'

He started, in the inconsequent way she found so baffling, to

hum a tune. At the same time he strummed his fingers across
her breasts. It seemed to her the mere echo of a tune: a single
note held, drawn out, held, repeated. That was the Schubert bit,
she heard him say. The bit where you could hear summer dying
away.

'Haunts you, doesn't it?' he said. 'It always does me.'

Yes, she agreed, it haunted her. The continuous rhythm of his
fingers across her breasts, repeated as the one drawn-out note,
drew her into the very fabric of the tune. For a long time after
the sound of his voice had quietened and she could hear nothing but her own suppressed breathing as he held her in one
long single kiss she could still detect the echo of the one drawn-
out note, haunting but uncomplicated, at the back of her mind.

'Never let it get complicated. Never let it – There's always tomorrow – '

Her breasts, by now, were bare in the afternoon sun. He
stopped caressing them with his fingers. Instead he kissed each
of them in turn, lightly.

'What are we going to do about love, today?'

'Well, nothing here, certainly.'

'How do you sleep at the cottage?'

'James sleeps in the room next to me.'

'Lucky James.'

'You can't come there, that's certain.'

Between alternate kisses of her breasts he let the conversation go on with casual lightness.

'What about the house? We still have a session to do in the
bedroom there.'

'We can't sleep in those beds.'

Nothing in all the world, he said, could make him think why
not. A bed was a bed, wherever you found or put it. It had
sheets and pillows. You drew the sheets back and slipped under
them and covered yourself with them and lay on the pillows.
You slept and made love and slept and made love and then it
was tomorrow.

'Go and make the bed and I'll be there tonight.'

'Oh! don't be impossible. I couldn't leave him, could I?'

'The word impossible should be struck from the language.'

'I don't care if it should. There's a limit.'

'Is there?' Head slightly to one side, he held her in a solemn, teasing gaze. 'There's that frown on your face again.' He drew his hand across the full span of her breasts and slowly back again. 'It shouldn't be there – '

'Oh! God.' Impulsively she pushed his hands away. Then even more impulsively she pulled them back again. 'God, do you know how I feel when you do that to me?'

She let herself be drawn away, without an answer, into another long current of soundless echoes. She lost count of time. Throughout the warm golden, afternoon she lay with eyes closed, thinking of nothing.

When she stirred at last it was to find him still lying on his back, blue eyes awake and on the sky. She looked at him for some time without speaking. The curious thought that he was still a stranger had been half dormant in her mind. Now it woke.

'We've heard a lot about me. What about you?'

'Me?' Ainsworth turned his head and gave a sudden ravishing grin. 'About me? What about me?'

'I don't know a thing about you.'

'Then let us,' he said, with another grin, 'remedy that: lazy, inconsistent, useless, jobless, aimless – Everything by starts and nothing long.'

'Be serious.'

'Especially inconsistent. Last year it was cave drawings in France. This year it's roads, old maps – Next year – Oh! who cares about next year?'

'I didn't mean all that.'

'Ah! am I married? I know.'

'Are you?'

'I'll pretend I'm married to you.'

'Will you? I don't know whether I like pretending.'

'Oh! I thought you did. Mr Pimm and all that.'

She had nothing to say. Her brown retracted eyes were not looking at him any longer.

'Oh! no, not married. Which does the nightingale prefer? The cage on the tree-top? Oh! no, freedom for me.'

She still had nothing to say.

'Getting really warm now,' Ainsworth said. 'I could do with an ice-cream to soothe the savage breast.'

'With what?'

She abruptly sat up, hands reaching for her tangled hair. 'Ice-cream. I left them in the shade – '

'Good Heavens, where's James?'

She leapt up. For a ridiculous moment or two she ran in a half circle, on bare feet. This actually made him laugh.

'We must have been here hours. Where on earth can he have got to?'

She stared wildly around, across the meadow, over to the car and up and down the river. Ainsworth looked with indifference at his watch.

'Half an hour at the outside.'

'James! It must be hours. James, where are you? Where on earth can he have got to?'

'My dear girl, he's a fisherman. You know how fishermen are. They fish on and on and never know what day it is.'

She started running towards the river bank. She then halted abruptly, looked this way and that, and started to run some way downstream.

'Not that way! Leprechaun. He's about fifty yards up there.'

'I can't see him anywhere. That's his trouble – he's always liable to go off somewhere – James! Where are you? James!'

Ainsworth stood watching her run along the river bank. She was still bare-foot. Her legs were pretty. There was something quite fresh, quite alluring, about the way she ran, her figure nervous against a background of tall brown-plumed reeds. It reminded you a little bit of a kitten in long grass, trying to find its way.

'How far did you say it was? Where did you leave him? I can't see him anywhere!'

Her voice, loud and piercing but not quite a scream, reached him as he was picking up a tub of ice-cream from under the shade of the ash-tree. He peeled off the lid, calling back:

'Oh! not far. Forty or fifty yards or so.'

The ice-cream had melted quite a bit. He dipped a finger into it, tasting it. It was no longer cold.

'I can't see him anywhere! He's disappeared completely!'

'Oh! he can't have.' He dug with a wooden spoon into the ice-cream. Underneath the surface it was still quite hard. After all, it had kept quite well in the shade. 'Probably playing Moses in the bulrushes.

Slipping spoonfuls of ice-cream into his mouth, he watched her start to run back, then stop abruptly and turn again. The likeness to a lost kitten struck him again by its aptness. He started to walk towards her with deliberate unconcern, quite slowly. Her legs were really awfully pretty but sometimes, as now, when she was startled or concerned, the brown eyes seemed altogether too uneasy and too large.

'He seems to have disappeared off the face of the earth. I can't see a sign of him anywhere. I'm getting scared – '

'Now don't panic.'

'But where exactly did you leave him? I'm always scared of water, I never leave him alone where there's water – '

'Now take it rationally. If he'd fallen in he'd have screamed. If he'd screamed we'd have heard him.'

'It's all very well for you. It isn't your responsibility – James, where are you? James! God, what would I do if he drowned?'

'They never,' he said, 'get drowned.' He followed her at a measured pace up the river bank, half-stopping now and then to peer and peck at the tub of ice-cream. The cream was softening nicely now. Quite inadvertently he had chosen the chocolate-and-raspberry one. The melting colours were suffusing and entwining into each other in brown and pink patterns, very attractively.

'There's something floating over against the other bank! It isn't a hat, is it? It couldn't be, could it?'

'It couldn't be,' he said and the words were almost more to himself than to her, 'because he wasn't wearing one. It's a paper bag.'

'I'm scared,' he heard her shout. 'I'm getting scared.'

Before Ainsworth could speak again she was almost beyond shouting distance, running fast. A few moments later he passed the spot where James had been fishing. The stick and papers that had held the multi-coloured super-duper lay on the grass there. He remembered the spot very well. A big low straddling thorn bush, already half-red with berries, leaned at a deep angle towards the river. Knotted to one of its lower branches was one of those strange grey, silken cocoon-like bags of caterpillars. He remembered it well because James had asked how the caterpillars, so imprisoned, eventually got out again and he remembered saying he didn't really know except that he thought they flew out, as butterflies. The rod, the line and the white and scarlet float lay there too, dropped in the reeds.

'There's a bridge up there!' She was shouting again, her voice piercing as she ran back to him. 'Perhaps he's gone over to the other side.' The brown eyes seemed pitifully, ridiculously large now. It struck him that it was she who might have been lost, not the child. 'Oh! my God, I'm frightened. I'm frightened what might have happened.'

'Don't, don't panic. Pull yourself together. I'll search the other bank – '

'It looks like an old boat-house up there too, past the bridge.' She was running rapidly away from him again, shouting as she ran. 'I'll look in that too.'

There was nothing inside the boat-house, a mere gas-tarred wreck of a shed forty yards beyond the bridge, but a half-submerged punt lay against the river bank outside it. Dismally she looked down into its green water-logged skeleton. For several hundred yards beyond it the river course became a straight, treeless canal-like stretch. There was nothing to be seen on that either except a heron standing with deathly stillness against a bank of reeds, a skeleton itself, a wintry spectre in grey.

She ran back to the bridge. It was a short hump-backed structure of brick. She stood in the centre of it and stared this way and that at the empty river. She felt steely and poised and tense, her nerves at full stretch.

'Have you seen him? He isn't up there. He's not in the boat-house – '

From what seemed an impossible distance downstream – she simply couldn't believe he had got that far – Ainsworth waved both hands above his head. It was a clear message of emptiness. She started running again, this time upstream along the opposite bank. Across the meadow a herd of cows, all black and white, stopped grazing and stood motionless and wooden staring at her. She ran for a hundred yards or so and then stopped too. Panting and out of breath, she stood and watched the heron rise from the reeds, the only moving thing on the river, answering with big pumping flaps of his wings her struggle for breath.

She walked slowly back to the bridge.'I would never forgive myself, I would never forgive myself, I would never forgive myself.'

She stopped and stood irresolutely against the side of the bridge, still panting. The coldly thumped monotonous words had just started to resolve themselves into images too frightening to face when she saw Ainsworth coming up the river path on long striding steps. For the first time he looked in the slightest degree agitated too.

'There's a bit of a spinney over there. I thought I saw something move along the side of it. Of course it might have been a dog but somehow it looked too big for a dog.'

'Why would he go over there? You don't think he's in here — in the – '

'God knows, the blasted little fool. No, he's not in the river.' Ainsworth was suddenly angered. 'He's too bloody fly for that. He's too bloody sharp to drown himself. Come on, let's get over to the spinney – the stupid idiotic little rat – '

'Oh! don't call him things like that. That doesn't help.'

'I'll call him something else when I – '

'Oh! God, I feel so sick.'

Ainsworth ran ahead. She followed limply, unable to keep up. From a point only a few yards from the spinney he turned and shouted something she could only half catch, something about 'I'll take the other side – you –' and then disappeared.

She walked, without heart to run, along the side of the spinney. A bird or two groped among fallen leaves. A pigeon fell from high up in an oak, beating its wings in swooping flight like a pair of clappers. Her eyes groped too and in return the spinney offered nothing but shadow.

'You shouldn't have called him names like that – that doesn't help – Oh! my God, what on earth have we done?'

Half-way along the edge of the spinney she stopped, weak from exhaustion, ready to cry. Once she actually opened her mouth in an effort to call something across the intervening space of trees but the sound never came.

Incredibly, not long later, as if in answer, she could have sworn she heard voices. Not one voice, nor the voice of the young man, but two voices, in conversation. She started to walk into the spinney. She picked up the sound of voices more distinctly as she walked and then, at last, heard one say:

'I tell you, mate, it's something cruel.'

'Too right. It bleedin' is at that, I tell you. How's the old brew coming up? – put plenty in, matey, I like the spoon to stand upright.'

James sat, legs outstretched, by the bole of an ash-tree. A great hole that might have been carved out by badgers went darkly back, deep under the grey knuckled exposed arms of the tree roots. Poised on the flatter edge of one of these roots stood an empty saucepan, the tea can. With chesty grumblings Mr Pimm leaned over it and stirred its contents with a stick.

'Jist coming up to the boil, matey. Nice an' hot. September tomorrow, they tell me.'

'Is it, be Guy? Bleedin' winter a-top on us afore we know.'

She was uncertain whether to laugh or cry. An urgent impulse to rush forward and pick him up in her arms was followed instantly by a cold desire to hit him across the face and bring him to his senses. The unexpected relief of finding him was at first like a surge of grief, as if in fact she had lost him. It died instantaneously in the hot flash of temper. Then that died too.

'James, James. How ever did you come to get all this way away? We've been looking everywhere.'

'I came back but you were asleep and then Mr Pimm came – '

'You shouldn't do a thing like that. Don't ever, ever do a thing like that again.'

'It's all right if I'm with Mr Pimm.'

'It's all right with Mr Pimm if you tell me.'

'I came to tell you but you were asleep.'

'You could have woken me.

'You were too fast asleep. I could see.'

'Well, don't ever, ever go away like that again. Without saying. Promise me.'

'It's all right with Mr Pimm. I was with Mr Pimm all the time.'

'Yes, but I didn't know you were with Mr Pimm. Don't you see? When I know, it's all right. It's when I don't know – '

'It's always all right with Mr Pimm.'

'Yes, I know it is, but – Say good-bye to Mr Pimm now. We must go.'

'Couldn't Mr Pimm come back in the car with us?'

'I don't think so. Mr Pimm had better walk back.'

'It's a long way.'

'Mr Pimm had better walk, I think. Say good-bye now.'

'All right. So long, matey.'

'So long.'

She took his hand. They walked out of the spinney. The receding rush of anger and relief had left her curiously cold and calm. With neither excitement nor any trace of surprise she saw Ainsworth striding towards her along the edge of the spinney, beating at the edges of hazel boughs with a broken stick.

'Not a sign of the little – Oh! for God's sake, there you are. Where in hell did you find the little bastard?'

'He was here.'

'Oh! just like that. Conjured out of thin air.'

'He was only with Mr Pimm.'

'Oh! marvellous. Only! Enchanting. God! – '

'Everything's all right now. It's all over. We'll say no more about it.'

With exaggerated gestures Ainsworth flung his arms in the air. So they would say no more about it. The little bastard had led them up hill and down dale and played hell's delight with everybody, but now, of course, it was all right. It was all over. Say no more about it. For a thing like that, he didn't mind telling her, he would have got a mighty good beating when he was a boy.

'And what good would beating do? It's all finished now.'

Oh! Naturally. Of course. Let him run wild and do as he liked.

Let him lead everybody a bloody good dance. Let him play Hamlet next time and drown poor bloody Ophelia in the reeds.

'Don't talk like that.'

And Pimm. Our Mr Pimm. Ainsworth had to confess he loved our Mr Pimm. The man who never was.

'Shall we walk back?'

It was the Pimm character, Ainsworth said, who really got him. Everything stopped for Mr Pimm. You were all set for a nice lazy afternoon by the river but then the amazing Pimm arrived. Scaring the living daylights –

'I know it sometimes seems ridiculous but it's very real to him.'

Ridiculous? The whole thing was wearing pretty damn thin, Ainsworth said, if you asked him.

'Then don't let's talk about it. I told you before it's just as real to him as –'

As what? Ainsworth begged her, again with an exaggerated gesture or two, to justify by some comparison the existence of Mr Pimm.

'Oh! it doesn't matter now.'

In silence, his irritation cooling, too, they walked back across the meadow, over the bridge and along the river to the car. Under the tree where they had picnicked she started to pack up, still in a mood curiously calm and cold, the few things left lying on the grass.

Suddenly, as she did so, there came over Ainsworth one of those inconsequent changes of mood that found her always unready. He suddenly appeared from under the tree with the two remaining tubs of ice-cream, carelessly tossing them from hand to hand with the ease of a juggler.

'Found! – two ice-creams. Isn't that luck? One for James and one for Mr Pimm.'

'Oh! no, don't. You'll drop them.'

Blandly Ainsworth ignored this and juggled on, finally giving both ice-creams to James, one in one hand and one in the other. Then he turned abruptly away from the boy, put his own two hands with all possible lightness on her shoulders and said simply:

'Sorry.'

The pain of this single word was enough to hurt her instantly. Her tears suddenly welled up, harsh and bitter. She did her best to cover them with her knuckled hands, then heard him say:

'Terribly, terribly stupid of me.'

She cried with miserable, discomfited silence into her doubled hands, unable to say a word.

'It was unforgivable. I didn't realize –'

He suddenly pressed his lips against the side of her hair as a new, gentle mark of apology. This affected her so deeply that she started to bite her lip in fear of making noises that sounded stupid.

'What is Gilly crying for?'

'Oh! I'm not crying now, James. I'm really not. Come on, have you got your things? Let's go.'

'That's it. Home for tea. Fish-and-chips for tea. Where's that big fish you caught?'

Religiously Gilly searched the grass for scraps of fallen paper. She saw them as if through splintered glass. There was a curious knotted ache across the centre of her forehead whenever she bent down.

'Well, are we all set?' With sudden, bouncing cheerfulness Ainsworth lifted James to the top bar of the field gate. 'Where's Gilly, the slacker?' He started beating with the flat of one hand on the top of the gate. 'Gilly's a slacker. We think Gilly's a slacker.'

Half-smiling, touched more by teasing even than apology, Gilly came slowly across the meadow.

'Slacker! That's what we think, don't we? Slacker! – Gilly's a slacker!'

'Gilly's a slacker! Gilly's a slacker!'

'I expect I am.' Her tears were more or less dry now. She gave her eyes a final irritated brush with the back of one hand. 'My mother always used to say I was a little on the slow side.'

'Well, all set now.' Ainsworth, with an almost tempestuous renewal of outward cheerfulness, lifted James over the gate and then vaulted over it himself, one hand. 'Slackers bring up the rear – ' He stopped suddenly and smiled at her as she slowly started to climb the gate, but whether in half-mockery or graciousness she simply couldn't tell. 'Sorry, madam – allow me.

With elegance he lifted up his hand. In that moment James said:

'I left my fishing rod and things up on the bank there – '

Ainsworth burst out laughing. Miserably, to her own amazement, she started laughing too.

All the way home she sat nursing the corroding conviction that James had died. It haunted her for long stretches of silence between conversations. She seemed to see him, in her mind's eye, drowned by the boat-house, below the green skeleton of the sunken punt and then somewhere on the broader stretch of water beyond, where the heron had stood guard like a grey wintry spectre.

When she told herself that these things were stupid it was merely to increase the already aggravated thought that she was careless. It was all her fault. She hadn't been watching. She should have known. You turned your back on a child and in ten seconds the world had swallowed it out of sight. In no time it was drowned or dead under a bus and all your life, for ever, you would grieve and wonder how it happened.

'I'll never let him out of my sight again. I never will. Never. I never will.'

Ainsworth, by contrast, soared into realms of enforced cheerfulness that merely made her still more thoughtful. Once, for a few minutes in the afternoon, she had lain stretched on the grass, warm and entranced, listening to the prolonged repetition of a single note played on an invisible instrument far away. The only note she could hear now was that of her own voice, dark and convicting.

She was even unaware for some time, that a game of make-believe was being played of which she was not part. James had caught a fish: a big fish, a marvellous fish, a spectacular fish, and they were going to have it with chips, for tea. Ainsworth declared it was so.

'How shall we have it? Fried? In batter? Or with tartare sauce?'

'Ta-ta sauce.'

'Good. Splendid.' Ainsworth gave repeated peals of laughter, drumming on the driving wheel with the tips of his fingers. 'Ta-ta sauce.' This too was a welcome joke, splendidly funny. 'Good. I think it's a salmon trout, don't you?'

'I had a bit of smoked trout once but I didn't like it.'

'Ah! this is different. This is salmon trout. Don't you think it's a salmon trout, Gilly?'

From her own hiding place Gilly aroused herself to say Yes, she thought it was a salmon trout.

'By golly I'll bet that took some getting in. How long to land it, James? It's big, isn't it – seven or eight pounds?'

'Oh! it took a long time. Ten minutes. More.'

'Oh! they always fight, those salmon trout. They fight like tigers.'

'Did you ever catch a fish as big as that?'

'Oh! Never. Never. That's the biggest fish I've ever seen.' With amused satisfaction, not untouched by pride, Ainsworth again drummed the steering wheel with his fingers and then slightly turned his head and said to Gilly, in a whisper: 'How am I doing? All right? Soon I'll be as popular as Mr Pimm.'

She retreated, not answering, further into herself. The game of the spectacular, mythical fish, the fish that never was, seemed to her too unreal, too dead, even to be silly. She remembered how, as a child herself, she had sometimes stood on the edge of a game, cold, outside, uninvited. All the time you stood outside the game you thought how ridiculous it was. But the moment you were inside –

'Suppose we'd better make it a fact, eh?' Ainsworth suddenly said. 'Those fish-and-chips will soon have to be. Didn't I see a fish-and-chip place in Market Easton?'

'I didn't see one.'

'I'll pull up on the market square.' Greatly pleased at suddenly turning fantasy into fact Ainsworth found himself equally amused at the idea of immediately turning back again. 'That is, unless you'd rather stand over a hot stove and – I'm sure you cook salmon trout beautifully.'

'I've never tried.'

'Good. I'll stop. I'm feeling not unpeckish for a spot of fish-and-chips myself.'

A mile or two beyond the town they finally pulled up to eat fish-and-chips, as a second picnic, on the roadside. There wasn't a shadow of doubt about it. Ainsworth said: the salmon trout was marvellous. With an occasional chip poised in his fingers like a cigar expressing supreme content, he was at pains to congratulate James, over and over again, on the wonder of the catch. It was a dream of a fish: not only the largest but by far the most delicious salmon trout he had ever tasted.

'Pass the ta-ta sauce, would you? Thank you. And after you with the vinegar. Much obliged. I wonder if Gilly would like vinegar? Vinegar, Gilly?'

Gilly ate slowly. The fish, she thought, was greasy. She had no heart even for imagining vinegar. By contrast Ainsworth was full of boisterous enthusiasm for vinegar, chips, salmon trout and ta-ta sauce combined. Eventually, a fat chip held in his fingers like a cigar, he was saying how it reminded him of a story, a thing he had once read in a book, about a small boy who had gone on a journey by himself and had to stop at lunch time to have his lunch at an inn; and how the lunch had all been ordered and even beer too; and then how the waiter who brought the lunch had stood over the boy while he ate it and how he couldn't eat it all because it was a man's lunch and how he couldn't drink the beer either because not only was beer not good for little boys but because only the day before a gentleman had come in and drunk a pint of that same beer and dropped down dead. So the waiter stole all the beer and most of the lunch and it was very funny.

'Does it make you dead, beer?'

'Well, in this case it was a joke, see.'

'Would the little boy be dead too if he drank the beer?'

'Well no, not quite. It was the waiter's way of getting the beer for himself.'

'Was it real beer?'

'Oh! yes it was real beer.'

'Then if it was real beer why did the waiter want to drink it when the other gentleman what drank it dropped down dead?'

'Ah! well, you see – in a sense – well, of course it's a story. It didn't actually happen.'

'I thought you said it did.'

Ainsworth wiped his mouth and then his fingers on his hand-kerchief. Then he looked out of the car window. Remarkably nice afternoon, he said, even more to himself than Gilly. And would anyone like a plum now, to take the taste of the fish away? He'd bought some very nice plums in the shop next to the fish shop. Nice big purple ones. Would James like a plum?

'I'd better peel it for him first,' Gilly said.

Slowly she sat and peeled a plum. The thin purple skin came smoothly away from it until she was holding a juicy golden egg in her fingers.

'What was the little boy's name?'

'David.'

'How old was he?'·

'Oh! about as old as you. Perhaps a little older.'

'What was the waiter's name?'

'I don't know. I don't remember. I don't think he had a name.'

'Everybody has to have a name.'

'I suppose so.' Ainsworth wiped plum juice from his lips and fingers and took a long covert glance at Gilly. 'What time do sparrows go to bed? Early, I suppose, when they're tired.'

'If the waiter drank the beer he must be dead. Will the beer you drank at lunch time make you dead?'

'Look! watch the plum.' A plum, held aloft for James to see, disappeared into Ainsworth's sleeve. 'Before your very eyes.'

'Magic!'

'The boy is right. Magic. Watch again.' Ainsworth slid the plum from hand to hand. It disappeared, with no great dexterity, up his sleeve. 'Gone! The plum is here, the plum is there, the plum they seek him everywhere.'

'You can do magic!'

'Only to order. You see? – gone, come back. Disappear, come back. Disappear – '

The plum rolled to the car seat. Ainsworth hastily picked it up and put it into his pocket.

'Magic! When we get home can you make my float come up out of the well? That disappeared too. The one like a kingfisher.'

'I think,' Ainsworth said, 'it's perhaps time we drove on.'

He started the car.

'We never got to your Roman site, did we?'

Ainsworth was too busy eating a last fragment of plum to answer and Gilly could only stare down, mutely, at her twisting hands.

'Why are you drawing the curtains?'

'Because the sun's still shining and you won't get to sleep if I don't draw them.'

'You never draw the curtains other nights.'

'Yes, but tonight's different – '

'Why is it different?'

'Because like I told you the sun's still shining and you won't get to sleep if I don't draw them. You want to get to sleep, don't you? You must be tired after that long day.'

Across the park, above the farthest of the chestnuts, lay a cloud like a lion. It was all golden, with a long tail that spurted orange fire at the end. All about it were smaller lions, gold too, fluffy-coated, crouching and waiting.

'Can I watch the clouds for a little while?'

'No, you can't. You've had a long day and you must be tired and it's time you went to sleep now.'

'You didn't read to me.'

'There isn't time to read tonight. We were late getting back. I've got a lot to do.'

Gilly gave the curtains final, impatient flicks with her hands. The sky disappeared. The bedroom became all dark, not real dark, but funny dark, browny-gold, with a long thin sword of light across the ceiling.

'Has Mr Ainsworth gone home yet?'

'I can't think why you keep on about Mr Ainsworth. That's the third or fourth time since you came upstairs.'

'Has he gone to get my float out of the well?'

'How on earth can he get your float out of the well if it's right down at the bottom? It's miles down there.'

'You can see it. It's floating on the water.'

'Well, I don't care what it's doing but nobody's getting it up tonight. Or tomorrow night. Or the next night. Or the next. So say good-bye to the float and shut your eyes. Before you can wink it'll be morning.'

Gilly straightened the bed-clothes, again with impatient flicks of her hands, pulling them tight, so that he felt all wrapped up and in prison, like a papoose he had once heard his father read about in a book. Then he heard her cross the bedroom, turn the knob of the door and go out of the room.

'Gilly.'

'Yes? For goodness' sake what is it now?'

'You didn't kiss me.'

With another flurry of impatience she came back to the bed and kissed him, once on the cheek and then on the forehead. Now this was the last time, did he understand? Positively and absolutely the last time. No more questions and no more playing games. It was late and it was night and it was time to go to sleep. Everything was asleep by now – everything. The birds, the geese, the fishes, the sheep – everything. They were all asleep, long ago.

'Are the mushrooms asleep?'

'Oh! for goodness' sake. For the last time –'

'Are the clouds?'

This time there was no answer. Gilly had gone, slamming the bedroom door. He was alone, wondering if the clouds slept and if they didn't why not? His mind was bright and alert and his thoughts sprang in all directions like bits of broken, coloured glass, falling apart and back again into strange brilliant patterns, like one of those boxes you had at Christmas and shook about and looked into and it was all like the windows in a church.

There was, after the long day, a great deal that he had to think about: the clouds that were like lions and all the smaller lions and the salmon Mr Ainsworth said he had caught and how they had had it for fish and chips and then the way the plum had disappeared and it was like magic and then the float that was down the well. He wondered greatly about the float down the well. He wondered if it was still there and if Mr Ainsworth could, by magic, get it up again. He didn't know if Mr Ainsworth was really magic or not. He couldn't decide. The plum going up his sleeve wasn't really magic. His father did that with a handkerchief. The first time he did it you knew it was magic but the second time you didn't but you said so because your father wanted you to and when you did he laughed very much.

It would be magic if Mr Ainsworth got the float from the well because Gilly said you couldn't. It was impossible. When it was impossible and you did it that was magic. When you knew something was happening and everybody pretended it wasn't and it was all the time that, in a sort of way, was magic too.

That was like Mr Ainsworth still being downstairs. He knew quite well Mr Ainsworth was still downstairs. Gilly said he had gone home but he knew that he hadn't, all the time.

If you listened very hard you could hear voices. Sometimes they sounded very far away. It might have been the clouds talking among themselves. It might have been the big golden-coloured cloud with the fiery tail that was like a lion, telling the smaller lions to go to bed. It wasn't funny that the clouds talked among themselves. When they were big fat purple clouds, like bears, they always made fat purple noises, rumbling and hawking like Mr Pimm did when he spat.

But now and then he knew that it wasn't the voices of clouds he could hear. It was Mr Ainsworth's voice and then Gilly's voice, in answer. Sometimes there were long stretches when there were no voices: only silence and everything sounded empty and there was no one in the house but himself. Even the voices of the clouds stopped then and all you could hear was a funny singing noise in your ears that seemed to make you float round and round in space, so that the house seemed emptier still.

Some time later he got out of bed to see, out of curiosity, if the clouds were still there. From a thin division in the bedroom curtains he stood and looked out across the park. The sky was a strange sandy green above the sunset. The clouds, all smaller now, so that the great lion was no bigger than a tortoiseshell cat and all the lesser clouds were no more than ginger kittens, seemed as if they were crossing an empty desert, very far away.

There were two windows in the bedroom. Presently he went to the other and peered through the curtains there, on the eastward side, over towards the farm. He knew that Gilly was wrong about geese going to bed. They never went to bed because sometimes you woke in the middle of the night and heard them making queer noises, croaking angrily or as if in pain. Sometimes he wondered if they were laying eggs when they made that noise. He knew that they did lay eggs because once, in the spring, he had walked across to the farm with Miss Garfield and was given a goose-egg by Mrs Barton, the lady there. The goose-egg was a joke because his father had pretended that it was a magic egg and that a magic bird had laid it. He knew quite well it was just a plain goose-egg because Mrs Barton said so but all the time his father went on pretending it was a big magic egg laid by a big magic bird and how it would have to be put into a basin when it was boiled for breakfast and eaten with a trowel. He remembered how his father had thought it very funny about eating an egg with a trowel and how he had gone on laughing about it afterwards, for a long time.

Now, to his surprise, as he looked through the crack in the bedroom curtains, he thought at first that he saw the farm on fire. Every window was alight with brilliant orange flame. In the few seconds before he realized that this was merely the fires of sunset amazingly reflected he felt a spasm of fright and started to dance up and down, shouting: 'Fire! Fire! The farm's all on fire!' only to hear the sudden angry sound of Gilly's voice sweeping upstairs:

'James! How many more times do I have to tell you? Go to sleep and stop banging about! What are you doing up there – having a nightmare? I'll nightmare you if you don't soon go down.'

He kept quiet. He didn't want to go down. For nearly ten

minutes longer he stood watching the flames of sunset dying in the windows of the farm. The sight of this was so real that he found it hard to imagine, over and over again, that the farm wasn't all burnt out: all burnt out and everybody dead. Mrs Barton was dead and Mr Barton and Arthur, who fed the cattle. The geese were dead and the cows and the old sheepdog named Trigger. The fire had burned them all. One day a big long black car would come and carry them away, all dead and sorry for themselves.

He knew one day you had to be dead, but only when you were very old. There were all sorts of ways of being dead but it didn't happen if you looked what you were doing. You could be dead in a fire, like at the farm, or falling into water or being striked. It was being striked when you stood under a tree and the lightning hit you. Then you were dead in no time. Then you could fall down the well and you could be deader than dead when that happened: Miss Garfield had told him so. You could be dead too by falling out of a window or being runned over by a car or eating poison berries and bad mushrooms or you could choke to death from not champing your food properly. He expected there were other ways. The worst of them all, he thought, worse even than being striked, was falling down the well and this was why he knew it would be magic, really and truly, if Mr Ainsworth ever got his float out of there.

After the orange fires in the farm windows had at last died down to the colour of ashes he listened for a short time longer to the sound of voices coming up from downstairs. It was quite clear, now, that there were two voices, Mr Ainsworth's and Gilly's. He went out at last to the landing and sat on the top step of stairs and listened. He sniffed hard at the air too, thinking that perhaps Gilly might be frying eggs and bacon, but there was no smell of frying in the air.

Nor could he hear distinctly what the voices said. For some time longer he sat there in a dream, half listening to the voices, half remembering the day behind him and all that had happened. This made him remember that there was yet another way of being dead: drinking beer. He found this hard to understand. His father drank beer and Mr Ainsworth drank beer and so did Mr Pimm, but none of them were dead. Perhaps there was beer that made you dead and beer that didn't make you dead. Or perhaps it was only as his father sometimes said: You didn't have to believe everything that everybody told you.

At last he went and sat on a step half way down the stairs. From there he could hear the voices of Gilly and Mr Ainsworth more distinctly.

'I've got a funny sort of feeling that boy isn't asleep yet.'

'Quiet enough since the fire scare.'

'Too quiet. The little monkey knows. Listen.' There was a long deep silence. 'What do you bet me he isn't still awake?'

'I'm a loving man, not a betting man.'

'Listen. You can hear him. You can tell.'

'Oh! stop being restless.' There was another long deep silence. 'Your ears are beautifully soft – just like shells – did anyone ever tell you?'

'Yes, and little pigs have big ones.'

'Then let's do the things that don't have to be heard. Come on, now –'

'No, no, I told you. Not here. Not while he's still awake –'

'Awake, my foot. Sleeping like a top and dreaming of fish-and-chips and Plymouth Hoe and Mr Pimm and all that stuff.'

'I don't think you should keep talking about Mr Pimm like –'

'Oh! I don't, I don't. Not really. The world is full of Mr Pimms. Millions of girls have Mr Pimms in their beds every night, wishing – only you don't have to wish.'

'Well, I tell you I do wish –'

'Wish what?'

'Oh! I wish I could get rid of that feeling of being listened to – of someone being always – James! aren't you asleep yet? James! If I come up and find you out of bed –'

There was now another long, deep silence.

'Dead to the world. I told you.'

'He's awake. He doesn't fool me.'

'Relax, relax. Kiss me –'

'What was that? Did you hear that? Wasn't that something creaking on the stairs? – James! –'

Going back upstairs, on sudden silent feet, on all fours, like a cat, James heard the last of Gilly's conversation:

'I'll tell you what. You go now. Go and have your dinner and come back. I'll make coffee. It'll be quiet by then. Really quiet by then – '

It was more than two hours before he was back again. Several times she stood in the garden, in darkness, listening for the sound of footsteps. It was nearly ten o'clock before she heard the sound of a car.

'I'd given you up.' She kept her voice to a whisper. 'I thought you were never coming.'

She was still in the garden. Like her voice the August night air, heavy with the scent of tobacco flowers, was breathless.

'You're quite cold.' Her hands, which Ainsworth held for a moment, were still restless. She kept twisting them together. 'You're in your dressing-gown.'

She laughed involuntarily, more out of relief than anything else. She tucked her hands into the sleeves of her dressing-gown and asked him to come into the house. When she drew him into the light of the sitting-room she saw, to her surprise, that he was wearing a suit. She had never seen him in a suit before. The cloth was a mixture of moss green and brown, the coat cut in at the waist, the trousers sheer and thin. Somehow, she thought, he looked taller in the suit. This added tallness also gave her a discomfiting feeling that he was beyond her. He seemed out of her range. Suddenly he was someone altogether too smart, too classy. When she twisted her hands together she felt not only restless but inferior and clumsy too.

'Sorry I'm late.'

Ainsworth kissed her, held her hands and apologized again. It was all, he explained, the fault of Mrs Fitzsimmons. He had happened to remark, quite casually, that he loved *soufflés*. All quiet, by the way, on the upstairs front? Good. Thank the lord for that. He was saying about the *soufflés* –

'Just a minute. I've got the kettle on for the coffee.' Her excuse to go into the kitchen was merely a fresh sign of growing nervousness. She came back with her hands tucked well into her sleeves and her arms closely wrapped about her. 'Sorry about that. I didn't want it to boil over.'

Well, the *soufflés*. It was just a casual remark but suddenly there she was, making one for dinner. Now the thing about *soufflés*, as she probably knew, was that the guest must wait for the *soufflé* and not the *soufflés* for the guest. That was the law of the Medes and Persians about *soufflés*.

'Yes.' She sat crouched in an easy chair. Her legs were drawn up and tucked away into her dressing-gown. 'I see.'

Cheese, of course. Now how, did one suppose, could she have know that all of the *soufflés* he liked cheese most? In fact, cheese only. It might have been chocolate, raspberry, peach, kipper, damn it, anything: he loathed most of them anyway. But cheese it was he loved and cheese it was she chose. How the devil did she know?

She sat watching him with grave brown eyes, with the pupils that, though so snail-like, were tight and coiled. She supposed that *soufflés* were something to eat but exactly what they were or why the guest had to wait for the *soufflé* not the *soufflé* for the guest, she didn't know.

And when it came – absolute dream, a miracle. Perfect. He'd read somewhere once that a *soufflé*, in order to be perfect, had to be a sort of floating poem. And that, he told her, just about described the *soufflés* of Mrs. Fitzsimmons. The cheese, of course, hadn't to be dominant. The taste had sort of to float through it so that you were always chasing after it, thinking you'd never get it back and yet you always did. And the whole thing, of course, as light as love.

She sat very quiet, her eyes downcast now, not watching him. In a strange way she felt suddenly detached from him. Even as a listener she felt no longer part of the conversation.

'Well, I suppose the claret helped too. Anyway the two between them helped get rid of the taste of those damn fish-and-chips. They were pretty foul, weren't they?'

If she was thinking coherently of anything at all it was of the kettle. She ought to go and take it off the stove and make the coffee.

'Why the deep thought? I don't believe you're listening. You didn't get cold in the garden?'

'No, I'm not cold. I'm listening.'

'My foot. You couldn't tell me the last thing I said.'

'You said they ought to be as light as love. *Soufflés*.' Her bemusement, in reality a new and deeper shyness, broke for a moment. The brown eyes momentarily lifted themselves. Then they looked down again. 'I was only thinking it isn't always like that, is it?'

'Isn't always like what?'

'Love. It isn't always light, is it?'

In his experience, yes. Just like the *soufflé*. The floating poem – enjoy it while you can. Oh! no, he didn't go for the heavy stuff. Lightness was all.

'I'll go and make the coffee.'

When she came back with the coffee, more than ten minutes later, her purposeful slowness in its making had only succeeded in making her more withdrawn and nervous still. In the sitting-room of the big house, in the car, by the river, in the car again, joking, conjuring, eating fish-and-chips: nothing of that had really troubled her. Now she was troubled and nothing could tell her why.

'Coffee's marvellous.' Ainsworth had made himself very comfortable, legs outstretched, on the couch. He sniffed the coffee and the air. 'Nice funny little house, this. Has a feeling.'

'James always says it's like a beehive. It smells of honey.'

'Not a chance of a spot of brandy by any stroke of luck?'

She seemed to shake herself out of herself a little. Yes, as a matter of fact, there was. She'd been going to make brandy-snaps one day for James – she'd learned how to do them at the cake-and-bread shop – and no amount of argument would make him believe that they weren't made with brandy. She'd had to go across to the big house and raid the sideboard there –

'Good for James. Full marks for James. Likes to get his facts right, that boy.'

She found the bottle of brandy. While pouring out a glass – no, she wouldn't have any herself, just perhaps a glass of brown sherry if she had anything at all – she looked up at him, breaking through her shyness again, to ask him with the slightest movement of her eyes if the measure was large enough. The smile he gave in return seemed to spark with a feigned reluctance: 'As my father used to say – "When asked, say yes, when pressed, say more" – just a *soupçon*.'

The unfamiliarity of the word caught her unawares. Hastily looking at the glass and then back at his face and back at the glass again, she filled the glass beyond the brim, spilling it over the table. He laughed and begged her not to worry. The mechanics for a situation of that kind were fully within his grasp. In a swift moment he was down on his knees, sipping brandy from the glass's rim, like a dog at a drinking bowl. 'As my father used to say again, nothing wasted where there's a family! Of drinkers, naturally.'

He finally sat back on the sofa, at ease with the brandy, praising it. Not only was it good, good that was in itself but it renewed acquaintance. He meant of the *soufflé*. Something of the aromatic nature of the brandy brought it back again. It was the old business, as he said, of the floating poem, chasing the taste, like an echo, thinking you'd lost it and you hadn't all the time.

'I really hated saying good-bye to that *soufflé*.'

'You did?'

'And if it hadn't been for you I wouldn't.'

She felt like a child tempted by morsels of food the heart wanted but the appetite refused. He seemed to drift farther and farther away from her. Or rather, as she slowly realized, she from him. The compliment about coming back to her was trite and dead.

Ainsworth seemed perhaps to sense this. He suddenly made noises and gestures of self-surprise. Stupid man, forgetful idiot – guess what? He'd clean forgotten something. He put both hands in his pockets and then withdrew them, clenched. Which hand? He'd give her a thousand guesses.

'Is it something for me?'

'Of course it's for you, girl. Guess.' His voice was mockingly harsh. 'Not unless you see anyone else around?'

No: she didn't see anyone else around. With a perplexity she didn't even remotely understand she sat biting her lip. For some reason that had no logical explanation either she felt ready to cry. Mechanically she pulled out a hand from the sleeve of her dressing-gown and tapped the fingers of his left hand and then hastily slipped her own hand back into the sleeve again.

'Wrong hand. Guess again. The night has a thousand guesses and the heart but one.'

'I'm no good at guessing. What is it? Just give it to me.'

'Heigh-ho, as we would say to James, and Presto. Magic – from the sleeve it comes! – '

'Perfume.'

All he could get, he explained, the only decent bottle. He'd got it at the chemist's, three doors from the fish-and-chip shop. It really wasn't bad. Not too sweet. The girl at the shop had let him try it. It was surprising what you sometimes found at these country shops. What was it called? *Rêves d'été?* Sounded better in French, of course. It always did.

She held the bottle in her two hands. She looked at him quietly for some time and then thanked him. It was the first time she had looked at him with full directness all evening. It might have been that she was looking at him either in gratitude or affection or merely with the beginnings of doubts about something. Ainsworth took it as an invitation to kiss her.

When after half a minute or so she broke away from him he said:

'I should call that *frigido moderato*. Something the matter?'

'Not that I know of.'

'That wasn't the sort of kiss you managed this afternoon.'

Something about the word managed brought her, for the first time all evening, to her senses.

'I'm sorry I couldn't manage better. Perhaps I'm not very good at managing.'

'Now, now. I didn't mean that.'

'What did you mean?'

'You know what I said – love's got to be light. Like a *soufflé*. Got to be light.'

'Got to be?'

'Well, must, is, should be, can be, ought to be, whatever you like, world without end. But light. As it always was, is and ever shall be.'

'I think it sometimes isn't.'

Once again she sat twisting and untwisting her hands. The force of uncertainty that had built up in her made her more than ever restless. She got up once on the pretext that the coffee was getting cold. Waiting for it to heat up in the kitchen she fell once again into the habit of tucking her arms into her sleeves, her arms wrapped about her.

When she went back into the sitting-room he was pouring himself more brandy. He raised the filled glass. He said something about her not trying the perfume. It was exquisite, the perfume. It was absolutely dead right for her. He had known it as soon as the girl had let him try it in the shop.

She started to try to unscrew the top of the perfume bottle. It was difficult. Her hands trembled and were clumsy. The top stuck tight and she couldn't get it off.

Ainsworth laughed and took it from her and sniffed at it. You could actually smell it, he said, without opening it. That showed it was powerful stuff. Like the *soufflé* and the smell of summer and all that – you could taste them all from a distance, sort of eh?

It didn't once occur to her that he might be mildly, effusively drunk. She merely felt once again like a child left outside a game, cold and uninvited. At last he unscrewed the top of the perfume bottle, sniffed at it again and laughed. It was pretty good, he thought, elusive sort of. He handed her the bottle. She took it and smelled of it lightly, and he said:

'Like it? Best I could get, anyway.'

'What's it supposed to be?'

'It's supposed to smell of dreams, dear.'

'Oh! yes. But it's a bit like lilac or pinks too or something. isn't it? You can't quite catch it, can you?'

'Dreams, dear, that's all. Plain dreams. Dreams of summer.'

Ainsworth suddenly took the bottle away from her. With his little finger pressed against the tip of it he shook out drops of scent. She felt his moistened finger tip touching her first behind one ear and then the other.

'Right? Isn't that where they put it nowadays?'

'I wouldn't know.'

As he touched her lightly behind the ears again she felt some of the constriction inside herself lessening, melting away.

'And where else would madame like it? Here?'

With infinite lightness he pulled away the front of her dressing-gown and bared her breasts. He touched them too, like her ears, with minute drops of perfume. Then he kissed first one and then the other. At the first brush of his mouth against her breasts her relief was so great that she felt like laughing. A great surge of warmth ran through her, driving out the last of her frigid uncertainty.

'And where else? They tell me they put it on the back of the legs too, nowadays.'

'I wouldn't know.'

Feeling the touch of his hand across her legs, she actually broke into a burst of outright laughter that was almost a pain. She felt delivered at last from all the things that had troubled and haunted her ever since the first moment when she had told herself that James was dead. Those were the things, she told herself, she could never bear again. In a sudden rush of half-laughing, half-sobbing words that he failed utterly to understand she begged him:

'Hold me so that I don't know anything. Hold me so that I just don't know anything any more.'

Ainsworth drove away about eleven o'clock. Still in his fingers a casual breath of perfume remained to remind him of the pleasures of the evening: the brandy, her breasts, the little house that, as the boy so accurately put it, smelled of honey. They were very lovely, her breasts. He approved of her breasts. He was pleasantly aware that they were breasts that had never been touched or seen before. They filled him with a sense of discovery. And as he remembered them he couldn't help wondering at the same time, lightly, how those of Mrs Fitzsimmons would compare.

In a mood of discovery he parked the car in the pub yard, at the back. It was nearly an hour past closing time but he was glad to see that lights still burned. As he switched off the engine

128

of the car a light, as if by response, shot out of a doorway and a long yellow shaft of it lay across the dark asphalt of the yard.

He could see the silhouette of Mrs Fitzsimmons, her hair illuminated at its blonde fringes by the backward glare of light, in the doorway. He was glad to see her there. She was always in her best friendly mood after closing time. She was the great late talker.

'I'd about given you up.' Her voice was like a mere soft echo of a voice on the night air. 'I'd just begun to think you were never coming and I'd have to lock you out.'

'It's a postcard, Gilly. It's a postcard, isn't it? The postman gave it to me.'

'Yes, it's a postcard.'

'It hasn't got a camel, though, has it?'

'No, it hasn't got a camel.'

Gilly sat at the breakfast table with her two hands wrapped round a tea cup, still in her dressing-gown.

'What does it say? What's on the picture?'

Well, he could see for himself what was on the picture, couldn't he? He didn't need a telescope, did he?

'There's a lot of palm-trees and people and a big house and a flag.'

'I expect that's the hotel. Yes, it's the hotel.'

'Read what it says.'

Gilly looked at the picture of the hotel, turned the postcard over, turned it over again and stared.

'What are you staring at? Why are you taking so long to read it?'

'I'm trying to make out what it says. It's shocking awful writing.' She stared again, hard, a curious, lost, withdrawn look in her eyes. 'Oh! yes. "Weather still marvellous. 95° in the shade. Man yesterday flaked out. Sunstroke. Far as we are concerned we can take it till the cows come home. Thinking of taking up permanent residence in fact. Heavenly. Don't expect us till you see us".'

'What does flaked out mean?'

'It meant somebody didn't feel very well, that's all.'

'What does sunstroke mean?'

Oh! it meant you sat in the sun and it sort of struck you because it was too hot and you weren't wearing a hat.

'Can you be dead like that? Like being striked by lightning?'

Oh! yes, you could be dead, but not often.

'You can only be dead once, can't you?'

Only once, thank God.

There were too many ways of being dead, he thought, even if it was only once, and sunstroke was another. He had never heard of sunstroke before.

'What does permanent residence mean?'

'Oh! it means they like it.'

'And what does expect us when you see us mean?'

'Oh! it means perhaps they'll stay a long time.'

'How long?'

Gilly stopped staring at the postcard, the table and her empty cup. At last she got up to pour herself another cup of tea. She found the teapot less than half full. With one groping hand she reached for the kettle and with the other the knob on the radio. When she switched on the radio a voice said something about the weather being changeable with showers in the afternoon. She automatically turned the switch off again and stared out of the window. The sky was blue.

james followed her stare through the window. Even if the sky was blue there were already across the park, low, long white strings of cloud. He half shut his eyes and, while Gilly poured her tea, squinted hard at them. He thought they were just like geese today. The big geese were all at the front and all the little geese, some still faintly grey, at the back. And if you looked very hard and shut your eyes so that your eyelashes came together like a curtain you could see that there were other little clouds like curled white crusts of bread and some like little loaves.

'Go and see if the paper's come, there's a dear. He sometimes leaves it on the doorstep.'

He went to the back door, opened it and looked out. There

was no paper. He looked briefly at the garden, the dahlias, the tobacco flowers that had already flopped in the morning sun and then wondered about his float that had fallen down the well and if he would ever get it back again.

Then in imagination he saw the postman coming back up the garden path. The postman had his brown light summer jacket on. His hat was pushed back from his forehead, as if he were very hot. The postman had a letter for him. He said he was sorry he'd forgotten it the first time. He was a nice postman. His cheeks were red and fat. He always whistled while he knocked on the door while waiting for you to open it and James said that was all right, mate, we all make mistakes some time.

Back in the kitchen he said: 'Look, I've got a letter. The postman forgot it the first time.' He held up the letter for Gilly to see.

'Oh! yes. Got what? Oh! a letter.'

He held up the letter again. She stared vaguely at his empty hands as he turned it over and over. Then he took up a butter knife from the kitchen table and slit the envelope open and took the letter out of it. Then he propped his elbows up on the table and stared at it thoughtfully.

'It's a letter from Mr Pimm.'

'It's what? Oh! from Mr Pimm, is it? How do you know it's from Mr Pimm?'

'He said he would write to me. When he went away.'

'Oh! he's gone away, has he? It's nice to be some folks. Where's he gone to?'

'He's gone down to the seaside. You know, where he went before.'

After another half minute or so of thought he started to read the letter from Mr Pimm. It was full of marvellous things, Mr Pimm's letter, not like the post-card, which didn't tell you anything, really, at all. Mr Pimm had been having a wonderful time, going on the dodg'ems and eating whelks and going out in a boat fishing and going round the pubs and buying rock. It was all wonderful. The weather was marvellous. Mr Pimm wished James was there. Not that Mr Pimm was lonely and all that. He had Mr Monday with him and Mr Monday had been fishing too. Mr Monday's arm was a lot better, the sea air was doing it good and they had a nice landlady. She cooked the fish Mr Pimm and Mr Monday caught for breakfast. It was all smashing, like Mr Pimm had told him before, and there was a band what played in a bandstand and a man what drew pictures in the sand and girls what came along sometimes and gave you packets of nuts and a balloon. Was Gilly listening?

Yes, Gilly was listening. But it was a bit like the Bible, wasn't it? It went on and on.

'There's a lot more yet.'

There was a pier. Mr Pimm and Mr Monday had been on it. It went a long way out to sea. You could fish from the end of it so that you didn't have to go out in a boat. Mr Monday was ever so clever fishing with one arm and he'd caught a cod weighing seventy pounds. It was the biggest cod anyone had ever caught off the pier. Mr Monday had cut it all up and given all the poor people each a bit for breakfast. Mr Pimm had given them loaves as well. Hundreds and hundreds of people had loaves and fishes for breakfast, thousands of people. It was like the Bible, like Gilly said.

'You're romancing a bit, aren't you? A cod weighing seventy pounds?'

'*It did weigh seventy pounds. It was. It did. Mr Pimm says so.*'

Gilly said nothing. She merely turned the post-card over and stared at the hotel and the palms. Expect us when you see us, was it? Whatever that might mean.

'P.S. It says P.S.!'

'Oh! it says P.S., does it?'

'P.S. and if you and your Gilly would like to come down one day and see us it would be very nice, like, and we would be pleased. It would not cost you no money because me and Mr Monday have got plenty because of the overtime, like, and we could all go on the dodg'ems and helter-skelter all the time, like me and Mr Monday do all day. Laughing our heads off. Please come soon. Yours truly and ever-loving friend Mr Pimm.'

While he read this Gilly seemed to fold herself farther and farther into a state of dreaminess. When he looked up at last it was to find her staring even more moodily into space and he wondered why it was that grown-up people so often didn't listen when you were talking to them. It was all very real and very important about Mr Pimm and Mr Monday at the seaside. The letter from Mr Pimm made you see everything they did and he longed to be with them very much.

'Can we go and see Mr Pimm and Mr Monday at the seaside today?'

Gilly suddenly thought she heard the sound of the morning paper dropping on the kitchen doorstep. She got up and went to the door and found the newspaper there and came back with it. Then she propped it up on the breakfast table, against the sugar basin, and started to read it, without a word.

'I was talking to you and you didn't listen. It's very rude not to listen when people talk to you.'

'It's what? Oh! yes. I was listening, I heard.'

Gilly turned the newspaper over and started to read another part of it.

'Could we go and see Mr Pimm and Mr Monday today?'

'What? No, not today.'

'Why not? Why can't we?'

'Because we can't. We've got a lot of things to do today.'

'What things?'

After another silence and after he had repeated the question twice Gilly said Oh! thousands of things. They had to fetch eggs from the farm and tidy up the sitting-room at the big house and go down to the village to get tea and bacon and things and he had to feed the geese, too, didn't he?

'Yes, but we could go after we've done all that.' Well, they could but not today. Besides, how were they going to get there? Give her a chance. Walk?

'Mr Ainsworth could take us in his car.'

'It isn't Mr Ainsworth's car. It doesn't belong to him.'

'Who does it belong to?'

'It doesn't matter who it belongs to. He can't have it and he can't take us, that's all.'

'Is he coming today?'

'How do I know if he's coming today? It's early. He's probably not up yet.'

'Why isn't he – '

'Here, go and feed the geese.' Impatiently Gilly flung an arm across the breakfast table, seized the loaf of bread from the bread-board and broke it in half. 'Go on. Call them. They'll come.'

He took the bread from her hands and went slowly to the kitchen door. When he opened it and looked out he saw, to his surprise, that there were now many more geese in the sky. A great flock of them had come up, wings stretched, necks craning, from the direction of the sun. There were so many now that he knew his small half loaf of bread would never feed them.

He called to Gilly: 'Is it enough bread?'

Of course it was enough, she said. It was more than he usually took. Scraps? No, there were no scraps today. He'd taken them all yesterday.

'I don't think it's enough.'

Gilly turned the morning paper inside out, almost burying her face in it. Why wasn't it enough?

'Perhaps if I broke it all up into little pieces like Mr Pimm and Mr Monday did and the man in the Bible did do you think they'd be enough then?'

Oh! yes, Gilly said, she supposed so.

'Do you believe all that?'

All what? Oh! about the loaves and the little fishes? Oh! yes, she believed all that.

'Do you believe it about Mr Pimm and Mr Monday and the cod and Mr Pimm giving all the people the loaves?'

Oh! yes, Gilly said, she believed that too.

'You said you didn't.'

Gilly didn't answer. He merely stood at the door, not speaking either, looking first at the garden, then at the park and the sky. In the park the grass was very wet, almost salty-coloured, with heavy dew. He slowly crumbled the bread into his hands and wondered how it was that people said they meant things and then the next minute said something that made you know quite well they didn't all the time. If it was true about the man and the loaves and the little fishes why wasn't it true about Mr Pimm and Mr Monday and the cod? He thought it was very true and he longed once again, very much, to be with Mr Pimm and Mr Monday by the sea.

As he stood at the wicket gate that led from the garden to the park, still slowly crumbling bread in his hands, his mind became filled with thoughts of the geese coming to be fed. The bright image of Mr Pimm and Mr Monday receded. The geese in the sky, in their long winged lines, white and grey, large and small, were just as real, just as they were every bit as real as the geese he now started to call from the farm, his voice almost singing.

Every morning the geese came when you called them. You called, waited a little while and then you heard them calling back. All at once their necks came craning across the grass and then you called again and they started running. It was like calling a dog. It was wonderful how they knew.

This morning he called twice, then three times, and then several times again, but there was no sign of geese in answer. He thought it ought to be a great morning for geese, with so many in the sky. It was strange that the grass was empty. Then he opened the gate and called again and then started to walk across the park, still calling.

The farm was a quarter of a mile or so across the park and he called the geese all the way to it, crumbling bread and getting no answer. At the side of the farm was a bullock-yard. It was always full of straw. There were big wooden sheds along the side. Once, in the middle of harvest, the bullock-yard was all piled high with straw that was new and yellow. When the geese went through it they disappeared. The straw jumped up and down until the geese came out at the other side, looking as if they all had their necks in broken baskets.

This morning Arthur was spreading fresh straw about the yard for young bullocks. James climbed the gate that led into the bullock-yard and sat and watched him. Arthur was a very little man with a face like a brown apple that had fallen and squashed from a tree. His skin was bruised and cracked. There was always a sort of icicle on the end of his nose. He wore his cap back to front. When he caught sight of James sitting on the gate he stuck his hayfork in the ground and leaned on it and called what did he want then?

'I've come to feed the geese.'

'Well, you'll feed on them. They've gone off to market.'

'Why? What have they gone off to market for?'

'They'll find out.'

Arthur spat into the straw, like Mr Pimm did. Then he poked about it with the hay-fork as if looking to see where the spit had gone.

'When will they be back from market?'

Arthur laughed. Then he spat again but this time he didn't rake about in the straw. He said the geese wouldn't be back today, nor tomorrow, nor the next day.

'Why not?'

This time Arthur didn't spit. He simply took off his cap, looked inside it and then banged it on his knee and put it back on his head again.

'Mrs Barton's bad a-bed. Couldn't stand the racket they allus kicked up. Couldn't git no rest.'

'What will the geese do at market?'

Arthur laughed and spat again.

'Make good dinners I shouldn't wonder.'

'Will they die?'

'They will if they don't mind their apple sauce.'

'Will Mrs Barton die?'

'Well, she's took to her bed, but that don't mean – No, no, she won't die. She's tough as old Harry, like the old geese. She won't die.'

James walked slowly back across the park. It was strange without the geese. He carried the bread first in one hand, then in the other, crumbling it. From the chestnut trees there rose and fell a continuous sound of pigeon voices. He liked that sound. It bubbled, like Miss Garfield used to do when she was dozing off after lunch.

He stopped, suddenly thinking that perhaps the pigeons would like the bread. He remembered his father saying once that pigeons were greedy beggars, they ate anything; but then when James said anything, like knives and forks, like tables and chairs? his father told him not to be silly, not that sort of anything. It was like when his father talked about dog eat dog: he simply didn't mean it.

It was the first time he had thought of his father for some long time. His father hadn't written anything funny on the post-card today, like the man whistling to charm the snakes, and it might not have seemed to matter very much except that he suddenly thought that it might be a good way of getting the pigeons down from the trees.

He picked up a dead stick from the grass and began to whistle a little tune on it. It wasn't any particular tune he knew or had heard. It just went on and on. Now and then as he played he looked up into the trees, where the pigeons were all hidden and still bubbling softly away like Miss Garfield, and hoped that, like the snake, they would be charmed and fly down to eat the bread. But all the time he played the bread lay on the grass and the pigeons never bothered to fly down.

At last he threw the stick away and clapped his hands several times, loudly. Instantly the pigeons flew out of the tree, clapping their wings in answer and then went on a strong, straight flight across the park, until they were joined with the clouds, grey and blue, so that he couldn't see them any more.

He supposed it wasn't true about playing music to charm snakes. If you could charm snakes like that you could charm pigeons and if you could charm pigeons you could charm geese. But music didn't work. It was much easier to clap your hands. So now he clapped his hands again, hoping that the geese would come suddenly back from market, but nothing happened, even when he clapped a second and a third time, and when he had finished he was still alone in the park. It was always like that. People either said things they didn't mean, like pigeons eating anything, or things that weren't true, like music charming snakes. He would rather have Mr Pimm any day. What Mr Pimm said was always true.

'Well, better get on, mate, and see what Gilly's getting up to.'

In the kitchen Gilly was still at the breakfast table. The morning paper had fallen to the floor. Gilly had a sheet of notepaper on the table and a pen in her hand and was writing.

'Are you writing a letter?'

'I was.'

Gilly stared into space. There was only a little writing, just a line or two, on the notepaper.

'Are you writing a letter to my father?'

'To who? Oh! good Lord, no – how could I write to them if I don't know the address?'

'They're in Tangier. Isn't that the address?'

'Some hopes. Besides they don't want to hear from us. Out of sight, out of mind.'

'What does out of sight, out of mind mean?'

He had meant to tell Gilly how the geese had gone to market because Mrs Barton couldn't bear the noise of them and how Mrs Barton was bad a-bed, but it didn't seem to matter now. Gilly was biting the end of her pen. Her lips were all knotted up and hard and she wasn't writing any more.

'Gilly, I tried to make the pigeons – '

Suddenly Gilly tore up the letter, screwed it up into a ball, very hard, and let it lie like a broken egg-shell on her breakfast plate.

'Why did you tear the letter up?'

'Oh! do you mind? I've got to get on. I've got ten million things to do.'

'Ten million? Ten million things?'

'Well, an awful lot. Can't you go and clean your teeth or something?'

'Who were you writing to?'

'Oh! it doesn't matter now. I'm no letter writer anyway. I'm no good at that sort of thing.'

He knew she didn't mean ten million things, but only perhaps one or two, perhaps a dozen. It was only that she was in a tizzy, as she sometimes said. She looked rushed and cross and awkward. Her hair was a mess and she looked all –

He couldn't think really what she looked like until he went at last into the garden and noticed the tobacco flowers that had drooped into complete listlessness with the coming of day. She looked just like one of those, he thought, all floppy and wrung out, and he wondered why.

For a time he looked down into the well. His float was still there, in the middle of the ring of water, blue and red like a kingfisher, exactly as it had been when he first dropped it there. Idly he wondered about getting it out. The wooden top of the well was always kept locked. When they were at home Gilly kept the key in a china mug with a king and queen painted on the outside that stood on the mantelshelf above the scullery stove. When they went out she hid it under the outside door-mat. If you could unlock the top of the well and drop down the line and the fish-hook Mr Ainsworth had given him he supposed it would be easy to get it out that way.

When he went back into the kitchen to talk to her about this he found to his surprise that Gilly was no longer there. After a few moments she came running downstairs, all dressed, her hair all fresh and brushed and her handbag on her arm. There was a nice smell about her too, like some sort of flowers, and for one impossibly joyful moment he thought that perhaps they were going down to the sea, to see Mr Pimm and Mr Monday.

'No, just to the village,' she said. 'We've got to eat, haven't we? We haven't got a thing in the house. You'd better write your list, hadn't you? My pen's on the table. Write your list.'

While he sat at the kitchen table, scribbling, and she went from kitchen to scullery and back again, finding a basket and repeatedly opening and shutting her handbag, he couldn't help thinking how strange it was that people changed so quickly. One minute they were all droopy and sorry and didn't like you speaking to them and said they had a million things to do. The next minute they were all gay and nice and you might have thought someone had given them a present or they were going off to a party.

When at last they were outside and Gilly was locking the kitchen door she actually looked down and smiled at him. She didn't look at all like a drooping night flower any more but at the same time, he thought, she seemed to smell like one.

'You smell all like flowers.'

'Do I? Do you like it?'

'You didn't smell like that yesterday.'

'Oh! no, it's new. It's something new.'

'It smells like one of those flowers that come out at night.'

'Does it? Yes, I suppose it does. Well, come on now.' She actually started running down the path, towards the garden gate. 'Last out, shut the gate.' Then as he reached the gate, a few paces behind her, she suddenly remembered something. 'Better take the umbrella. It's clouding up a lot. Will you run back? You can manage the key, can't you? The umbrella's hanging behind the door, with my raincoat.'

The umbrella was red, with a little black pattern all over it. Once he had seen a moth or a butterfly exactly like it, sitting on some grasses in the park.

'That's a good boy. I don't think we'd better go without it. You can never trust this weather. It's treacherous. Did you put the key under the mat?'

'What's treacherous?'

She didn't bother to tell him what treacherous was. Instead she twirled the umbrella round and round by its handle, the cord on her forefinger, so that it flew in the air rather like a butterfly. Then she went on to say, quite gaily, that if he was good they might have coffee at that cakeshop just near the post office. He could have an ice-cream or one of those funny dough-buns with eyes in them, shaped like little men.

She actually laughed quite loudly, as if something about the little men really amused her, and then all of a sudden he remembered that he still had the back door key in his hand. He hadn't put it under the door-mat after all.

'Oh! my goodness. It's just as well you remembered that. What if we'd lost it? We wouldn't be able to get in again, would we?'

He didn't say anything. He wished only that, one day, the key would also open the lock on the top of the well.

'You must have a sort of sixth sense.'

'Me? Why?'

'How else did you know I popped across here every morning

at eleven o'clock for coffee and a cheese roll or something? I always do. I never have breakfast, you see.'

'I don't know about sixth. When I got up this morning I felt short of numbers one to five. Felt as if somebody had put me through the wringer and forgotten to take all of me out.'

'Charming compliment. Is that the effect my company has on you?'

'You know what I mean.'

They were all three, Gilly, James and Mr Ainsworth, in the little cake shop that stood beyond the post office at the far end of the street. James had a pink and white ice-cream and a dough-man with three black waistcoat buttons and two black eyes. He sat for some time wondering if to eat the waistcoat buttons first or the eyes. Then he decided to save the eyes until last. Otherwise if he ate them first the dough-man couldn't see.

'I very nearly wrote to you today.'

'Good God, *wrote* to me?'

Gilly simply nodded; it was no more than a flicker of her slow brown eyes.

'But what on earth could you want to *write* to me for?'

In a low voice, almost a whisper, Gilly said she hadn't anyway, had she, so it hardly mattered now.

'But my dear girl, *writing* –'

Gilly slowly stirred her coffee. When she lifted the spoon out of the cup a few golden grains of brown sugar clung to the sides of it.

'I didn't sleep half the night –'

'But that was no reason for *writing* to me, was it?'

'How did you sleep?'

'Oh! me? Splendidly. Like a top. I always do.'

James noticed that, after this, Gilly didn't speak very much for a time. Mr Ainsworth was wearing a brown woollen jacket with yellow sleeves. It was fascinating because it looked as if someone had first started to knit it in brown wool and then had run out of that colour and knitted the rest in yellow. It made Mr Ainsworth look very smart, though. Gilly stared a lot at him, with full brown eyes.

Presently James decided to eat two waistcoat buttons, the

top and the bottom ones. They were really currants. They were rather hard and crusty. As he ate them he remembered how, a long time ago, he had picked up what he thought was a currant off the kitchen table and how it wasn't a currant at all but a peppercorn. It was hot and nasty and burned his mouth. Ever since then he had been very wary of currants. But today they were nice. He ate them very slowly.

All the time he was fascinated because Gilly's eyes somehow looked rather like the eyes of the dough-man. They stared straight in front of her, dark and shining, and hardly ever moved. And sometimes as he watched them he couldn't help wondering how it would be if you didn't have any eyes. He supposed it would be all black, like night, or perhaps just like nothing. Once or twice he was tempted to eat the two currants that were the dough-man's eyes just to see if his face looked all empty and like nothing when the eyes were gone. But each time he let the two eyes alone, saving them till last.

It was wonderful what a difference it made to things if you screwed up your eyes when you looked at them. The more he looked at Gilly with his eyes screwed up the more she looked like the dough-man. She seemed a long way away from him. Her voice seemed a long way away from him too.

'I just wanted to pack it all in. I suppose it was the postcard.'

'Pack it all in? But why – '

'It was just that one bit – "expect us when you see us". It made it seem like ages and ages. It suddenly put years on me – years – '

'But what made you want to *write*, for God's sake?'

Gilly said something about it all being silly. You knew how it was after a bad night's sleep and how things seemed all twisted and upside down. All night you had processions marching through your mind, nagging at you, all bright as day and enough to drive you barmy, and whenever you thought you were going to sleep they came parading back again, worse than ever.

All the time James watched her with screwed-up eyes, slowly chewing currants. He couldn't think what she was talking about.

'But where on earth did I come into all this?'

'Well, I don't know – it's hard to explain. But I somehow

142

thought if I gave up the job – you know, the – him – I'd be free, sort of – '

'But you just couldn't walk out, I mean just like – I mean and leave him – it's all right, he's not listening – he's busy with his ice-cream – '

James took the third currant off the dough-man's waistcoat. He bit it carefully in half and then put the two halves into the ice-cream to make two new black eyes. He expected any moment that Gilly would suddenly start scolding him and tell him not to be a messer and to eat things properly or she'd never bring him out again, but for some reason she never did. She didn't even seem to know he was there. Her voice was low and far away.

'But I don't get the writing.'

'I know you don't. Nor do I, now. But at the time – I was going to write to the solicitors, too.'

'Solicitors?'

'Yes. I've got an address of some solicitors in London in case anything happens or goes wrong or I have to – '

'Funny girl. Like some more coffee? I'd like some. They make it very well here. For a wonder.'

Gilly shook her head. The two halves of currants sank into the melting ice-cream. They had almost disappeared before James spooned them out again. When he had eaten them the ice-cream didn't seem to have any face. It was all empty and cold, like the moon.

Mr Ainsworth attracted the attention of a waitress and ordered more coffee.

'Certain persons seem to be very preoccupied this morning.'

'Oh! yes. I thought at one time we were going to have a long song and dance about Mr P. and Mr M.'

'Oh? What about Mr P. and Mr M.?'

'S - e - a - s - i - '

'Oh! I see. Yes. Well, today I'm afraid I can't do a thing about it. Mrs Fitzsimmons is taking driving lessons this afternoon and needs the car. She never used to drive but since her husband died – '

'Oh? When was that?'

'I gather vaguely it was some time last year. They were on

holiday in Belgium or somewhere. Not having the car sort of ties her down. Of course she's still – '

'Still what?'

Soon it would be a question of eating the eyes. Already the dough-man's feet had gone, together with all three waistcoat buttons and the ice-cream. It wasn't going to be easy to leave the eyes much longer.

'Well, still young. I say young – thirty-three, thirty-five.'

'I always fancied I saw her once in the post office, drawing her pension. A big, dark woman. A lot of hair – '

'Oh! no, not Katie – not Mrs Fitzsimmons. Very fair – smooth skin – a real blonde.'

'I just thought it might have been her. I must have been mistaken.'

'And that real Irish chin – rather long – '

James slowly ate the left eye of the dough-man. With only his right eye the dough-man looked lop-sided, funny and rather sad. It made him look a little as if he were winking, rather cross-eyed, at someone behind you.

The waitress brought another cup of coffee to the table. Mr Ainsworth said 'I'll pay you for all this. Save you running.' The waitress smiled very pleasantly. It would be four-and-three, sir, altogether, she said. Mr Ainsworth smiled too. When Mr Ainsworth smiled the corners of his mouth quivered very slightly upwards, as if pulled by invisible threads, leaving an expression behind them that shimmered with light, compelling attraction. The smile always seemed to hover for a few final seconds on the verge of mockery without ever slipping into it completely. In the same way his eyes somehow smiled without ever revealing that they had purposely done so.

The waitress stood held for some seconds by an apparent inability to count the change correctly. At last Mr Ainsworth told her to keep it. As he did so Mr Ainsworth smiled again. He looked the waitress up and down and said how good the coffee was, he had to congratulate her on the coffee. But then he always said that, didn't he?

'You do, sir, but then that doesn't mean you needn't say it again.'

'I'll try,' he said, 'to remember that.'

The waitress seemed to drift away. The one remaining eye of the dough-man stared out, shining and sad and odd. James couldn't bring himself to eat it. Once the eye had gone it was all over and dead and there was nothing there any longer.

'Well, so the s - e - -a - s - i - d - e is out. What now? Any plans for this afternoon? I mean nice plans.'

'Chores. What else? I've still got all that clearing up to do.'

'Over in the house? I'll come and help.'

'Help is the word. And exactly what plans?'

James at last detached the remaining eye from the dough-man. Then he swiftly decided he couldn't bear the odd emptiness of the face and put it back again. While he was doing this Mr Ainsworth spelt out the words b-e-d and l-o-v-e, looking at Gilly with a combination of mockery and suspense, waiting for an answer that didn't come.

James knew perfectly well that the answer didn't come because they were watching him. He always knew when people were spelling out words that they didn't want him to know. They always thought you didn't know but all the time you did.

'You'd better think of something else. I don't like spectators.'

'Pity Mr P. and Mr M. have gone off. They always kept him amused.'

'I think we're being listened to.'

'Oh! yes? I see, yes. Perhaps we are.'

After a few moments of silence Mr Ainsworth suddenly said he wondered how the light was. He took his light meter from his pocket. In a flash the dough-man and his one eye were replaced by the winking finger of the lightmeter, which Mr Ainsworth held out for James to see.

'It's a sort of watch. It tells you how light or how dark it is. So you know when to take a photograph. So you get it just right.'

'Is it just right now?'

'Oh! not bad. Of course we're indoors.'

'Does the watch take the photograph?'

'Oh! no, the watch doesn't take the photograph. It only tells you.' Mr Ainsworth started smiling, inspired by a sudden bright idea. 'Have you got a camera? If you had, the watch would tell you when – '

'No. My father has, but he's taken it away with him.'

'Tell you what.' Mr Ainsworth turned on Gilly a slow, almost steadfast stare. With light amusement the corners of his mouth flicked upwards. 'I've got a little one I'll lend you.'

'Yesterday you gave me the float and the fishing rod – '

'Yes, but not giving today. Only lending.'

Gilly looked at Mr Ainsworth with uncertainty. Was he sure that he should? A real camera? It was really a bit young –

'A d-u-d really. I accidentally dropped it getting over a gate, one day last week. The l-e-n-s got cracked. One of my old ones. Very careless of me. I was really rather attached to it.'

Gilly started to ask if it didn't take pictures? but Mr Ainsworth interrupted and said with a blank expression on his face.

'Oh! pictures, yes. Of course. Pictures of all those sheep in the park and geese and cows – Oh! anything you like. Pictures by the ton – '

'You can't take pictures of the geese because they've all gone to market to be killed.'

'Oh! that's bad. Poor old geese. Still, I suppose it's Michaelmas and – ' Mr Ainsworth was smiling again. The blank expression on his face had gone completely. 'But you can take everything else you like, dead or alive, and all in colours, all afternoon.'

'All afternoon?'

'All afternoon.'

'Will it take a picture of a snail?'

'Ah!' Mr Ainsworth said. He paused, reflecting. He seemed to think it curious that anyone should want to take a picture of a snail. 'A snail? Yes, yes, of course. A snail, yes.' All of a sudden he laughed. 'But you'll have to be quick.' He laughed again. It was of course a great joke, being quick about the snail. 'Very, very quick. Won't you? Very, very quick.'

'Yes, but snails are – '

It reminded him. Mr Ainsworth said, of a story. It was about three men who went out to hunt snails. One was away hunting for two whole days and got one. One was away for three whole days and got two. The third was away for a week and got none. 'I would have caught him,' he said, 'but he got away.' Mr Ainsworth laughed again.

Gilly started to say it was time they went home for lunch. The quicker they got home to lunch the quicker James would be able to start taking pictures with the camera.

'Yes, that's it. Quick,' Mr Ainsworth said. He laughed again. 'You see a snail and you have to be quick – like that!' – Mr Ainsworth made swift, snapping noises with his fingers. 'Like lightning! Before he gets away.' Mr Ainsworth laughed yet again. 'Mustn't on any account let him get away.'

'Have you got the camera with you now?'

'No, I'll bring it after lunch. I'll have it all ready. Film and all. Everything ready.'

'Will you and Gilly come to take pictures too?'

No, no, Mr Ainsworth said. He didn't think so. This was a special treat, just for him.

'What will you and Gilly do this afternoon?'

Oh! they would find something, Mr Ainsworth said. They would amuse themselves.

'Like playing games?'

Something like that, Mr Ainsworth said. Something like that. That sort of thing.

'I'm glad.'

Glad? Mr Ainsworth said. Why glad?

James shut his eyes. In the darkness under his lids he could distinctly see a snail, a butterfly, the float that had fallen down the well and the snake that his father had drawn for him on the picture post-card. He was going to take pictures of all of them. It was marvellously, wonderfully exciting to see them there already.

'Glad?' Gilly said. 'Why will you be glad, James?'

'Because then I'll be alone and you won't be a nuisance.'

Now Gilly laughed too, her voice rising on a sudden peal of excitement.

'Funny boy,' she said. 'Always the funny boy.'

In the park was a forest. It was all tall white grasses and dead brown dock stalks and white skeletons of thistles. In the middle of it was an ant-hill. When you crouched down behind the ant-hill and half shut your eyes and peered over the top of it you could see how the grasses and docks and thistles were just like trees, tall and waving or big and crusty, and how they went on and on, thicker and thicker, until the end of the world.

James had the camera slung over his neck by a strap, in just the way Mr Ainsworth wore his. The light was exactly right. He knew the light was exactly right because Mr Ainsworth, just before he and Gilly had climbed the stairs in the big house and waved good-bye and told him not to go too far away and not to lose himself, had looked at his lightmeter and told him so. The lightmeter was like a watch. What it said was always right. It was a wonderful thing.

After he had crawled several yards through the forest, over the other side of the ant-hill, on his belly, he rested for some moments on his elbows and cupped his hands to his eyes and looked through his binoculars. His father had a pair of binoculars. They were in a big black leather case with a red velvet lining. It was very important to have binoculars. They made little things suddenly seem like big things. They also made things that were a long way away seem as if they were terribly near you.

Through the binoculars he could see a snake. It wasn't a very big snake but it was sitting up, just like the one on the picture postcard. It was dotted all blue and yellow, with a black arrow on its head. After watching the snake for some moments he started to whistle and he was sure the snake sat up a little more and turned its head. You could see its eyes very large through the binoculars and its tongue frisking out of its mouth like a black dragonfly. When he whistled a little more the snake sat up even higher, all rigid, now its head back, as if it were listening.

This was how he wanted to take his picture. He dropped the binoculars to his knees. He clicked the camera shutter sharply several times, just like Mr Ainsworth did. Then the snake seemed suddenly to take fright and slithered off in a flash through the forest, so that he couldn't see it any more.

In its place was a butterfly. It was sitting on one of the thistle-heads that were silver all over except for a few last faint hairs of purple on the crest of its head. Through the binoculars he could see the butterfly panting and quivering like a great scarlet and black and orange bird that had come down into the forest to rest after a long flight through the sky. Part of its wings were dusty. Once or twice he thought that the trembling of the wings would shake the dust away. Instead the butterfly sat there for a long time, delicately shimmering, making no move to fly away even when he excitedly clicked the camera shutter, taking its picture over and over again.

When the butterfly had flown away at last he crawled on through the forest. Now and then, above the jagged bone fringes of thistleheads or red-brown steeples of dock seed, he caught a glimpse of the afternoon sky, cloudless, intensely tranquil, very blue. It winked above him as part of a world forgotten. Once or twice he heard a descending flap of pigeon wings as a bird flew and floated from a tree. Otherwise there was nothing to distract him except the things he wanted to photograph: the poised and slithering snake, the butterfly, a great bumble-bee half-falling like a dark and drowsy climber from a towering yellow head of flower, a crowd of ants scampering across a hill half-carpeted with thyme.

After the forest had finally cleared away the grassy plain of the park, empty of sheep today, stretched before him. Partly crouching, camera slung over his neck, he started to cross it like a traveller searching for new horizons. He was out to discover a river and a frog. He wanted very much to take a picture of a frog. His notion of taking a picture of a snail had faded. Something, perhaps Mr Ainsworth's joke about having to be so quick in case it got away, a joke that now didn't seem to be very funny, had driven it out in favour of a frog. He liked frogs. They reminded him, in some way, perhaps because they were all fat and wrinkled round and under the eyes, of Mr Pimm. And perhaps because they reminded him of Mr Pimm they also seemed very real, very friendly.

His thoughts of Mr Pimm, the frog and the river reminded him in turn of a kingfisher. The kingfisher in turn reminded him of his float that had fallen to the bottom of the well. He wanted very much to get a picture of a kingfisher as well as a frog. Above all he wanted a picture of the float that was like a kingfisher. He knew he might have to wait a long time before he could find a kingfisher that would sit and wait for him – it wasn't like the snake, which sat quite still while you whistled and charmed it – but he knew too that the float at the bottom of the well was always there. But with everything, the frog, the kingfisher and the float, it was only a question, as Mr Ainsworth said, of being patient. The camera would take thousands of pictures, tons, millions, if only you were patient and took your time.

He finally reached the river. He sat down on the bank to wait for a frog. It was no use getting the binoculars out to look for a frog because frogs appeared mostly all of a sudden, out of the grass, when you least expected. You simply had to be patient.

He didn't quite know why it was, but he had always had an idea that frogs could talk. Perhaps again it was because of the eyes that looked so like those of Mr Pimm, or the big wide mouth or the hands that were so like people's. Would a frog do the things you wanted, like the snake, when you whistled? He stared for a long time at the dark still water under the crowded alder branches that were already shedding leaves that floated downstream like so many light brown flotillas, now and then whistling gently, and waited with patience for an answer.

The frog that finally came and sat on the bank was so remarkably like Mr Pimm that James actually took out his binoculars and stared at it for some moments to make sure that it was true. The same rather weary, wrinkled eyes, the toothless sort of mouth and the floppy skin of the neck, all magnified by the binoculars, prepared him slowly for the truth that the voice which eventually spoke to him was that of Mr Pimm too.

'Ah! there you are, old matey. What you bin up to? Where you bin?'

'Oh! busy. Up to my neck. Got this camera.'

'Camera, eh? Some folks are lucky.'

'Run off my feet, taking pictures. Like me to take your picture?'

Mr Pimm said he would, very much. The camera clicked, several times.

'Just get you from a different angle. Hold still – that's a beauty.'

'Fancy you having a camera. You ought to have bin with me and old Monday down at the sea this week.'

'Too busy. Run off my feet as it is. Pictures of this, pictures of that. Spent all afternoon getting a snake and a butterfly. Now I've got to wait for a kingfisher.'

He chatted for several minutes to Mr Pimm, unaware of time. Once Mr Pimm wanted to know when his pictures would be ready, but James said strike a light, not yet, the best he could do was Tuesday. He had thousands and thousands to do, millions. When would Mr Pimm be back? Mr Pimm said he doubted he'd be back afore Wednesday but anyway he'd look him up when he was.

'You do that, matey. We'll blow a bit o'bacca together and chat up a bit. So long now, though. Got to give the kingfisher best, I reckon, today. Got to get on and get a few shots of that float of mine.'

'Float, eh? New float?'

'The one I dropped down the well. Never get it up again, so I'll get a picture or two. So long now, old matey. See you Wednesday.'

'So long, Jamesy.'

Mr Pimm seemed to drop the lid of one wrinkled, frog-like eye. Ten yards away, at the same moment, a water vole dropped into the river, flattened out and started to swim in silence downstream. The reality of the vole set the camera clicking madly. In another ten seconds the vole had disappeared. Nothing was left to break the surface of the water except a thin rippled arrow, barely light.

'See that, matey? A water rat. No, no, he's gone now. Disappeared. You got to be quick, matey, eh? You got to be quick.'

Mr Pimm too had disappeared. The river bank, breathlessly captured by the swift dark course of the vole swallowed in shadow, was hushed, frogless and soundless now.

He stood for some moments on the river bank in the sun, wondering whether to go upstream to the little house, where the float lay at the bottom of the well, or downstream, following the vole. He knew that rivers ran eventually down to the sea, because his father had once told him so. Now he found himself suddenly entertained by the idea that if only he walked on and on, downstream, he would come in time to the sea, where Mr Pimm still was, with Mr Monday. There he could take pictures of Mr Pimm and Mr Monday, fishing boats and dodg-'ems, steamers and whelk stalls, people swimming in the sea and men wearing funny hats. He had no idea how far the sea was but it couldn't, he supposed, be very far. He had no idea, either, of which way it was. But all he had to do, he told himself, was to follow the river.

It would be a little difficult at first, he knew, because at the far end of the park the river flowed into a lake. He had been to the lake only once before, with his father. He remembered how it was a dark, cold, frosty, bitter day, in winter. His father wore big white sheepskin gloves. He kept slapping them together. All round the lake glassy fringes of ice, jagged at the edges, locked the banks. White frozen reeds stood everywhere like forests of whips. Now and then they too slapped together, in the freezing wind.

His father told him how big pike lived in the lake. One day, when summer came back, he and James would come down and catch them. But now it was too cold and too icy for fishing. His father at last pointed to a dark strip of unfrozen water winding its way centrally through the frozen lake. He said that this was the river, flowing through the lake and out of the lake and down to the sea. When James wanted to know what would happen when the water of the river froze too and it couldn't flow any longer his father didn't answer his question except to say suddenly that it was getting beastly cold and they ought to be starting back for tea.

Then he remembered asking his father if the river, when it

152

froze over, would go to sleep under the ice, and if the fish would go to sleep too and if the sea, wherever it was, would miss the water from the river coming down and soon feel thirsty? His father really didn't answer these questions either, except in the way Gilly often did by laughing and saying he was the funny boy, always the funny boy.

Now the lake was clear and unfrozen. It looked very big and wide. It was impossible any longer to see the course of the river flowing through it. The water was a single, silent sheet. All about it the forests of reed that had slapped together in winter like white frozen whips were still green, with heavy soft brown plumes, like foxy tails, at their tips. On the water itself green islands of water-lily leaves lay so close together that in places they were joined into one island, thick enough, he thought, to walk on.

Always have the camera at the ready, Mr Ainsworth had told him, you never knew what you might see. So now he stood by a gap in the reeds and peered through them to where, close beyond, moorhens were actually walking on the lily leaves. They were lightly strutting and peering about from leaf to leaf as if on solid ground. They seemed to be utterly unconcerned that they might sink or drown. He could even hear their voices, casually chatting.

It seemed to him a remarkable thing that birds could walk on water. It would be great fun, he thought, to do that. He would like to try it himself. All you had to do was to put your feet gently from one leaf to another, as the birds did, and then go on and on. In that way he could follow the course of the river through the lake, walking all the way across it, and eventually come to the sea. He would have to tell Gilly about it.

He was actually on the point of stepping into the water when the air was suddenly carved apart by great creaking, straining sounds. A wide white cloud soared out of the lake, followed by another. The pair of swan necks rising slowly towards the sun had the strong lift of planes taking off, forging into air with stretched white power.

He stood transfixed, amazed, partly afraid, watching them. His stunned astonishment was so great that he even forgot the camera. There was no need either to magnify the vast lifting white wings with binoculars. He simply stood locked in disbelief, staring in wonder.

When he at last remembered the camera and started madly to click the shutter the swans were rising high past a wall of poplars, far down the water. He could hear the sound of their wings squeezing with power through the sky. The strong forward flight carried them above and past the poplars until finally he could see them no longer. Even then he could hear the machine-strong test of wings tirelessly cleaving the air.

Their final disappearance, high beyond the lake, filled him with a greater wonder than their first sudden uprising from the water. He now told himself they were far over the sea. The swiftness of their passage left him not merely locked in amazement. It uplifted him so completely that he instantly forgot all notion of walking on the water. He was filled simply with a longing to follow the swans.

As he turned and walked slowly away from the lake the idea of flying with the swans, far down to sea, never once seemed at all improbable. It sprang simply out of the world of Mr Pimm and Mr Monday, the snake that lifted its head to the sound of music, the frog that spoke in the voice of Mr Pimm. It was one with the many things that the eye of the camera found and held and transfigured. It was one with the world of the vole, the butterfly, the ants scuttling about their hill of thyme, the moorhens walking on water. It was even part of the world of the snail he hadn't caught yet and the float that he couldn't reach.

Nor did the notion of following the passage of the swans seem any less remarkable than the idea of his father flying to Tangier. That too was a long, long way over the sea. He knew because his father had told him so. He knew too that it was quiet up there. You hardly heard a thing. Sometimes you didn't see a cloud. His father had told him that too.

'Just as if you were sitting in a great big bird. Just like that. Just the same.'

All the way back along the river, across the park, his mind was so caught up by the magnetism of the swans' flight that by the time he reached the little house it came to him with slow surprise that neither Gilly nor Mr Ainsworth were there. He had forgotten them completely. It came to him only slowly, too, that they were still at the big house, amusing themselves, as Mr Ainsworth said, playing games. Even then it hardly seemed to matter.

He remembered the back door key under the mat outside the door. He thought for a moment of getting the key, going into the house and getting himself a drink of water. The autumn afternoon still seemed to stretch about him unafflicted by hours, a territory all his own. He decided to look instead down the well. He would take a picture, perhaps several pictures, of the float. Perhaps there would come a day when it wouldn't be there any longer. It would disappear altogether, like the snake and the water rat and the swans. No, he thought, not like the swans. The swans would always be there. He could see them now. He didn't care so very much, after all, about the water rat and the butterfly and the snake and the frog. He could, after all, see those any day. It was the great reality of the swans' flight that really mattered. He found himself thinking more and more of it in the way he thought of clouds and their shapes. Where were they going? How far would they go?

He finally lay flat on his face and looked down the well. The float was still there. It was still a thin streak of blue and copper, exactly like a kingfisher. It seemed odd that it never went away. He tried to fix the eye of the camera on it, but the crack in the wooden top of the well was too narrow and too awkward. After trying to fix the camera against it several times he at last gave up and took it away.

He now had a better idea. He had once heard Gilly say that the key that fitted the back door also fitted the well. If it did it was all too easy. He could open the top of the well and take the pictures that way.

'Every time I undress you it's like the first time. You didn't mean that about writing to me – that was silly – '

'Not now. I did then, but not now –'

Gilly lay back at full length on the pillows of one of the beds in the big house. Her bare arms were outside the coverlet. With brown relapsed eyes she watched the sky. The fragment of blue she could see through the upper area of one of the long windows had remained unblemished for so long that it gave her a feeling of unshaken permanence. She had been in bed with Mr Ainsworth, making love, not merely for the whole afternoon but for ever.

'I've got a funny sort of feeling we live here, you and me. Do you know what I mean? That it's ours. We live here and we always have lived here and we always will.'

Mr Ainsworth responded with drowsy half-kisses. His mouth pressed itself against her bare shoulder. One hand lightly held her left breast, his fingers too lazy to stroke it any more. Live here in permanence? Always? There was something to be said for it perhaps.

Gilly found herself listening for sounds, drowsy too. That was another strange thing about the afternoon: its soundlessness. There were days in the country when you heard, even from a distance, every tick and whisper of sound. The air was so clear and quiet that you could almost hear a wisp of sheep's wool break against a twig or a feather dropping from the mouth of a bird. But this afternoon there was a total lack of sound. The air was deep but empty. It was a kind of miraculous nothingness.

In the early part of the afternoon she had wondered, several times, about James. It was, she couldn't help agreeing with Mr Ainsworth, a wonderful thing to have given him the camera. It was wonderful to have thought of that. Mr Ainsworth's repeated assertion that the boy would play with it for hours was actually delivered in such a way that she even thought it was funny. Mr Ainsworth made it seem not as if it were a trick or a deception. It was some sort of amusing gift, given affectionately.

'Oh! he'll love me for ever for that camera. That'll make quite a mark on his little mind.'

'It will? You think so? What will he say when he finds it doesn't take pictures?'

'Not a damn thing. I remember once when I was about his age my father's gardener let me play all day with a pistol. Old German war-time relic sort of thing, barrel all bunged up, about as lethal as a spoon. I killed a million Indians with it that afternoon.'

'You did? You think he's all right then? I just can't help wondering now and then.'

'I'll make a bet with you.'

'A bet? What about?'

Ainsworth laughed softly. He stroked her breast with light fingers. A bet? Oh! yes, the bet. He was willing to bet her that James was just below them, happy as a sandboy, playing on the terrace. That was all. He was sure he had actually heard, several times, the click of the camera. Just to prove it, just for her sake, if she was worried, he would get out of bed and go to the window and look.

'It isn't that I'm all that worried. It's just that I don't want him to wander too far away.'

'I tell you he's on the terrace. Want to bet? Shall I go and see?'

'What do you want to bet?'

Mr Ainsworth lifted himself on one elbow. He laughed with a bemused softness, his lips seeking the tip of her bare breast.

'Whatever's on the menu.'

Gilly laughed too. That, she thought, was the great, wonderful thing about Mr Ainsworth. You never knew in what new, entrancing way he was going to put things. With typical light-heartedness he had already spoken casually of the first feverish act of love as breakfast, something quick and hot and unprolonged, to satisfy the appetite; the second as savouring more of a long, elegant, blissful drink, a lazy draught of the wine of afternoon. And the third? He looked forward to the third. Not the food and wine of love this time, he suggested, but more of a theme, perhaps, with variations?

'Well, what about your bet?'

'Ah! yes, the bet.'

Ainsworth slipped out of bed. He walked naked to the window and stood there for a full minute or more, looking out.

'Well, is he there? Have I lost my bet?'

'Yes, he's down there. You've lost, I'm afraid.'

'What's he doing?'

Ainsworth stared down at the completely empty terrace. Then he looked beyond it to the park, tranquil and empty too in the September sun

'He's taking pictures of a bird. A starling cracking a snail. Ah! yes, that's the snail he was after.'

'I didn't think starlings cracked snails. It's thrushes.'

'Ah! yes, a thrush. That's right. Anyway the snail's having a tough time.'

'Poor snail.'

'Ah! well, everything has to eat. The snail feeds on leaves, the thrush feeds on the snail, the cat feeds on the thrush. Everything must live. We all get hungry.'

'If you're hungry come back to bed with me and don't talk so much.'

She felt him slip back into bed with her. His body was cool but newly eager against her outstretched legs. His mouth slowly sought the tips of her breasts, holding them briefly in turn, delicately. With almost the same slow, delicately relapsed but awakening sense of a new experience she let her eyes hold the sky beyond the window, encompassed again by a great tranquility, and heard him say:

'*Allegro vivace? Con spirito?* or the slow movement?' She listened without an atom of comprehension. It was always the same. She was always a little outside his world of music. 'Yes, I think *pianissimo*. Softly, long drawn out.'

He laughed quietly. His mouth again brushed the tips of her breasts. Her response was simply a sigh, deeply relapsed. The fact that she had no response in words hardly surprised him. The thematic notion with its infinite variations was, perhaps, too subtle. He couldn't expect too much. The fact that Mrs Fitzsimmons had responded with greater spirit late the previous night was hardly surprising either. She was altogether more experienced in musical matters. She had, he thought, a certain quality of *coloratura* about her. She knew exactly what he was speaking about. When he offered her the rhythm of a long *cadenza* of his own she was only too glad to accept it for what it was, something unserious, impromptu and brilliant, to be enjoyed and never taken seriously. Perhaps it was the Irish in her.

'I wish we didn't have to get up. I wish we could stay on all afternoon and all night like this.'

'Even symphonies have to end.'

'Do they? You didn't bring your transistor with you today.'

'I looked at the programmes and there really wasn't a decent thing to listen to.'

'Did that piece ever come on again? The one you missed. The one with the one long note repeated all the time. I often think about that. It wasn't long after I met you. It always sticks in my mind.'

'Ah! the Schubert. The distant horns. No, that's never been on again.'

'I'd like to hear it some time.'

He barely stirred on the pillow. His arms were clasped above his head. He lay at ease, satisfied. By contrast she had begun to feel unexpectedly restless. The angle of light across the sky started to trouble and then irritate her. She began to be sure it was altogether later than she dared to think. The spell was breaking.

'I suppose,' Ainsworth said, 'we ought to think about going. He'll have taken enough pictures of that snail by now.'

'No, no, don't go.'

Her restlessness suddenly expressed itself in a powerful desire to keep him there. The embrace of her hands against the bare flesh of his back was strong and pained.

At first he felt casually embarrassed by this. He half tried to restrain her. She seemed to try to harden her grip on him. She partly buried her face against his shoulder. In turn he only partly heard her say something about how wonderful it was to have someone to love who was actually there, someone you could touch –

'What on earth are you talking about?'

Hesitantly she started to explain what it was she meant. She supposed it sounded silly. Perhaps it even sounded stupid, but it was terribly difficult to explain to him how she had been in love once before.

'Nothing very special about that. We all have.'

Yes, but this, she said, was different. She agreed it wasn't at all the first time it had happened to anyone. It must have often happened, but that didn't make it any the less – She broke off, paused and then wrapped herself into silence.

'Well?'

The difficult part to explain was, she said at last, that she had been in love with someone who wasn't there. Well, not exactly, not really like that. Actually it had all come back to her again that very morning, in the tea-shop, when the boy had sat there wondering whether to pick the eyes out of the dough-man. It had brought it all back to her.

He listened to this incredible piece of inconsequence as if he were watching someone trying to unravel a knotted piece of string. It seemed fascinating and pointless. Eventually the string, would be straightened out, the knots all unravelled, and then what? What could be more boring than a straight piece of string?

'Well, we've got to someone who isn't there and now the doughman. The great romance – '

Please, she begged him. It wasn't so easy. It wasn't so simple as all that. She knew it sounded terribly silly to say that she had been in love with someone who wasn't there – no, no, not quite that, but at least someone she had never spoken to.

'Oh! that often happens. That's quite common.'

This man used to come into the shop, the baker's, she said, every day. Mostly to buy cakes. Sometimes bread. He was about thirty, she thought. She didn't know. Perhaps married. It was always in the lunch hour, about half past twelve or so. It wasn't that she served him or spoke to him or anything of that sort. Most of the time she couldn't even bear to look at him. He always looked rather ill. Even in summer he wore a white silk muffler. He was in the shop, every day, for perhaps three or four minutes, even less. She never knew which was worse – the agony of the moments when he, the shop, the figures in it and she herself stood locked together, or the tension of waiting for it to happen, or the moment when the tension started to unravel itself and he was no longer there and it was all over.

Ainsworth wound a brown length of her hair round his forefinger. Slowly he made a loose knot in it, against her bare throat.

It was impossible to explain what it felt like to be in love with someone you never spoke to, she went on to say, someone you never even touched, but that was the way it was, that was how it had been with her. Perhaps it was just as well, after all, that he never had spoken, had never come within a million miles of touching her.

'There's a name for all these things.' The loose knot of her hair looked, Ainsworth thought, like the tail of a squirrel. 'Very sinister, the eyes of the dough-man – '

She didn't know, she said, about names. Her grip on him tightened again. 'I used to feel my body melting sometimes. I used to feel everything go black.'

He unravelled the curled knot he had made of the few strands of her hair, then curled it up again and then again let it go. The curl had a slight but fascinating spring to it. It almost seemed to knot itself of its own accord.

'And now everything's much simpler.'

She didn't know about simpler. It seemed to have some point to it now, that was all. There was no despair about it now. There was none of that pain of telling yourself that you were up a blind alley, that you'd never get anywhere. It was all so much more real, now, not a nightmare. If that was what he meant by being simpler she understood. Perfectly. It was all so beautiful.

She gave a deep uneasy sigh. She turned in the bed and smiled at him, full in the face. The curl of hair dropped away from her neck as she moved. At the same time she shook the rest of her hair with a sharp twist of her head, almost as if in self-reproach.

'I shouldn't have bored you with all that. But it helped, getting it off my chest. I've never told anyone before.'

Having no word to say, Ainsworth said none.

'That was why I left the shop. I couldn't go on any longer. I felt I couldn't bear it another day. Then I saw about this job – you know, looking after the boy – and it seemed like the right thing. It got me away from people.'

'Thank you.'

'No, you know how I mean. I didn't mean it like that. I mean it was just Providence, sort of – coming here to get away from people. And then you, that afternoon by the river.'

'Well, that's it, isn't it? You wish terribly hard for a thing and it never happens. You meet someone casually, a few silly words, mean nothing – and damn, there's an explosion.'

'You've exploded me all right.'

'Really?'

'Really. Every part of me.'

'Well, well.' His hands stopped playing with her hair. His fingers ran down her neck, over her breasts and down, slowly and strongly, to her thighs. 'The parts I can feel seem to have stood the explosion pretty well.'

'You like my body, don't you?'

'I'd say it's pretty high on my list.'

'It's yours for keeps if you want it.'

She waited for him to say something in reply to this. Nothing happened. She waited a little longer. Then, out of the casual stroking of his hands, she felt much of her restlessness come back. Again it was later than she thought. Again she felt disturbed. The spell was breaking. There was something uneasy about the angle of light in the sky.

Suddenly she sat bolt upright in bed. He tried as suddenly to draw her back to him but she swung her legs to the floor.

'Oh! why the hurry? Don't go. Why the sudden departure?'

'I've a funny feeling about that boy.'

Her underclothes were strewn about the bottom of the bed. Casually he watched her as she started to put them on. One of the things he liked most about her was the extraordinary smoothness of her skin. The arms and legs were hairless. Her whole body was as clean as the skin of a pear, the flesh gleaming and almost golden. Even the minute blue veins across her breasts seemed to melt under the skin.

Suddenly he laughed. She turned, half dressed, in the act of pulling on her girdle. She looked at him almost in an attitude of alarm.

'What's so funny now?'

'I was only thinking that a body like yours deserves a rather better girdle.'

'You might well laugh. Hardly call it Paris fashion. But then I never get a chance to get out and buy myself another.'

'I'll buy you one. What colour?'

'Oh! any colour.'

'Black? Or purple? What about purple?'

'What? Don't make me laugh. Me in purple?'

'Why not? I rather fancy you in purple.'

She was still drawing the white, plain, rather tattered girdle up over her thighs when he said:

'Better tell me the right size. Then I'll bring it when I come back.'

She turned full front to him, rigid and alarmed.

'When you what?'

'When I get back. Don't you know your size? Or do you want me to measure you?'

'Get back? Get back from where?'

'London.'

'You're going to London? Why?'

'Business – well, you could call it that. Couple of visits to the British Museum. Some things I want to look up. A couple of days, that's all. After all, I came down here to do a bit of research and so on – '

'Oh! your roads and things.'

He suddenly got out of bed, good-humoured, laughing again.

'You seem to have difficulty with that thing. May I help? No – I've hardly done a damn thing about the roads and it's time I did. The trouble is the scenery keeps getting in the way.'

'Scenery?'

'Yes, among other things.' His fingers once again sought the tips of her breasts. 'This sort of scenery.'

He started to fondle her again. He made light efforts to help her to dress, kissing her several times with unprolonged tenderness on the lips. When she finally parted her lips it wasn't to accept or question or reproach him but merely to utter the flat low statement:

'I never thought of you going away.'

'Well, it has to be thought of now.'

'When?'

'Tomorrow.'

'And two days? Is that all?'

'I'd be back in one if I had my way.'

'I love the way you say that.'

'How else should I say it? It's natural.'

She said nothing. After some moments she went on with her dressing. As she sat on the edge of the bed, pulling on her stockings, she turned and saw that he had draped a blanket over his shoulders. He was now standing by the window, looking out. She thought at once of the boy and said:

'Is he still there? I'll warm him if he's wandered off somewhere.'

'Oh! yes, he's still there.'

'Still playing with the camera?'

'Still playing with the camera.'

Ainsworth flattered himself it was a great idea, the camera: stroke of genius. He stared idly at the park, rather ragged, he thought, after the summer, empty of sheep, nothing much moving, the chestnuts showing rusty fire down the avenue. He often thought that a herd of deer would have set it all off to perfection. He supposed they had them in the old days. Yes: the deer too were quite a thought. He would send the boy off to photograph them another day. With Mrs Fitzsimmons he hadn't, of course, to think of these subterfuges. She was quite free, her own mistress.

He smiled. Mrs Fitzsimmon's skin was remarkably white. It had a quality of exciting purity. Thinking of it he smiled again and was then suddenly taken unawares by the presence of Gilly, just beside him.

'I thought you said he was still down there.'

'Just skived off like nobody's business round the corner.'

She said nothing. She went back to the bed to finish her dressing. For the first time she was aware of a slight shadow of doubt.

She finally ran her hands across her untidy hair. Then she went across to the bedroom door, pausing just long enough to look back at him, still standing naked by the window.

'I'm going to look for him. If I'm not back in five minutes you'll come too, will you?'

'Oh! you're surely not alarmed or anything?'

'I don't know what I am – '

'I tell you he was just down there. Only a minute ago.'

'I'll be happier in my mind if I go and see.'

She vaguely heard him begin to say something about being a slow dresser, no point in hurrying, and then she was gone. As she ran down the back stairs the chill of doubt suddenly enveloped her completely, a black shadow now, touched with anger.

The terrace was empty. Suddenly the park, empty too, seemed vast. She half-ran, half-walked the full length of the terrace. Then she ran back again, calling as she went. In the act of running down the steps she was suddenly arrested by a voice from overhead. She turned, looked up and saw Ainsworth at the open bedroom window, buttoning his shirt.

'Find a snail and you'll find the boy.' Ainsworth laughed. 'Remember? You have to be quick or they get away.'

For a second or two she halted on the steps, her anger divided between Ainsworth and the boy. Then the divisions of her anger suddenly fused and turned furiously back on herself. She gave a shout of impatience that was directed as much at herself as at Ainsworth and said:

'What's so funny about it? Oh! no, it's not your responsibility. – '

Even before she had finished them the words sounded pointless. She turned away swiftly. She ran down the steps and partly across the gravel drive at the foot of them. The notion of hunting a snail in the empty acres of the park, ridiculous though it was, suddenly had the effect of changing her anger to fear. She was aware, also, of being cheated: cheated first by the boy, then by Ainsworth, and then by the final ridiculous notion that the snail and the boy were one, elusive, impossible to find, faintly mocking –

She ran aimlessly for two hundred yards across the park before being struck by a sudden spasm of relief. He was, of course, where he always loved to be: in the glass-house, talking to Mr Monday and Mr Pimm. She suddenly felt pitifully and profoundly grateful for Mr Monday and Mr Pimm. All this time they had never really existed. Now they were suddenly here, very real, when she most wanted them. She ran back to the glass-house. Almost before she opened the door she knew that that was pointless too. She went in, stared at the fig-tree and the vines, listened to the drip of a tap from somewhere under a shroud of ferns, smelled the dark dank odour of water and then ran out again.

As she ran back across the park she felt equally cheated by Mr Pimm and Mr Monday. The sudden figures of salvation had as suddenly let her down. She remembered the past vivid realities of Mr Pimm: having Mr Pimm to lunch, playing dominoes with Mr Pimm, sitting on the river bank with Mr Pimm, fishing. Mr Pimm, in those days, had actually existed. She had believed in Mr Pimm through every word and breath. She had even talked his language.

Out of this new confusion and unreality of Mr Pimm sprang a single coherent thought: the river. For the first time she was frightened. She stopped running. She half-started again, changing direction. Then she saw, from behind the trees beyond the little house, a cloud of smoke rising in a thick grey-blue column. The fear of the river was abruptly replaced by fear of fire. She started running again. At the same moment, from some distance behind her, she heard a shout and turned to see Ainsworth half-way between herself and the terrace, hands in pockets, neck-tie still half-knotted, strolling casually.

'Take it easy!' she thought he called. 'Take it easy now – ' and then something about a snail.

Her throat was dry with running. More with the idea of trying to appear casual too, unworried by it all, she dropped into a walk, her only sign of agitation an occasional quick brushing of her hair, with first one hand and then the other.

The little house at last came into view from among its barricade of trees. The smoke, she now saw, was well beyond it, a bonfire. Running again, she felt cheated by that too.

She started to shout. The sound of her voice, hoarse, falsely high-pitched and loud, struck oddly on the calm expanse of the windless afternoon. To her infinite astonishment a dark blue figure on a bicycle, a hundred yards or more beyond the house, turned its head and shouted back in answer:

'Sorry. Nothing for you today!'

She stared at the postman. He waved a hand. She thought of shouting again and then, at the last moment, let him go.

Half exhausted by running, she walked slowly into the garden. She stopped for a moment to lean on the open gate, anxiously getting back her breath.

The sight of James lying flat on his face, staring down the well, the top of the well unlocked and open, come to her slowly at first, like a slightly distorted vision unfolding incredibly from a surrounding forest of flowers. For a wild moment or two she saw the prostrate figure as dead. Then she saw a twitch of the hands. A moment later she heard the camera clicking madly.

She hauled him to his feet. She struck him several times about the face and head before actually realizing she had moved at all. He looked at her in wild response. His stare of surprised and enormous innocence was his only protest. It angered her so much that she furiously knocked the camera from his hands. It fell clattering on to the flagstones of the garden path. Instinctively he stooped to pick it up. Before he could reach it she struck him fiercely about the head again, half-knocking him down, shouting:

'You do that once more to me and I'll beat you into Kingdom Come! You hear me? I'll leather the life out of you – '

He stood stunned and tearless, without a word. It was only some long time later that the lack of tears started to haunt her. In the moment when she stood there and saw him slowly pick himself up from the garden path, not crying at all, one hand vaguely searching for the dropped camera, she swiftly felt that his lack of tears was yet another form of cheating. Why didn't he cry? He had to cry. It was his right to cry.

'And don't stand there all blasted surprised and innocent, my lord, either! You know what'll happen to you if you get into the well, don't you? You know! You'll die – you won't be here – I told you, didn't I?'

She raised her hand to strike him again. Then in a savage change of mind she picked up the camera and swung it towards him as if to hit him with that instead.

'You hear me? I told you forty times, didn't I? You know, don't you? Don't tell me you don't know – it's wicked and wrong to do things like that – don't tell me you don't know. You're old enough to know. The well'll get you if you do things like that – the well'll get you. And then you won't be here, will you? You won't be here.'

To Ainsworth, coming in by the garden gate, she looked more like the ghost of the girl who had spent all afternoon with him, with much pleasure, in the bedroom. Her face was taut and white. As she raised the camera for the second time in the act of striking he strode forward to take it from her hands. As he did so she suddenly threw the camera down on the garden path, shouting:

'Who are you to interfere? You and your damn camera! Who are you to interfere?'

The camera fell with a crash. The force of it striking the ground broke it open. It lay there like an empty and useless cigarette case. The boy seemed for a brief moment as if he were about to stoop and pick it up. His hand stopped stiff in air. His eyes fixed her with an appeal stunned but brilliant. It too haunted her long afterwards. She started to cry. Her tears came more from sheer relief than anger. All the time she hoped the boy would cry too but once again he showed no sign of crying and all Ainsworth could say was:

'Take it easy. Take it easy now. It might have been worse. Much. Infinitely. Be thankful for that.'

Ainsworth knotted his tie. He hated, above all things, dressing in a hurry. With a final movement of both hands he smoothed the tie into place and she took it as a gesture of comfort.

'James.' From the foot of the stairs Gilly's voice forced itself up like sharp, probing wire. 'James. If I catch you awake and out of bed again – James! You can hear me, can't you? If I have to come up again and I catch you out of bed! – Don't pretend you can't hear me. I know you can.'

James lay with his head completely covered by bed sheets. Outside, though the sun had set, the evening was still not dark. Under the sheets it was like being once again in the depths of a forest, except that now there was no snake or frog or butterfly to watch or even the flicker of a shadow. It was all grey under the sheets. It was all nothing. He was in a prison, a trap of grey darkness, with no way of getting out.

Mr Ainsworth had gone away with the camera. He knew that he wouldn't see it any more. The pictures he had taken had all gone too. He knew they were dead. The snake was dead too and the butterfly and the ants and the frog and above all the swans. From the moment Gilly had dashed the camera to the ground they were all dead and destroyed. You had to keep the camera closed and dark inside so that the pictures could live. The moment it opened and the light got in they were dead. He knew all that because once his father had told him so.

It was bad enough that the snake and the frog and the ants and the butterfly and the swans were dead, especially the swans. But now he felt that Mr Pimm and Mr Monday were dead too. He was alone. When he spoke to them they didn't come out of the darkness. He tried several times to speak to Mr Pimm in the old familiar way, smoking shag, spitting, calling him his old matey, but nothing happened. It didn't seem the same any more. Mr Pimm was one with the great grey darkness that covered everything and from which there was no way out.

In the same way he tried vainly to recapture his vision of the swans. He would seem to see them for the fraction of a second as they rose white and splendid across the lake. And then as suddenly they were there no longer. The strange, soaring, squeezing sound of their wings flying down to the sea was broken. He longed once again to hear that sound. It was all wonderful, that powerful squeezing rise of wings, taking you into the sky, down to the sea, to somewhere you had never been before.

The only things that were real any longer were the camera breaking open on the path, the grey trap of darkness and the voice of Gilly now and then probing up the stairs. The voice of Gilly, he thought, was a new voice. He had never heard that particular voice of hers before. It seemed to come from altogether another person. It was as if she had made herself a deliberate stranger. Sometimes it seemed even worse than that. Somehow, for some reason he couldn't fathom, something to do with the camera and Mr Ainsworth, he knew that he and she were enemies. He knew that she hated him because of the well, the key he had stolen and above all because of the camera. In the grey darkness he could hear the continual sound of her voice, hard with hatred.

After a time, under the sheets, it was like being under a tight, black umbrella. The greyness had gone. He knew that it was really getting dark outside. Unable to sleep, he pretended he was asleep. I'm asleep, he told himself. I'm asleep, Mr Pimm, are you? Since there was never an answer from Mr Pimm he concluded at last that Mr Pimm was asleep. He said good night, matey. Mr Pimm didn't answer. He knew then, once again, that Mr Pimm wasn't really there any more, neither asleep nor awake. There was a sort of strange blank cave where Mr Pimm had been. It was all hollow inside. Its echoes sang and pounded in his head, gloomy and haunting.

He remembered how echoes had sung and pounded in his head once before, when he was ill and Miss Garfield said he had a temperature. The echoes drove him into a world of frenzied glassy dreams. He was climbing up endless steps, all alone, into a glassy, cruel sky. Soon the sky was a sea. On the sea were tall ships, like storming skeletons. He was shrieking with terror because their sails were white lips, nagging at him with snarling, beckoning voices.

Much later, for a moment or two, he fancied suddenly, out of half asleep, that he heard them beckoning him again. He half roused himself with a jolt of terror. The cruel white lips of sails seemed suddenly to snatch at him. They were weaving and seething in front of his face. They were mocking and terrorizing him, ready to take him away.

He realized presently that these voices were in reality one voice: the voice of Gilly. She was saying good night to him. Her voice was quiet and low. She was saying how sorry she was about what had happened, about the things she had done and said. She said she was sorry she had to hit him like that but she was angry and he knew it was wrong to take the key. He didn't want to drown, did he? He didn't want not to be here any more? What did he suppose she would be left to say if a terrible thing like that happened? She could never face it. She would never forgive herself. She would die of shame.

He listened, pretending sleep. He waited in vain for her to say something about the camera. That was the all important thing, the camera. The camera was dead and destroyed. It was because the camera was dead that everything else was dead: the snake, the butterfly, the ants, the frog, above all the swans and Mr Pimm and Mr Monday.

Gilly said nothing about the camera. She repeated, instead, several things about the key. She had hidden the key. She had put it away somewhere so that no one, not he nor anyone else, not even God himself, could find it. He knew that that was wrong. He knew that God could find everything. It didn't mind where you put a thing, a key or anything. In any case he didn't want the key any more. The key wasn't important any longer. It didn't matter.

He was aware of her leaning over the bed. She was moving the sheets slightly and pressing her lips against the side of his forehead. Still in a pretence of sleep, his face remained solid and stony. She said she knew he wasn't asleep. She knew he was listening. That was why she had come up: because she knew he still wasn't asleep, because she had to say how sorry she was and because she couldn't sleep herself until she did.

'Aren't you going to kiss me? Aren't we friends?'

He lay still, saying nothing. He knew that, because of the camera, they would never be friends again. She was like the voice that had come probing up the stairs. It was a voice that belonged with the snarling voices of the skeleton lips of the ships' sails in his old glassy nightmare. She was foreign and strange. She hated him.

'You're nearly asleep, aren't you? I'll say good night now. Don't get out of bed again. If you don't hear me about for a few minutes it's because I've walked as far as the garden gate to meet Mr Ainsworth. He's going away for a day or two tomorrow. I'll only be gone a minute. Only a little way.'

He still lay quite motionless, breathing deeply. Her words meant nothing. He had nothing to say.

'Good night now. I won't be long. Mr Ainsworth's just coming to say good-bye, that's all. Then I'm coming to bed too. I'm having an early night tonight.'

She said this as if everything, now, were solved and simple. An early night was a piece of great self-sacrifice. Now everything would be the same, she seemed to say, as it had been before.

'Good night.' Her voice was down to a low, caressing whisper. 'Nice dreams. And mind, no getting out of bed again.'

It was deliberately in response or defiance of this last sentence of hers that he got out of bed, some long time later and went to the window. He drew one of the curtains back an inch or two and stood looking out. Lights still burned in the farmhouse across the park. The night sky was clear and without cloud. There were many glittering stars. There was no breath of wind and all he could hear as he stood there, at first watching nothing but the lights of the farmhouse and the stars, was the sharp repeated click of something in the garden below, almost like the agitated rapping of a thrush killing a snail on a stone.

When finally he pulled back the curtains several inches wider he could clearly see Gilly standing in the garden below. She was standing by the gate, absently clicking the latch up and down. The harsh click of it was something like a signal repeating itself over and over again to someone who wasn't there.

As he watched her and listened there rose up in him a grave, taut defiance of her. It was almost an exultation. He was suddenly glad that she was all alone there, waiting, in the darkness.

The better part of a week later he sat eating his breakfast, as he had done on previous mornings, as if nothing had happened. The sky was calm. Thin shoals of minute upper cloud were quickly drifting far off, like grey-white fish-scales. He searched among them, in vain, for one like a swan. Only once did Gilly say, from behind the paper, her voice thin and far off too, that if he didn't eat up soon his egg would get cold.

Searching through the kitchen window for the swan-like cloud, eyes half closed, he caught sight of the postman cycling up the road in the park. Purposely he put on an air of formality, almost grace, to ask:

'There's the postman. May I go to meet him, please?'

'Yes, you can go to meet him.'

By the time he reached the garden gate the postman was already cycling past the house. The postman was a podgy man. His red ears were big and stiff and crinkled like rhubarb leaves. His eyes were like blue marbles. He smoked on duty. His favourite word was chronic. Everything was chronic. The weather was chronic. The news was chronic. The harvest was chronic. The outlook was chronic. All was chronic.

'Anything for us today?' James opened the gate and stood waiting.

The postman, cigarette in mouth, got off his bike and said he didn't think they was. It was nothing but an old, chronic, no-good load of tripe today. Bills and circulars and pools and free offers and God knowed what. Chronic. Mail was late too on top on it. Chronic. It was a sharp old morning too. Nearly a frost down the hill.

He stood sorting through his mail bag. He unleashed a big elastic band that held a bundle of letters. He sorted through them too. No, they wasn't nothing. Was he expecting something from his Ma and Pa? When was they coming back? All the time the cigarette stub, three parts burned, bobbed up and down between his lips like a fat white ant.

'We expect them when we see them.'

Oh! it was like that, was it? The postman betted it was hot where they was.

'They'd like to stay there for ever.'

'Would they be God? The postman took his cigarette out of his mouth. He stared at it with an air of heavy surprise, as if there were something wrong with it. Then he spat briefly and put it back again.

It was a very poor spit compared with Mr Pimm's but it had the effect, temporarily, of almost bringing Mr Pimm to life again. Briefly the postman became Mr Pimm. James spat too. For a few moments he and the postman were old together, talking man to man.

Had his Gilly heard about Mrs Barton? the postman said.

'I don't think so.'

Dead. Passed away.

'But she went to hospital. They were going to make her better.'

Chronic, the postman said. They made her take her vest off. She couldn't bear her vest off. She'd never been used to it without her vest. Died. Chronic. Snuffed it, like a light. Old, of course, but not that old.

'Chronic,' James said.

Funeral Thursday, the postman said. Service in the church. Crematorium afterwards. James must tell his Gilly. Perhaps she'd like to go.

'Yes, I'll tell her.'

Funny how many people went to hospital and snuffed it afore you could wink, the postman said. Very funny. He betted they gave 'em a shot of somethink to help 'em on. Chronic. Shortage of beds he shouldn't wonder.

'Mrs Barton used to give me cheese-cakes when I went to the farm.'

Ah? Well, she wouldn't make cheese-cakes no more, the postman said. You could bet on that. Terrible, not having her vest on. Chronic. No, no more cheese-cakes.

'Will they let her have her vest on when they take her away?'

Everybody, the postman said, everybody he talked to had been on about it. Thought it was a scandal. Vest on? It was a bit late in the day for that. He rubbed his hands together. He said he'd be damned if it didn't feel half-tidy frosty still.

James stood watching the postman rubbing his red cold hands together. He tried to conjure a vision of Mrs Barton without her vest on. It wasn't very easy. The postman said well, that was how it was. Third in the village in a week. Thick an' fast. Chronic. That was hospitals.

He got on to his bike at last. He started to ride away, saying 'So long,' lifting one hand, the cigarette still ant-like between his lips.

'So long,' James said.

Better luck tomorrow with the postcards, the postman said. He betted they'd got caught up somewhere. Chronic, the mail, these days. Chronic. Like hospitals.

James went back into the house. Still at the breakfast table, Gilly was hidden behind the morning paper. He could feel a cold, sullen withdrawal in the air. He started to say first how there was nothing for them in the post today, then how Mrs Barton had died and how it was because she hadn't had her vest on. He felt a strange sense of unhappy dread whenever he thought of the vest.

It was some time before Gilly moved or answered. At last she lowered the paper and stared.

'What were you on about just now?'

'Mrs Barton.'

'What about Mrs Barton?'

'She died. She didn't have her vest on.'

For some moments Gilly simply stared at him with a curious, thin-lipped hostility, without a word. He knew then that they were still enemies. He knew even before she folded the paper suddenly and rustled it down into her lap and said:

'Are you trying to be funny?'

'The postman said so.'

'One of these days you'll stop making things up. Mrs Barton? She was alive and well yesterday.'

'She went to hospital and they took her vest off and she died.'

Gilly suddenly got up from the table. She started to clatter cups and plates and cutlery together in a flurry of cold impatience. He stood still and watched her, failing to understand.

It was all so simple about Mrs Barton. It was strange that Gilly didn't believe him when he told the truth.

'Listen, are you trying to make a monkey out of me? You know it's wrong to tell tales about people.'

He started to say again, simply, how Mrs Barton was dead –

'Then why didn't you tell me straight out? Instead of a lot of nonsense about – poor soul, you might think it was a joke or something. Haven't you finished your egg?'

'Not quite.'

'Then sit down and finish it for God's sake. Mooning and maundering about – breakfast on the table half the morning. And don't crumble your bread all over the place.'

He sat down at the table. He scooped a spoonful of boiled egg from its shell. It was cold and stiff and glassy. He chewed on it slowly, without relish, and she said:

'And don't be so dainty. Eat it up if you want it. And if you don't want it don't maul and mess it about. It makes me sick.'

Before he could speak again she snatched egg and cup and plate and spoon away. She took them all out into the scullery together. He heard a brittle sickening sound as she crushed the egg-shell. Then she came back and picked up the paper, unfolded it, folded it up again and furiously banged it into the seat of a chair. With irate hands she swept his crumbled bread into a heap and just before she took that away in another gesture of near-fury he said:

'Could I have the bread for the birds?'

'Oh! do what you like! Do anything – bread for the birds, bread for the fish, anything, do as you like. What do I care? But I won't be told fairy tales. You hear me? I will not be told fairy tales.'

He stood stunned again, speechless.

'People die of pneumonia and accidents and heart attacks and things like that. But not because they don't have their vests on. I tell you – I will not have fairy tales.'

He withdrew into his own sullen retreat to the far side of the table, a half-crumbled slice of bread in his hands.

'I will not be lumbered with fairy tales. You understand? Just now and then I'll have the truth.'

He started to go to the kitchen door. He held the bread hard in his hands, afraid to crumble it again.

'Of course I know the truth is hard for some people. It chokes them. They'd rather make things up. But just now and then I'll have it, I'll tell you that. I was brought up to tell the truth and I'll have it from you too. Or God help me.'

He started to open the kitchen door. When it was wide open he hesitated, at a loss, and held it there for some seconds.

'And let's either have the door open or shut. One way or the other. You want me to catch my death too? There's a draught blowing in like winter. Go on! – either get in or out. Do what? Do what you like – I don't care. Only get out from under my feet – I've got something else to do besides listen to people who tell lies.'

'I didn't tell any lies.'

'That's the trouble with some people. They don't know lies from truth. Do they?' She whipped the table cloth from the table like a white flayed skin. 'You should know.'

A sudden barrier, black and from that moment immovable, fell between Gilly and himself. He walked into the garden. His steps were slow. He stood for some time and stared at the well. The well was locked. He would never look into the well again. The key was hidden away, in a place where he could never find it. The camera had gone too. It was dead, like Mrs Barton.

'And don't you wander away! I'll limb you to bits if you wander away.'

He stood by the gate, in almost the identical attitude in which Gilly had stood there in the night. His hands were nervous on the latch. His world was narrowed. A wall had sprung up between himself and everything outside. All the things he wanted were outside the wall: Mr Pimm and Mr Monday, the snake and the frog, the butterfly and the river, the lake and the swans. He felt it all to be forbidden. The farm was also forbidden, its windows shuttered. He supposed the park and the glass-house were forbidden too. He mustn't wander.

The only thing left open to him was the sky. He stared for a long time that morning at the sky. The air was still windless and quiet after its breath of frost but in the sky, far, far up, hosts of fish-scale cloud moved with the strangest speed, now sprinkled white with sun, on an upper wind.

On these high currents of air the clouds changed their shapes with confusing rapidity. Sometimes they seemed like white wind-blown faces. Sometimes they were like crowds of swimming eyes. Sometimes they were like flocks of white-winged birds. Once or twice he tried to imagine that in swift moments of whiter congregation they assumed the shape of swans. Always, just as swiftly, the wind blew them apart again, into a new flight of separation. The flight became, once, a host of butterflies, white too, sprinkled with flecks of blue. He saw it once also as a flight of wings much smaller, exactly like gnats nervously dancing in the sun, golden signs that the day would be fine. They even seemed, at one breathless moment, to become like so many berries all dipped in sugar, glistening, waiting to be eaten. Once they became white fern-patterns, a silver imagery of leaves and flowers, exactly the same as you saw on window panes after a night of frost, when it was winter and you wondered how the white ice-forest on the glass ever came to be made.

Out of all these things the pictures that recurred most sharply in his mind was of objects flying, hurrying into far distances. He longed to follow them. His impression was that far up, a million miles in the sky, there was a sort of platform. It was a great cliff-edge, opening out to vast new spaces. He could imagine that when you reached this great edge of cliff, with the endless space below, you simply spread and lifted your wings. Then you were away on your own flight, with no one to tell you not to do this or that or not to wander. You were all alone and flying just how and where you wanted, like a swan. He was convinced you had to be like a swan because you needed the vast white swan-wings. You needed the great squeezing sound of power, to take you right away.

His illusion about the swans was so compelling that he actually opened the garden gate, some time later, and started to wander idly away outside. For a few moments he was free. He was beginning to feel a first breath of escape when suddenly Gilly's voice cut the air, calling shrilly from the abruptly opened kitchen door:

'And where do you think you're going now? How many times do I have to tell you? I said not to wander, didn't I? Don't you ever listen? *I said not to wander!*'

He walked slowly back to the house. He stood on the threshold of the kitchen door. Inside she was sitting at the table, still in her dressing-gown, still reading the morning paper, hair still unbrushed. Her eyes were smoky, as if she hadn't slept well. She was still distant, he thought. She was foreign and cold. Her lips were still thin and unloving. He knew that she was still his enemy.

'Well, don't stand gawping with the door open. I told you – either come in or out. Get something to play with – get your chalks out or something. Colour some pictures. Don't hover about so. You grate my nerves.'

Slowly he was troubled by a curious notion that in some way he had done wrong to speak of Mrs Barton and her vest. It was hardly strong enough to make him feel that he was sorry and he simply said:

'Could I go to the farm?'

'Farm? Farm? What on earth do you want to go to the farm for? What makes you think they want you at the farm. You're the last person they want to see.'

'I thought I could say I was sorry about Mrs Barton.'

'Sorry? Sorry? Are you trying to be funny again? Well, don't. Sorry about Mrs Barton? – it's me you should say you're sorry to. Me. I'm the one that's made a monkey of.'

'Where are my chalks?'

Chalks, chalks! They were where he left them, weren't they? In the box under the stairs, where they always were. He could find them for himself, couldn't he? He could look for himself for a change, couldn't he? Did she always have to find every damn thing for him?

'Is the blackboard there too?'

The blackboard, my God, the blackboard! Yes, wonder of wonders, that was there too. It hadn't walked, had it? And he'd better, she warned him, take it outside. She wasn't having chalk all over the place and dust and scratching.

Without a word he went to where, under the stairs, the blackboard and the chalks were kept. The dark triangular hole under the stairs smelled of onions, floor polish, paraffin, things old and friendly. He longed suddenly to stay there, shut away, secure in the partial darkness. He longed to invent a game. He longed to conjure up someone he could talk to. He wanted to stay there in a comforting prison of his own making and not come out for a long time.

But after less than half a minute Gilly's sharp voice warned him:

'I don't know what you're up to in there but come out and don't do it. You're not touching that electric light switch, are you?'

Once before, in the half darkness, he had pulled a lever. Much later, when Gilly went to switch on the lights, there were no lights.

Without a word he came out from under the stairs. He carried his small square blackboard in one hand, his box of chalks in the other. He went through the kitchen. Gilly had nothing to say. She seemed if anything, he thought, farther away from him than ever, more distant and more cold. She was more and more his enemy.

'Does the baker come today?'

'If it's sweets you're thinking of I can tell you now you've had that one.'

The baker was a lady. She was fat and dark. She wore trousers and a collar and tie, like a man. In the baker's van she kept bars of chocolate, packets of peppermints and gums, buns with ice on them. He liked her. He knew, now, that she didn't come today.

He went outside. He shut the kitchen door behind him and sat on the doorstep. He held the small square blackboard on his knees and stared at it. He stared at the sky too, his eyes half closed. It seemed a funny thing but now the high upper clouds were no longer like anything he had seen before. The many small white objects that had been birds and butterflies and gnats and berries and patterns on a frosted pane of glass had disappeared. They had simply become one object, a grey ceiling, closing in on him, shutting away his notion that there was a great platform up there, a great space, from where you flew away.

He picked up a white chalk, thinking he would draw the sky on his blackboard. Then he hesitated and changed it for a blue one. He sat for some long time holding the blue one in his hand. Then he changed the blue chalk for an orange one. Then with the orange chalk he drew a house. It was a big tall house. It wasn't like the farmhouse but much more like the one in the park. He drew green grass in front of it, then blue squares for windows. Then he took a red chalk and scribbled all over the walls and roof of the house a maze of jagged angered lines, with burning brilliant clouds, not at all like the shoals of moving cloud in the upper sky but exactly like the angry red colour you saw at sunset.

Soon the house was burning. It was all on fire, all orange and crimson, from the grass to the chimneys. All its windows were angry with dancing flame. And inside them, if you looked carefully, you could see people, all nasty and sorry and burning and shrieking and not knowing what to do with themselves.

When he went out to meet the postman on the following morning, and the morning after that, the postman had nothing to offer again except the same casual, empty hand.

'Nothing for you today, my old sport. Your folks running out of stamps? I shouldn't wonder. Sharp again. Chronic.'

This neither surprised nor disappointed him. He waved his own casual hand, untroubled. The post-cards were all the same: the same sand, the same palm trees, the same sunshades, the same hard bright blue sky. They didn't matter any more.

It was only when he went back to the kitchen that he found himself face to face with things that did. Every morning the barrier between himself and Gilly came down again, black and cold. Every morning they were enemies again.

'Well, where's the post?'

'He said there's nothing today.'

'Nothing, my foot. He said that yesterday. He's always saying that. You mean to say there isn't a post-card?'

'He said nothing today.'

'That's what he always says. He doesn't look, half the time. He hides them in his bag.'

Always she sat at the breakfast table, in her dressing-gown, hair unbrushed, reading the morning paper, sloppy cup of tea in her hands. Always she looked at him with the same grey, disbelieving sharpness, as if she half suspected him of hiding the letters too.

'What else did he tell you? You were out there chatting long enough. A lot of rubbish I expect. He always talks too much, that one.'

'He says they're keeping Mrs Barton till Friday.'

'First it was Wednesday, now it's Friday. What are they keeping her for?'

'He says they have to wait for the *post-mortem*.'

'*Post-mortem? Post-mortem?* What do they want with a *post-mortem?*'

'What's a *post-mortem*? Is it what she died of?'

No, it wasn't, she said. It didn't matter. She dropped the newspaper on the floor, reached across the table for the tea-pot and poured herself another cup of tea. He watched her drop several lumps of sugar into the cup and then stir them hard. Then he said:

'The postman says it's been three white frosts and now it'll rain today.'

'Oh! he does, does he?'

'He says it always rains after three white frosts.'

'Oh! he does, does he? The great prophet. It looks fine enough to me.'

'If it rains you'll have to get a new umbrella.'

'Will I? And why?'

'The last time it rained there was a hole in it and it rained on your face.'

'Well, it can rain on it again for all I care.'

He went to the kitchen window and stared at the sky. Clouds of a peculiar shape, something like fat, creeping hedgehogs, grey at the crest, dark blue underneath, were coming in from the west. He watched them for a time, silently. He didn't want it to rain. Rain would imprison him in the house. He would never be free all day. On the other hand, in a way, he wanted it to rain. If it rained it would prove the postman was right. It would prove too that he didn't tell lies about what the postman said.

'Will you get a new umbrella?'

'Oh! don't keep on about the umbrella.'

'They have nice umbrellas at the shop in the village.'

'Oh! do they? Well, they can keep them. The old red one will have to do for me.'

'It isn't any good if it's got a hole in it and it doesn't keep the rain out.'

'It's good enough for me.'

'Could I play with it for a while and make a tent in the garden?'

'No, you could not. And for the fifty millionth time stop going on about the umbrella. You're enough to give anyone the green willies – you drive me up the wall.'

'It would make a nice tent and I could play in it for a long time.'

'Oh! for God's sake shut up about the umbrella and the tent and everything, can't you? I'll tent you into Kingdom Come if you keep on and on and on.'

He was quiet. He had nothing to say. They were going to be enemies again all day, as they had been the day before and the day before that and the day before that. They had been enemies ever since she had taken the camera away from him and struck him in the face. The black barrier had never lifted. Whenever he tried to lift it by talking of things like rain and frost and the umbrella and what the postman said she turned on him like a cat from a corner, dark and spiteful, sometimes savage.

He had spoken once, but only once, of Mr Ainsworth. When was Mr Ainsworth coming back? Her face, as he spoke of Mr Ainsworth, became glassy, with queer harsh lines about her eyes and mouth, as if someone had thrown stones at it and broken it into splinters.

183

Suddenly, without the slightest warning, in that strange and unexpected way he found grown-up people so often had, she seemed to change. As she started hurriedly to clear the breakfast table she became amazingly talkative and bright.

Yes, perhaps after all he was right about the umbrella. It was pretty awful really, the old red one. Was it at Sharman's he had seen the nice ones? or Hetherton's? It was probably a good time to have a new umbrella anyway, with autumn here and soon the winter coming on, though sometimes she was blessed if it didn't seem to rain more sometimes in the summer than the winter. Anyway it was a good time. They could go and see. It didn't cost anything to look. There was no harm in looking. They'd take the old one with them anyway, in case it did rain on the way. And if he was good, and didn't pester, he could carry it.

He listened to all this amazed, without a word. He thought of the snake that you charmed with a whistle. He thought of how it went into a trance as it listened to the music. Now it was just as if Gilly were trying to charm him with talk of the umbrella. He could only listen, unaffected, and wonder why. He could only guess why she changed so much, so quickly. It was strange how grown-ups changed like that, all of a sudden, unexpectedly, as if nothing at all had happened, and expected you to change too.

As they walked together to the village he was stubbornly aware of not changing. He carried the red umbrella stiffly. He carried it because she said he could carry it, not because he wanted to or because it gave him any pleasure. Once a few spots of rain started to fall. As he felt them fresh on his face, she actually gave a short laugh and said he was right after all. It was raining. He could put the umbrella up if he wanted to.

He put the umbrella up. The hole in it was quite small. Underneath it, he thought, it was suddenly like being in a tent, with the sun shining through it, warm and crimson. It seemed, if anything, to shut him even farther away from her. He was stubborn and stiff and alone under his own bright roof and he listened indifferently as she said, again with her own new brightness, as if nothing had happened:

'What colour shall we get? What colour do you fancy?'

He said he didn't know what colour he fancied. The umbrella wasn't for him.

'I like coloured ones, don't you? They're gay. They make you think it isn't raining.'

He liked some coloured ones. He liked green.

'Oh! not green. Green's unlucky.'

Why was green unlucky?

'Oh! I don't know. It just is. It somehow always has been.'

The grass was green. Was that unlucky?

'Oh! well I don't know about that. About grass. It's only in things you wear, sort of. No, we won't have green. What about blue, or orange?'

Orange and blue were all right, he said, but he liked white too. White suddenly reminded him of swans. Yes, he liked white the best.

'Oh! not white. We can't have white. Not for umbrellas. That's for sunshades. Sunny days. Not rain.'

Why couldn't you have white for rain?

'Well, it somehow isn't right. You have black and colours and things for rain. Not white.'

Why? It kept the rain out just the same.

'Well, just because – Well, we'd look silly going to Mrs Barton's funeral with one white umbrella and one red one, wouldn't we?'

Why would they? Would people laugh?

'No, not exactly laugh. I don't mean silly that way. It wouldn't be right, that's all. Not nice. Not the thing.'

Did they have to go to Mrs Barton's funeral?

'Yes, I think so. She would like it.'

How could she like it if she was dead and she didn't know?

'Well, here we are. Shall we look in at Hetherton's first? I see by the church clock it's past eleven already. Put the umbrella down. It doesn't rain now.'

She stopped. He put the umbrella down. They were in the centre of the village street now. Suddenly, for the second time that morning, in the strange way that grown-ups so often had, she again seemed to change. Unexpectedly she retreated from him, not dark and hostile now but nervous, very quiet, with nothing to say. Her eyes again took on a glassy, uncertain look, so that when at last it was time to stand and look in at the shop window, at the umbrellas, he knew that she wasn't really seeing them at all.

'Let's look at Sharman's instead, shall we? I think it's better there. They have better things. Better quality.'

Sharman's stood at the far end of the street, between the post office and the café where you could have coffee and the dough-men with currants for eyes and buttons on their waistcoats. He stared in at the window. There were no umbrellas in the window. There was a yellow sheaf of corn, with a shotgun standing near it. There was a leather bag and a dead pheasant lying beside it, all brilliant with brown and scarlet and green on its feathers. He stared at the pheasant and wondered why it was there. He supposed that somehow someone had shot it but quite how it had come to die in the window he couldn't imagine. Perhaps it had flown into the shop to escape from the man who was shooting it. The dead eye of the pheasant, like Gilly's, was dark and glassy.

It was funny to have a sheaf of corn in the window too. It was the first time he had seen a sheaf of corn in a shop window. He turned to ask Gilly about it. He found her staring dumbly across the street. Her eyes appeared to be in a sort of trance. He knew it was a trance because that was how the snake was when you played music to it: it became all lost and drowsy and sleepy-dead.

He said something about the umbrellas. After several seconds she said 'What?' and then went on staring glassily at the opposite side of the street. By now it had started to rain again. Thin bright spits were coming down. He started to try to put the umbrella up. Even when he managed to open it fully, with a sudden tight snap, she hardly noticed it at all. She seemed instead to be looking for someone either going into or coming out of the pub on the opposite side of the street. She was staring terribly hard and no one was there.

The umbrella sat on his head like a crimson mushroom. He

liked it like that, low down, a red tent to hide in. But when she suddenly came out of her trance and saw it she was very annoyed and said:

'Put that thing down for goodness' sake. Why will you act so stupid? We're going into the shop. You can't get into the shop like that, can you? Besides it's unlucky, putting an umbrella up indoors.'

Again he wanted to ask why it was unlucky. She simply snatched the umbrella from him and snapped it shut again. A moment or two later they were in the shop. It was rather dark in the shop. He sat on a high, thin-legged chair, by the counter. A lady in a white jumper floated out of the shadows at the back of the shop. She was very tall. The white sleeves of her jumper were long. Her arms spread out like wings.

He thought as he watched her that she too was like a swan. Suddenly there were rows of umbrellas on the counter. When they were unrolled they looked like dead birds with blue or green or red or black or speckled feathers. They reminded him of the dead pheasant in the window. He wanted to ask the lady in the white jumper about the dead pheasant and how it had come to be shot and died in the window. The lady in the white jumper seemed kind. She had a white necklace round her neck with beads shaped like big shining teeth. He wanted to ask about that too but every time he made up his mind to speak she was busy talking with Gilly, tall, out of reach, beyond him.

All the time they were talking he knew that Gilly was, in a sense, even farther away. She picked up the umbrellas one by one, stared at them and put them down again. She felt them dreamily and cautiously. They too might have been the feathers of dead birds. There was one which had a pattern of blue and orange all over it, just like the float that had fallen down the well. This was the one he wanted her to choose. In the end she chose a plain simple black one and the lady said:

'I always say in the end there's nothing like black. You can't beat it. It's got that elegant look. That is something. You can't go wrong with black.'

Even before she had finished speaking Gilly was saying:

'Would you wrap it up while I'm gone? I'll be back in two minutes – '

'But it's raining. Wouldn't you like to carry it?'

'Perhaps I will. No, just wrap it. I'll be back. James, sit still now, don't fidget. Talk to the lady – I just want to make this call across the street – Oh! yes and the bill. It'll give you time to make out the bill.'

When Gilly had gone out of the shop James stared at the lady wrapping up, with her long swan-like arms and long white fingers, the black umbrella. He stared at her making out the bill. He stared too for long periods at the necklace, so that at last she said:

'Ah! you're looking at my necklace. All the children look at my necklace.'

'What is it made of?'

'Teeth. Sharks' teeth.'

He had heard of sharks. They were fishes. He thought they were very big fishes but this was the first time he ever knew that fish had teeth.

'Did you have to kill the shark to get the teeth?'

The lady laughed.

'No, no. Not exactly – '

'Did the dentist pull them out for you?'

The lady laughed again.

'He would have to be some dentist to pull teeth out of a shark.'

'Who pulled them out then?'

'Oh! I suppose somebody did – at some time – I never thought'.

'Have you ever seen a shark?'

The lady seemed to retreat a little. She started to fold away the various umbrellas that lay on the counter like so many green and red and black and speckled birds. No, she said, she had never seen a shark. Except of course in pictures.

'How do you know they're sharks' teeth then?'

Well, she'd never stopped to ask. She'd always sort of taken it for granted. That was what she'd been told and there it was.

'They look like claws.'

What did, the teeth? Oh! yes, so they did. Now she really came to look at them they did. Exactly like claws.

'I've got a book about the jungle which shows you all about claws. Eagles and tigers and leopards and polar bears.'

Oh! that was interesting. That must be a nice book.

'In it it says kill or be killed.'

Did it indeed? Well, that was interesting.

'It means it's the law. In the jungle. If you don't kill something else and eat it then something else eats you and you die. So you have to kill things first before something kills you or else if you're not quick – '

You caught it all ways, didn't you? the lady said. You hadn't much chance, one way or the other.

'Could you catch a shark with worms?'

Did he go to school yet? the lady said No? Perhaps it was time he did. Worms? Well, no, she supposed not –

'Would you want a float?'

Well, no, the lady didn't think so. She thought you would have to be very big and strong to catch a shark, terribly big and strong. Well, here was the parcel –

'Like Mr Pimm? He's strong. I could ask Mr Pimm to catch a shark for me.'

Ask Mr Who? Pimm? Was he a fisherman?

'Oh! yes, he's a fisherman. We go together sometimes. I caught a smoked salmon once. But not with Mr Pimm.'

The lady laughed again. She must, she said, go fishing with him some time. It must be nice to catch smoked salmon. To go out and catch smoked salmon, just like that, and come home and have it for lunch. That was the way.

'We don't have it when Mr Pimm comes to lunch. We have liver and bacon and fried onions when Mr Pimm comes.'

Came to lunch, did he, Mr Pimm? That was lucky. Who was Mr Pimm? She couldn't say that she'd ever heard of him. Did he live in the village?

'Oh! yes, he lives in the village but you don't see him very often.'

No? But if he came to lunch –

'Ah! but he comes in secret.'

Oh? In secret, eh?

'Only for me and Gilly. Gilly likes him too.'

Oh! Gilly liked him too, did she?

'She likes him but he doesn't come so often since Mr Ainsworth started to come.'

Oh! there was a Mr Ainsworth too, was there?

'Oh! yes, and Mr Monday.'

Three of them? It must be a bit crowded for lunch sometimes.

'Oh! they don't all come together for lunch. Mr Ainsworth nearly always comes at night.'

Oh! at night? Well.

'And sometimes in the afternoon. When they play games.'

When who played games?

'Gilly and Mr Ainsworth.'

Oh! they played games, did they? That was nice. What sort of games?

'Playing the piano and laughing and – '

Oh! yes?

'And sometimes undressing.'

Oh! really? Indeed? The lady suddenly picked up the parcel containing the umbrella and turned it over and over quickly, as if not knowing quite what to do with it. Instead of laughing again she gave a slight uneasy giggle. Then she put the parcel back again on the counter. Then she picked it up again. Well, this was the parcel. It had the umbrella in it, he understood? The black one. He could hold it until – she'd wrapped it nicely, he must hold it tight –

'What did you wrap it up for if it's still raining?'

Well, they usually wrapped things up. It was the custom.

'I like your necklace. It shines. It looks like a crown.'

The lady, with her long white fingers abstractedly fondling the necklace, seemed to come out of her retreat at last. Her eyes were very alert and bright and she laughed again.

'I'm glad you like it. Well, here's the parcel. Hold it tight.'

She leaned across the counter to give him the parcel.

'You smell nice.'

'Oh! do I? Thank you. It's my new perfume. Thank you.'

'It's just like Gilly when Mr Ainsworth has been.'

The lady, her long white fingers travelling round the teeth of the necklace in rapid scales, as on the notes of a piano, had nothing to say and could only laugh again.

In the bar of The White Hart the barman, Harry, a tall thin man with chocolate brown sideboards and short-sleeved yellow pullover and a half-burned cigarette in his mouth, stood behind the bar-counter polishing glasses with a crimson cloth. The bar, at that mid-morning hour, was otherwise empty except for a single customer in a soiled cream polo-necked sweater and creaseless baggy trousers that looked as if rudely knitted from unwanted shreds of flaky dark tobacco.

'Morning, madam. Something I can get you?'

'No, thank you. I didn't really – I just wondered if I could speak to Mr Ainsworth?'

'Ainsworth?'

The barman lifted an empty glass to the light. The customer in the soiled polo-necked sweater was drinking whisky. He lifted his glass too. The barman, open-mouthed, looked for several moments as if he would breathe on his glass. He then changed his mind and polished it with the cloth instead. Rain rapped sharply on the windows.

'Ainsworth? Arranged to meet him here?'

'He's been staying here.'

'Ainsworth?'

The barman picked up a second glass and held it up to the light.

'That's right.'

'Staying here? Long?'

'Oh! some time. Quite some time –'

'Ainsworth.'

The barman, still polishing the second glass, turned to the figure in the polo-necked sweater.

'What about you, Captain Drage, sir? You know just about everybody.'

'What name?'

'Ainsworth.'

The Captain stared at his glass.

'Ainsworth. Regular? Ainsworth? No, I draw a blank there. Most likely one of the summer crowd.'

Captain Drage sucked lovingly at his whisky. Out of a sort of suspended politeness he gazed dreamily at the minute orange level of what remained at the bottom of the glass and then drank that too.

'I don't think we've met.' He looked at Gilly with moist, charming eyes. 'Drage. Could I offer you a drink?'

'No, thank you.'

'Pleasure. Glass of sherry?'

'No, really, thank you.'

'No? Not even if I pressed you?'

The Captain laughed. It was a joke. She failed to see it as a joke.

'Well, what's no for the goose must inevitably be yes for the gander.'

It was another joke. The Captain was very fond of jokes. He laughed again.

'If he was in here very often the Captain would know him,' the barman said.

That was right, the Captain said. Little escaped his eye. He pushed his empty glass across the counter, looked at Gilly. He pleaded again to be allowed the pleasure of buying her a drink and seemed hurt at the shake of her head.

'Pity. Now if it was Miss Philpot, one could understand. She's reached the age of refusal.'

It was yet another joke. Gilly stared. The Captain laughed again.

'Where is the Philpot anyway?' The Captain looked crisply at his wrist-watch. 'Ten to twelve. It's about her witching hour.'

'She always goes to market on Tuesdays, Captain Drage. She never comes in till late.'

'Oh! don't rush away, miss, don't rush away. What name did you say again?'

The legs were interesting, the Captain thought. He'd noticed them at once when the girl first came in. Pretty legs, delicate. There was something interesting about the eyes too, though he couldn't say quite what.

'I just remembered,' the barman said. 'Appleton – we've had a Mr Appleton here. Some weeks now. You're sure it wasn't Appleton? You're sure you didn't make a mistake about the name – ?'

'No,' she said. 'I never made a mistake.'

The pretty, delicate legs disappeared through the door of the bar. The Captain watched them with approval and the barman polished another glass.

'Appleton – Ainsworth. I couldn't have made a mistake like that, could I. God, I couldn't have made a mistake in the name.'

She was carrying the new black umbrella across the park, on the way to church. The horizon had a white-grey autumnal collar of mist on it, like a ring of fur. James was carrying the old red umbrella. It was almost the only colour of any brightness in a windless afternoon of wet grass, trees still stooping under a long night rain, a river flowing full of muddy yellow cream.

She had allowed him to carry the red umbrella only as a great concession. It was hardly the thing for church. You didn't go to funerals with red umbrellas. Then at the last moment, just before they left the house, a dark rumble of thunder belched out from the mists across the park. Reluctantly she relented: he could take the umbrella if he liked but only then, she said, if he kept it well out of sight. At the last moment she made him change his anorak too. A bright blue anorak with a yellow lining wasn't the thing for church either, and she made him change it for a dark blue roll-top sweater.

In the morning there had been a post-card. It was almost eleven o'clock, long after breakfast, before the postman arrived. He snapped about rain, trains being late, a landslide somewhere down the track. She stood waiting, half irritable too, and actually said, as she took the post-card:

'Is that all? Nothing else? I mean – '

'Lady, I don't write the mail.'

'No, no. I didn't mean for us. I wondered if you had anything for Ainsworth – at The White Hart – '

'What name? Ainsworth? Never heard of it. They come and go there. Come and go.'

She turned, went into the house and slammed the door. She put the post-card on the mantelpiece without reading it. It had the same bright blue sky on it, the same sand, the same big green palms.

'What were you saying to the postman about Mr Ainsworth? Is Mr Ainsworth coming back?'

'Mind your own business. Your ears are too big. Too big by half, I tell you, too big by half.'

Now, she with the black umbrella carefully rolled up, he with the crimson one flapping continuously undone as he used it for a walking stick, they were almost the full distance across the park, with the squat stone tower of the church in sight beyond the stone bridge that went over the river and the tall yellow-leaved limes that stood over the bridge.

'And not in puddles! If I've told you once I've told you a million times. Not in puddles!'

He wanted to ask about Mrs Barton. He had seen, that morning, a big long black car slowly driving across to the farm and then, some time later, driving away again. He understood one thing about being dead: it meant you weren't there any more. What he didn't understand about was where you went when you were dead and they came with the big long black car and took you away.

Reflectively he poked the ferrule of the red umbrella into a puddle and, turning it round and round in the water, stirring the reflection of himself, thought about the dead.

'If you go into puddles once more I'll take it away from you. You shan't have it. I warn you! I'll take the wretched thing away.'

When they came at last to the curved stone bridge over the river James stopped and bent down and looked through the spaces between the balustrades to where, below him, the river was flowing away in flood, a churning yellow spate.

'Is the river going to the sea?'

'All rivers go to the sea. In time.'

'In time? How long does it take it to get there?'

'Watch what you're doing. How do I know how long it takes to get there? Don't lean over! You'll lose the umbrella. You'll fall in. And then where would you be?'

The necessity of answering the question didn't bother him at all and he said:

'Could I have a dough-man?'

'It's a fine time to ask for a dough-man. Just as we're going into church. No! Why?'

'I'm hungry.'

'You should have eaten your lunch up. You played about and messed and mucked it, didn't you? You didn't want it, did you? It was a perfectly good lunch. I warned you you'd be hungry.'

'I don't like stew.'

'Oh! we don't like stew. What do we like?'

'A dough-man.'

'God, a dough-man. A dough-man. A dough-man.'

'I won't eat it in church. I'll save it till we come out again.'

'Till we come out again. That'll be the day.'

'What day?'

'Don't ask me what day! The day of reckoning I shouldn't wonder. The day – God, how much are dough-men?'

Soon he was in the tea shop. He had two shillings in his hand. Gilly stood outside waiting. The strange, dark, splintered look was on her face again.

'The lady said I could have two dough-men.'

He held the two dough-men aloft, in a paper bag, laughing. Everything suddenly seemed splendid. Everything was right again.

'Where's the change?'

'The lady didn't give me any change.'

No change, no change, no change? So that was it? You went in for one thing and they gave you two and you got no change. That was how they worked it. You were too young to know. You were too young and simple and in no time they had you.

'I've a good mind to go back – working a thing like that on a child. A wangle like that. I've a good mind – no, it's too late now. They're teeming into church as it is. It's ten to four already.'

She walked, almost marched, ahead. He followed, the bag of dough-men in one hand, the umbrella trailing in the other.

'Wasn't I lucky to have two dough-men?'

'And keep that umbrella up. Keep it out of sight. If I half-catch you playing with it in church –'

It was all purple and white and gold and black in church. There was a long purple box and beyond it tall white candles burning in long gold sticks. All the people everywhere, on all sides, wore black. The lady who had worn the sharks' teeth round her neck was there in black too, but without the sharks' teeth today.

Gilly knelt on her knees and buried her face in her hands, exactly as if she were crying. He pushed the crimson umbrella far under the pew-seat, so that she shouldn't be angry. A man in black and white standing in a high place with a big brass bird in front of it, with folded wings, began to say things that floated after each other on long stony echoes. As he spoke Gilly seemed to bury her face deeper and deeper into her hands, as if she were crying once more, and he said:

'What are you crying for?'

His whisper was loud but she made no answer.

'Why are you crying? Are you crying for Mrs Barton?'

Without lifting her face from her hands she struck him sharply with her elbow. The blow might have been deliberately savage. The pain of it sprang through his body, up through his mind and into his eyes. His first impulse was to cry but somehow he managed not to cry. Instead he gave a hard sharp indrawn breath and she said:

'Shut your eyes. Don't you know where you are?'

He shut his eyes. He clasped his hands over them and it was all dark inside. Then he opened one eye and looked through his fingers and shut the eye quickly again. It was like a camera taking a picture. There was a flash of purple and white and gold and black, all bright, and then it was dark again.

He started to try for a second time the trick of looking swiftly, with one eye, through his fingers. He had forgotten

196

the paper bag with its dough-men inside and now, with a rustling crash, it fell to the floor. This time she didn't strike him with her elbow. As he opened both eyes he could see only her fist, clenched, tight-gloved, black with threat.

'One more sound,' she whispered, her voice black too, 'and I'll – '

He sat transfixed and rigid on the pew-seat, not daring to pick up the paper bag. Long stony echoes rose and pursued each other and quarrelled in the great vault of the church roof and fell and rose and died again. In a sudden interval of silence he heard the chatter of sparrow voices beyond an open window and the light sound of them was almost a mockery of the congregation at last rising from its knees with a smothered sigh. With her fist she prompted him to stand up. He stood up stiff, eyes and lips not moving. As he got to his feet he remembered the paper bag. He stooped to pick it up. Instantly her eyes turned on him, threatening again, dark and hostile. He remembered the time when her eyes had been dreamy and brown, like snails, and you couldn't tell, sometimes, whether she was listening or not. Now he couldn't for the life of him understand what had happened to change them so much.

He left the paper bag on the floor of the pew, not daring to pick it up. Its importance to him grew as the big purple box, borne on the shoulders of four men in black, approached down the aisle, and all the time he had a growing fear of leaving it there. As the box slowly approached, passed him and was borne away towards the outward shaft of light coming through the church door, a great hush came down on everything and he had a sudden odd vision of the two dough-men skulking in the paper bag, silent, embracing each other, afraid to make a sound.

'Wait. There's no need to rush. Let people go first. And don't forget your paper bag. Hold it carefully. Don't rustle.'

He felt small in a crowd of giants. The giants moved slowly, hemming him in, whispering and shuffling. It was like being in a slow black prison of skirts and trousers. Faces were far up, far beyond him. When he looked up to them he could see only the shadows of their chins. Once he thought he saw the lady who wore the sharks' teeth but the figure passed him, aloof, dark, its arms no longer like swans' wings, and there was no hint of recognition.

His sense of relief at being outside, free in the thin afternoon sunshine, prompted him to give a short whooping sound of escape and begin rustling at the paper bag. Gilly swooped on him like a dark bird, with hissing noises:

'Not in the churchyard. Not in public, not in the street. You'll eat them properly, when you get home.'

Soon they were going home. He was gradually freed from the prison of skirts and trousers. The sun, after a long struggle, had broken at last through the mist that had gathered low down on the horizon after night rain and now hung in the mist, a vast tender face of copper and rose. Below it, across the park and the fields, newer, whiter areas of mist were gathering, some long, like the airship his father had once told him about, some shorter, like sheep, but all white and ghostly. He stared in fascination at these shapes, clutching hard at his paper bag, and said:

'Look, all the clouds have come down to sit in the fields.'

'Oh! have they?'

They reached the bridge over the river. He wanted very much to stop at the bridge. The notion of the river driving and swirling and flooding onwards, down to the sea, fascinated him so much that he actually broke free and ran the last thirty yards or so to the bridge and was already clinging to the parapet over the open balustrades, peering over, when Gilly arrived.

'Watch what you're doing now. You wouldn't want to drop your paper bag in the river, would you?'

No, he said, but he wanted to sail a boat. He turned to pick up an empty cigarette packet from the gutter and she almost screamed:

'Not that dirty cigarette box. Take a stick or something, a leaf. Look, there's a conker shell.'

He picked up a conker shell. It was split in half and shaped like a round boat, pure white inside. He stooped and peered through the balustrades of the bridge and threw it into the water. Then he picked up a twig with a few half-brown leaves still on it and threw that in too. The conker shell leapt and danced on the creamy flood water and the twig raced up behind it, swimming and twisting. He knew suddenly that the twig would never catch the conker shell. It was a long way to the sea. The dancing green-and-white boat would be there first.

'Look, the conker shell's laughing. The twig can't catch it.' He danced excitedly up and down. 'The conker's the fastest. It's laughing.'

'Is it? It's lucky.'

Today everything was wrong; everything had to be so particular. Without another word he watched twig and conker shell racing each other downstream until at last the twig caught itself, strangled, against the bank, and the conker shell was too far away to be laughing any longer.

In that moment, the race over, he suddenly remembered something.

'I left the red umbrella.'

'What next? For pity's sake you'll be leaving yourself next. Where did you leave it then?'

'Under the seat.'

'One of these fine days you'll leave yourself and then you'll turn round and you won't be there.'

'I'll run and fetch it.'

'No, no. Wait. I'll come back with you.'

'I can run. I know where it is. I'll go.'

A moment later, free again, he was running back to the church, laughing too.

The door of the church was open. He went in. The long aisle was empty. The tall candles were still burning at the end of it, on the altar. There was no sound except the rustling of his paper bag.

A figure emerged from somewhere beneath the candles. It was all alone and black. It stood completely still and watched him as he walked up the centre of the nave. It held a thin stick in its hands and after watching him for some moments longer it moved, held up the stick and extinguished one of the candles. Then it stood still again, staring at him steadily.

At this moment he became aware of being afraid of two things: first of the figure itself, then of not being able to remember the pew where the umbrella was. He looked into one pew and then another and then a third. The rustling of his paper bag was followed by the clap of his feet as he stumbled up a pew-step. It was as if the bag had suddenly burst and there was a great echo.

The figure came down from the altar. It stopped and spoke. Its voice was a croak in a vast cavern. What, it said, was he looking for?

'An umbrella.'

Ah! umbrellas. If you had as many pounds as umbrellas people left in church you'd be worth a million. What colour umbrella? Where had he been sitting? The voice's echoes rumbled in the cavern.

'Red. I think we were sitting here.'

Red, eh? Well, that was easily seen.

Suddenly, for some reason, the figure seemed indifferent to all thoughts of umbrellas. It started to creep away. It was old, its feet imprisoned somewhere under the big black garment it wore.

When it finally reached the big wooden doors at the end of the nave it stopped and turned and spoke again. The voice now seemed to come from a greater distance and expand itself, with still greater echoes, into an even greater cavern than before.

When the boy had found the umbrella would he go out by the little door at the side?

'Which door? I've found the umbrella.'

The little one down there. On the left hand side. It was open. Would he go out that way? It was time to shut the big doors now.

'Yes.'

With the umbrella in one hand and the paper bag in the other he watched the big doors close. They met like slow black jaws. In the vast dark space of them the figure on its old creeping feet was suddenly no longer visible. For a fearful moment or two even the face was lost. By the time it had reappeared James was walking away, up the nave.

Not that door. Not that way. Didn't he know his left hand from his right?

'Oh! yes.' He stopped and turned and held up the paper bag.

Wrong hand, wrong hand. The one with the umbrella was the left.

'Oh! yes, I forgot.'

Just as well. Important to know the left hand from the right. Even if the one didn't know what the other was doing. Yes: the left was the right way. The figure laughed at this and the laugh echoed about and through the church like the cracking of a great dry nut.

That was the way people sometimes talked: in riddles, so that you couldn't understand them. But now he felt sure of his left hand and that the left way was the right way and so as not to forget it again he clutched the umbrella tightly, almost fiercely, as he went the rest of the way up the nave and then firmly to his left and then finally through the door at the side.

Now he was in the graveyard. All about him gravestones stood like sheep, grey, dead in the act of grazing. A few were lying down. Letters and words were printed on their faces that he couldn't read.

After staring at them for some moments he turned left, the way the umbrella led. He mustn't forget, as the figure in the church had said, the difference between his left hand and his right. The left was the umbrella; the right was the paper bag. He held the umbrella slightly aloft and felt secure.

He felt secure also because there was a path and he could follow that too. He didn't expect at that moment to see Gilly, the bridge, the shops in the village street. It was important to follow the umbrella and the path and in time he would arrive at things and places and people he knew.

Soon there was a long low stone wall in front of him, with a gate in it and a row of trees beyond it, tall but lopped at the tips and with leaves like floppy yellow handkerchiefs slowly dripping from the boughs. He went through the gate and turned left again. Beyond the gate was another path. It went slightly downhill and he followed that too.

Presently he heard a familiar sound. It was the sound of water running. Even before he had listened to it for several moments he knew too that it was the sound of the river. It excited him and he started running. After twenty or thirty yards he saw the river running below him, parallel with the path. It was the same muddy yellow, curdled, prancing stream that he had seen leaping under the bridge, taking his chestnut boat away.

He stopped to pick up a fallen tree branch. It was rather big and he put down first the umbrella and then the paper bag before he could pick it up. Then he hurled it two-handed into the river. It fell with a great splash and then raced away, a black arm crooked above the flood water.

After watching it for some moments he stooped to pick up the umbrella and the paper bag. At first, not thinking, he picked up the umbrella in his right hand. Then he stopped, not sure of his way. Then he remembered the figure in the church. He remembered what it had said and how it had laughed about it: that he mustn't forget the difference between his right hand and his left and that the left was the right one.

Suddenly it struck him that this was not merely odd but not true. If the right hand was right then the left hand couldn't be right as well. You couldn't have two right hands. There must be a difference because the figure in the church had said so. If the hand that held the umbrella was the left and that was right then could the other hand be right too? If he now picked up the umbrella in his right hand he could only suppose in fact that that was just as right as his left hand and he had only to follow it to come to the right place in the end.

He finally picked up the umbrella in his right hand and the paper bag in his left and started running. After ten minutes or so of running he found that the path suddenly went steeply downwards until it skirted the very edge of the river. On the bank above it there was now a wood. Through the trees at the crest of the wood the sun appeared, dancing and bouncing like an enormous scarlet ball. It was exactly as if he had thrown it up the bank and it was following him, in and out of the trees, as he ran by the river.

Soon he not only found the ball of sun exciting to watch but he discovered also that if he swung the umbrella over his head he could hit the ball and send it faster on its way. It was like playing ball with his father or Gilly. But now it made it more fun because the umbrella and the sun were the same brilliant colour of orange-red. They were part of each other. Once he actually stopped and for a moment or two played with the idea that if he opened the umbrella and swung it high enough he could catch the sun as you caught a fish in a net and if he shut the umbrella quickly enough he would have the sun inside and never let it out again.

He tried this briefly and found that it didn't work very well. The paper bag fell to the ground and one of the dough-men half fell out of the paper bag. After that he let the sun roll or bounce and dance along on its course while he occasionally aimed a great swish at it with the umbrella and helped it along.

He knew that if he kept on for a time like this, hitting the sun at such a pace on its way, he would presently arrive at the bridge. This must be so: the bridge was on the river. It was only when he suddenly realized that the sun was no longer a brilliant ball dancing beyond the woodland that he became puzzled and stopped altogether. The way the sun disappeared was rather like the figure in the church suddenly disappearing, faceless, into the two black jaws of the closing doors.

All at once it occurred to him that the sun was probably sleeping. Once his father had assured him that this was so: that at the end of the day the sun slipped round the edge of the world and went to sleep, just as everyone else did, for the night. This didn't at all mean that it wasn't there any more. It was very much there but it too had to rest and it wasn't until it had had a rest that it appeared again, fresh and real in the morning, in the way people did.

The idea of this kept him still untroubled. The sun was merely resting. Like everyone and everything else there were times when the sun naturally got tired. This undoubtedly was such a time. He supposed there were other times when it rested behind clouds, either briefly or for longer, according to whether the cloud was like a bird or an ice-cream or a bear. After its rest it would surely come out again, shining and fresh.

When it did come out again, appearing suddenly from a great

unrolling bank of mist, it seemed larger, closer, more a ball of crimson-orange fire than ever. The burning essence of its light lay with smouldering brilliance on trees and leaves and grass and the fast creamy flood course of the river. It transformed everything with a great glow that, above all, seemed to him very friendly.

Except for the prancing noise of the river it was remarkable also for a great stillness. He stopped and stood still and listened to it. The extraordinary thing was that when he stood still the sun stood still too. It was aware of him. It too was his friend. It was moving and stopping and doing as he did, all the time.

At this moment he realized suddenly how good it was to be by the river. It was marvellous to be beyond reach of the nagging, rasping, booming voices. It was a joy not to be told, in a bad-tempered snapping voice, what to do and what not to do; to escape, at last, from a world where all you did was wrong and you didn't know why it was wrong. He couldn't think why people weren't always the same, why they were all sweetness and kindness one day and then, without explanation, sour and dark and revengeful the next.

The wood suddenly ended. Beyond it was a broad flat meadow crossed by hedgerows and a dyke feathered with reeds. He divined that this was the meadow where, earlier in the afternoon, clouds had come down to sleep. Now the only clouds he could see were gathered far off across the fields, more than ever like sheep waiting to be counted, and over them the sun, free of mist now, was less sleepy and crimson, more and more golden and awake.

All the time he kept steadily to the river bank. As the world of church and voices and bridge and voices receded he began to think, presently, of Mr Pimm. Mr Pimm was down at the sea. Mr Monday was down at the sea too. Both Mr Pimm and Mr Monday, having been away so long, seemed at first a little vague and far away but he didn't doubt that they were having a good time and that soon, with luck, he would be with them, his old mates, and hearing all about it.

Presently he stopped, sat down on the grass, set the umbrella and the paper bag down beside him and picked up a stone. This stone was a shell and he put it to his ear. Immediately he could hear the strange noises you always heard in a shell: the sea, waves, the wind, voices.

Clear as anything was the voice of Mr Pimm. You could fairly hear the spit in it. It was all smoky and full of shag and grunty breathing. It had been a rare spell of weather by the sea, Mr Pimm said. Rain? No, no rain. Hadn't had no rain, had they, Monday old sport, since the week afore last? Not a bleedin' drop.

Yes, the fishin' had been pretty fair. He and old Monday went out at nights a good deal. There was a good lot of cod about and Mr Monday had caught some dabs. Oh! yes they had them fried for breakfast. Very good landlady who cooked for them, with chips and tomato sauce. Oh! yes, and prawns too. You got the prawns at the little stall by the harbour, and the whelks and the mussels too, where the lady who had gold earrings in her ears measured out the prawns and shrimps and things in a pint pot. You could smell the fish smell and the drying sea-weed and boats lying on the mud when the tide was out, all strong and thick and salty on the air.

They'd missed their old matey, he and Monday. When was he coming down? Pretty soon now? That was the stuff to give the bleedin' troops, Mr Pimm said. They could do with some news. Their digs, the place where they were staying, was just a bit along from the harbour, near where the old lifeboat house was. You couldn't miss it. It was where the old cannon stood and the fish nets hung out to dry.

How had things been with him? Mr Pimm said. Rough? Well, have to take it with the smooth, like they all did. What was that? Fed to the teeth with it? He'd better come away then for a few days, hadn't he, and make a change? Nothing like a change. Good as a bleedin' rest. He'd better come afore the weather changed its mind too. He could take it from Mr Pimm the grub was as good as you'd get anywheres and the landlady never minded what you asked for. No complaints, everything free and easy. Far? He'd be there in no time at all! Like Mr Pimm said, it was just there by where the old cannon stood, not so far from where the river come into the sea. He knew the place, didn't he? It was where there was a bridge and it could screw round on a swivel like, Mr Pimm said, so that ships and boats could go through.

He knew the place. The vision of it, remembered from when he had once seen it with his father and had marvelled at the way the bridge swung and opened to give sea passage to small ships rose in his mind with dazzling clearness. He could see the ships and the cannon and the lady with the earrings selling the prawns. He could smell the sea-weed, the boats and the sea-mud drying in the sun.

He picked up the umbrella, making sure that it was in his left hand. Then, with the ball of sun safe on its glowing course across the meadows and Mr Pimm and Mr Monday safe in the paper bag, he started to walk again.

He was all set, now, for the sea. He knew, now, that it was only beyond the next bend of the river.

Gilly leaned on the bridge, waiting. The postman came from the direction of the park on a red post office bike, whistling. He stopped on the bridge and without getting off the bike he too leaned on the bridge, supporting himself with one hand.

'All on your lonesome?'

'Just waiting.'

The postman hitched his post-bag farther across his shoulder, looking at her. She was leaning with her back to the bridge. He had been used to seeing her in the mornings, in her dressing-gown, hair unbrushed, mouth without lipstick. Now her dark blue woollen dress and long new outstretched black umbrella gave her a certain elegance. He stood surprised.

'Sorry there's nothing for you this afternoon.'

She was quick to grasp at the word sorry and the corners of her mouth twitched in a smile. It broadened still further when he suddenly went on to say that he was sorry about the morning too but she knew how it was. Landslide, mail all held up, weather, enough to drive you round the twist. He was afraid he'd –

'I was a bit hasty myself.'

They smiled at each other. Then she looked down the long straight line of the umbrella to where the ferrule met the wet gravel on the bridge. He followed the line the umbrella took and with it the line of her legs. They were very good legs, the postman thought, and the tips of her black patent shoes were splashed with mud.

'Funeral go all right?'

'A lot of people there.'

He looked down at her legs again. She was aware of it and moved the umbrella the merest fraction.

'Saw the wreaths going in this morning. Scores.'

'Hundreds.'

'For a woman who never went anywhere she'd got a lot of friends.'

She made a tiny circle in the wet gravel with the ferrule of the umbrella.

'You can stay at home and be friendly.'

The postman grinned. He'd never thought of that. He was out and about all the time, himself. He'd have thought it might have been a bit boring, at home, like her, you know, all day long.

'All depends what you mean by boring.'

She smiled again and started to make a slightly larger circle in the wet gravel with the ferrule of the umbrella. He stared at the umbrella and her legs again.

'What was that name,' he said suddenly, 'you were asking about this morning?'

The umbrella became frozen. Her lips were thin.

'Was I asking about what?'

'Some name. A letter. Some name like – '

'Me? A name? I didn't think I was.'

'Only,' he said, 'I got one here for Appleton. Was that it? Was that the name?' He took a letter from his bag and held it out, between the two middle fingers of his left hand, 'c/o The White Hart. Appleton.'

'Doesn't mean a thing to me.'

'London post-mark.'

He moved to put the letter back into his post-bag. She moved too, shifting the umbrella with apparent indifference from one hand to the other.

'Could I see the writing?'

The postman held out the letter again. Without touching it she stared at it, almost aloof, for several seconds. There was nothing in the entire world she could compare with the writing on the envelope.

'No, it's nobody's writing I know.'

Suddenly she lost all aloofness. She looked down at the umbrella and then half over her shoulder and then completely away from him, uncertainly, in the direction of the village.

'Didn't go down to the crematorium then?'

'No, we didn't go. I had a job to keep him quiet in church as it was.'

'Ah! yes, James. Didn't see him in the park or up the road nowheres.'

'He's gone back to the church for an umbrella.'

The postman seemed about to make an effort to push himself and his bike, boat-wise, off the bridge. He hung poised, hand outstretched.

'Want me to tell him to get a move on if I see him?'

'He'll be here.'

'Met somebody to play with.'

'He'll come.'

'Or talk. Great one for talking, that boy. I used to see him talking to the electricity men. Ten to one he's chatting somebody up in the village somewhere.'

'Let him chat.'

'Best way. Leave 'em alone and they'll come home, I always say. Bringing their tails behind 'em.'

'That's what they say.'

'I got four. I should know. Kids, they know where home is.'

The postman seemed about to make another effort to launch himself and his bike from the bridge. Again he hung poised, staring at the elegant line of her umbrella, her shoes and her legs. Again she was aware of it and slightly moved the ferrule of the umbrella, this time drawing a triangle in the gravel. The postman looked at the triangle, then across the meadows where long horizontal rolls of mist hung like white suspended pillows, and then back at the triangle. He watched while she drew a cross through the triangle and then said:

'Going to be foggy tonight.'

'Think so?'

'Got to expect it. Time of the year.'

She supposed so.

'We've had the summer. Three frosts this week.'

Without a word she stood with her head to one side, in an attitude not merely of listening but of listening to something, a voice, a sentence, a note of music, of summer, far away.

'That's it,' the postman said, 'winter round the corner.'

She supposed so. Not that she cared. She wouldn't be here much longer anyway.

'No?' The postman, nose quickened again, spoke as if much surprised. 'They coming back then?'

According to the postcard this morning, yes, they were coming back. Ten days from the time the card was posted. A week from now.

'Well, he looks well and happy enough. They won't be able to say he don't.'

She supposed he did. She supposed they would too. Plenty of sun. No responsibility.

'Wonderful, what you can do with money.'

Suddenly, turning her head to look across the meadows she became, for the first time, uneasy. A sharp run of mist thickening and rising quickly swallowed the ball of sun. An impression that the afternoon was already later by some hours started to oppress her, at the same time bringing a chill to the air. In a few seconds the fog marched forward like a wall of ghosts, cutting off the green of meadows, the flare of autumn boughs and at last the curl of the river, like a severed yellow worm.

'It's like a cold hand on you suddenly,' she said. 'I'd better walk part of the way back with you.'

The postman got off his bike to walk with her. The air was chilly. His breath, grey as a puff of smoke, added to the swirl of fog. In a few seconds the afternoon, its daylight and its suspended air of summer died completely. The quietness, away from the noisy flood of the river, seemed deathly.

'Mind the kerb here,' the postman said. 'Meaning, you can't see a hand in front of you.'

She felt her way forward with the ferrule of her umbrella, lost, hardly sure of the division between path and road until suddenly the postman clutched at her arm, steadied her and guided her like a child. For some moments she felt as if handcuffed to his arm, a groping prisoner, gripped by a chill terror of being actually trapped and drowned in fog. Then she suddenly heard the postman say:

'Blimey, would you believe it?'

In another instant the sun was shining. She saw the fog roll itself up, like a blanket, and swirl away, leaving blue areas of sky.

'That's how it comes up from the river. Up and down in no time. Up and down.'

'Where is that boy now?' she said. 'For heaven's sake where is that boy?'

In bright sunshine the church, at the end of the village street, stood out with brilliance, its stone cream-white, a square loaf of homely bread.

The postman halted his bike. Under a big yellow elm at the end of the churchyard a queue of schoolchildren were waiting for a bus. The churchyard stood deserted except for several jackdaws hopping from gravestone to gravestone. Leaves fell like yellow snow from the elm and the postman leaned his bike against the churchyard wall.

'I'll go and round him up for you. Probably playing with some kids back there.'

The postman opened the gate and started to walk across the churchyard. Jackdaws flew lazily up, clipped over a few headstones and alighted again. She called after the postman:

'It's a red umbrella – you can't –'

She walked up and down, her own umbrella nervous on the path. A bus arrived. She watched half the queue of children climb into it, heard a bell ring. The postman came out from the main porch of the church, looked this way and that and then disappeared behind the tower. The bus disappeared too and in what remained of the bus queue two girls struggled with a boy, giggling, knocking his cap off.

The postman appeared again. Jackdaws again rose, flopped from stone to stone and again alighted, arrogant, never far away. The postman started to walk up the church path, towards the street, then changed his mind, walked some way back and then changed it again.

'The big doors are locked,' he said. 'The side door's open – '

'You mean he's not – ?'

'The verger saw him. He took the umbrella and went. Twenty minutes ago.'

'Oh! my God he must be there.'

A second bus arrived. As it pulled up a boy's cap flew over the church wall. There was a long crackle of laughter. A boy vaulted the low stone wall and a bell rang. The bus started, giving off hysterical laughter, the boy running behind to catch it.

'What exactly did the verger say?'

'He remembers telling him to go out by the side door.'

'He must .be in the street somewhere. We could have asked the children. They've gone now.'

'No, there's two left.'

Two girls still waited at the bus stop. The postman walked over to them, spoke for a few moments and then came back.

'One girl says she remembers seeing a boy walking on the church wall. But not with an umbrella.'

'That could be him, walking on the church wall. He'd lose the umbrella anyway. He'd drop it somewhere.'

The postman got on his bike.

'I'll look all the way round – all round the back.'

The postman disappeared. She walked up and down, nervously prodding the umbrella into the path. The two girls at the bus stop stared. She suddenly recalled the cake shop, half-started to walk down the street towards it and then saw a woman pushing a pram overloaded with loaves, bags of apples, cabbages, an old can and two children coming up the path.

'Lost who? Well, they was two on 'em licking the steam off the cake shop window just now. A boy and a girl.'

She almost started to run.

'Drive you scatty. Disappear like bloody eels afore your back's turned. And sit still, blast you! You'll have me in the gutter.'

The postman, appearing suddenly from a side lane on his bicycle saved her from running. Two children, a boy and a girl, hand in hand, came up the street. A heavy, grey-haired man, jovial, in moss-green tweeds, paused in the act of getting into a car and called with stentorian voice across the street:

'How are the chrysanthemums?'

She recognized Captain Drage.

'He means me,' the postman said.

'Any anemone centres this year?'

'Not this year. I give 'em up.'

'I've got you on a plate,' the Captain said. His face laughed with fire. 'Practically got you scuppered.'

'The show,' the postman said. 'He always tries to beat me at the show.'

'What's the secret mixture this year?' The Captain's fascination at a possible answer was so great that he now gave up the notion of getting into the car and started to come across the street. 'Gin and something? I swore it was old brandy last year.'

'Not seen a little boy with a red umbrella?' the postman said.

'No. What's he supposed to be doing? Waving the warning flag?' The Captain laughed uproariously, at the same time half-raising his green tweed hat. 'Belong to you, madam?'

'Yes. No, no, not really –'

'Ah! Good God, it's you. Of course. We met. In The White Hart. How could I forget?' In sudden recognition the Captain beamed with charm, then went on with new, heavier jocularities. 'Steer clear of this feller. Don't let your little boy be part of it. What is it this year? Come on, postie, come on, come clean. Guinness? I tried mine on whisky and purple hearts for a time but they wouldn't stand up straight! Couldn't hold their heads up! Much trouble with leaf miner?'

The postman stood silent.

'Like an oyster, this feller.'

'That woman said she saw –'

'Small boy coming up the street now,' the Captain said. 'Eat-

ing a pink ice-cream. That him? They all eat ice-cream in the
street nowadays. Can't tell one from t'other. Not him?'

'He's smaller than that. About six – '

'Too much nitrogen, I suppose, in the purple hearts? Made
'em all look like reeds shaken in the wind.' Abruptly the Captain
arrested his flow of laughter. 'You serious about this boy? You
mean you've lost him?'

'I think the Captain knows your people,' the postman said.

'Ah! Yes. Good God, of course I do. Ah! yes, the Tangerines.'
The joke flared brightly. The Captain took off his hat again,
looked inside it and put it on again. 'How are they doing out
there? Pretty warm, Tangier, I suppose. Oh! it's their boy is
it? I thought it was a girl they had. Well, if he's gone absent
without leave we must get him back into the guard-room. That's
clear. Where was he last seen?'

'He'd been to this funeral,' the postman said, 'he went back
for an umbrella – '

'Ten to one he's at your place,' the Captain said. 'Red umbrella, eh? Using the damn thing to shade the blooms, I expect.
Trying to hold 'em back.' The continual skein of jokes amused
the Captain so much that he played with it like a kitten. 'Like
the girl who went into the perfume shop. "Got anything to
hold 'em back?" she said. Always been a favourite joke of
mine. Of course you have to see the girl – '

'I'm worried, I'm getting worried – '

'Never worry about children, girl. They have an instinct.
They're animals. Their noses tell them.'

'You don't know this one. He's fly – Oh! my Lord, yes, the
sharks' teeth – '

The Captain stood amazed. None of his own jocularity
matched for a moment the singular madness of sharks' teeth.
His mouth fell open. For fully half a minute, as he watched
Gilly running, it made no sound. It was only some moments
after she had disappeared into the shop across the street that
he suddenly said:

'Good God, the girl's distraught.'

'Sharks' teeth?' the postman said. 'What did she mean by
sharks' teeth?'

The Captain, not laughing now, confessed himself scuppered.

'Sharks' teeth? Hell. Did she say sharks' teeth?'

He started to stride across the street, jokes, chrysanthemums and purple hearts forgotten. As Gilly reappeared from the shop, her face blank of expression, brown eyes sunk in a mask of white, he said:

'Was I hearing properly just now? Sharks' teeth?'

'It was just a necklace – the woman – he saw the woman wearing it in the shop.'

'Curious thing for a boy –'

'He talked such a lot about it – I just thought –'

The Captain seemed suddenly to address himself, rather than anyone else, with vigorous reproof.

'We must get ourselves organized. No use standing here. The thing to do is to keep a base. Not to move from base. Where were you when you saw him last?'

'On the bridge.'

'Then back to the bridge. At the double. Back to base.'

'Yes, but he could be anywhere – miles by now –'

'Back to base.' The Captain was suddenly taut with efficiency, keen to forge into action. 'I'll take the north end of the street. You get back to the bridge. It's if he comes back to the bridge and finds you're not there that the trouble starts – Ah! there's the Philpot.'

He waved a broad hand of greeting. From the other side of the street a figure in denim trousers the colour of cow manure, a red flannel shirt, a yellow neckerchief and black gum boots folded over at the tops like a labourer's waved in reply. The face of Miss Philpot had an extensive red and purple brilliance broken by distinct dark moustaches on her upper lip. She came across the street with manful strides, hands in the frontal pockets of her trousers, a cigarette glued at an angle to her lower lip. The eyes, brought to perpetual watering point by smoke, glowed with a blue moist innocence that was somehow lost and sad. She coughed with the dry bark of an old horse condemned to long winters in sodden fields.

'Ah! Miss Philpot. Haven't seen small boy running loose? Red umbrella –'

'I see millions of kids. Swarming all over the damn place. Red umbrella?' She coughed, ejected the cigarette from her mouth by sheer force of breath and somehow caught it, before it fell, in a quivering hand. 'Good God.'

'He's about six,' Gilly said. 'Yes, he's got this red umbrella – '

'Bloody good distinguishing mark. Ought to be easy enough. They mostly look like dirty little flies crawling about.'

'Belongs to this young lady here. Well, if you see him – Where's the post? Ah! there you are, postie. You'll be around?'

'Just going into the office now, sir.'

'Good man. If you find him see that he sticks here, by the post.' The Captain found irresistible the temptation to untangle another joke. 'That's it, nail him to the post.'

'I will, sir.'

'Where's that damn girl careering off to?' The words were blasted from Miss Philpot's flabbily quivering lips between hard rattling coughs. 'Why the panic?'

'Back to the bridge. She last saw him there.'

'No need to run like a bloody deer if she did.'

Miss Philpot's cough was like the shabby bark of a dog roughly roused by something hostile. It seemed to split open the otherwise tranquil village street so fiercely that it brought a butcher running to his shop door with a cleaver in one hand and a half severed lump of flesh and bone in the other.

'I'll get my steed. I'll go with her.'

Miss Philpot strode back across the street. A half rusty skeleton of a cycle, her steed, weighed down by a basket at the front and a carton of tins and bottles at the back swayed into action as she cocked over it a swinging beefy leg. The exertion caused her to cough with lumbering barks again and to spit between the barks with something like venom, so that she failed completely to hear the Captain's final injunctions about the bridge:

'Make her stay at base! Not to move – that's the drill.'

The heavy skeleton of Miss Philpot's steed, propelled by coarse booted legs, surged forward up the street. The Captain followed its course for some moments without speaking. It finally seemed to remind him of something. It was the war, he suddenly said, and he turned with another joke to the postman:

'Always remember how she turned out at the first air-raid. By the time she got gas-cape, gas-mask, tin-hat, whistle and whisky bottle strapped to the bike you could bet Jerry was back over Bremen. Always last at the turn-out. The chaps used to call her arse-end Aggie.' The Captain stood watching the muscular cycling figure of Miss Philpot as it reached that of Gilly, half-running at the far end of the street. He laughed, appropriately saving yet another joke until the last: 'Always said she had the parson's nose for disaster.'

The wood came to an abrupt end on a sharp ledge of land. The horizon became wide, with an immense space of pale blue sky stretched above and across it, tent-wise. Below this lay the sea. It was clear that it was the sea for two reasons: it was everywhere an expanse of grey-white waves, with minute white crests on them, as you always saw it in pictures, and also because here and there, dotted among the waves, were dark boats and sometimes, even darker, ships without sails.

James sat on the grass by the open ledge, and while looking at this vision of sea, decided to eat a little more of Mr Monday. He took Mr Monday out of the paper bag. It wasn't too hard to bring himself to eat Mr Monday. The figure of Mr Monday, as compared with that of Mr Pimm, had always been a little confused and vague. He had never spoken much with Mr Monday. The amount of communication between himself and Mr Monday had always been a little thin. Mr Monday, except for his broken arm, had never achieved the robust, spitting, guttural, lovable reality of Mr Pimm. His voice was never there. Accordingly it wasn't easy to tell Mr Monday that he was about to be eaten and in the end it didn't seem to matter.

Munching on Mr Monday's left leg James sat with contentment and looked down at the wide grey-white expanse of sea. His confidence that it was Mr Monday's left leg he was eating arose from the fact that he had sat Mr Monday on the grass, facing outwards over the ledge, so that he too could look at the sea. Mr Monday's severed leg was clearly on the umbrella side. Mr Pimm was sitting on the other.

Presently it became clear that there was something odd about what he supposed was the sea and also about the boats and ships that sailed there. It came slowly to him that this was not the sea: that instead it was a flat stretch of marshland covered with packed low cloud. You never knew what shapes the clouds would take from day to day and now, he thought with great surprise and wonder, they had taken on the look of the sea. Another great surprise was that the boats on the waves were not boats; nor were there any ships. The boats were black cattle revealed as contentedly munching between odd gaps of cloud The ships without sails were two giant scoopers, orange-coloured, the nearer working on a dyke.

This, he thought, was more wonderful than the sea. With fascination he watched the giant orange arm of the scooper rise, the tip at first half hidden in mist and then, groping upwards, carrying away a pair of muddy, dripping jaws. Now and then the cabin of the scooper became clear of mist too. It was a great swivelling box, with a man in it. When cloud swirled in the man disappeared. The scooper became a huge clockwork toy, working on its own. Then the mist momentarily rolled back again and there was the man, back as if by magic, working the levers with big gloved hands.

His discovery about the cattle and the scoopers brought him the discovery also that it wasn't very late yet. Men were still working. The sun had disappeared again, swallowed somewhere by the sea of cloud, but now and then he caught a touch of light dimly reflected in a broken stretch of water in the dyke. Then he made another discovery. Nearer to him, much nearer than the scoopers, in the last of the fields below the ledge, sat a third object. It looked at first like a windmill that the wind had uprooted, carried away and dumped down at last, sails wrecked and askew, half in cloud.

He pondered for some time on this object while eating Mr Monday's other arm. Now and then the mist crept in, exactly as a wave creeps in across a shore, and half-drowned the object, leaving only the wrecked sails exposed. He was about to convince himself that this was a wreck when suddenly the cloud drew away, abruptly lifted itself and left the sails newly exposed in a shaft of sun. Before the cloud whipped across the sun and wiped it out again he suddenly knew what the object was: the wreck of an old harvest binder, abandoned, sails tattered, at the gateway of a field.

It was exactly, he told himself and then Mr Pimm and then what remained of Mr Monday, like the one Mr Barton had in the barn, half-derelict too and unwanted. Mr Barton sometimes let you climb into the seat of it. As you sat there, in the shadows of the barn, you could imagine you drove an engine, a plane, a racing car. You could even imagine, he now told Mr Pimm and Mr Monday, that you were driving the great scooper.

Looking from the binder to the scooper, emerging from time to time like a monster out of the mist, he wondered if there were fish in the waters of the dyke. He imagined the scoop as a great net, bringing fish to land. In another rise of mist he saw a cloud of sea-gulls rising and crying, white and blue, about the scooper. Excitedly he called the attention of Mr Pimm and what remained of Mr Monday to the remarkable fact that the scooper was fishing. Every time the great jaws came out of the water they were loaded with fish and Mr Pimm distinctly said blimey, what would they think of next and how he fancied a bit of haddock for tea.

He watched the scooper for a long time. At last it stopped. The man in big gloves climbed down from the cabin. Then he walked some distance along the bank above the dyke and got on to a blue motor-bike. When the motor-bike started there was a puff of strong blue smoke in the air.

When the motor-bike had disappeared there were fewer seagulls about the scooper. Most of them were swallowed in mist. Slowly, after a time, the mist began to lift a little, but irregularly, so that islands of it were left scattered across the marsh. The mist lifted mysteriously, without wind, and from somewhere there came the small barking of a dog.

James put Mr Pimm and what remained of Mr Monday back into the paper bag. Then he grasped the paper bag in his right hand and the umbrella in his left and started to walk down the slope towards the marsh. At the foot of the slope ran a narrow track and beyond the track lay the field where the binder stood.

He climbed on to the binder and sat on the seat. He made buzzing cracking noises, as of engines starting up. He made swishy, windy sounds, as of sails beating into corn. He spat over the side of the binder and looked over his shoulder, watching falling sheaves.

After ten minutes or so of this he called 'Whoa!' and the binder stopped. He climbed down from the seat and tinkered with a nut on a wheel. To his joy there was actually a rusted spanner lying loose in the grass. He got hold of it and lay on his back underneath the binder and tinkered with another wheel. From somewhere quite a distance off the dog barked again, testily.

The mist came down again. Under the binder canvas it was like being in a house, all alone and sheltered and shut away. There was actually a sheaf of corn there, still dry but soft, a spongy cushion. In the intervals of tinkering with machinery he sat on it and spat again and imagined how tough it all was and how he'd never get things working. He put a length of old straw in his mouth and chewed on it and sometimes sucked, puffing smoke. The entire enclosure under the canvas was a new world marvellously far distant from all voices except, at broken intervals, the little voice of the dog.

He forgot about the sea. Like Mr Pimm said, it wouldn't run away. This was his home, under the shelter of the binder. Once or twice he peered out from under the canvas, looking this way and that. There was no one in the wide world, now the driver of the scooper had gone home, to molest him, to tell him what to do or what not to do, to scold or warn or punish or annoy.

The voice of the dog seemed presently to come much nearer. In a funny sort of way the mist seemed to wrap it up. It was like the dog barking in a bag. When he looked out from under the canvas there was nothing to be seen except mist. It was as if the dog wasn't really there at all, but only the bark of it.

Then he heard, suddenly, another voice. It was a woman's, scolding. He thought of Gilly, shrill, scolding too.

'Come out of that! Inquisitive, inquisitive. Not in there! Inquisitive boy, bad boy.'

He felt uneasy and guilty but not afraid. He wondered how the woman had found him there, in his hiding place. Her scolding voice was suddenly like that of all the others, sharp, accusing, breaking in on the world he lived in. He laid the spanner in the grass. He picked up Mr Monday and Mr Pimm in the paper bag and then the umbrella, ready to run.

He was aware of the dog, near now snuffling in the grass. The voice of the woman scolded again:

'No, now. You heard, didn't you, you heard? Inquisitive boys are bad boys, you hear me? You know what I say. Out of there!'

The dog was snuffling about the wheels of the binder, picking up scent. Its voice sounded like panting bellows, large. It seemed to lap up great mouthfuls of air and mist and grass and straw. While still invisible it seemed like a figure both grotesque and hostile. It would discover, bite and even eat him.

It appeared finally as a toy, a puppet, a clipped lamb, all white. It appeared suddenly under the canvas of the binder, curious and then affronted. It looked down on him with disdain, as at a mongrel, lost and skulking. It gave him a few further glances of pity and then sniffed, first at his feet and legs and then, coldly, at his hands and face. It ignored them all, suddenly, for the paper bag.

It snatched at it. James snatched back and the dog snatched in return. It might at first have been playful. Then the dog growled. His nose foraged at the mouth of the bag. A fear that Mr Monday and Mr Pimm were about to be golloped up made James snatch the bag away, high now, over his head. The dog regarded this as a gesture of playfulness and laughed openly, with a panting whimper, half sitting up to beg. As the boy lifted the bag still higher the dog sat completely upright, front paws dancing, pink tongue laughing and darting.

The voice of the woman scolded from out of the mist: 'Georgie! You hear me, don't you? If you get dirty coatsie there'll be no meatsie. No bonesie. You hear me? No bonesie, no walksie tomorrow.'

The dog laughed, begging. In the voice of the woman pretending playfulness, exploring the mist, the boy caught the echo of all other voices, pretending one thing, concealing another.

He decided to give the dog a piece of Mr Monday. He could spare the other leg. He started to open the paper bag and the dog barked in a yell of joy. The severed leg of Mr Monday hung in air. The dog yelped again, laughing, prancing up and down. From out of the mist the voice of the woman scolded new threats and at last the dog rose and took the leg of Mr Monday in a neat, single grab.

'No more now. Off, off! No more – I can't spare any more. That's my supper.'

The dog, finding Mr Monday satisfying, sat on his haunches, paws playful, begging for more. His sudden act of growling might have been playful too but it was enough to alarm the boy into breaking off Mr Monday's arm, leaving him limbless altogether. A spasm of sadness at losing so much of Mr Monday and seeing him suddenly so defenceless made him screw up the paper bag and say suddenly, fiercely, into the dog's face:

'She'll beat you if you don't go back. Go on, go back. She'll beat you. No meatsie, no bonesie, nothing. She'll take it all away –'

The dog snatched at Mr Monday's remaining arm and snuffled in the same moment at the paper bag. In despair the boy leapt to his feet, holding the bag high over his head. All at once, as if by a miracle, the woman clapped her hands.

The clash of them split through the mist like a signal. Suddenly cowed, the dog became lamb-like, limp. It gave a final docile, delicate sniff at the air and then squeezed itself out from under the binder wheels. From somewhere more distantly in the mist the woman's voice sounded almost musical:

'Good Georgie. Good boy. There's my lamb. That's my treasure. Mumsie doesn't like to hurt but sometimes Mumsie has to if boys are – there, there, run now. Keep to the path!'

Under the shelter of the binder James again took Mr Pimm and what remained of Mr Monday out of the paper bag. He looked at them for some time without speaking. Then he picked up the rusty spanner, and put it to his ear like a telephone.

Indistinct buzzings and echoes told him presently that Mr Pimm was on the other end. Beyond these noises he could distinctly hear the sound of the sea.

How were things? he asked Mr Pimm

Mr Pimm said they were half-tidy like, if you knew what he meant. The weather was dodgy, though, sort of. What was it like back up there, with him?

Bit misty.

Mushroom weather, Mr Pimm said. Had any lately?

'No, but he was going to have a few for supper tonight. With bacon and sausage and fried bread.

That was the stuff to give the troops, Mr Pimm said. Were they horse ones? or the real natives? The little 'uns? The real thing?

The real thing.

Better munch up then, Mr Pimm said, afore too many people fell over theirselves, getting their feet in the gravy.

Too right, matey. Better munch up.

He started to munch up. He divided the rest of Mr Monday into mushrooms, bacon, sausages, and fried bread. There was plenty of gravy and he hastened to dip Mr Monday's head in it. The mushrooms were all the better for plenty of pepper and salt on them but he kept Mr Monday's three waistcoat buttons until last. They made very good blackberry tart, for afters, with cream.

When he had finished eating he lay down and put his head on the old dry sheaf of corn. The sheaf was rather like a mouldy pillow, damp but comfortable. He lay on his back, with a straw in his mouth, and now and then puffed at it, like Mr Pimm. Among other things he thought about the little dog. It was worse than awful, like Mr Pimm said, being a dog. It was even worse than being a boy. You couldn't do anything at all without somebody, some woman, scolding at you that you wouldn't have no bonesie and no meatsie and no walksie either if you didn't behave and do as she wanted. There was no freedom for a dog. It must be awful being a dog. He was glad he wasn't a dog, having to eat another dog.

When he went to sleep at last it was to the distant sound of sea-gulls across the marsh and to the repetition of those sounds he always heard when he was alone and there was no one there to interrupt them: the strange and mysterious sounds of the sea, waves, the wind, voices.

Miss Philpot rested her steed against the bridge, hitched up her trousers and leaned over the parapet, staring at the river below.

'Good God, it's like a mountain torrent. Yesterday when I came by there was hardly a trickle. You couldn't have drowned a mouse in it.'

'Drowned what?'

'Look at the water. Look at it coming down.'

'I hate water. I've always hated it.'

'Fascinates me. Always has a queer bloody marvellous fascination.'

With floppy, clumping strides Miss Philpot started to march up and down the bridge, steps regular, sentrywise. Once or twice she halted, stared again at the river and marvelled again at its swollen, curdled course.

On the third of her turns of duty a dark sudden swirl of mist slid across the bridge, cutting her off the farther end of it, from the girl and the chestnut trees beyond. Imprisoned in black-grey cloud she shouted in a cracked gargling voice:

'Stay where you are. Don't move. You'll get run down. I'll switch my bike lamp on.'

The river too disappeared. Mist curled over Gilly's shoulders and arms, wet and cold, like a slipping eel. She gripped the stone balustrade of the bridge, cold too, and suddenly called in panic:

'Where are you? I can't see anything. Where have you gone?'

Miss Philpot groped along the bridge, feeling her way with heavy finger-tips, swearing in grunts.

'Good God, there you are.' Her big hands, rough as toad skin, clutched Gilly's bare arm. The girl shuddered and Miss Philpot said: 'This is a bloody nightmare. We'll get run down. Where's my bike lamp?'

She stumbled against her steed, groped for the lamp switch and flicked it on. In the white beam of the headlight the face of the girl looked flat, grey-white and skeletonized, the eyes deeper and darker than ever. The mouth hung open, locked in the act of saying something, without a word.

'This is sheer bloody madness,' Miss Philpot said. 'We're on the wrong side of the road for a start. We'd better move over. We'd better get back.'

The mist thickened and darkened. The light of Miss Philpot's lamp reflected back from the pall of it like a woolly moon. Miss Philpot groped with her steed across the bridge. Gilly started to follow her and then, half-way across the road, heard the sudden roar of a heavy lorry coming down the hill, its brakes grinding.

She ran the last few yards across the road, half falling against Miss Philpot and her steed. Miss Philpot swore in grunts again. The brakes of the lorry whistled like a screeching bird. Its headlights appeared from the screen of afternoon darkness with no more power than two feeble orange candles. Miss Philpot, more in vexation than fear, swung the beam of her headlight to and fro, ringing the bell of her steed furiously, shouting.

A lumbering red monster of a two-tonner, piled with timber, came to a halt on the bridge. The mist at the same moment danced, lifted a little and let in a shaft of light. The face of the lorry driver grinned down from the cab, its eyes squeezed up in rising cigarette smoke.

'Trouble?'

'We lost a boy. A small boy,' Miss Philpot said. 'He has a red umbrella. You haven't – '

'I better get off the bridge. You'll get yourselves bleedin' coffined up here.'

The lorry crawled over the hump-back of the bridge and came to a halt thirty yards on the other side. The mist thinned for a second time, revealing a brief apricot line of light beyond the river. The face of the lorry driver leaned out of the cab and called:

'You lost what? A kid?'

Miss Philpot came running with her steed, the headlamp still shining. Gilly ran too, calling:

'He's about six. He might have come this way –'

'They always go home,' the lorry driver said. 'Like my kid – missing for a bleedin' day once. Come home good as gold for supper. Eating a toadstool. His ma was half scatty.'

'Toadstool?' Gilly's voice came in a hard giggle, half-laughing, half-frightened.

'Big red thing. "Nice cake," the little bastard kept saying. "Nice jam cake." He'd eaten half of it. His ma went up the wall. Crazy. Lucky I was there. They got the stomach pump.'

The mist suddenly lifted completely. It was afternoon again, all blue and apricot across the meadows. The eyes of the driver were blue too, careless in the sudden wide expanse of light. He flicked his half-smoked cigarette into the road.

'I'd help you look for him only I'm due up in Doncaster tonight and I'm late as it is. It was black as hell back there. Where's he live?'

'Oh! he lives just back there – not far – you might – if you see him –'

'Go back home. He'll be there. The little perishers have got this instinct. Like bleedin' pigeons. He'll go back.'

'Exactly what I have said,' Miss Philpot said. 'They thrive on it. It's this instinct for self-preservation.'

'I didn't know whether to leather the living daylights out of him or cry like a nit,' the lorry driver said. 'His ma had guts-ache for a week.' He actually laughed, at the same time revving up his engine, his hand ready on the brake lever. 'Go home and wait. Sit down and get yourself a nice cuppa tea and wait –'

'Very sensible advice,' Miss Philpot said. 'Very sensible. It's very nice of you. We're sorry to have troubled you.'

'He's got this red umbrella – in case you – and a blue roll-top sweater – dark blue –'

The driver lifted a hand in farewell, grinning. The engine revved loudly, suddenly died down again and the driver said:

'Tell you what. If I see him I'll pick him up and drop him at the first caff I see. How's that?'

'Very practical,' Miss Philpot said. 'Very practical. Splendid.'

'He'll probably want to go on to Doncaster with you,' Gilly said. 'He's very friendly.'

'Not to worry,' the driver said. 'I'll buy him a choc-ice and dump him.'

The lorry moved off. A smear of dark smoke from its exhaust lifted, spread itself and instead of disappearing merged with a new running cloud of mist. The sun became darkened again. The two women stood silent in the centre of the road, staring at the retreating lorry. A flock of starlings, direction lost, whirled up from the meadows and over the bridge, wings whistling as they disappeared.

'It's very sensible advice and I think we ought to take it,' Miss Philpot said.

'The Captain said we were not to move – we'd got to stay here – '

'The Captain? – who on earth takes any notice of the Captain? He never gets a trick. Good God, if we depended on him – '

'All right – we'll go back by way of the farm. I never thought of that. That's a place he might be – '

The mist lifted again. The sun shone weakly, dark at the edges. Miss Philpot switched off the lamp of her steed and the two women moved off the bridge, starting up the road.

'I'll murder the little devil. I'll kill him if he doesn't soon come back.'

Miss Philpot laughed with a dry, coughing crackle. It was a funny thought, she was about to say, killing the boy if he didn't come back, but the words never managed to form themselves on her loose, quivering lips. Instead she reached across the kitchen table and picked up the bottle of whisky she had been lucky enough, she told herself, to have in her shopping bag on the back of her steed and started to pour herself a third half-tumbler.

'I don't see what there is to laugh about. I nearly killed him once before. I felt like murdering him anyway – I tell you – that day I found him half-way down the well – '

'Have a drop more, dear? Do you no harm. Help you to collect your thoughts a bit.'

Gilly sat suddenly dumb, staring, elbows on the table, having no thoughts to collect. Mutely she watched Miss Philpot pour more whisky, then lifted her own tumbler, automatically and drank. The whisky ran about her veins like a scalding worm, her muddled brain a grey ditch.

Some considerable time later she was aware of Miss Philpot pouring still more whisky. After a gulp or two at the second glass she suddenly felt the scalding worm multiply into a stark red tangle that invaded the grey ditch of her mind with a stab of torment that brought her sharply to her feet, saying:

'God, he must be upstairs somewhere – he must have climbed in somehow – got through a window – '

She rushed upstairs. Less than half a minute later she was coming down again, aware of nothing but of how prematurely dark it suddenly seemed. The figure of Miss Philpot was a mere hunched bag in the gloom of the kitchen. The mist outside was the colour of slaty smoke.

She switched on the kitchen light. Miss Philpot's eyes blinked at the impact of its sudden brilliance, smoky too, red at the edges.

'You look better now, dear. Done you good. Wasn't he there? I had a thought. I thought we should – got a telephone? – '

Miss Philpot's words stuttered away, half incoherently.

'Telephone? We haven't got a telephone.'

'Good thing, dear. Had mine cut off years ago. Expensive luxury – bloody – '

'You think we should call the police? There's a phone at the farm – '

'Police, my foot.' Miss Philpot said, pausing in the act of pouring more whisky, laughed again on a note cracked, old and dry. 'Oh! he'll come back – not to worry, like the lorry driver said, they always do – '

'I didn't mean that – you know, what I said about murdering him – I – I shouldn't have said that.'

In distraction she ran her fingers through her hair, took another gasping gulp of whisky and began suddenly, for no reason at all, to think of Ainsworth. His voice, casual, drawling, slightly reproachful, seemed now to wander through the kitchen.

227

'In the big house, sweetheart. Or the glass-house. I should say the glass-house. Obvious retreat. Wasn't he always there with that chum of his – Mr – '

'Mr Pimm!' She leapt up from the table, startling Miss Philpot into an open-mouthed stare. 'Good God, yes, of course, the house – '

'Find a snail,' she seemed to hear Ainsworth say. 'And there's the boy. You've got to be quick to catch him – '

When she and Miss Philpot reached the glass-house it was completely dark. The watery, froggy smell was thick and dank. A drip of water dripping slowly into a tank was the only sound inside.

'James? Are you there? James, are you hiding in there? Come out if you're hiding!'

'Let me get my lighter,' Miss Philpot said.

She stood at the door of the glass-house, fumbling, muttering something about the head-lamp of her steed and how she should have brought it. Her hand struck the lighter a series of uncertain blows in the darkness. A spark or two sprang up and then, at last, a light.

'I'll hold it well up, dear. Then you'll see – '

'James! Are you there? James, are you hiding?'

The glow of Miss Philpot's cigarette lighter fell with greenish candescence on ferns and water-tank, the big branching green skeleton shapes of fig-leaves and on the upper tracery of vines. The light seemed to attract movement in the shape of shadows inside the glass and then of something indistinctly grey and grotesque in the darkness beyond the glass. A face, followed by another, seemed to resolve itself, stare woodenly and retreat again. A wheezy gasp from Miss Philpot made Gilly cry out too. A second later the faces of sheep withdrew from beyond the glass into darkness, ghostly, aroused and frightened before they finally disappeared.

All the way back to the big house Miss Philpot kept muttering between wheezy coughs: 'I ought to have brought my bike lamp. Let me go back and get it.' By now she had snuffed out the cigarette lighter and several times stumbled uncertainly in the darkness. A moment or two of suddenly uplifted fog served to draw the high fabric of the house out of the autumn night like a broad sketch in white chalks. The steps to the terrace became clearly visible. As Gilly led the way up them Miss Philpot came fumbling several steps behind her, muttering that it was all right, there were sure to be lights in the house, it was all right.

'God, I remember now I switched the mains off. That day – '

Gilly halted inside the threshold of the house, her hand on the dead light switch just inside. Her voice echoed about the empty hallway and then, sepulchrally, up the stairs. Miss Philpot's panting breath following it like a quickened echo.

'I'd better go and get my bike lamp – '

'No. Wait a minute. I'll call.'

Gilly called into the house. The second and third calls 'James! James! Are you there? Call if you're there!' rang like enlarged echoes of the first, over-loud, clapping back at her.

Miss Philpot stood fumbling in the darkness, trying to get the cigarette lighter to work again. As it sparked and spluttered, Miss Philpot coughed and swore gently, more at herself than the lighter, under her breath. The lighter leapt into flame at last and Miss Philpot held it aloft, the glow expanding into a weak yellow arc in the big hallway, hardly reaching the nearest wall.

'If he's anywhere he's upstairs – '

Gilly began to walk across the half-lit hall way, Miss Philpot following with the uplifted lighter.

'I'll go and fetch the bike lamp. I just remembered – I forgot to fill the lighter up today. I should have filled it up.'

She thrust the lighter into Gilly's hand. Gilly took it and halted and then started to give it back.

'No. You take it. You'll never see your way in the dark. You take it.'

'I shall see. It never works outside anyway. It'll never last that long.'

Miss Philpot, wheezing and coughing, disappeared into the night. Gilly, alone in the hallway, stood with the hand that held the lighter fully extended. Then she walked round the hallway, halting at last at the stairs.

'Me? I never lose sleep over anything.' Again she started to remember, with perfect clarity, scraps of conversation with Ainsworth. She remembered too how she had stood at the foot of the stairs and Ainsworth crouched low with the camera, had taken her picture.

'He seems to take his Mr Pimm very seriously, doesn't he?'

'Yes, but he's only six.'

'Funny, this talking and playing with someone who isn't there.'

When she presently walked upstairs it wasn't difficult, either, to hear the notes of a piano.

'Nice instrument. Beautiful piano.'

'Haven't I heard what you're playing before?'

'Oh! this. You might have done – '

It was again our old friend Schumann. It was the transistor playing by the river, in the summer afternoon. It was the five-finger exercise, the basis of it all. It was Schubert too, the distant horns coming from immensely far away, very gentle, in calls that haunted you and could hardly be heard.

'Beautiful instrument, I said. Quite exceptional.'

'What is it you're playing?'

She seemed to hear too the voice of a wood pigeon, swooning, breaking, pausing and swooning on again, the single repeated voice of full summer.

'Oh! just making it up as I go along. Extemporising – '

Noisily Miss Philpot blundered back. The light of her battery bike lamp swung into the hallway like the white stab of a searchlight. For a second or two, as it swivelled, it struck Gilly straight in the eyes, partially blinding her. Miss Philpot called where was she? she couldn't see her, oh! there she was, half-way up the stairs.

Gilly came down, half-blinded, putting out the cigarette lighter as she came. Lamp in one hand, whisky bottle in the other, Miss Philpot skated uncertainly across the bare wooden floor.

'Thought we could do with another nip before – '

In the darkness on the way to the house Miss Philpot had been struck, for the first time, by true fear: that the boy might be dead. She seemed to see him dead somewhere in the big house. She remembered stories of children climbing into chests, playing hide-and-seek in cupboards, only to be found, long afterwards, as skeletons. She began to be sure, now, that it was something like that: some twisted accident of lock and key, the mistake of a second, in the dusty darkness somewhere upstairs.

She had to admit to herself that she was afraid of the stairs. She uncorked the whisky bottle and prepared to resist the stairs with jocularity.

'I thought at first a man was following me. It was the sheep again. Much the same thing I suppose.'

She laughed with a voice from which both bitterness and jocularity had dried out. It was no more than a flat beat of an old cracked tin.

'Hold the lamp, dear. I took the liberty of bringing a glass – took the liberty, by God, what am I talking about? I don't mind confessing – confessing! I never confessed to anything in my life.'

With a quivering hand she poured whisky into the glass, holding it out to Gilly. She had been about to confess that the stairs haunted her, that she was frightened now to go up them. She said instead, laughing again on the cracked low beat, the words out of her mouth before she could stop them:

'Knock it back, dear. I'll have one with you. I can't say I care all that for empty houses.'

With amazement, pouring herself the next drink, she heard Gilly say:

'How do you know it's empty?'

'Now don't start that. My thoughts are bad enough as it is – You think he's somewhere up there? I mean –'

'Houses aren't always empty when they seem –'

Miss Philpot drank, looking with inquisitive uncertainty at Gilly, her face strangely withdrawn in the curious backward half light of the lamp.

'Are you going up? You want me to come up with you?'

'You see it with children sometimes.'

'See what with children?'

'They play where you think it's empty and it really isn't. He used to play with people who weren't there. A lot.'

Miss Philpot drank again, utterly at a loss to grasp at the conversation, her mouth loose, unable to cough.

'A lot?'

'All day sometimes. Long conversations. Coming to lunch, fishing and smoking and playing games and going to the sea. We both did.'

'We?'

'Oh! yes, me too. I did. I had to.'

Miss Philpot, unnerved, pouring herself another half measure of whisky, searched the face of Gilly again, but now more sharply. It was the sort of talk, she told herself, that made you wonder. It was the sort of talk that verged on –

'He's probably in his own world somewhere.'

'Own world? What world? Where?'

'Oh! somewhere.'

'I don't know how you – You mean you know where to look?'

'Not exactly.'

Staring at Gilly, prompted again by her own suddenly magnified fear, Miss Philpot was astonished to find no fear at all in the face still rigidly held behind the lamp. It struck her instantly that the nature of its withdrawal was more than merely strange and cold. It had an alarming air of being calculated.

'Well, if we're going to look up there, we'd better – '

'I'll go by myself. You stay here.'

'No, no. I ought to go with you.'

'You have the lamp. I can manage with the lighter.'

The exchange of lamp for lighter left Miss Philpot groping for the foot of the stairs. Her hand quivered convulsively as she set whisky bottle, glass and lamp on the bottom step. She wanted very much to sit down. Instead she gripped the bottom curve of the banisters in much the same way as Gilly had gripped the balustrade of the bridge and realized all of a sudden that there were thoughts in her head impossible to bear.

'Shall I shine the light up the stairs for you? Are you sure you wouldn't rather I – '

'I can see. I know the way.'

As Miss Philpot watched the flame of the cigarette lighter disappear upstairs she felt herself gripped by a second phase of fear: this time not merely fear that the boy was dead but fear of Gilly. You heard stories like that so often. When people were missing and you started searching there was always someone, she told herself, among the searchers –

She sat down at last, heavily, on the bottom step of the stairs. She stared at the broad white beam of the bike lamp spreading arc-wise across the empty floor. She recalled the withdrawn cold face behind it and in recollection found it colder and more withdrawn than ever.

For some time she sat with one hand gripped across her knee, the glass held tight in the other. From time to time she drank, stopped and then grabbed the bike lamp and shone it upstairs. She was overwhelmed at last by a conviction that suddenly she could hear voices.

The sharp realization that they were not voices but the notes of a piano being picked out, one finger, four or five of them, slowly, brought her to her feet. The notes too seemed to be oddly cold and distant, somehow unreal. The pattern they made was less like a tune than speech, an exercise in monosyllables flatly repeated.

She listened to the notes of the piano for some time without moving. The pattern of them repeated itself a dozen times, lingered on a solitary note and then stopped. Some moments after it stopped she stood once again amazedly convinced that she could hear voices. This time she was so sure of it that she even told herself that she caught a word or two, a dismembered sentence that ended up, like the music, on a single broken note.

Presently there was the sound of a door shutting and Gilly, still carrying the cigarette lighter, came downstairs. Miss Philpot advanced a step or two to meet her, starting to say:

'What was it? What did you find –'

Gilly kept on downstairs, face blank and distant at first, with no word to say.

'Were you talking to someone? I thought I heard a piano.'

'Oh! yes there's a piano up there.'

'I thought I heard you talking to someone.'

'Me. Just me. Talking to myself.'

'You? – was it you playing the piano?'

'One finger. *Every week day* – yes, it was me. You like music?'

'Oh! yes in a way. Some music. Do you play? I mean do you like music yourself?'

'I didn't used to.'

Soon they walked back to the little house, Miss Philpot carrying the whisky bottle and the lamp. The mist had lifted a little. In the stark light of the lamp the wet grass shone white, as if already frosty.

They sat at the kitchen table again, the girl withdrawn and quiet again, and Miss Philpot poured more whisky. She suffered from the illusion that drink heightened her powers of perception. It made her mind sharp and clear. Now, with bleary eyes she peered at the girl and again told herself how quiet she was and also, now, how suspicious the quietness was. There was something, it seemed, hiding behind the cold withdrawn stare that you couldn't get at, couldn't define.

'I think someone else should know how we're getting on,' she said. 'I mean I think we should tell – '

'Tell who?'

'I thought the Captain might have been along by now.'

'He didn't say he would.'

'Yes, that's what I mean. I think he should know – I mean that we haven't found anything. You don't think he might be staying with friends? – the boy, I mean?'

'No, he's not with friends. We really haven't made any friends.'

Miss Philpot gave what she thought was a friendly laugh, croaking wheezily. It wasn't easy to make friends in the country, she said, but it was wonderful how enemies cropped up from nowhere.

The laugh infected Gilly, who laughed too. It seemed, Miss Philpot thought, a strange sort of laugh and the sentence that followed it seemed stranger still.

'It would be nice to think he was with Mr Pimm.'

'Mr Pimm? Who is Mr Pimm.'

'He isn't really.'

Miss Philpot squinted hard.

'How do you mean?'

'He is and he isn't. Him and Mr Monday.'

'Monday?'

'Yes. They're friends – I mean they're friends of each other as well as being friends of the boy.'

'I thought you said you hadn't made any friends.'

'Well, this was different. They really weren't there but we used to talk to them. We used to have long conversations.'

Miss Philpot squinted hard again.

'Long conversations? The four of you?'

'Well, the three of us mostly. Not Mr Monday. They were very funny sometimes really. They made you laugh.' She sat with her eyes widely staring, brightly lost in recollection. 'No, not Mr Monday. He didn't come so often. He'd broken his arm. That was funny –'

'Funny?'

'I mean it was funny how the boy went about with his arm broken too.'

'Oh? He had a broken arm? I didn't know that.'

'Well, not really. Not actually – I mean it was real for him but not –'

Miss Philpot thought it time to pour herself more whisky. This time she measured it slowly, her eyes downcast, watching the glass with care.

'So you think he might be staying with these – '

'Oh! no, no. He wouldn't be, not if they weren't – '

'You don't think one of them might have come and taken him away?'

The very suggestion made Gilly laugh again, more loudly this time and, Miss Philpot thought, still more strangely.

'It's the sort of thing men do sometimes,' Miss Philpot said. 'I mean to boys. You don't think one of them might have – '

'Oh! no, no, no.'

'Did they used to come here very often?'

'Oh! often. Mr Pimm came every day.'

The air of locked bewilderment on the face of Miss Philpot

made Gilly laugh again. She sort of laughed privately, Miss Philpot later said, when asked, a sort of private joke laugh, sort of mocking, secretly.

'I don't think you can really understand,' Gilly said. 'It's one of those things between two people and when you try to explain – it sort of isn't – I mean it isn't real, not in the same way.'

Miss Philpot, earnestly sipping whisky, said nothing.

'Didn't you ever speak to people who weren't there when you were a child? Didn't you ever play with a Mr Pimm?'

Miss Philpot said she didn't think she had. Not that she could remember.

'Well, I didn't mean with Mr Pimm exactly. But you know what I'm getting at.'

No, she didn't, Miss Philpot told herself. At the same time her greatly heightened powers of perception, so apparently clear and sharp, seemed to tell her that she did. She was growing more and more aware of a tension of strangeness, of unbalance, in the air. She was caught in a maze, finding it no longer possible to say who existed and who didn't, what was true and what was not. And without realizing that she had already asked the question once she suddenly said:

'You say they used to come here a lot? The men I mean.'

'Oh! they came to lunch nearly every day. At least Mr Pimm did.'

'In the evenings too?'

'Oh! not in the evenings. He'd be in bed by then. The boy I mean.' Gilly laughed again; and again, Miss Philpot thought, with a certain unbalance, strangely. 'Oh! not Mr Pimm and Mr Monday. Not those two. They were strictly for the day.'

And the night? Miss Philpot wanted suddenly, and very much to ask about the night. But at first it was difficult to frame a question about the night; and when at last she did so she asked it casually:

'I suppose you found the evenings a bit tedious all alone?'

'Sometimes.'

Ah! sometimes, Miss Philpot thought. That was a word to conceal a mountain.

'Have another nip?' Casually she half-lifted the whisky bottle.

The girl shook her head. More casually still Miss Philpot said: 'When are they coming back?'

'Who?'

'Your people.' Miss Philpot poured herself another whisky, less carefully this time, slopping it over the sides of the glass. 'His people I should say.'

'They'll let me know.'

'Or ought I to say exactly that? His people?'

The fixed, formerly withdrawn eyes of the girl, alerted themselves with a sudden flash of interest. The quick change of subject, Miss Philpot thought, had instantly worked wonders.

'What's their name?' she said. 'I'm ghastly at names. I can never remember. His, not theirs, I suppose I should say. I met him a couple of times at the pub. Rather nice, I thought. On short acquaintance – '

'His?'

Miss Philpot, startled at the incisive whip of the word, proceeded to mop up a patch of spilt whisky with her handkerchief, almost as if she hadn't heard.

'You said his?'

'Well, they're not married, are they, as I understand it?'

The girl shot up from the table, trembling and white. For some moments she stood there blindly staring, quite unable to speak. Later Miss Philpot had an expression of her own for this violent change of attitude:

'She'd been quiet and sort of not quite there all evening, as if she didn't really grasp what was going on, and then suddenly there she was, in this bone-white rage. I thought at first I'd dropped a brick.'

Miss Philpot, trying again to appear casual, started to apologize for the brick.

'Did I say something I – '

'They might have told me. That's cheating. They should have told me. That's letting me down.'

'Well, of course it may well be one of those things – '

'They just sailed off. Calm. Cool as you like. Not giving a damn.'

'Her name's Porteous,' Miss Philpot said. 'That I do remember because the name's so odd. She – I mean the wife – the boy's mother, I mean – went off and busted somebody else's arrangements up – Of course they weren't married, the second pair, but it was beastly. They had an arrangement. It was hardly fair.'

In what Miss Philpot later described as her bone-white rage, her insupportable fit of trembling, the girl stood unable to speak again. Her normally slow brown eyes had become, Miss Philpot said, frighteningly wild and large.

'Well, I mean, they're the rough details as I understand it,' Miss Philpot said. 'I got it mostly from the Captain's sister. Of course it may not be – but then, every day – you don't even know with your friends.'

The words that the girl finally spoke seemed to be bludgeoned out of her by inner rage:

'If the boy's gone then he's gone and I'm glad he's gone – It'll serve them right – '

'Now dear, you don't mean that. You're a bit upset – '

'I mean it and I'm glad I mean it. If that's the way they cheat you. Cheat you? – why should I give a damn?'

'Sit down, dear, and let me pour you another nip.'

'Why should I worry? Let them have him on their conscience for a bit – conscience? Did I hear somebody laughing?'

She suddenly sat down at the table, the knuckles of her hands white and contorted for a moment and then suddenly spread out, strengthless and limp.

'They sail off and they trap you. You're nothing but a little squirt of a paid mouse and they leave you in a trap.'

For a few painful minutes Miss Philpot too sat down, not speaking. The increase in the apparent brightness of her perceptions had stopped, receded and left her fogged in uncertainty. Only a single sentence remained with anything like clearness out of the mad scrabble of voices heard and remembered, distant piano notes, figures there and not there, conversations held and not held, making her feel a little mad herself:

'If the boy's gone then he's gone and I'm glad he's gone – '

The whisky Miss Philpot had poured for the girl remained on the table, untouched. Miss Philpot pushed the glass across the table.

'It'll do you good, dear. Where are you going to spend the night.'

'They cheat you all along the line. They cheat you. They leave you in a trap.'

'I could give you a bed at my cottage.'

'I made a mistake. I know now. One mistake. But not like that. Not in that way. Not cheating. Not deliberately.'

'Let's be rational about this. Let's go back and see what the Captain's heard.'

Miss Philpot sat staring at the girl with what she thought was sympathy, with the best of intentions, a slight half smile on her uncertain lips, her whisky-sopped eyes groping helpfully.

'And what are you sitting there staring at me like that for?'

'Me? Staring. I wasn't aware of staring. I only – '

'Only what?'

'I don't know, I just wondered – '

'Wondered what? You sit there looking at me as if I'd hidden the poor kid somewhere.'

'Poor kid? You said if the boy was gone he was gone and you were glad he was gone but I know you didn't mean that – '

'Glad? Let them be glad. Lolling in the sun. Let them be glad.'

'If you could get a few things together now I think we ought to be going. I think we should.'

'I made a mistake about the camera. I know now. That one mistake. I'll never forgive myself for that.'

Later, as they started to walk together across the park, Gilly pushing the bicycle, the crumbling figure of Miss Philpot clinging on to the back, Miss Philpot became more and more solicitous. Several time she even implored Gilly, lugubriously, to admire the stars.

'Not to worry, dear, not to worry. Aren't the stars beautiful? So many of them. I'm sure everything will come all right. I love the stars. Not to worry. I've great faith in the stars. Do you believe in horoscopes and all that?'

To Miss Philpot's infinite surprise the girl's answer came in the form of another question:

'I suppose you go – you're in The White Hart a lot?'

'I read mine every evening. In two papers. Scorpio – not a very good lot. Do I do what, did you say?'

'I wondered if you ever came across a man named Ainsworth in The White Hart. I said did you go in there a lot?'

'The damn place would fall down without me. It's been a bad year for Scorpios. What are you?'

'He stayed there for a while. I wondered if you ever met him. Ainsworth?'

Gilly felt a long clumsy pull on the back of the bicycle. Unconsciously, thinking of something else, she had been pushing the bicycle rather fast. Miss Philpot stood panting, broken-winded, trying to get her breath.

'Silly. Shouldn't try to talk and run at the same time. What were you saying?'

It wasn't all that important really, Gilly said. She stood waiting for the groping figure of Miss Philpot trying to get back her breath. The harsh arc of the steed's headlamp was white on the road and Miss Philpot suddenly said:

'Oh! Ainsworth did you say? No, I can't say that I ever did.'

'Well, perhaps it wasn't Ainsworth. I couldn't be too sure – '

'That place is packed stiff with people in summer. All strangers. You never know anybody. What sort of man was he?'

'It doesn't really matter.'

Miss Philpot's breath almost normal now, gave a coughing laugh that ended in a dribbling giggle.

'You do rather go in for the elusive figure, dear, don't you? Some here, some there. Some with names, some – '

Gilly started to push the bicycle forward again. Miss Philpot grabbed at the frame, missed it and hung on with shaking finger tips to the edge of the mud-guard.

'Ainsworth, Ainsworth.' Miss Philpot repeated the name several times between lugubrious gasps for breath as they came to within sight of the village. Once or twice more her laugh dribbled into a liquid giggle. 'Another friend of Mr Pimm?'

'No.' Gilly seemed to be talking half to herself. 'Not quite.' Miss Philpot, clinging to the back of the bicycle, now moving rapidly again, wasn't sure she heard. 'In fact you might say they didn't get on very well sometimes – '

'Didn't what, dear?'

'There was a bit of jealousy – oh! it doesn't matter.'

'Jealousy?'

Out of the tangle of words, half heard, sometimes mis-heard, Miss Philpot was sure she heard this one at least correctly. She chewed on it for some time like a morsel of tender meat, again sure that her brain was working with sharper perceptions. At last her words fumbled their way out:

'I think I'd better drop into The White Hart for a second or two. The Captain's sure to be there. There may be something. It's amazing the way the instinct goes. I remember when I was a child we lost my sister once. At Scarborough, on holiday, after morning church. I thought my mother would go crazy. When we found my sister she was having a poached egg on toast in a policeman's kitchen. Always the way –'

Again Miss Philpot, emerging into something like sobriety, laughed with a liquid giggle. Gilly, listening as if to a voice not there, gripped the handlebars of the bicycle and stared at the white arc of the bike lamp lying whitely across the street ahead.

'You'll come in for a moment too, won't you?'

'No, I'll wait outside.'

'It isn't late.' Miss Philpot's massive arm crooked upward, uncertainly, under the street lights. 'Good God, it is though. It's nearly ten. Have we been talking all this time? Sure you won't come in?'

'I won't come in.'

'I won't be long. Just – Only a minute.'

In the succeeding ten minutes Miss Philpot bought herself, in The White Hart bar, a double whisky and another for the Captain. The Captain, it seemed, had news that was reassuring. A woman had reported seeing a boy of five or six travelling on a south-bound bus with something red in his hands that might have been an umbrella or a parcel or possibly a book. The Captain was waiting for further news on the blower now. The boy was wearing a sweater too, but there was some doubt as to whether it was green or blue. It all seemed hopeful, the Captain thought, if not certain. The trouble was, he declared, that a lot of people were colour-blind.

Miss Philpot, perceptions heightened again, suddenly assured the Captain that there was also blindness in other directions.

'Some people see,' she said, 'what they want to see.'

The subtleties of this sentence, delivered in a low voice to a bar in which a man was in heavy, despondent lament at the decline in the rabbit population and hence of good, cheap dinners, was lost on the Captain, who merely licked his lips and stared.

'They also see,' she said, 'things which are not there.'

'Elucidate,' the Captain said. 'Elucidate.'

Miss Philpot's method of elucidation was to take the Captain aside, to the far end of the bar, and embark on a heavy passage of her own: a fumbling story of two men coming to lunch and yet not coming, of strange voices heard in an upper room, a few broken notes on a piano, something about a snail. From this she darkly deduced for the benefit of the Captain that there were times when those who pursued the fox actually had the animal already hidden in a bag.

'N'est-ce pas?' she said, 'N'est-ce pas?'

The Captain simply stared at a glass case of an otter with a fish in its mouth mouldering greyly among yellowed reeds and wondered what on earth she was driving at. He didn't often come as far as this rather shadowy corner of the bar.

'She talks a terrible lot about men. One gets the impression – '

The Captain stared at a steel engraving of a nymph-like figure hanging next to the otter, nude, breasts coyly turned away, reclining on the floor of a stretch of woodland. He couldn't recall ever having consciously seen it or the otter before. The buttocks of the nymph shone pure and white and immediately below them a passing wit had scrawled across the glass, in tipsy letters, with scarlet lipstick: *To Tulip, with love.*

The Captain was just beginning to wonder with a kind of amiable excitement who Tulip might have been when Miss Philpot said:

'She talked a lot about a man named Ainsworth. You know every face in this bar. Does the name mean anything to you? Ainsworth?'

Still half lost in wonder at the identity of Tulip, the Captain confessed that it didn't, very much. Still, one couldn't keep track –

'And Pimm. There's apparently a man named Pimm. It seems the boy used to see a lot of him – I mean, one gets the impression – '

'How do you spell it? Of course there's Admiral Pym – '

'Oh! no, I don't think like that. I think more to rhyme with dim – I mean with an "i" – '

'Ah! spell it with an "i", Samival,' the Captain said, 'and a millimetre.'

Miss Philpot, the extent of her sharpening perceptions having suddenly limited again, said she didn't quite understand about the millimetres. The Captain, relishing for a moment longer a new private joke, merely laughed in his throat, with subtlety, and said:

'Mm, mm.'

'I've a shrewd suspicion she thinks the boy might be with this man Pimm.'

'Good God. We'd better ask Harry. Harry'll know.' The Captain prepared to call across the bar to where Harry, the barman was still listening with patience to the lament of the declining rabbit. 'Har – '

'No, no, leave it for a minute. She's deep. One gets the impression she's deep.'

'The girl, do you mean?'

'For example when I asked her about the boy's parents – the father I mean. She flew into a blind rage, bone-white, absolutely blind. You're not going to tell me she didn't know. Your sister knows. I know. Everybody knows. It's common knowledge – '

The Captain, listening with some vagueness, stared at the nymph. He wondered if the nymph herself was Tulip or if Tulip was in fact a girl – strange name for a girl, you rarely heard it, but rather nice. Miss Philpot, seeing the Captain's eyes wildly fixed on the rotund white proportions of the nymph, suddenly accused him sharply of not listening and said:

'You said elucidate. Well, listen when I elucidate.'

The Captain, in an injudicious moment, said he was sorry but he was in fact wondering who Tulip was.

'Tulip? Who on earth's Tulip?'

The Captain said that that was the fascinating question. Who was she? Was she? – he seemed about to give a flea-like wink at Miss Philpot, but at the last moment restrained himself and drank, with a joke, instead. 'Was she or was she not? Tulip or not? Tulips better than one? –'

'She's slightly off-balance if you ask me –'

'You don't mean the girl?'

'Otherwise why should she fly off the handle like that when I merely mentioned the boy's parents, I mean the father. After all the relationship's got nothing whatever to do with her. It's merely her job to look after the boy. I imagine they pay her well –'

'Imagine so.' The Captain, once again absorbed by the nymph, asked himself why it was that nymphs, especially those of the eighteenth century, were always so fleshy in the keel. 'Probably bored.'

'You've put your finger on it.'

Miss Philpot gave a trembling giggle. The Captain, still gazing at the nymph and still half lost in conjecture about Tulip, wondered for a moment what in fact he had put his finger on.

'It explains the men, I mean. It would do, of course. It mightn't be extraordinary, one – but three.'

'Three? Who's three?'

'There's a third. Named Monday.'

'Monday? Good God. We'd better ask Harry. Three of them?'

'Three of them. Ainsworth, Pimm and Monday.'

'She seems to have gone it a bit rich.'

'Well, some of them do, don't they? That,' Miss Philpot said, suddenly accusatory, 'is all that's in their minds. It's all they think of. Isn't there a name for it?' It was suddenly as if she were not only laying bare the minds of others but that of the Captain too. 'Nymphomania – isn't that it?'

The Captain, visibly disturbed, looked into his glass and attempted with enthusiasm to drain what he thought was the last of his whisky. It wasn't there. Was Miss Philpot psychic or something? It seemed the slightest bit unfair of her, he thought, to read his mind about the nymphs. The impulse to turn the whole affair into a joke was nevertheless irresistible and he suddenly said, laughing in anticipation:

'Isn't there a fly called a nymph? Eh? Always been a good lure.'

'Nymphomaniacs, that's what they call them. Of course.'

'Nymphs and shepherds – '

'I don't think shepherds. I don't think in this case shepherds.'

'Well, we'd better pump Harry. If they're locals Harry'll know.'

'I suppose it's the eyes. They go with the type. They sort of fold back inwards and look inside, if you know what I mean.'

The Captain had no way of either knowing or understanding about eyes that folded inwards, and merely looked first into his own glass and then at Miss Philpot's and said:

'Another? Yes?'

To his astonishment he discovered that her glass was still more than half full. Odd. Talking too much, he supposed. Odd too that they should both be talking about nymphs, he thought. Curious coincidence.

'I don't suppose you had time to notice. But look next time you see her. They're brown and yet sort of not. They're not always with you.'

The Captain, lost, begged Miss Philpot to drink up. He would go and get her another and at the same time ask about those chaps – what were their names again?

Miss Philpot told him and drank up. The Captain took her glass and went away to the bar. For a moment she thought she would join him at the bar and then decided it would be more prudent to remain in the corner, where it was darker. In the interval while the Captain got the drinks she felt the best of her bright perceptions come back, again giving her the necessary sharpness to elucidate, to dissect both a situation and a character. Being a woman oneself, she told herself, made it that much easier to know a woman. The solution to the problem of the eyes that were brown and yet sort of not, that folded back into themselves, and of the voices heard and yet not there – it all began to seem a great deal more simple now.

'I brought you a double malt. Harry doesn't always have it. I know you like it. No, he's never heard of those coves.'

'Curiouser and curiouser.'

Miss Philpot, thanking the Captain for the whisky, stood looking at it in vague contemplation.

'Never got the taste for it. Nor for Irish. Mrs Fitzsimmons did her damndest to convert us all to Irish when she first came, but I could never take it.'

'By the bye, is she still away?'

'On the jaunt still, I imagine. I must ask Harry. Haven't seen her in a longish time.'

In contemplation too the Captain stared at his own whisky, then at the nymph on the wall, thought for some moments of Tulip and then was suddenly struck by what he considered a piece of staggering elucidation of his own. The bright figure of Mrs Fitzsimmons, blonde, gay-eyed, smooth-skinned, suddenly appeared before him, a nymph too. The comparison with the figure on the wall struck him as one of startling interest. She too was great with the men. The bar constantly palpitated with her presence: it was never quite the same without her. He didn't delude himself for a moment that she was the actual Tulip mentioned in dispatches but he had no doubt, in his own mind, that the deeds of valour were there. It seemed, anyway, as good a time for a joke as any:

'You suppose the Fitzsimmons is a nymph too?'

'I shouldn't bandy that word around.'

The Captain was set back. He had possibly, he thought, intruded into territory not quite firm. He laughed, drank sharply and let the whisky tickle the depths of his throat.

'Well, perhaps that's a bit strong. I meant more the amorous eye.'

'It isn't the same thing at all.'

'No, no? Really?'

'It's deeper. It goes much, much deeper.'

'Well, I'm damned.'

'It's more even than that.' Miss Philpot's mind clarified again, searched the depths of her glass and secured from it the one word that had troubled and so far eluded her all evening. 'It's an obsession. It's something they can't help. A complete mad obsession. Mad.'

246

The Captain involuntarily let his mouth fall open, without reply. Not even the thought of Tulip had the effect of brightening his own whisky-brooding eyes and he was finally saved from both the necessity of words and thought by the voice of Harry, the barman, calling, holding one hand to his ear:

'Captain Drage! Wanted on the blower, sir. Police at Easton Green.'

'Good show. News at last. Coming.'

'I wish I knew what she was born under.'

The Captain crossed the bar. The barman lifted the flap of the bar counter. The Captain went through the gap and into a room behind. After three or four minutes he came back, speaking with relish, saying to the barman as he passed:

'Give us one more for the road, Harry. The police at Easton Green say they've a chap there whose wife found a boy crying his eyes out in a bus shelter. She took him home. About the right age and build – '

'What about the red umbrella?' Miss Philpot said.

'Oh! not a bee's wing about the red umbrella. But otherwise it seems to fit. They want us to get over there – someone with a car, that is, to collect – they're pretty short of staff – '

For Miss Philpot the evening seemed suddenly deflated.

'I suppose I ought to go and tell the girl. She's waiting outside – '

'I've got the car. I'll come too. I'll drive you both over.'

'The Captain, pausing at the bar to drink and pay for the final whiskies for himself and Miss Philpot, inquired with jovial interest how Mrs Fitzsimmons was faring and when could they expect to be seeing her back again?

'Not much news, sir,' the barman said. 'Only what the cat tells us.'

Ah! the cat, eh? It was like that, was it? the Captain said. The cat-call, eh? The bar rang with the jocular echo of the Captain's laughter. And what did the cat call when the cat called?

'You know Mrs Fitzsimmons, sir. Wherever she is it's not dull, sir. And not dark either.'

'Cats see in it.'

'They do, sir, Captain Drage.'

'Dark doings, Harry? We shall see, we shall see.'

The street outside was quiet and empty. The Captain called to Miss Philpot that he would get his car. Miss Philpot stood watching and waiting. By the time the Captain came back with the car Miss Philpot was walking in strident circles, up and down the street.

'She was here – I left her here – I haven't had a single glimpse of her.'

'I'll call – Miss – God damn it, I don't even know her name.'

'Nor me.'

The Captain called 'Hullo, hullo there,' and 'Miss!' into the lighted street, several times. There was no answer.

'Significant,' Miss Philpot said, 'significant.'

The Captain stood waiting whoozily, for an answer to his calls, thinking of the nymph, Tulip, and whether Mrs Fitzsimmons was a nymph too.

'Blast the girl! One goes to all this trouble and – God, girl, where are you?'

Neither the stars nor the lights in the street gave any answer and Miss Philpot, staring up at the stars, could only say it was no more than she thought, no more than she expected, and then:

'I wish I knew what she was born under. I wish I knew what she was born under. It could explain.'

'It may take some explaining,' the Captain said.

James woke, crawled from under the canvas of the binder and looked at the morning. The mist of overnight had lifted completely. Hoarfrost like the delicate white icing on a cake lightly covered the marshland. The sun was rising, burnt orange, into a sky of thin lofty blue, clear of cloud.

He looked at once for the man on the dredger. The orange arm of the dredger was motionless above the dyke. He listened for the sound of a dog barking. There was no sound of a dog barking.

He crawled back under the binder. The air was cold. He wondered if Mr Pimm was cold too and took him out of the paper bag. Mr Pimm didn't seem unusually cold. He looked much the same as he had done the previous evening. For a moment or two he wondered if he should start to eat Mr Pimm and then decided against it. He said 'Hullo, Mr Pimm, it's very early I think' and put Mr Pimm back into the paper bag. Mr Pimm didn't say anything but with his shining black currant eyes he looked content and thoughtful and friendly.

Some time later James heard a church bell begin to ring from somewhere across the marsh. It was the sound of a single bell and the slow ding-dong of it made him sleepy. He lay down again, shutting his eyes.

When he woke again the sun was well up the sky. Dark patches and stripes of melted frost lay across the grass. The sound of the church bell had stopped. Instead he could hear the noise of a motor-bike. He looked out and over towards the dredger. The motor-bike had stopped by the dredger. The man on it was wearing a big white sheep-skin coat and a crash helmet and a pair of goggles.

A great sense of freedom came over him. He was glad he wasn't a dog. Dogs had to be chained up or sit in baskets or wait in kennels until they were told to have meatsies or walkies or bickies or something. They had to beg and do as they were told and follow their masters and keep to the path and not run away. It was like him with Miss Garfield. They had to be scolded and told to eat up and be struck on the head when they were doing things they liked. It was like him with Gilly. He didn't like the thought of being a dog. It reminded him of what his father had said: dog eat dog. If you were a dog another dog might eat you.

He watched the man working the dredger. The big orange arm swung and swooped and fished in the dyke. It came up dripping with water and yellow clay. Farther along the dyke a big grey-white bird stood on the bank, watching. Its beak and legs were very long. It stood there without moving for so long that at last he told himself it was a dead bird or perhaps the ghost of a dead bird. All the time the big orange arm of the dredger kept swooping and fishing in the dyke.

There were many sheep in the marsh. He was glad of this. He liked sheep. You could never be lonely when there were sheep. He said 'Hullo, sheep, how are you?' but there were so many of them and some of them were so far away, far under the huge spread of sky, that he knew they couldn't answer.

A man appeared among the sheep in the nearest field. With him was a black and white dog which ran up and down and then round and round, in circles. It was a very nice well-behaved dog. It was enjoying itself. Now and then the man whistled. Finally all the sheep gathered themselves together in a ring and were very still and quiet, like people in church. Perhaps, he thought, they were hungry and waiting to be fed. But presently the man whistled again and the dog ran. The sheep ran too and nobody fed them.

He knew what the man was called: he was the shepherd. The man on the dredger, the shepherd, Mr Pimm, the dog, the sheep and the big bird sitting on the dyke: it was getting to be what Mr Pimm sometimes called a bit crowded in these 'ere parts. He laughed to himself. It was great fun, being free, by himself, far from people who scolded and punished and took away the things that gave you most pleasure, like cameras and things. He wished he had the camera now but he supposed you couldn't have everything. It was enough to be free.

He decided, presently, that it was time to piddle. Just before he piddled against the wheel of the old binder he asked Mr Pimm if he would like to piddle too. Mr Pimm said he thought he'd better, it'd be that much easier, and he too proceeded to piddle against the wheel of the binder.

He thought Mr Pimm seemed to be a long time doing what he had to do but Mr Pimm assured him it was the cold weather. Anyway it was as well to get it over with afore they got started. When Mr Pimm was finished at last James put him back into the paper bag.

Soon the shepherd and his dog started walking away across the field. When they had finally climbed the fence in the far corner James decided to start walking too. The sheep were all scattered now, in different directions, grazing peacefully.

He started walking. He was going to walk first, he told himself to where the big grey-white ghost bird sat on the edge of the dyke. That would take him away from the man working on the dredger. He didn't want to be seen by the man on the dredger because it would mean being like a dog. The man would tell someone who would tell someone else who would tell someone else who would tell Gilly. It would be just like being a dog: they would put him on a lead and scold him and punish him and take him home and not let him out again. He didn't want that. It was all so nice and simple as it was.

As he walked he knew it wasn't far now to the sea. You could tell the sea was near because the sky was very big and blue and high up and clear. The marsh was very flat and he knew, some-how, that the sea began at the very edge of it. There seemed to be a sort of sparkle in the air and the sun was warm.

He clutched the red umbrella firmly in his left hand and Mr Pimm, in the paper bag, in his right. Along the banks of the dyke, where the dredger still had to work, were high fringes of reed, with brown soft tassels at the tips of them. He walked half-hidden by reeds. The big grey-white bird had become hidden too by reeds and he seemed to walk a long way without seeing it again.

Finally he stopped and walked down to the edge of the water. He started poking at the water with the red umbrella. From not a dozen feet away a great wing-clap suddenly split the air. The heron, the grey-white bird, rising on wings that seemed for a moment as wide and high as the arms of the dredger, swung over him, low over the water and swept across the marsh. He let out a startled half-scream, slipped on the bank of the dyke and dropped the red umbrella.

By the time he had recovered his feet again it was in the water, floating away.

'Now I'd like to go back over this again, Miss, if we may. No, no more tea for me, thank you. Perhaps Detective-Constable Pierce would like another cup, though. That's quite all right. Plenty of time.'

Gilly took the tea-pot from the kitchen table, went into the scullery and filled it up with hot water. She came back, filled up the Detective-Constable's cup and her own and then sat down at the table. She pushed the sugar-basin across the table and Detective-Sergeant Broadbent said:

'I'd like to take the man Pimm again, if I may. I think we didn't mention any Christian name?'

'I told you before. There isn't anyone named Pimm.'

'George perhaps? Bill? Jim? Arthur?'

'I tell you he was just known as Mr Pimm.'

'No Christian name. You've been looking after the boy now for six, seven weeks. Right? No Christian name. Just Mr Pimm.'

'It's like I told you before –'

'I've got a note here about a conversation we had yesterday. You said you could describe him if given a bit more time.'

'I can't describe him – I –'

'You said he smoked a pipe, but otherwise you can't describe him. He comes to lunch quite frequently. He goes fishing with the boy. You all play dominoes together. But you can't describe him except to say that he smoked a pipe – Is this correct?'

'No, it's not correct – it's like I told you – it's a question of being and not –'

'Then we'd better correct it, hadn't we?'

Detective-Constable Pierce, sitting on the far side of the table, poured himself his fifth cup of tea with his right hand, at the same time deftly producing from his jacket pocket a packet of cigarettes with his left. He offered the packet to Gilly, who shook her head.

'I've another note here which refers to the sea,' Detective-Sergeant Broadbent said. 'Something about Mr Pimm staying for a holiday by the sea. Was this correct?'

'The boy believed he was staying by the sea. That's what made me say it – how I thought he might have gone down there –'

'Where could this be? Margate? Brighton?'

'I tell you – it's like I said before – it's all part of his imagination – I only just remembered the sea because I thought –'

'I see. Pimm is part of the boy's imagination.'

252

'That's it. That's right. It was real, though.'

'How do you mean? It was imagination and yet it was real.'

'Yes, it was. That's right.'

'Very well. He exists only in your imagination but he's real. Let's leave it at that for a moment. I've a note of a conversation here, which I had with Miss Philpot. There was another man, Monday.'

'Yes. He – '

'You say you can't describe Pimm. But Miss Philpot seems to be more definite about Monday. She says you told her Monday had a broken arm.'

'That's right. But – '

'I see. That seems to be very definite. You couldn't add more? What sort of age man, for instance. Middle-age?'

'I never saw Mr Monday, I tell you. I never saw him.'

'According to Miss Philpot these two men came to lunch every day. Or nearly every day.'

'Well, once perhaps Mr Monday came, just once. I may have seen him just once.'

'I see. Just once. Real or in imagination?'

'In imagination, I tell you. I've told you a thousand times.'

'All right. In imagination. Mr Monday has a broken arm in imagination. Well, we'll leave it at that for the moment. Perhaps I will just have another cup of tea after all. And Pierce, I'll have a cigarette.'

Detective-Sergeant Broadbent paused while Gilly filled his cup with tea. He took a cigarette from the packet offered him by Detective-Constable Pierce, lit it with a silver lighter and leaned back from the table, inhaling smoke. Through the cloud of exhaled smoke he sat with an air of comfort, even reassurance, and stared at Gilly. In turn she stared down at her cup and for some moments he was unable to catch for himself a direct glimpse of the eyes that Miss Philpot had remarkably described as being 'brown but sort of not. They're not always with you.'

'All right, Miss. Let's go back a bit on another matter. I'd like you to tell me a little more, if you will, about Mr Ainsworth.'

'Why don't you keep out of my private life? My private affairs – what's it to do with you?'

'You say this Mr Ainsworth stayed for some time at The White Hart. Late August, early September, you said.'

'If you say so.'

'Any idea for how long?'

'I told you yesterday.'

'Two weeks. Perhaps more. Perhaps nearly three. You couldn't quite remember.'

'If you say so.'

'Not surprisingly you couldn't quite remember. The White Hart has no record of a Mr Ainsworth ever staying there. I've looked at the register.'

'I tell you he was there all right! God, I was with him every day. I should know.'

'Real? or in imagination?'

'Why don't you ask Mrs Fitzsimmons? Why don't you ask her? He used to talk to her after the bar had closed, every night.'

'Mrs Fitzsimmons is away. We'll contact her if necessary.'

'If necessary! If necessary! God, when? If it isn't necessary now when is it necessary?'

'You said yesterday that Mr Ainsworth had gone away too. Any idea where?'

'You tell me, you tell me.'

'No idea of an address?'

'He just left. For two days. He had business. He was coming back. He just went.'

'Down to the sea, perhaps. Catching up with Pimm and Monday.'

'Don't keep on about Mr Pimm and Mr Monday! They were as real as he was! – God, I sometimes wonder if he was here either! – God, I wonder, God help me, I wonder –'

She suddenly buried her head in her dry, contorted hands. Now and then she stopped the contortions of her hands and struck her forehead, blindly and rigidly. When at last she looked up again, after nearly five minutes, Detective-Sergeant Broadbent had a clear good look at the eyes that were 'brown but sort of not'. They were, as Miss Philpot had rightly said, not with him: nor were they wet; and he was unable to say which surprised him more.

He walked to the window and stood looking out. A little rain in the morning had cleared by noon and now the sky was rippled with white, western cloud. The frost of the previous morning had cut the last of the dahlias, singed the leaves of the wind-broken tobaccos. The borders of the garden, each side of the well, were black.

'Why don't you go out and find him and stop going over and over things? Over and over!'

Detective-Sergeant Broadbent stared at the blackened garden, without reply.

'You think I've hidden him somewhere, don't you? You think I know where he is, don't you? You think it's me – that's what Miss Philpot tried to say!'

'Let's not take too much notice of Miss Philpot.'

'You took notice of her just now!'

'Yes, but let's not take too much notice.'

The detective-sergeant came away from the window and sat down. He stubbed out his cigarette into his saucer.

'All right, Miss. We'll suppose there is – or was – an Ainsworth. Perhaps he had a Christian name?'

'Yes, he did. Alex.'

'Ice-cold in Alex.' Detective-Constable Pierce gave a short laugh that slightly checked his pouring out of his sixth cup of tea.

'Was that supposed to be funny? A joke or something?'

'It was just a remark.'

'Well, if it was a remark meant to take the mickey out of me you know what you can do with it, don't you?'

'Now, now, Miss. No need to get excited.'

'That's what you want to do, don't you? Get me excited. Get me all mixed up. Get me – '

She suddenly grabbed the tea-pot and poured herself more tea, slopping it into the saucer, glaring.

'All right. The name was Alex. Would you mind telling me what your relationship with him was?'

'Yes, I would. That's my private business, my private affair.'

'Affair?'

'Yes, affair if you like. Affair, affair.'

'When you say affair – '

'I do say affair, don't I? You can hear me, can't you? Affair. Is that plain enough? Affair!'

'Try not to shout, Miss. All right, we'll leave it at that. I won't ask you if you were lovers – '

'You're asking, aren't you? That's exactly what you are asking, isn't it? Well, isn't it? You'll be asking me next how many times I slept – go on, why don't you ask? There's nothing left, is there?'

Detective-Sergeant Broadbent made gestures of apparently great patience, spreading out his hands across the table, palms upward.

'All right, let me ask you something else. Did Ainsworth – I'm still assuming there is or was an Ainsworth – get on well with the boy? Were they friends?'

'Quite well. He gave him things.'

'Things?'

'Like the camera. He went off all one afternoon with it. Taking pictures. That was my big mistake, my one mistake.'

'Mistake?'

'Yes, mistake, mistake. I told you yesterday.'

'I can't recall that you told us yesterday.' Detective-Sergeant Broadbent looked without haste at Detective-Constable Pierce, who looked without haste into the depths of his tea. 'Do you recall anything of that, Pierce? A camera?'

Detective-Constable Pierce looked immensely thoughtful, sipped his tea and said he couldn't say he did.

'Well, you say a mistake. What mistake was this? Something to do with the camera?'

'Yes, it was something to do with the camera. I took it away from him. I was mad with him. I thought he'd fallen down the well.'

'Did you indeed? You were mad with him. He resented it?'

'It was a mistake, I tell you, a mistake. A mistake. My mistake.'

'I asked you did he resent it?'

The question came as she lifted her cup in the act of drinking tea. The knuckles of her hands, no longer contorted now, were bone-rigid as she grasped the cup. Instead it was her eyes that showed contortion now. They were no longer remotely like brown snails, turning back and inwards on themselves. They writhed with listening anguish.

'For God's sake why must you keep on and on and on and on and on at me?' She started banging the table with her clenched fists. The cups on the table rattled as under an attack of hammers. 'Why aren't you out there with the rest of them, looking for him? There's a big enough crowd of them out there, isn't there? With their bloody sticks and dogs and boy scouts and bikes and God knows what. Why don't you go and join them? Go and hold Miss Philpot's hand or something. She'll love that. I daresay she knows where he is! She knows all right – she'll say I've told you!'

'Now, Miss, do sit down – '

'Sit down, for Jesus' sake, sit down, sit down? You get me all worked up so that I don't know whether I'm crazy or not crazy – whether I – '

She sat down. Her body, suddenly limp, slumped like a weighted sack on the chair. Her head fell forward on her outstretched hands. Merely staring, dead silent, she sat for several minutes without moving. At length, with patient aggravation, the voice of the detective-sergeant began again:

'Yes, we've got a lot of people out there looking. But we think you can help us too – '

'How? You want me to light a torch or something and guide you?'

'You don't by any chance, I suppose, know Mr Ainsworth's address?'

'How should I? Why should I?'

'It wouldn't seem unusual, would it? You were very intimate – you were – '

'He left without giving it.'

'He seems to have left The White Hart without giving it too.'

'He left in a hurry. Why do you keep asking about him? What's he got to do with it? What's he – '

'I don't think I said he had anything to do with it.'

'No, but it's there. In your mind. You think it. You want to make me believe he had don't you, you want to – '

257

'I don't want to make you believe anything. I merely asked you if by chance you knew Mr Ainsworth's address – '

'No, I don't. What's more I wouldn't give it to you if I did.'

'Well, it's perhaps not important.'

'Oh! it's not important now? One minute it's important, one minute it's not important, another minute – Oh! yes, go on, go on, go on. Put words into my mouth that aren't there. Put a rope round my neck. He resented him too. Yes, he resented him. What's his address? Where is he? It's a clear case of kidnapping now, is it? Oh! yes, he resented him. Work on that.'

'He resented him? Can you explain?'

'He resented him for one thing because of Mr Pimm and Mr Monday. He didn't believe in them.'

'Who didn't believe in them?'

'Alex – Mr Ainsworth – oh! what does it matter?'

'Perhaps it does matter. Let's get the point clear. On the one hand you tell me Pimm and Monday don't exist. On the other you tell me that the boy resented it because they did and Ainsworth didn't believe in them. Is that how it was?'

'You've got it all pat, haven't you? It's all plain enough, isn't it? It's all clear.'

'All right, I accept that. It's plain and clear.'

'All right, you accept it, you accept it. You drive me round and round the twist until my head's raging like a dynamo and I hardly know what day it is and then you accept it – do you mind if I go out a minute? Do you mind if I get a breath of air! I can't stand it much longer.'

'By all means get some air.'

'I'll just go upstairs and get my scarf. It looks like rain again.'

She turned, unexpectedly calm, eyes averted, and went upstairs to fetch her scarf. Watching her go, Detective-Sergeant Broadbent fully expected her to cry. When she showed no sign of crying he walked to the window again and pondered there, looking at the blackened burden in the garden, on a state of disturbance more disturbing than mere tears and said at last to Detective-Constable Pierce, now pouring his seventh, luke-warm cup of tea:

'Well, say something.'

'I jotted down a note here. About the mad bit. The well.'

'Yes?'

'I wondered about physical violence. Difficult to explain – but the idea that he might have been down the well might have set her thinking along those –'

'It's worth a thought.'

'She might have started to resent the boy too. I mean if she and Ainsworth were lovers and all that – the boy, I mean, could have got in the way. Assuming there was an Ainsworth.'

'Oh! there was an Ainsworth all right. Only his name was Appleton.'

Gilly came downstairs, tying her scarf over her head as she entered the kitchen. The scarf was a bright crocus-orange in colour, with repeated spots of sepia brown. Its very brightness, closely framing her face, seemed to force the tired eyes more and more inward, back on themselves. She suddenly seemed, Pierce thought, to be grieviously alone. He stirred four or five spoonfuls of sugar into his tea, remembering Appleton. He had a very sweet tooth and he took yet another spoonful of sugar, unable to look up at the face.

'So it's all right if I go out into the garden for a moment, is it?' she said.

'It's all right. But don't go away.'

'I'm not going anywhere. I've nowhere to go. Not even hell. I'm in that already.'

She smoothed her scarf with her hands. A strange air about her, very quiet, gave the impression that she was locked in resignation. She paused at the door, her hand on the latch, and Broadbent said:

'There was just one more little thing.'

Yes? She stood looking down at the door latch, face hidden. What was that?

'That day when you made what you say was your mistake. The day you thought he'd fallen down the well. What made you think that?'

'He had the top of the well open and the camera and he was trying to take a picture of a float that had fallen down –'

'A float? You mean a fishing float? You wouldn't have this camera?'

'Would it matter? There was no film in it anyway.'

'No film in it?'

'That was the mistake.'

She lifted the door latch. It clicked. The door opened. Heavier, bluer cloud was coming up now from the west. The incoming air was chilly. Pierce started to light another cigarette and Broadbent said:

'You say he made you angry. Mad, you said. Did you use any sort of physical violence on him that day?'

'Children have to be punished sometimes. It was the only time I ever hit him.'

'And did he resent it?'

She stood still, looking down, not answering.

'Or was the resentment perhaps on your side?'

She opened the door to its full extent and stepped outside, still without an answer. She walked slowly up and down the garden path, not bothering to shut the door. Strike a light it was freezing with the door open, it was half-way to flaming winter, Pierce thought, and went to the door to shut it.

'Hullo, there's a station car driving up. It looks like Greaves. Yes, it's Greaves.'

A police car, coming up rather fast across the park, drew up, sharply beyond the garden gate. A young policeman, rufus-haired, half-knocking his head against the roof of the car as he got out, straightened his cap and came up the garden path, eager for duty, only half aware of Gilly standing there.

'They've found the red umbrella, sir.'

She turned her head sharply, her eyes very bright. She stood for a moment frozen between the blackened borders, scarf brilliant against the lowering sky. Then she suddenly screamed, turned wildly and started running.

'Stop her, Greaves, get her! – No, don't bother. Let her go. Where was it found, the umbrella?'

'A chap working a dredger on the marsh –'

'Turn the car – no, let her go. Pierce! drink your ruddy tea up and shut the door. Let her run. She's not important. It'll do her good to run.'

The yellow scarf fluttered across the park like a bird driven by the wind. The wheels of the police car, turning, crunched on gravel. Pierce came out of the house running, hatless, and Broadbent, for the first time losing patience, shouted at the lowering afternoon:

'The trouble with this dam' place it's got no telephone! You're out of touch!'

'Did you say she's not important?' Pierce abruptly stopped running and came slowly back to the door.

'That's what I said. Not important. Can't you hear?'

She walked along the lakeside, head down, hands locked inside the front of her coat. October leaves were beginning to fall on the lake, mostly the leaves of poplars, yellow, swimming down exactly like fish in the windy air.

Presently she started to remember a conversation with the boy.

Could you walk on water?

No, you couldn't walk on water.

But the birds on the lake walked on water, the moorhens.

Yes, but moorhens were different.

How were they different?

Because they were light and they didn't sink and they could swim anyway.

If you could walk on water and walked through the lake would you get to the sea?

No. You couldn't do that.

Why not?

Because you just couldn't. It wasn't possible.

Why wasn't it possible? Miss Garfield had read out a story once about some fishermen in a boat who saw another man walking on the water.

That was different?

How was it different? They saw the man walking on the water. Miss Garfield read it out.

It was because the men in the boat had faith. They believed the man who walked on the water. They believed it and there it was.

If anybody believed hard enough could they do it too?

Oh! if you believed hard enough you could do anything.

Like walking on the water to the sea?

That was the funny boy.

She walked on along the lake, head always down, hands locked underneath her coat. The wind stirred the poplar leaves in sudden whispers. The yellow leaves, like birds driven by a common impulse, suddenly took flight. They fell slowly, turning gently in air, dropping on grass and reeds and water.

Half-way down the lake she stopped, lifted her head for the first time and stared at the expanse of lily pads. They too were turning yellow. Between them reflective spaces of dark water were caught by sudden ripples. They ran among decaying leaves like scattered brilliant coins. At the same time the delicate sound of leaves rippled by wind ran across the air like disjointed notes of music. They were like a few careless scales blown in from some distant part of summer.

She looked for moorhens walking on the water. She stared in search of them for a long time. It was only as it started to grow dark that she could hear the voices of them, far across the other side of the lake, settling down, unseen, among clumps of reed. They too were like distant notes from summer.

As she listened to them she stared with withdrawn brown eyes as if the sounds were actually visible. They might have been a crowd of faces watching her from among the reeds. It was only when it began to grow fully dark at last that she tied her scarf completely over her face and started to walk down, blindly, to where the water was.

'It was a good show,' the Captain said. 'There was some pretty fair staff work.'

At a few minutes past six the Captain walked into the bar

of The White Hart, pleasantly exhausted, laden with a variety of accoutrements left over from more belligerent and active days: haversack, whistle with lanyard, water bottle, torch, *alpenstock*, oil-skin cape and cap, a pair of goggles and a long yellow-handled spring-bok rake.

The bar was already full of men, with a few women, some armed too with implements of search. The air was full of anecdote, of talk of coincidence, of narrow misses, false alarms.

'The extraordinary thing was that I'd just made up my mind I'd have a stab at the marsh myself – free-lance sort of – I suppose some sort of instinct working. Then this copper came haring up and said they'd found the kid. Said to stop operations.'

'I was working like a beaver in a rat-hole down behind that old bacon factory place when a chap came up and stopped the show.'

'You sound disappointed.'

'Well, that's a bit strong. I was merely just getting into the meat of the thing. Sort of worked up. I gave up a whole day.'

'I was absolutely convinced all the way along he was in that ruddy culvert at the back of Jameson's place. It ought to have been bricked in long ago. I've always said so.'

'You know where they never looked? Every damn place they searched but not that one.'

'The church belfry.'

'No: that underground cave-place behind the big house. Vast affair. Kept meat there in the old days.'

'Ah! sort of prehistoric refrigerator.'

'Underground you mean? No, I'd no idea it existed.'

'Oh! my goodness yes. Stored carcasses by the ton there. I played there myself as a kid. Splendid hiding place. Ah! there you are, Captain. Fit?'

'Now that I've renewed acquaintance with my friend J. Walker Esq., yes.' The Captain held up his whisky as if partly in relief, partly in celebration. 'Cheers. It was a damn near shake.'

'Anybody know the details?'

'Are there details? I thought it was all pretty straightforward.

Get outside that one, Captain, and let me get you another. The last time I saw you was at the top of that haystack. You looked practically stymied I thought.'

'You know what they say?' the Captain said. 'When you see anything you've never got your gun. There was I, half-way up this perishing haystack, when out came this pheasant, full in my face. Last year's bird. Cock.'

'You mean up a ladder? Damn funny. Same?'

'Many thanks.'

'A double, I trust?'

'Are there trebles?'

'A treble if you so desire, sir. Say the word and I'll give the order. Far be it from me to deny – God, honestly you worked like a black.'

'Ah! splendid, at last,' the Captain said. 'Miss Philpot.'

He couldn't help thinking of the old days when he suddenly turned and saw Miss Philpot, the old days of the phoney war. He recalled in untarnished vision a picture of her scrambling to duty, gas-cape flung about her like a pudding cloth, tin-hat askew, stirrup pump in air, as always too late with too much.

'Ah! Madame,' the Captain said. 'A little solace for the tired spirit?' He laughed with low jocularity. 'Or a little spirit for the tired solace, perhaps?'

Miss Philpot, with tired hands, raised a glass already drained of all content except a mere millimetre of amber. 'Thanks, but I already – '

'It looks, if I may say so,' the Captain said, 'a trifle exhausted.'

'Like me.'

'I will renew, dear lady, I will renew.'

'What news?' Miss Philpot said. 'Oh! none, I suppose, now that they've found him. Is it true he's absolutely all right?'

'Absolutely all right,' the Captain said. 'I've seen him. Merry and bright. Quite happy. Still had food.'

'After three days? Good God.'

'Seems he'd made the rations last damn well. He had this bun affair he was still clinging to.'

'Good God. Bun?'

'It's the old survival thing. It's what I told you all along.'

'Well, I suppose it's a load off that girl's mind.'

'Didn't box too clever, that girl, I thought,' the Captain said. 'Now if she'd got the brain to match her legs – '

The Captain went away to the bar. There he demanded of Harry to know how tricks were. Harry, surrounded and half-deafened by customers, said you might think it was VE Day, what with this and that, and he'd got something to show the Captain in a minute when he had the time. A treble again? This was something new, a treble.

'Pardon,' the Captain said, pushing back through the crowd with Miss Philpot's full, upraised glass. 'Pardon. Steady she goes – '

'I never knew the kid at all myself,' someone said. 'Odd how you can get so worked up about someone you've never seen. It was like losing one of my own.'

The Captain presented Miss Philpot with her glass, jocularly.

'A treble from Tulip, with love.'

'A what? From who?'

'A treble. A celebratory treble. It was Parkinson's idea, wasn't it, Parkinson?'

'And from whom, did you say?'

'Tulip.'

'A treble, great Heavens,' Miss Philpot said. 'You'll have us all on the floor.'

'And who,' Parkinson said, 'is Tulip?'

'That,' the Captain said, 'is the great undercurrent question.'

'Tulip?' Miss Philpot said. 'A dark new girl-friend?'

'It was a triumph of organization,' the Captain said. 'You get nowhere unless organized. Who was what? Tulip? – I've an idea she's Parkinson's mystery mistress.'

'You took the joke out of my mouth, Captain.'

There was suddenly much laughter.

'Now, now,' somebody said. 'Come clean. Who is this Tulip?'

'It's for the Captain to say. He introduced her.'

'Shall we say she is better unidentified?'

'Miss Philpot's right,' someone said. 'She's the new dark lady. The dark, dark Tulip.'

'I do not know,' the Captain said. 'I cannot tell.'

265

'And what the hell is that supposed to mean?'

'It's supposed to mean,' the Captain said, 'to Tulip, bless her, with honour.'

'Well, let's hope she's satisfied.'

There was again much laughter. The Captain, empty glass upraised, sought to elbow his way back to the bar. On the way he was momentarily held up by a farmer holding a great tankard of beer who said, nudging fatly past him: 'You know the kid's parents? Oh! I just wondered. They say they're on their way back, that's all. They say he sat there in a car dump, cool as a flea.'

'What's all this, Harry? Said you'd got something – sorry, there's an awful battle. Can't hear.'

'Telegram, sir – '

'A what, Harry?'

'Telegram, a wire, Captain Drage, sir. I pinned it up at the end of the bar. Thought it might interest you, as you were asking – '

The Captain pushed his way through a half-circle of drinkers, to the end of the bar. The telegram was pinned up on a shelf behind it.

'*Married today stop Drinks on the house stop Don't stop stop Love Alex and Fitzie Appleton.*'

'Appleton?' the Captain said. 'Who is Appleton?'

Harry, busy at the far end of the bar, didn't hear.

Back with Miss Philpot and her attendant crowd the Captain raised his glass again.

'More cause, it seems, for celebration.'

And what, they asked, could that be? The more the merrier. Might as well make it a day.

'This time,' the Captain said, 'it's from Fitzie with love. Married today. To a fellow named Appleton.'

'Appleton?'

'I can't recall him,' the Captain said. 'Probably one of the summer crowd.'

'Appleton. Oh! yes, I remember him. He was in here sometimes.'

'Oh! yes, I remember now. The rather self-to-self type. Not the eager beaver.'

'No, I don't recall. Nevertheless smart work.'

'I always said she wouldn't be long. After all, bloody attractive – '

'Perhaps,' someone said, glass raised, 'she took a leaf from Tulip's book?'

'A petal,' the Captain said, 'a petal.'

There was again much laughter. The Captain was certainly on form, they all said, great form. The Captain laughed in appreciation, said he wouldn't say no to another treble, since Miss Philpot had been good enough to ask, and thus encouraged, permitted himself another joke:

'To Fitzie with love. To Tulip with love. And, I think also, to our Philpot.' He stooped to kiss her lightly on the cheek, half mocking, half in gratitude. 'For helping to bring the lamb back to the fold.'

'That's enough of that. Save that for Tulip.' There was again a burst of spontaneous, ringing laughter. 'It's all over now.'

James stood on the terrace of the big house, looking across the park. It was late afternoon. A sharp, dark wind was blowing. In the distance, beyond bared chestnut trees, the clouds were like grey dirty sheep.

He was trying not to hold Miss Garfield's hand. Once or twice she extended it towards him, bony, skinning and dry, and each time he took his own away. Nor did he want to speak to Miss Garfield. Once or twice he had asked her questions and to each question there was no real answer.

'Where has Gilly gone?'

'We shall come to that later.'

'Why don't I have Gilly now?'

'We shall come to all that in good time.'

Now he had no more questions for Miss Garfield. He simply stood apart, alone, determined not to hold her hand.

From the remote end of the park, from beyond the bared dark skeletons of chestnut trees, a car presently swung out at speed, like a white swift mouse.

'Get ready to wave, James.'

He stood still, determined neither to wave nor answer.

'Get ready to wave. They'll want to see you wave.'

The car, not a distant white mouse now, but more like a big white rat, ran across the park, round the steep curve in front of the house and stopped at last under the steps below the terrace.

Two figures, hands and faces brown as the dead chestnut leaves that had fallen along the full length of the avenue, got out, waving with excitement, smiling greeting.

'Wave, James. Wave.'

His hands were stiff at his side, his eyes stiff ahead.

'Who is it?' he said. 'Who are they?'

Miss Garfield offered no answer, cold wind blew at the bared chestnut trees. Dead leaves on the road underneath swirled upward in rings and blew away like scales. Clouds like grey dirty sheep, others like scurrying lambs, were herded away together on the farthest rim of darkening sky.

FOR THE BEST IN PAPERBACKS, LOOK FOR THE

In every corner of the world, on every subject under the sun, Penguin represents quality and variety – the very best in publishing today.

For complete information about books available from Penguin – including Pelicans, Puffins, Peregrines and Penguin Classics – and how to order them, write to us at the appropriate address below. Please note that for copyright reasons the selection of books varies from country to country.

In the United Kingdom: Please write to *Dept E.P., Penguin Books Ltd, Harmondsworth, Middlesex, UB7 0DA*

If you have any difficulty in obtaining a title, please send your order with the correct money, plus ten per cent for postage and packaging, to *PO Box No 11, West Drayton, Middlesex*

In the United States: Please write to *Dept BA, Penguin, 299 Murray Hill Parkway, East Rutherford, New Jersey 07073*

In Canada: Please write to *Penguin Books Canada Ltd, 2801 John Street, Markham, Ontario L3R 1B4*

In Australia: Please write to the *Marketing Department, Penguin Books Australia Ltd, P.O. Box 257, Ringwood, Victoria 3134*

In New Zealand: Please write to the *Marketing Department, Penguin Books (NZ) Ltd, Private Bag, Takapuna, Auckland 9*

In India: Please write to *Penguin Overseas Ltd, 706 Eros Apartments, 56 Nehru Place, New Delhi, 110019*

In Holland: Please write to *Penguin Books Nederland B.V., Postbus 195, NL–1380AD Weesp, Netherlands*

In Germany: Please write to *Penguin Books Ltd, Friedrichstrasse 10–12, D–6000 Frankfurt Main 1, Federal Republic of Germany*

In Spain: Please write to *Longman Penguin España, Calle San Nicolas 15, E–28013 Madrid, Spain*

In France: Please write to *Penguin Books Ltd, 39 Rue de Montmorency, F-75003, Paris, France*

In Japan: Please write to *Longman Penguin Japan Co Ltd, Yamaguchi Building, 2–12–9 Kanda Jimbocho, Chiyoda-Ku, Tokyo 101, Japan*

A CHOICE OF PENGUIN FICTION

More Die of Heartbreak Saul Bellow

'What drives this book – and I mean *drives* – is the exultantly sour views of modernity, sexuality, women, the local and international scene' – *The New York Review of Books* 'Brilliant and funny . . . Bellow's ideas at their most astute and trenchant' – *The New York Times*

Very Good, Jeeves! P. G. Wodehouse

When Bertie Wooster lands in the soup, only the 'infinite sagacity' of Jeeves can pull him out. 'A riot . . . There are eleven tales in this volume and each is the best' – *Observer*

The Good Apprentice Iris Murdoch

At Seegard there is something rich and strange, with the power to change people's lives – for better or worse. 'Iris Murdoch is here very much at her formidable, myth-making best; inventive, comic, moving' – Elaine Feinstein in *The Times* 'A heaving, sprawling, headlong spiritual thriller' – *Observer*

Milk and Honey Elizabeth Jolley

'It is a novel about those who had to leave Europe and who never put down roots in the earth of the new hemisphere into which they were blown . . . a quirky, brilliantly written study on the amorality of ignoring reality' – *The Times* 'A truly exotic mix, a little as though Edgar Allan Poe had been transported to the outback and set to Straussian music' – *Guardian*

Charlotte's Row H. E. Bates

With its superbly realized industrial setting and cast of memorable characters, *Charlotte's Row* is one of H. E. Bates's best novels in which he reveals his deep understanding of the ambitions and dreams of ordinary men and women. 'He is the Renoir of the typewriter' – *Punch*

A Sport of Nature Nadine Gordimer

'The mature achievement of a fiercely intelligent writer . . . grand-scale, rich and demanding' – *The New York Times Book Review* 'Compulsively readable . . . a genuinely picaresque novel' – *The Times* 'Vast as the veld and teeming as a township, *A Sport of Nature* expansively encompasses over forty years of South African experience' – *Independent*

A CHOICE OF PENGUIN FICTION

Fireflies Shiva Naipaul

The story of Trinidad's most venerated Hindu family, the Khojas, *Fireflies* is Shiva Naipaul's ferociously comic and profoundly sad first novel. 'A masterpiece . . . anyone who misses reading Shiva Naipaul's *Fireflies* will miss an entirely delightful experience' – Auberon Waugh in the *Spectator*

The News from Ireland William Trevor

Twelve superb stories from William Trevor that exemplify his precision and subtlety. 'One may turn to him always for artistry, wisdom and wit' – *Sunday Telegraph*. 'Mr Trevor's imagination brings everything to life with a marvellous vividness and glow . . . voluptuously readable' – *Spectator*

Natives and Strangers Louisa Dawkins

Only as she becomes a woman does Marietta, born in Songo, Tanganyika Territory, realize that she cannot change the whiteness of her skin. Just as marriage to the tormented Jonathan Sudbury cannot save her from loving Michael Kagia, the brilliant young African politician – and loving Michael cannot stop the tragedies of the future or correct the mistakes of the past.

Roger's Version John Updike

'Updike at full power, a truly astonishing novel. It is a sort of modern fantasia on themes from Hawthorne's *Scarlet Letter*' – Frank Kermode in the *Guardian*. 'He is a writer of charm as well as one possessed of staggering gifts' – Anita Brookner in the *Spectator*. 'A complete original, and full of energy and optimism . . . a highly recommended read' – Lynton Lesserday in *Punch*

Maus Art Spiegelman

'I can't find superlatives adequate to describe it. It's the best cartoon book I've ever read . . . Very direct, very powerful, very moving . . .' – Steve Bell. 'Anyone moved by *When the Wind Blows* . . . will appreciate Spiegelman's genius for dealing with a subject many would say cannot be dealt with at all' – *The Times*.

Fair Stood the Wind for France

'*Fair Stood the Wind for France* is perhaps the finest novel of the war . . . The scenes are exquisitely done and the characters – tenderly and beautifully drawn – are an epitome of all that is best in the youth of two countries. This is a fine, lovely book which makes the heart beat with pride' – *Daily Telegraph*

The Triple Echo

H. E. Bates tells movingly the strange tale of a lonely woman and her love affair with a young deserter, of their intrigues and their deceptions and the elaborate web they weave to outwit the Military Police.

Love for Lydia

'Bates at his best . . . I read the tale with a sense of eager dread, so real are these folk, so torn and buffetted, and finally so humbled under the winds of passion and the even more terrifying peace which comes when the storm is over . . . A book likely to be one of the most-read love stories of our time' – Richard Church

The Wild Cherry Tree

These ten stories show Bates at his most tense and immediate; observing with baleful accuracy just what happens when people are 'thrown suddenly with neither direction nor compass into territory utterly strange and unexplored'.